The Garden of Earthly Delights

A novel

Robert Dodds

About the author:

Robert Dodds grew up in Yorkshire and Kent. He went to Oxford University to study English, and then became a teacher and lecturer. After several years working in England, Mexico, and the USA, he settled in Edinburgh. In the mid 1980s he set up a new degree course in film and television production at Edinburgh College of Art, which he led until later becoming head of the School of Visual Communication in the college. In 2008 he left academia in order to devote more time to writing. In addition to his books, he has had a variety of work performed and broadcast for television, radio and theatre.

Visit robertdodds.com to read more of his writing

For Isobel and Laura

ISBN-13: 978-1503332652
ISBN-10: 1503332659

Cover image:
Marinus van Reymerswaele (c.1490-c1546) *A Moneychanger and his Wife* (detail). Photographed by the author.
Rear cover image:
Hieronymus Bosch (c1450-1516) *The Last Judgement-fragment of a lost triptych* (detail). Photographed by the author.

ACKNOWLEDGMENTS

This novel was inspired by the late 15th Century painting 'The Garden of Earthly Delights' by Hieronymus Bosch. It started life as a proposal for a radio play, and then over a period of several years it went through seven drafts as a stage play and six drafts as a novel. Along the way I was encouraged and given valuable feedback by BBC radio drama producer and dramatist David Ian Neville, and by my literary agent Kathryn Ross. I would also like to acknowledge two excellent sources of ideas and information: Laurinda Dixon's 'Bosch' (Phaidon Press 2003) and Paul B. Newman's 'Daily Life in the Middle Ages' (McFarland 2001)

AUTHOR'S DISCLAIMER

This is a work of fiction, and cannot be read as an account of events in the lives of actual historical figures.

CHAPTER ONE

DEN BOSCH. 1490

Aleyt stands in the darkened room, hidden, as if in a long-ago childhood game with her older sister or her cousin. Inside her head is the same remembered sound: a surging rush, like liquid being poured away, over and over. Her blood, pumping.

Today it is the world outside that she hides from. But the noises and smells of that world are finding her out anyway, creeping cunningly through the gap in the heavy shutters: the stench of packed bodies and quick-fried sweetmeats; the tolling of a bell; the voices of the massed people of Den Bosch, a low *ruh-ruh-ruh* pierced occasionally by shriller cries. Drawn unwillingly by a horrid curiosity, she peeps out at the town square below.

The bearded man at the centre of it all draws her eyes at once. He is clad only in a loin cloth with his hands bound behind his back. Like Jesus in the images of the Passion, he is surrounded by a howling, jeering crowd that is gripped by lust for his death. But he doesn't wear Jesus's serene expression, the look that speaks of transcending all earthly torment. No, this bearded man's face is an open book of terror. His eyes dart from place to place, and his tongue works at his parched lips. The loin-cloth is soiled a filthy brown.

Aleyt's breath feels trapped in her throat. She moves

1

slightly so that the narrow gap in the shutters lines up with a different part of the scene. There is a tall, thin figure, like an island of black-robed calm in the broiling bustle. Beneath his cowl, most of his face is hidden. On a lectern before him is a Bible, and only his mouth moves. Surely, no one will be able to hear him in the hubbub. This is her first sight of the man. For weeks his reputation has stalked the town. Even now that he has finally come out into the open, he is still partly concealed. In spite of her fear, she is curious to see his eyes.

Behind him, on the steps of the Stadhuis are ranged the monks and nuns of Den Bosch, a mass of brown and black cloth. Dotted amidst this loamy soil like the flowers of the year's early spring are the more colourful robes of the cathedral clergy. They all have the best view of the proceedings, and, in contrast to the Inquisitor's pious concentration, they are busy gossiping and eating nuts and haggling with the street vendors who offer cups of watered-down brandy from small barrels strapped to their backs.

Aleyt moves again, trying to free her breathing, her gaze skimming over the mob. *Ruh, ruh, ruh...* like the sound of an angry sea, surging even to the wall of their house directly below her. Thank God the cottage at Roedeken will soon be finished. If the future is to bring more such abominations to the market square, they will be able to lock up this house for the day and escape.

She is startled by the door opening behind her, and turns quickly to face it. Of course: it's Jerome. He has been back for more than a week from his long absence in Reims, but she still forgets that he is in the house. The silence in his studio is the same, whether he is there or not.

He remains standing in the doorway, peering uncertainly into the gloom of the shuttered room.

"Aleyt?"

"Yes, Jerome. I'm here by the window."

He moves forward carefully, eyes adjusting, irises opening. The pale oval of Aleyt's face forms itself in front of him, like one of the phantoms that any darkness conjures in his mind's eye.

"Why are the shutters closed?" he says, knowing why.

Aleyt begins to fumble with the catch, but Jerome is taken by an impulse of pity, which grows instantly to rebellion, and he steps forward again and puts his hand gently over hers.

"Well – let them stay closed, why not?" he says.

She feels now that she can draw on his strength to face what is out there.

"But you know we must watch."

"Perhaps they may not know we're at home," he says.

"Of course they know we're here. Where else would we be?"

She is right. He puts aside her hand and himself unhooks the heavy metal latch and lifts the crossbar. He pushes the shutters outwards and the hinges groan as if they too have a voice in this matter. Noise floods into the room, and the square below is framed by the opening like one of his paintings, teeming with vivid little figures. From all the other houses around the market place, the most prosperous citizens of Den Bosch look out from their windows. They will be seen by all now, the Master Painter and his wife, watching in approval, it might be, as God's soldiers go about their work.

"Come..." he says, making room for Aleyt beside him.

In the heart of the square, a wooden platform has been erected with a few steps leading up to it. Projecting upwards through the centre of the platform is a stake, the straight trunk of a felled pine stripped of its bark. Below and around the platform are heaped scraps of timber, trimmed tree branches, bundles of twigs, and gashed hay bales. Sometimes someone edges forward to throw on their own small fagot, buying remittance from time in purgatory. The bearded man is being dragged towards the platform by three of the town's tipstaffs, sweating and conspicuous in their bright red tunics. He fights them with every step, flinging his body backwards against their tugging, and they look angry, as if they feel he is making fools of them in public. One of them cuffs the man hard on the head, making him scream out something incomprehensible. *Speaking in the Devil's tongue* will be entered in the official record, since he has confessed to witchcraft. But Jerome and the rest of Den Bosch have known this harmless moon-witted beggar for years, since long before the arrival of Jacomo and his Inquisition. He'd always talked nonsense, and regularly had fits of screaming and shouting. You gave him a groat, from time to time, or a scrap of bread, and in bad weather the monks somewhere would take him in.

Aleyt moves closer to his side, and he senses her agitation from the catch in her breathing. He sets his jaw and tries to face with fortitude the scene outside. This poor loon in the square could be expected to act thus, but would any man do better? What if he himself were being dragged to a post to be burned? Wouldn't he be screaming and struggling, with a soiled loin cloth? And what about the Inquisitor himself, this Jacomo, who has now left his Bible and climbed onto the platform to wait beside the stake? How would *he* fare, if places were exchanged? Anger suddenly brings the blood up into his face.

The bearded man is finally heaved up to the platform, all flailing limbs, and the black-cloaked Dominicans on the front rank of the Stadhuis steps commence the slow sonorous chanting that will continue until all is done:

Adoremus in aeternum sanctissimum Sacramentum.

Laudate Dominum omnes gentes: laudate eum omnes

populi...

For a few moments the townspeople fall quiet, and the chanting predominates, but then the mob resumes and even increases its noise. Women shriek like banshees and men whistle, roar and jeer. The calls of excited children twitter like marsh birds. Some of the onlookers have brought drums and crumhorns and bladder-pipes, and the cacophony bounces off the surrounding houses and blares up into the sky above.

"They make a noise like a farmyard," Jerome mutters. He squints so that his eyes go out of focus, and sees geese with human heads, blood-faced pigs hoisting their handkerchiefs in the air, and cows capering on hind legs with their calves on their shoulders.

Aleyt has closed her own eyes completely. Let me not be haunted in dreams, she thinks. In her darkness, the proximity of her husband feels strange to her. Their elbows are touching. Why does he not take her hand, or put his arm protectively around her shoulders? Would that not be natural and affectionate? But, of course, it would not be appropriate. They should appear to be praying, at such a moment.

Jerome lets his eyes focus once again. The tipstaffs are tying the bearded man's hands behind the stake. His knees refuse to support him, and he slides down onto his haunches, his head bowed. The tipstaffs haul him up again, but as soon as they step away, he subsides once more. The crowd boos.

"Why do they do that?" Aleyt asks, not looking.

"They want to see his face when he burns," Jerome says.

"Why are they like this?" Aleyt whispers, as unwilled curiosity forces her eyes open once more. These are the people with whom they live side by side every day; the same ordinary people who have bakeries and breweries and do laundry and build walls and till the fields around Den Bosch and eat and drink and pray, just as they do. Now it is as if they have lost all their

5

singularities, and become a composite, many-headed monster.

The Inquisitor, still dark and faceless beneath his cowl, briskly removes the waist cord from his black gown and grabs a handful of the man's thick unruly locks. He loops the cord tightly around the clump of hair and hands the end to one of the sweating tipstaffs. They force the man back to his feet, and lash his hair to the stake so that his neck strains backwards and he can't sink down. Then the Inquisitor makes the sign of the cross and begins praying, leaning in towards the condemned man's ear.

Jerome's gaze escapes down the steps of the platform, where a brazier of coals glows redly. The executioner, a fat carrion crow, thrusts a long stick wrapped in rags into the brazier and holds it there until bright flames lick upwards. Then he withdraws the firebrand and stands in readiness. The Inquisitor gathers his cassock up around his knees and picks his way carefully down the steps. When he is clear, the executioner thrusts the flaming brand into one of the bundles of hay at the base of the platform.

It catches light immediately, and the crow hops swiftly around the edges of the pyre, touching the brand here and there until flames leap upwards on all sides of the platform. A solemn hush finally falls upon the crowd.

Aleyt, closing her eyes once again, hears beneath the chanting of the Dominicans the crackling and snapping of wood as it catches the fire from the hay. Closer to hand, she is surprised by the sudden cooing of some pigeons on their own rooftop, unperturbed by the scene below.

"Jesus! Jesus! Jesus!"

The cry jerks her eyes open, and she sees the flames climb higher around the bound man. Was he commending his soul at last to God? Or was *Jesus* just a word for unbearable pain? Now a long, high-pitched

6

and wordless scream punctures the sky, and a dense pall of smoke obscures him from view. He makes no other sound.

Aleyt buries her face in her hands, sobbing.

"A sight to remind us of the torments of Hell," Jerome says. He feels sick inside, sullied by his mute, tacit approval of what has passed in the square. He is disgusted with himself and his fellow men. How far they have all fallen, together, since the original sin in the Garden of Eden.

The chanting of the Dominicans ceases, and for a long moment only the crackling of the burning pyre can be heard. Then the crowd comes vigorously back to life, as if each person experiences their own miraculous resurrection. The buzz of excited chatter grows louder and louder, until the market square seems filled with a swarm of bees.

These beasts and insects that we are, Jerome thinks, and turns back to face the comfortable room behind. The new tapestry from Arras, earliest fruit of the Reims commission, moves sinuously in the mild breeze that comes past them from the open window, and a whiff of acrid smoke is carried to his nostrils.

"Well, we haven't shirked our duty," he says. "No-one can say that the Master Painter and his wife are impious."

Aleyt feels suddenly exhausted. She goes to sit on the carved oak settle against the wall, her grandfather's wedding gift. Jerome remains standing, silhouetted against the window. She can't make out his expression.

She needs to clarify something. With a glance at the closed door of the room, she speaks very quietly.

"You don't believe that man was possessed by devils, as the tribunal decided, do you Jerome?"

Jerome looks at her in surprise.

"Need you ask? What do you think?"

"I think... I think that we must act as if we believe that. Even in front of Mary."

7

Now Jerome understands her. He nods.

"I agree."

"Not that Mary would ever say anything deliberately against us, but..."

"She's a goose," Jerome completes her thought, "and she could let slip any nonsense to anyone."

He sighs. Before Inquisitors came to the Duchy of Brabant, there had been little need to worry what tittle-tattle went about. Now, even a loose word from a servant could bring danger.

He gazes out of the window behind him again, and then comes to sit next to her. The lines on his forehead are drawn together, and his cheeks are slightly flushed.

"Half of the monks out there are drunk, and no one cares! The Church whips up this... this smoke of fear to hide its own vices."

Aleyt raises a hand, palm outwards.

"You mustn't speak such thoughts."

"I know, I know. Well, let my paintings speak for me."

"You must take care."

"I'm licensed to tell unpalatable truths, in my own way. My patrons inside the Church – they, at least, understand the need for that."

Aleyt cannot share this confidence, although she will not question it aloud. Her father, a great prophet of doom in political matters, mutters darkly of shifting sands in Den Bosch and the rest of the Duchy of Brabant. The big towns squabble for primacy, and no-one knows when or if the young Habsburg, Philip, will assume effective control of his lands. Meanwhile, unquestioned by civil authority, the Church powers flex their muscles and seek out new enemies, in all ranks of society. She wishes Jerome paid more heed to all of this, but he only accuses her of borrowing her father's unfounded anxieties.

She picks up her sewing basket from the floor beside the settle. There is a little time before supper. She needs to do something that will calm her down. Just now, she can't imagine having an appetite for food. She will just sit quietly in this room, avoiding the window. She suspects there will be noise and drunkenness in the square until nightfall, the celebrations of the unburnt. She pulls out from the basket the little lace cap she is working on.

"What's that?" Jerome asks.

"For my cousin Frida's baby. You remember? It's due any day. I'm making a little hat."

She holds it up. It's nearly finished, a sweet little white cap to keep the baby's head warm at night. Their eyes meet for a moment, and the unspoken thought they share is like a ghost passing through the room between them.

Aleyt decides to detain the ghost before it has dematerialized. She returns her eyes to Jerome's.

"It's eight days since you came home, Jerome…"

She lets the remark hang in the air and returns to her lacework.

Outside, the first bells of Den Bosch begin to call the monks and nuns to Vespers. Moments later, as always, the great bell in the cathedral tower joins in with its deep, measured, serious tone that seems to chide the other bells like unruly children. Jerome, uncomfortable after their exchange, sends his eyes wandering around the tidy room. He notices something he can't identify lying on the table and goes to look more closely.

A scroll of parchment.

"What's this?"

Aleyt looks up from her sewing.

"Oh – I'm sorry Jerome, I forgot. Mary came dashing in with that, while you were in your studio. She was afraid to disturb you, and she was in such a mad rush to get out to the square. A messenger gave it to her at the door."

Jerome turns the scroll so that he can see the seal. It is dull red, vesica-shaped: an ecclesiastical seal.

9

"This has come from Overmaas!" he exclaims.

Eagerly, he breaks the wax apart and unrolls the parchment to read it.

To the Master Painter Jerome van Aachen, known as Hieronymus, of Den Bosch:

The Cathedral Chapter of Overmaas sends you greetings and good tidings. From the seven submissions received for the design of our new window at the north transept of the cathedral, your depiction of the nativity of Our Lord Jesus Christ has been chosen. Our bursar will visit you next week with the primus payment to secure your services, and to agree a date for completion of the drawings and colour plan, to be no later than the end of mensis Januarius the Year of Our Lord Fourteen Hundred and Ninety One. The assembly and installation of the window is to be completed by Easter of Fourteen Hundred and Ninety Two, and your supervisory services during the period of making and installation will be secured by a separate stipend to be agreed after the design work is accepted.

Benedictio Dei,

Sigismond,

Amanuensis to the Cathedral Chapter of Overmaas

His head is bent over the parchment, but Aleyt can see the furrowed lines on his forehead gradually smoothing out, and when he lifts his face to her he is smiling.

"Well?" she says.

"The cathedral chapter at Overmaas has chosen my design for their window!"

In this moment she is suddenly reminded of how he looked at their wedding festivities, seven years ago. On an impulse she puts aside the cap, and all complications too, and stands up to embrace him.

"God be thanked!" she says.

He smiled the whole day long, that day. In some unheeded moment during the intervening years, a different, more serious spirit crept into him. The spirit settled in gradually, scoring lines on the forehead, hollowing the cheeks a little and turning the mouth down at the corners. Jerome became a man of forty, and she has come to thirty, but just now she can discern the bridegroom again, and feels younger herself.

They step apart again, a little awkwardly. Jerome still has the parchment in his hand, and holds it up between them.

"My pleasure in this is the greater because it's unexpected."

"Oh? Weren't you confident?

"I would have been confident but for what was whispered to me by the Dean at Overmaas when all the submissions were in."

"What, before you went away to Reims? Why didn't you tell me?"

"I promised to tell no-one. The Dean actually said *don't even tell your wife, Jerome*."

An unnecessary injunction, Aleyt thinks. Is he going to tell her now? She looks at him with eyebrows raised, inviting more.

Jerome shrugs.

"Well, I suppose it doesn't matter any more. I've got the commission. But you'd still better keep what I tell you to yourself. There is no proof."

Aleyt nods. The bridegroom has retreated back into the past, and Jerome's brows are knitted crossly again.

"Apparently the Abbess Dominica secretly offered a large donation if the cathedral chapter preferred her candidate."

"Bribery?" Aleyt says. "So who was her candidate?"

"He didn't go as far as to tell me that."

Aleyt only knows the Abbess Dominica by sight, but she has a thorough knowledge of Jerome's views of her character.

"Well, I suppose it comes as no surprise that the Abbess would do such a thing?" she suggests.

11

"No. It's typical of the woman's devious ways."

He dwells for a moment on the animal images he reserves for the Abbess Dominica. A warty toad hopping. A fat worm tunnelling. A sow snouting in a trough. All in nuns' wimples.

"Well, it's a happy coincidence that I sent a message to Hameel yesterday and invited him to share our supper tonight," he goes on, dismissing the unpleasant creatures. "I didn't want to say anything until the chapter voted."

"Why is it of concern to... to Hameel?"

"I'm going to ask him to work as my assistant on this project."

"But... surely... he works as a Master in his own right?"

"Of course, but this is different. A commission with such prestige – he'll feel honoured to be asked, and it will be an opportunity to advance his craft. He's never worked on a window of such a scale. By the way, I thought he'd be here by now. I said to come at the Vespers bells."

Aleyt's left eyelid goes into its flutter, as if a butterfly has landed there. She stands, and turns that side of her face away from Jerome.

"I'll go and see if Mary's back yet. There's things to be done in the kitchen."

She's through the door and onto the landing, but Jerome calls out as she begins to descend the narrow wooden stairs.

"Oh, Aleyt! There's a cloth bag of dried mandrake fruits in the pantry."

She steps back to the door of their parlour.

"Where did you get those?" she says.

"Well, from my good friend Izaak the apothecary on Brugstraat of course. He got them from Spain two weeks ago, and he knew I was coming home soon, so he kept some back for me. Anyway, don't let Mary mistake them for something else and make a fruit pudding out of them!"

"You should keep them safe somewhere else," she chides him gently. "I expect your good friend Izaak charged a pretty price."

"I'll use them soon. I'll make up a new potion. You'll take some?"

Aleyt nods. She has tried to decline in the past, but then Jerome delivers a speech, and she must give way. For many hours – even as long as a day and a night - after taking the mandrake potion they will lie like broken dolls on their bed. The room will spin giddily around her like a spinning top losing momentum, and strange apparitions will fly through the air. Periodically, as the potion twists her guts, she will vomit violently into one of the wooden buckets placed beside the bed.

"You know how I hate it," she says, anyway.

"It's a small price to pay, if it keeps Saint Anthony's Fire from our door," Jerome replies, as he always does.

These mandrake fruits, she knows, are supposed to be a powerful protection against the hideous plague that rages intermittently through the land, seizing rich and poor alike. But she feels that Jerome is overly zealous to use them. God sends him visions when he is sick with the potion, which he uses in his paintings. For her own part, it's mere misery. Even after the worst has passed, for days afterwards she feels as if the whole house bobs on a swelling sea.

No more to be said on the matter however. She turns and makes her way down towards the kitchen, thinking she must be sure to visit her cousin Frida with the finished baby's cap before the potion is ready.

Jerome listens to the sound of his wife's feet descending. Each step on their staircase has its own distinctive creak. It's almost a musical scale – or an unmusical scale – as a person goes up or down through the heart of the house. When he hears the sharp *crack* of the final stair he goes to the little recess in the wall where their simple carved wooden crucifix hangs. He must thank God for what has just been bestowed upon him. Making the sign of the cross over his forehead and chest, he kneels. He gazes at the crucifix and then closes his eyes, making that image stay as if burned into his mind's eye like a glimpse of the sun, letting go of the sounds from outside the window, concentrating on God, who is always there, ready to listen to him. When he feels that the stillness in his heart is sufficient, when he feels that God has entered the room, he speaks aloud, letting phrases from the Psalms flow through him slowly. He lingers on the sounds and dwells on their meaning, so that God will know they are his own words, and that they come from his heart as well as from the Bible.

"Lord, by thy favour thou hast made my mountain to stand strong. To the end that my glory may sing praise to thee, and not be silent, O Lord my God, I will give thanks unto thee forever. I will walk within my house with a perfect heart. I will set no wicked thing before mine eyes. Whoso privily slanders his neighbour, him will I cut off. Him that hath a high look and a proud heart I will not suffer. Mine eyes shall be upon the faithful of the land, that they may dwell with me. He that worketh deceit shall not dwell within my house. He that telleth lies shall not tarry in my sight. Make a joyful noise unto the Lord, all ye lands. Serve the Lord with gladness, come before his presence with singing. So be it. Amen."

He finishes, but remains kneeling in his self-imposed darkness. The image of Abbess Dominica drifts into his mind's eye. She of the high look and the proud heart, the worker of deceit. He has a sudden pang that his prayer has been sullied by resentment. He hasn't chosen the most appropriate words to thank God for his good fortune. So he makes her image walk away along a long dark road, and when she has finally disappeared, he says a silent Lord's Prayer in atonement. He wants to appear grateful before God, not tainted by bitterness.

He adds a prayer to Saint Gummarus, patron of the childless, whose tomb he visited in the chapel of the abbey at Lier, on the way home from Reims. Should he have left a larger donation there? The monks at Lier seemed serious and pious, unlike so many in Den Bosch.

As he ends this prayer, he hears feet ascending the stair. It's Aleyt again – her tread is lighter than Mary's or Hameel's. He makes the sign of the cross once again, and gets back onto his feet as she opens the door and enters, closing it behind her.

"Mary's just come in from the square now," Aleyt says.

"We're too lax with her," Jerome replies, meaning that Aleyt is too lax.

"I know, but she's back now, and the supper will be ready soon."

Now comes the sound of wooden clogs striking the stairs, like an approaching hammer. Jerome and Aleyt share an amused look. There is a knock at the door, but before they can call out, the knock is followed by the door opening just enough to admit the flushed, pretty face of their maidservant.

"Yes, Mary?" Jerome says.

"Hameel has come, Master… and Mistress," Mary says breathlessly. "Shall I send him up?"

"Well, what else?" Jerome says.

Mary shuts the door. Immediately they hear her voice braying down the stairwell.

"You're to come straight up!"

There is the sharp crack of the bottom step as a measured tread begins its passage upwards. A moment later there is a cascade of noise as Mary's clogs begin their descent. Midway on the narrow stair there is a pause in both sets of steps, a shuffling of feet, and a giggle from Mary, then both the upward and downward movements resume.

"She goes down those stairs like a fall of crockery!" Jerome remarks.

Then Hameel's signature light triple rap sounds on the door, and Jerome calls out, "Come in!"

Hameel enters, taking off his cap and running a hand through the luxuriant dark curls on his head. His brown eyes, usually frank and fearless, seem to flicker across the room without focussing, and there is a look of unease on his handsome face.

"I'm so late! I'm embarrassed!" he says, looking at nothing.

Jerome holds out his arms.

"Hameel! At last I set eyes on you again! Where have you been since I came back from Reims?"

Hameel shrugs, his face inscrutable, and steps awkwardly into Jerome's arms. Inside the Master Painter's embrace, he seems to crumple a little. Then he breaks away quickly to take Aleyt's hand. She feels a tremble in his fingers as he takes hers, and a pressure just too strong as he presses his lips to her knuckles. She has given him the hand that bears her wedding ring.

"It'll be dark soon! Would you have us lighting expensive candles for you?" she chides the top of his bowed head.

Hameel steps back and sweeps an arm towards the window.

"I was coming directly here after the burning, but the Abbess Dominica caught me in a corner near the Stadhuis. There's no getting away from her when she's got a bee buzzing inside her head."

"What did she want?" Jerome asks, always on the alert for new stones to pelt her with in private. Hameel waves an arm dismissively.

"Oh, it was all about the costs of the stone font for the convent chapel. The usual things."

Jerome nods. Some years ago, when Dominica first became the abbess, he had been already in the midst of executing a commission for the convent's refectory at her predecessor's behest. Her carping and haggling over the price soon set the tone of mutual antipathy that had

16

festered ever since.

"Abbess Dominica chisels down the costs of everything except her own robes and meals!" he says. "And then when it comes to paying up…! Do you know how long it took me to get the money out of her for my painting of the Passion?"

Hameel smiles wryly.

"Eight months…"

"…and three weeks!" Aleyt interjects.

They all laugh. The old joke seems to have eased the tension in Hameel's shoulders and face. Jerome turns to Aleyt.

"Am I such a bore?"

"Of course you are," she says, "and that's why Hameel has stayed away!"

She makes a smile and moves towards the door.

"I'm going to chivvy Mary. Hameel – you know it's just cold meats? We must use all up before Lent."

"Of course! I wouldn't expect a feast at night-time. I ate well at midday."

"Well – for now I'll leave you poor put-upon artists alone to discuss your grievances."

CHAPTER TWO

"Hameel – make yourself comfortable."

Jerome gestures to Hameel to sit. Hameel takes the less comfortable of the two oak box-chairs, out of politeness, and listens to Aleyt's footsteps receding down the stairs. He runs his eye appreciatively around the familiar room. This room – indeed, the whole house – embodies the idea of a 'home' for him. His own lodgings, a cramped pair of rooms beside his workshop, are no more than a place to live in. Not that he should complain. His lodgings are a step up from the overcrowded kennels that cram his neighbourhood. But they feel bare and lifeless, and for five years he has lived in them as if he will move to something better in a few weeks' time.

Jerome takes the other seat. Hameel looks tired, he thinks, and he hasn't noticed him fidget like this with his fingers before, as if there is some substance clinging to them. He is fully seven years younger than himself, but he seems to have wrinkled slightly in the few weeks that they've been apart. How unlike Aleyt, who has bloomed like a flower while he was away, her skin gaining a beautiful peachy healthiness after the wan looks of the fruitless winter. He should have thought to say this to her – tonight, he will say this.

"So, Hameel, is it the Abbess I must blame for your

absence from our house since I returned from Reims?"

"It is."

"I have to say - to be blunt - you look worn out, Hameel."

Hameel nods.

"She wants my nose at the grindstone day and night."

"Oh, yes. A tight deadline for you to work to, and then you can go dangling for payment."

"She's given me a good advance in fact."

Jerome hoists an eyebrow.

"You should consider yourself very favoured, Hameel! Well – you'll at least take time off for the Holy Company's Shrove Tuesday feast tomorrow?"

"I don't know, Jerome. There's the expense of it as well. I haven't put my name down."

"That's a pity, I'd have liked your company. Do you want me to ask Wiggers in the morning if there's still room? Let me make up a half of the subscription for you."

Patronising, as ever. But Hameel keeps his brow unfurrowed.

"That's a kind offer, Jerome, but no, you'd better not."

Jerome has observed the supressed hint of a frown. Was he tactless to offer money? Surely he can do so much for a friend of such long standing? He sighs inwardly at the prospect of the feast. A day lost to his painting, and an unwanted flirtation with the sin of Gluttony.

"No doubt the Abbess will be there herself, feeding like the very picture of Gluttony!" he says, following the thought through to an image.

Hameel snorts and nods. The Abbess has the appetite of a horse. But he doesn't want to be drawn into this old topic.

"Did you eat well at the Abbey of Saint Denis in Reims?"

"In moderation, but well, yes."

"And your brother Goessens remains there?"

"He does. He's set up a studio there and will execute the figure of the saint, and incorporate my sketches for the background landscape, with the Abbey featuring prominently as the Abbot requires."

"But surely the Abbey of Saint Denis, by definition, only came into being after the saint's death?"

"That's not a matter that troubles the Abbot. He's more exercised by the dilemma of the saint's halo. Poor Goessens is driven around in circles by the matter."

"Why is that difficult?"

"Hameel – perhaps you're forgetting that Saint Denis was decapitated?"

"Ah…"

"And the painting for the abbey's chapel is to show his subsequent miraculous preaching, with the head cradled in his arms."

"So the halo…"

"Could be where the head used to be, or could be carried along with the head. In my view haloes are best dispensed with altogether."

"You never give your saints haloes."

"No. But these French monks are old-fashioned. The Abbot is determined upon a halo, but torn by doubts as to where it should be. I'm delighted to leave it all to Goessens. At least the Abbey of Saint Denis is prosperous, and the Abbot will pay well for his halo. I doubt he's as rich as our Abbess Dominica, however."

There is a cheer from the square outside, where the buzz of excitement still persists. Perhaps some juggler or conjuror has started to entertain the crowd, Jerome thinks with distaste. Folly and levity springing up like mushrooms out of death.

"Since you've been away, perhaps you don't know about her latest source of income?" Hameel says.

"What's that?"

"The Inquisitor."

"What, the Spaniard?"

"Yes, Jacomo."

"How is she making money from him?"

"She's lured him from where he was staying, to lodge at the convent."

Jerome considers this. Her audacity can still surprise him.

"A man lodging in a convent!"

"It's of the Dominican order. Their nearest monastery is too far from Den Bosch for his convenience."

"But do neither of them have any care for propriety? And he's paying a good price, I expect?"

"Oh, Jacomo won't care about the price. Rome will foot the bill, as long as he unmasks his quota of heretics and witches."

A quota? Would the Papal authorities be so cynical? It's possible.

"You really think Rome sets a quota?" he says.

Hameel shrugs.

"Well, nothing would surprise me," he adds.

"You've not met Jacomo, have you?" Hameel says.

"No – I believe he arrived on the same day as I left for Reims. Have you?"

"The Abbess introduced us, the last time I was at the convent to discuss the chapel with her. That was when I found out he'd moved in there – he and another Dominican, who acts as his assistant. *Outriders*, Jacomo said, *Just a start*. Apparently he expects more inquisitors to follow him here in due course, once he's got established. Answerable to him."

"And how did you find him?"

"Terrifying. Do you know why he's come to Den Bosch?"

"Well, to hunt out witches I assume."

Hameel waves a hand expansively.

"He can find them anywhere in Brabant. No, it's because of our famous ironworkers."

21

"What – at the bell foundry do you mean?"

"That's right. As it happens, Master Diederik left Den Bosch just after you went to Reims. He's casting bells for churches up in Zwolle and Groningen. But Jacomo told me he's eagerly awaiting his return."

Jerome tries to put these elements together: bells and inquisitors. He gives up.

"I haven't a clue what this means, Hameel. Is he ordering new bells for Rome?"

Hameel shakes his head. If only he could shake out of it the images that have plagued him since his conversation with the inquisitor.

"No. It seems he's spent years dreaming up new ideas for torture, and he wants our ironworkers to cast implements from his designs. What's worse, the Abbess put the suggestion to him that I could make precise drawings from his own sketches. She showed him some of my work on the font and the gargoyles. Now he's got hold of the idea that I might liaise between him and Diederik. Christ! You should have seen his eyes light up, Jerome, when he told me his idea for a device that would slowly twist a man's head until he was looking over the middle of his own back."

Jerome slaps a hand angrily on the arm of his chair.

"What right have such men to claim to represent God? God the just, God the merciful! The punishment of sinners in the next life is reserved to Him alone, and here in this imperfect world, we have civil authorities to punish crime."

He thinks of the Burgemeester, the thin-lipped Theofilus Piek. There is a man rigorous enough, and with powers enough, to keep Den Bosch as free of robbers and rapists and drunken brawlers as any city in Brabant.

"Does Theofilus Piek know of these intentions?" he says.

"I don't think it's likely. I think Jacomo is waiting for the return of Diederik before going any further."

"Well, our Burgemeester will be at the Feast tomorrow. I'll look for a moment to bring this up. Does he want Den Bosch to be known for such works? He shouldn't lie down and let these monks from Rome trample where they will!"

Hameel, as usual, is left between admiration and irritation. Jerome is so sure of himself. But why does he think it his business to interfere in matters of church and state? Why does he think the Burgemeester will heed the advice of a painter?

But Jerome is looking to him for some response, so he raises an invisible cup into the air, making a wan smile.

"I'll drink to that!"

Jerome smiles back, letting go of his anger, for now.

"How remiss of me! Let me fetch you a goblet of red wine."

"Better still, could we go into your studio to drink our wine? I'm curious to see how your painting of Hell progresses. I haven't seen it since... what, the Feast of the Epiphany at least."

"Of course, yes – by all means come down and visit Hell with me! But first, Hameel, I have some news."

He gestures at the scroll still lying on the table.

"Hameel – the commission for the window at Overmaas is mine!"

Hameel has no place to hide from the beaming face of the Master Painter, whose eyes demand his approbation and admiration. He glances back to the scroll awkwardly, and feels a flush rising to his face. He summons the will to look back into Jerome's eyes, and sets his mouth into a smile.

"That's wonderful news, Jerome! Congratulations!"

His voice sounds toneless, like a flawed bell. But Jerome doesn't seem to notice his awkwardness. For an artist, Hameel thinks, a man with an acute eye on the world around him, Jerome can be surprisingly blind. Just now, his gaze is blurred by excitement at his triumph.

23

"I'll be starting in the autumn, when I've finished my triptych for Saint John's. It's a big job, and I'll need help. Hameel - I want you to work on this as my assistant!"

He looks expectantly at Hameel.

In clumsy confusion, Hameel jumps out of his chair and walks to the window, where he feigns a sneeze. Surely Jerome cannot fail to see through the poor thin mask he is wearing over his feelings? He stares out of the window, trying to compose himself. Out in the square the crowd is diminishing now as the light begins to fail. The pyre has burned out, and tipstaffs are throwing buckets of water on the embers, and at each other. They are drunk. At the stake, which is solid enough to have survived the flames, he can make out the warlock's skeleton hung with clinging fragments of charred flesh.

He turns his gaze back into the room, looking towards Jerome, but not at him.

"I'm...I'm not sure Jerome. This commission from the Abbess... the font, the gargoyles..."

"Small beer, Hameel, compared with this work!"

Small beer for him, Hameel thinks, but the biggest commission that's ever come *my* way. He takes a deep breath. Jerome's intentions are good, and it's entirely thanks to Jerome that he has become an artist himself. He must focus on that fact, remember the debt he owes to the Master Painter of Den Bosch. Still, in this instance, the morsel he has been thrown is too gristly to swallow easily.

"But I'm contracted... I'm contracted well into the autumn."

"Hurry it along, Hameel. The Abbess is an impatient, hasty woman anyway. You can have your job done by the start of the autumn."

Hameel turns away again and looks up at the sky above the square. Behind him, the Master Painter brings their agreement to a conclusion.

"You and me, Hameel! It'll be wonderful to work with you again. Come on, I'll get you that wine, and we'll go down to Hell together!"

CHAPTER THREE

Jacomo, the Inquisitor, crossing the bridge towards the bell foundry, finds his attention caught by the enormous wheel being driven by the river's current. Coming to a halt, he glances in either direction out of habit. He has no enemies in Den Bosch yet, as far as he knows, but that will change. Since the early days in Seville under Father Torquemada, when once he was ambushed in a street in the Jewish quarter, he has preferred to have an armed man at his back. For now, in Den Bosch, where his inquisition has barely begun, he will depend on his concealed dagger and his sharp eyes and ears.

Satisfied that his surroundings are innocent, he leans his elbows on the stone parapet and gives his full attention to the wheel. Mechanical devices of all kinds fascinate him, and his eye savours the construction and shape of the massive wooden paddles as they dip into the hurrying green water and are propelled upwards again, dripping copiously and glistening in the Spring sunlight like the scales of some extraordinary fish. The wheel's strong, inexorable movement speaks to him of the power that God has put at Man's disposal. He is himself such an engine of His will. It flows through him, like the surge of a river.

The large, stolid and unadorned brick building from

which the mill wheel projects emits a loud panting noise, as if an enormous beast were stabled inside. Jacomo permits himself this fantasy for a moment, imagining some monstrous creature with horns and serpent tail straining at its chains. Behind its surfaces, the world is filled with the Devils' hidden works. But he is familiar with the interiors of foundries and forges, and knows the monster's breath is in reality the regular huffing of gigantic bellows driven by the power of the water. Other sporadic sounds ring out: metallic clangs and sharp impacts. The sweetish smell of burning charcoal is in the air. Jacomo feels a pleasant thrill of anticipation. The bell foundry of Den Bosch is famous throughout Brabant for the quality of its craftsmen, and he is confident that he will bend their master to his will. God's will.

Moving on from the bridge, he comes to the side of the brick building. There is a low archway. It doesn't look like the main entrance, which must permit the passage of a horse and cart at least. However, it appeals to Jacomo to make his way into the foundry unseen, and he slips under the arch into a passageway. He follows a sound of quietly clinking metal to an open door, and peers in at a small room with one barred embrasure. A man wearing a thick leather apron looks up startled from sorting through tools on a bench.

"I'm here to speak with the Master," Jacomo says. "Where is he?"

The man looks at him in a disconcerted way, and then puts a finger to his mouth and shakes his head, making a grunting noise. Jacomo surmises that he is mute. But presumably he isn't an idiot, or he wouldn't be working here. The man gestures with his palm in the air for Jacomo to wait, and goes out quickly through the door.

The room seems to be a store and workshop for tools. Jacomo enters and looks approvingly over the neat racks of tongs and hammers, pincers, pokers, and metal

27

implements and contraptions of all kinds, some of whose functions are obscure to him. He picks up a small vice, and turns it a few times. The screw is well-greased, and it feels heavy and balanced in his hand, a good quality implement. He wonders if they make their own tools, and looks closely at the handle to see if there is any identifying mark.

Outside, he hears footsteps approaching, and he puts down the vice and turns to face the entrance. A powerful square-built figure fills the doorframe.

"Brother Jacomo? I was expecting you – but not here!"

The man smiles. Jacomo chooses not to.

"Master Diederik?" he says.

The man nods, and looks uncertain whether or not to offer Jacomo his hand, so he puts the matter out of doubt with a benedictory sign of the cross in the air between them. He prefers to avoid touching human flesh. Even the physicality of his own body and its functions is a matter for regret.

The bell master bobs his head downwards a little in acknowledgement of the blessing, and then makes the faintest sketch of a second smile, his closed mouth like a bent pin on his fleshy face, which is flushed with the heat of the foundry. His brow is damp with the sheen of his disgusting sweat – could he not have wiped himself with a towel before appearing?

"I hope that your work in Groningen and the north went well," Jacomo says. "I've been waiting eagerly for your return, and looking forward to seeing your foundry in operation."

"And this is a good morning for you to call, as I said in my reply to your message. A bell for Saint Paul's of Antwerp is in its casting pit, and we'll be pouring the bronze within the hour. My foreman will come to tell me when the molten metal in the crucible is at the right heat. Would it interest you to see that process?"

"That would be most interesting, yes."

28

Jacomo waits, and Diederik examines his hands for a moment.

"Your message said that you wished to discuss some business proposal with me, Brother Jacomo?"

Jacomo nods. He prefers to save words, when a gesture will do. Besides, a nod or a movement of the hand can hold more meanings than a word.

Diederik steps aside from the doorway.

"Come with me then, Brother. We'll go to my office where we can be more comfortable."

He follows Diederik's broad back along the passage. When he was a boy, and still a foolish prey to Satan's promptings, he delighted in goading boys of such dimensions into fighting him. His reputation grew with each one that he bloodied and humbled. Caught off guard by this memory, he suppresses the sinful pride that still accompanies it. He will don his hair shirt tonight, in penance.

They emerge into an ample yard filled with wooden frames of all kinds and sizes, broken ends of clay castings, and boxes piled with sand. Brick buildings enclose the yard on three sides. Smoke rises thickly from a wide chimney at the far end, and drifts in a curling dark plume into the blue sky above.

"The furnace," Diederik says, glancing back at him and pointing towards it.

They pass through a doorway to a large, bright room. There are tables scattered with plans and papers, and more tool racks on the walls. The bell master gestures to a settle with an upholstered seat against one wall. Jacomo sits, and Diederik pours beer into two mugs from a pitcher that stands in a tub of water for coolness.

"I always drink beer, Brother, in preference to water, and I make sure my family does the same," he says.

"You believe that the plague is carried in the water?" Jacomo says, drawing the most obvious conclusion.

"Yes. Thanks be to God – and beer – we are untouched as yet."

"I think it's God you should thank indeed," Jacomo says. He has no time for such theories. Saint Anthony's Fire is visited by God upon the sinful, and no-one can avoid it by any of the many measures touted about by the ignorant.

He takes the merest sip of the beer, and sets the mug down on the ground beside him. He looks at the bell master without speaking. Most men will speak quickly, and sometimes rashly, faced with his stillness.

"Well…" Diederik says before long. "What exactly is it I can do for you, Brother Jacomo?"

"That depends on what you *can* do, Master Diederik. That's what I've come to find out. Your reputation is excellent. Your bells are considered the best in all Brabant. The bell that calls me to prayer at the convent of Saint Agnes is a most sonorous instrument."

The bell master looks pleased, and lowers his head a little to hide it.

"The first bell I had the overall charge of when my father had died. A lucky beginning. Is it a bell that you want us to make, Brother Jacomo?"

"No, it is not. What else than bells do you make here, Master Diederik?"

"Well, sometimes we cast bronze statues and effigies for the inside of churches and cathedrals. We've made hundreds of crosses of course – simple work – and sconces for candles. We also make large cauldrons and cooking vessels for the big kitchens of the nobility. And in our forge we make implements for our own foundry, and to sell to blacksmiths and other metal workers. We make quite a range of instruments – both standard ones and bespoke ones."

"So – both forging and casting – and from the largest of bells to the merest pair of pincers to pick up a hot piece of metal?"

"Yes, although of course we specialize in the larger work – the bell casting. Our biggest bells have to be cast in the location where they'll hang. We dig a casting pit at the base of the bell tower. But here in Den Bosch we cast all sizes of bells that can be transported on a cart. We have a special strong cart, which can be drawn by four donkeys."

Jacomo nods. This has all been reported to him, more or less, from the investigations of his assistant, Brother Bartelme. But he prefers to confirm anything that comes from Brother Bartelme, or any other source, with his own eyes and ears.

Diederik takes a good swig of his beer and wipes his mouth. Jacomo continues to wait.

"But what have you in mind, Brother Jacomo?"

Jacomo gives him a long look. Diederik puts down his beer mug, looking as if conscious of some unintended sin.

"You must be aware, Master Diederik, that torture is a necessary part of an Inquisitor's work. Those suspected of heresy, witchcraft, or other heinous crimes against God must often be tortured to extract confessions and information. And it is my own belief, and that of some of my brothers in this work, that torture can also be used to drive the possessing devils from the bodies of those who are confirmed in their wickedness."

He pauses, the better to observe the bell master. The sweaty sheen has dried out now, and his face is a cold white with blotches of redness on his cheeks and forehead. He wonders how much beer Diederik drinks, during his working day. But the man seems sober enough.

"We use, in God's work, a range of instruments," Jacomo goes on. "You might know some of their names, by repute. Some implements we can carry about with us from place to place - devices such as the heretic's fork and the pear. Others are large and heavy things – the Judas chair, the Spanish donkey, or the stretching rack, for example – which are kept only at a few centres in the largest towns. Generally we have access to the dungeons of the civil authorities – as I have here in Den Bosch. But I have bigger plans for Den Bosch, Master Diederik. I would like to set up here an inquisitorial dungeon, wholly under the control of the Church of Rome, for the investigation and punishment of heresy and witchcraft. God knows I suspect enough such sinners abide in these parts. The Abbess Dominica, of the convent of Saint Agnes, owns a highly suitable building, with thick walls and an extensive cellar, used at present as a storehouse. It's conveniently adjacent to the gaol cells behind the Stadhuis. Den Bosch is the largest and most important town of all Brabant, and, by great good fortune, is home to the skilled workers with bronze and iron who will be needed for such an enterprise."

Diederik looks like a man about to vomit. His eyes are wide but sightless, as if focussed on something unpleasant inside himself.

"You want us to make torture devices for you here?" he says.

There is a suggestion of incredulity in his tone, but Jacomo treats it as a brisk statement of fact.

"Exactly – and, Master Diederik, they will be devices such as the world has never yet seen!"

He can see that Diederik has been surprised by his tone. He can't keep the enthusiasm out of his voice on this matter – but then, why should he?

"What do you mean, Brother?"

"I mean that between us – with my ideas and your skills – we can create the finest array of implements that any inquisitor has yet had at their disposal."

"I don't understand – I thought that… well, I thought there was a fixed range of such…things."

"There is. But new things are added to God's world by the powers he has invested in Man. He has given us imagination, to seek and find new ways of serving him. This is my way – my own gift to God. You must understand that when we torture a witch or a heretic, it is not the human being, the child of God, whom we torture. It is the demons that possess him – or her. Those demons are tenacious. They will not yield their prey without a fight, and if they are not driven from the body they inhabit by the most excruciating pains, they will hold on and carry the soul away to Hell."

Jacomo pauses, and waits patiently for some response from Diederik.

The bell master reaches for his beer mug, and then changes his mind.

"What sort of things do you have in mind?" he says slowly and quietly, as if he would prefer the words unspoken.

"I have many ideas, but they are united by a single principle. I want the torment of these devils to be conducted in the most elegant and fitting way that is possible. The crushing of bones and gouging of eyes and ripping away of genitals – while all necessary and appropriate in many circumstances - are crude work, butcher's work. Let me give you a story that illustrates my intentions. Have you heard of the name of Perillos of Athens in ancient Greece?"

"I'm not a highly educated man, Brother," Diederik says apologetically. "I can read a piece of Latin, and make my measurements of course, but..."

"Oh, he's not a well-known figure," Jacomo says, waving a hand dismissively. "He was a brass founder, who worked for Phalaris, a tyrant king. He proposed a new means of executing criminals – the brazen bull. He cast a bull as large as a real bull from brass. It was hollow, with a door in its side. The condemned man was pushed into the interior through the door, which was then locked. A fire was set under the bull, and so the brass heated up until the man was slowly roasted inside. Phalaris would himself be feasting with his courtiers while this was in progress, and Perillos designed the bull in such a way that its smoke rose in scented plumes. Even more clever was a complex

33

system of tubes that he devised in the head of the brass animal that made the prisoner's screams sound like the bellowing of a real bull."

"How horrible!" Diederik mutters.

"Yes, horrible," Jacomo agrees. "To inflict such torment merely for its own sake. And Perillos paid a heavy penalty for his imagination – when Phalaris was completely satisfied with the design and construction of the bull, he made sure that Perillos was the first man to suffer death within it."

Diederik pulls a face.

"And you wish to persuade *me* to make torture implements!"

Jacomo smiles.

"Of course, the fate of Perillos is hardly an encouragement. But those were ancient, heathen times, when Christ had not come among us to redeem our immortal souls. I only describe to you the device of the brazen bull to illustrate how imagination and elegance can be employed in such a matter. That is what I seek in the service of God. But a brazen bull would not suit my purposes at all. Do you know why?"

"Why?"

"Because if I am torturing a devil that has taken up residence in a man or a woman, then I must know that they have been driven away before death. Otherwise I have lost a soul to Satan. I must hear the words of renunciation on their lips. It is my duty to guide them to their final utterances. They must die commending their soul to God. The infuriated bellowing of a brass bull would be of no use to me."

Jacomo is watchful of the effect of his words on the bell master, who now picks up his mug of beer again and drains it. When Diederik speaks, avoiding his eyes, it is as he expects.

"We have as much work as we can handle in our own line of expertise, Brother Jacomo. I have orders for bells that will keep us busy the rest of the year."

34

Jacomo listens patiently. He will allow the worm to have its wriggle before impaling it on his fisherman's hook.

"So – although of course I appreciate the high opinion you have of our foundry, and the... the... high moral value of what you aim to do..."

Jacomo keeps his eyes on the bell master's face. A moist sheen is reappearing on his forehead.

"... I fear that I... we... must decline to branch out into a line of work that is... is not really in our field."

The wriggling is over.

"So you *decline*, do you, Master Diederik?"

Diederik straightens his back a little, as if to draw strength from a good posture.

"Yes."

"You are a married man, I believe, Master Diederik?"

Now he has him. He looks completely perplexed. You can read in his face: *Married? What has that got to do with anything?*

"I am, Brother Jacomo."

"Your wife's name is Birgit?"

"It is..."

"But you also have a particular friend in the town, I believe?"

"A friend? I have many friends, I hope, in the town, Brother."

There is sweat beading now on his forehead. The fool begins to see where this is going.

"Your *particular* friend is called Catalyn. I had her brought to speak to my assistant, Brother Bartelme, yesterday. The Abbess Dominica knew where she was to be found."

Now Diederik flushes red to the roots of his sparse, curly hair.

"The acts you engage in with Catalyn – and I know all the details - are not sanctioned by God's laws, Diederik. Were they lies that she told to Brother Bartelme? I would deal harshly with a liar."

Diederik shakes his head, looking at his hands. His flush is so intense that Jacomo would not be surprised to see blood bursting out of his pores.

"So – you must think of your wife. Your good wife, Birgit. I hear nothing against this pious woman; a good church-goer, the mother of your children. You must renounce this sinful liaison henceforward. I imagine you can do this, and the matter can pass quietly into the past?"

Diederik's eyes are closed now, as if he could hide thus from the shame. He nods his agreement.

"Good. We must prefer that to a public denunciation and all the attendant unpleasantness for a man of your standing in the town. Dealing with common adultery does not fall within my own remit, of course, but I'm aware that the authorities in Brabant punish it harshly, when it raises its ugly lustful head. So - let me just say this: your new work will take precedence over your existing orders. You will be paid very well for your skills – and *enthusiasm*. I expect your fullest co-operation. God has chosen you for this Diederik, just as he has chosen me. Do not set yourself against the will of God."

He pauses. Diederik has opened his eyes again.

"Perhaps the idea of torture fills you with horror and repugnance?" Jacomo says.

Diederik nods mutely.

"That is a natural and understandable reaction. But remember what I've told you. It's the devils within that I torture, not the heretic. I have overcome my own horror and repugnance by prayer and meditation. I know that what I do is for the glory of God. That must be your own guiding principal, Bell Master."

There is a knock on the open door. A bearded face looks in.

"I believe our metal is ready to be poured, Master," the man says, and then, catching sight of Jacomo, he bobs a bow at him and crosses himself.

Jacomo stands up.

"Excellent. Now that our agreement is made, I look forward to learning much more about your working methods!"

Diederik stands too, and leads the way towards the casting pit. He trudges along with head bowed, as Jacomo has seen some men trudge towards their place of execution.

CHAPTER FOUR

Jerome makes the short walk to the Meeting House of the Holy Company of Our Lady with a foretaste of anxiety, and an apprehension of disgust to linger on the palate later. It's Shrove Tuesday, and today's feast is the last occasion before Lent for the eating of meat. The Company's chef, Maarten, will have been working all through the night, with his kitchen assistants scurrying exhausted about him. Jerome's own share of the feast's subscription would have fed his household comfortably for a week; perhaps two. There will be a degree of ostentation and excess that sits awkwardly, to his mind, with the Company's charitable purposes. For certain there will be a swan stuffed with a goose stuffed with a partridge and so on down to the tiny bony larks that some adore, but he finds disagreeable. He wished they could all come to life, bursting out of each other and flying about the hall. What consternation!

The quick, squabbling lives of birds fascinate him, and he enjoys sketching their colours and fleeting shapes. He tries to picture a swan snatching a goose and swallowing it... a streak of ripples, a flash of white, a mysterious vanishing. But swans are not cannibals. It's wrong, this calumnious dish.

Today is given over to the sin of Gluttony, that greasy-chinned gobbler of good intentions. God gave us pleasures and appetites, but didn't he also give us guilt? And why? To guide us. Our earthly delights can be modest companions on the road to Heaven, but too often they are tempters on the road to Hell.

As he enters the hall, he stuffs these reflections away. His status in Den Bosch requires him to belong and participate, not to carp and moralise.

The dining hall is filling up. Perhaps two thirds of the guests – some seventy or so souls - are already present, and many have already taken their places on the benches. A small boy's pale face materializes beside him, at the height of his elbow. His cap, bearing the Company's swan emblem, is a little too big and has settled over his ears.

"Spiced wine, sir?"

He picks up a cup from the tray and inhales the sweet aroma of cloves and grapes. God whispers *gluttony*, and he barely moistens his lips with it. He stands still for a moment, struck by how the midday sunlight from the high side windows divides the hall into zones. There are vivid areas glowing with the rich colours of the company's fine clothes, and dark shadowy places where indefinite figures lurk like ghosts.

Wiggers, the Holy Company's servant, comes up to him. He's not tall, but his square muscular body conveys an obscure sense of menace. His tunic looks too tight, and his head pops redly out of the collar, like a pimple ripe for squeezing. Above his flushed features, his hair, generally a mousy, sandy colour, is an orange fire raging out of control, and Jerome wonders what dye he has used to colour it, and why.

"Welcome, Master Jerome. How are you?"

"I'm well, thank you Wiggers. You're looking very... different."

Wiggers smirks a little and touches a hand to his crown.

"It's in preparation, Master Jerome, for a certain honour that's to come my way.

39

"Oh – what honour's that?"

"Oh – you'll see at the end of Lent, Master. I'll be wearing a cap out of doors until then. I'll say no more for now."

Jerome nods, unable to make any sense of this. Over Wiggers' shoulder he observes the Burgemeester, Theofilus Piek, entering the hall. The small white dog that he dotes on is trotting at his heels on a leather leash. It's the wrong dog for Theofilus Piek. It should be a wolf hound, a lean, loping animal like himself. Piek surveys the hall, his thin lips compressed. Jerome nods to Wiggers, and makes his way briskly over to him, before he can be engaged in conversation by anyone else. Piek is one of the tallest men in Den Bosch, and his bony head looms above him, only just on the friendly side of neutral.

"Good day, Theofilus," Jerome says. Here in the Company's house, they don't stand on ceremonial titles.

"Good day, Jerome."

"How is your family?"

"Well, well thank you. Down, Moses!"

The little dog subsides.

"And your family, Jerome? Your brother? The family workshop?"

"They are well. But I rarely go into the family workshop. I prefer to work alone, in my own house."

"Ah, yes, I think I had been told that. And then your secretive creations spring out at us, unexpected and shocking."

"My sponsors specify my subjects, in general."

"But they get something they could never have specified, don't they Jerome? That's why your work is so sought after. You're at work now on the commission from our own cathedral here, aren't you?"

"I am, yes. The triptych for the nave."

He pauses. Theofilus is already looking around again. He must move him on from small talk while he has the opportunity. At any moment they could be interrupted.

"Now, Theofilus, what do you think of this Inquisitor that we have here in Den Bosch, this Dominican, Jacomo?"

Theofilus turns his pale blue eyes back to him. He looks surprised by the abrupt change of topic.

"What do *I* think of him? What does that matter? The Spaniard is sent by the Pope. It's no affair of mine."

Or yours Jerome can read easily in his look. But he'll have his say.

"But doesn't his jurisdiction overlap with your own? All criminals are sinners, and some sinners are criminals. Who is to punish, in this life, such people? The Church or the Civil Arm? And what should be left to God to punish?"

The Burgemeester looks at him warily.

"These are complicated matters to raise, Jerome, especially at the start of a festivity. We should be taking our seats. What is really on your mind?"

Jerome lowers his voice a little.

"What I've heard is that Jacomo wants to establish Den Bosch as a centre for the Papal Inquisition in Brabant. That would mean this town, *our* town, becoming a place of cruel torture and public executions. You saw for yourself the burning of that poor madman yesterday! Is that the kind of thing you want to see more of in Den Bosch? If Jacomo is given his head, there will be an influx of these meddling monks, creating God only knows what misery with their investigations and zealotry. In short, the man is obviously a fanatic, and I'd implore you to do all in your power to make things less comfortable for him here."

Jerome catches a glimpse of orange out of the corner of his eye. Wiggers. How long has he been standing there, within earshot? Wiggers leans forward and speaks deferentially to the Burgemeester.

"If you'd care to take your place, Burgemeester, then the others who are standing will take their cue to sit.

41

The first dish is ready to come out, when prayers are said."

Theofilus nods, and makes a forced smile down at Jerome.

"Well, we must leave this Jerome. I've heard your views. Enjoy the feast!"

With a little tug at Moses, he lopes off. *Did I achieve anything?* Jerome asks himself. Well, even if he has planted the smallest seed of a question in the Burgemeester's mind, that is something. He has prayed himself, this morning, for the soul of that poor man burned alive.

Wiggers remains next to him, looking at him in a peculiar way, he thinks. A pustule with froggy eyes.

"Where have they put me?" he enquires.

Wiggers consults his list and points out his place on the bench. Then he bobs a quick bow and bustles off to deal with a late arrival. Jerome looks at his allotted seat. He is almost at the top of his table, but there is one place above him. Who have they placed there? A weasel, dressed in a purple tunic with a dark fur collar. He stares. Then he remembers. He has seen this thin faced man before – it's the Frenchman, the cloth merchant, De Bouilly. Well, he's a recent arrival in town and just elected to membership, so that's why he's honoured with the top place on this occasion.

He gets his legs over the bench next to De Bouilly and sits, exchanging a greeting and a nod, and watches as the last arrivals take their places. Among them, he is unpleasantly surprised to see the Abbess Dominica manoeuvring her not inconsiderable bulk into position at the end of the high table, just on the other side of De Bouilly and facing across them down the hall. What is she doing there? It's not that he himself feels slighted – he is contented enough to take his place – a high place – among the successful merchants, craftsmen and minor clergy on the side tables. But *her!* Venal, conceited, scheming: it sickens him that she has most of Den Bosch at her feet. How has she bought or cajoled her way to the top table?

The weasel turns his way, and Jerome shakes away his irritation to attend to him. He has met him only once before, when he struck Jerome as being predominantly sanguine but with perhaps a touch too much of yellow bile. Not that he is expert in the humours, but he enjoys categories and classifications.

De Bouilly's Flemish is slow and deliberate, larded with a thick French accent.

"Master Jerome – I have been hoping to meet you again. I am interested to learn something more of your craft. What are you working on now?"

He suppresses a sigh. This kind of question he is always running up against. He riffles through his pack of well-practised evasions, playing the usual cards of generality and vagueness. His work is alive for him, it has its own voice to speak with, but until it is in the presence for the first time of its commissioning patron, it should speak only in private. As he talks, he is half attending to the Abbess, who is in his line of sight beyond De Bouilly and already eating olives from a small bowl and sucking her fingers. No waiting for grace before *she* tucks in. Being at the very end of the high table, she has only one dining companion, at her left elbow, another cloth merchant, Meerdink. At the moment they are conversing animatedly, but there is always the danger – and the feast will be a long one – that discourse in that direction will dry up and she will direct her conversation forwards and downwards to De Bouilly and himself. On his right hand side, Jerome has observed from the corner of his eye Meister van Dorff settling into his place. He is a bore, nominally a lawyer but too rich to bother practising. He is obsessed with his alchemical experiments, which are always failing to bear fruit through no fault of his own. Well, he will just have to subject himself to van Dorff's retorts and condensations if the Abbess is the alternative.

43

Now they must all stand, as the Lord and Lady Dreyer de Middelrode promenade down the centre of the hall in clothes that would look very fine from a greater distance, and take their places at the centre of the high table. Theofilus Piek, the Burgemeester, greets them there in a way that somehow combines the required degree of deference to the nobility with a suggestion of assertiveness, as leader of a civic authority with less power than they used to have, but more than they are ever likely to have again. Jerome watches the performance carefully, but he still can't put his finger on how the Burgemeester pulls off this act of complex ambiguity so adroitly. Bishop Andreas says grace, and then waves over a servant to take away his mitre as if proclaiming to the world in general that he is now off duty.

Jerome takes advantage of the break to start De Bouilly on a new tack.

"Now that you've been here a month, are you finding yourself settling to our ways?"

De Bouilly shrugs. Jerome has seen that same Gallic movement of the shoulders many times from the Abbot in Reims.

"It is not so different here than my home town. Perhaps your whores are not so pretty."

Jerome's hand, half way to his mouth with his cup of spiced wine, halts for a moment in consternation. It might be that whoring is a topic for open conversation in Chartres, where De Bouilly comes from, but he will quickly find that things are different here.

"I wouldn't know about that, of course," he replies. He knows he sounds priggish, but the topic must be changed. "I'm a married man, myself."

De Bouilly's eyebrow, a little miniature weasel itself, wiggles sinuously.

"Ah, but you have a pair of eyes, Master Painter. You can look at a pretty face without committing a sin."

Jerome allows himself a nod of what might look like

44

complicity. He still feels uncomfortable. He wouldn't want the Abbess to overhear him apparently condoning whoring. De Bouilly goes on, leaning towards him confidentially.

"Perhaps these naked women I have heard that you paint, perhaps they are not only from your imagination?"

"My subjects are drawn from the scriptures," Jerome says awkwardly. He knows he's expected to banter, not sermonise. "If I sometimes depict nakedness, then it's because it's a necessary part of the scene."

De Bouilly, disappointed, gives him his Gallic shrug again, letting the matter drop.

"My own wife and children follow me here after Lent," he says, "by which time I hope to have secured a house on the square – like your own fine house, Master Jerome. It was pointed out to me. You say you are a married man – do *you* have children?"

"Not as yet," Jerome admits. This man De Bouilly seems to have been sent as a trial to him.

"Ah – well, I am sure you will have sons one day soon to carry on the family tradition. Was your father a painter?"

"He was."

The room where his father died last year floats across his mind's eye like a mote. The grey half-light. The bony fingers clutching at the bedsheets. The feeble voice urging him and Goessens to sire sons.

The ewerer and towel boy arrive, and they dip their hands into the offered bowl of tepid water and wipe them dry. As soon as the boys have passed on down the table, the first food arrives – some sort of small individual pie, and Jerome takes out his simple knife, noting that De Bouilly has brought a silver one with a carved bone handle. The Abbess has gone one better, as usual, and he catches a glint of some jewel in the handle of her knife as she thrusts it eagerly into the pie in front of her.

"Mmm – squab, I think?" De Bouilly enquires, indicating the pie with his free hand.

Jerome nods. He thinks of the large dovecot at the Convent of Saint Agnes, the top of which is visible over the wall. Has the Abbess bought her way to the high table with a gift of tender young squab for the pies?

They eat in silence for a few moments, so he can't help but overhear the Abbess, who is speaking in answer to some question from Meerdink on her left, but in tones designed to carry.

"Yes, we took delivery of the sacred bones on Friday last, and so we hope to be ready for our first pilgrims when the season begins after Lent."

"Which saint did you say?" Meerdink queries, wiping squab gravy from his chin.

"Saint Alonsus – a martyr of the first rank. He was put to death by the Romans, who began by chopping off his feet, and so he's particularly efficacious in alleviating lameness and all disorders of the lower limbs."

"And do you have the, er… the feet themselves?"

The Abbess shakes her head sadly.

"The feet were never found. But we have the next best thing: both thigh bones! At their previous resting place, in Zwolle, the chapel is completely festooned with the crutches and walking sticks that pilgrims left behind after their miraculous cures. We think we'll get a lot of interest. Do put the word around, among any friends or acquaintances who are afflicted."

"Where will you…er… put the, er…"

"For the present, in our chapel. But we're constructing a shrine in the east yard, with a roof against inclement weather. Pilgrims will be able to access that through our back door in the east wall, which will have a small tollbooth."

"Ah, so – there will be a fixed charge?"

"A nominal charge, just to keep out beggars and time-wasters. Pilgrims will be expected to leave more substantial gifts at the shrine itself – the usual things."

46

Meerdink nods. De Bouilly of course has heard everything too, and he now addresses the Abbess.

"Permit me, madam. May I introduce myself? Monsieur Pierre De Bouilly, of Chartres. I am making my home in your beautiful city, and I hope to visit this shrine of which you speak. I have a constant pain in the knee, especially during the damp and cold weather."

"I'm delighted to meet you Monsieur De Bouilly. I am the Abbess Dominica, of the Convent of Saint Agnes."

She turns slightly to her left.

"And this is Meister Meerdink, one of our most eminent cloth merchants."

De Bouilly acknowledges him with a nod that takes his head almost to the table's surface, like a seated bow.

"Enchanté, Monsieur."

Meerdink nods more perfunctorily, and permits himself a strictly provisional smile. As the most important cloth merchant in the town he is reserving judgement on this newcomer who is in the same trade.

"Welcome to er... Den Bosch," he mumbles half-heartedly.

Jerome, awkwardly on the edge of this interchange, glances to his right to see if he can avail himself of the van Dorff option, but van Dorff is already droning on to his neighbour on the other side about some minor explosion that has occurred in his laboratory. Reluctantly he turns his attention, although not his face, back to the threesome that has formed to his left.

"The Abbess Dominica," Meerdink explains to De Bouilly, "is at the head of our most prestigious convent here in Den Bosch." He lowers his tone slightly, and Jerome can imagine him glancing off down the other side of the hall, where there are various clerics, monks and a handful of prioresses and abbesses. "We have *dozens* of monasteries and convents here, Monsieur, but the Convent of Saint Agnes outshines even the...er, Franciscans and the Benedictines. Associated with the

47

convent is the best infirmary in the whole of Brabant for the sufferers of Saint Anthony's Fire. I believe the affliction... er... afflicts your countrymen also?"

"It does, Monsieur. It is a plague."

"In my opinion - and nothing is done about this - it's a result of the Jews poisoning our wells. I tell our Burgemeester – you see him along here to my left, the tall man, Theofilus Piek - I tell him that a watch should be set. Tipstaffs should watch the houses of these Jews at night, catch them red-handed as they sneak out to our wells with their poisons..."

The Abbess cuts in.

"Really, I can't go along with that, Meister Meerdink. How would you account for so many cases of the Jews themselves suffering with the Fire? It's clear to me that the sufferers are those singled out for punishment on earth by God. The fire of Saint Anthony is visited upon them for their sins."

Meerdink looks thwarted, but inclines his head in polite deference to her opinion. He addresses De Bouilly again.

"However the disease arises, the infirmary at the Abbess's convent is the best in the whole of Brabant."

"You're too kind," the Abbess simpers.

Jerome can bear no more.

"Have you *cured* any of your patients yet, Abbess?" he interjects, turning in his seat. All three of them look at him in surprise.

The Abbess favours him with a smile as cold as a knife in the ribs.

"We cannot hope to *cure*, Master Jerome. We can only make the poor sufferers as comfortable as they can be, and keep them safely apart from the rest of the community."

"*Poor* sufferers?" Jerome replies, with a smile as cold as hers.

"I speak of their condition, not of their means. Of course the doors of such an infirmary, which offers the very best that is to be had, cannot be thrown wide open. We would be overwhelmed."

Meerdink catches De Bouilly's eye, to offer an explanation.

"The Abbess's infirmary is a refuge expressly for those of... er, gentle birth and good family who are unfortunate enough to be afflicted with this terrible scourge. It's important not to er... exacerbate their suffering by plunging them into a rabble of the poor and uneducated in their dying days."

"Quite so!" De Bouilly nods and appears even to shudder. "The ranks of society must be observed, especially in the face of such distress."

The squab pies are now finished with, and the platters and fragments of crust are taken away by the boys. More boys appear immediately, and trenchers of bread are set in front of the company, each filled with a rich pool of golden sauce in which little islands of meat glisten. Jerome looks down into his trencher as if at a little world, imagining the tiny inhabitants of these islands. Fisher folk, setting out in canoes to fish for spices.

The chef has appeared at the screen that masks the kitchen door, and is looking around the hall. Lord Dreyer de Middelrode spots him and stands briefly to lead a round of applause.

"What are we eating, Maarten?" he calls out.

The hum of chatter falls quiet. The chef smiles and bows, first in the direction of the high table, and then to left and right tables.

"You have just had pies made with the finest squabs from the Abbess Dominica's dovecote..." (here there is a smattering of applause, and the Abbess raises a deprecatory hand) "... and now you have before you a dish of boiled chicken, smitten and hacked small, seethed and served in a sauce of galingale, milk of almonds and grains of paradise."

There is a renewed burst of clapping, and the chef,

looking relieved, slips away behind the screen with another bob to the company in general. The eating resumes - with gusto in the case of the Abbess, and conversation is held in abeyance for a time.

Now there is an interval of entertainment. Accompanied by a flautist, and playing a psaltery, a minstrel gives them a selection of short songs, both religious and secular. Some subdued conversation continues around the hall, but Jerome simply listens to the music. The sunlight creates a halo that outlines the singer's head and shoulders, and he thinks of poor Goessens struggling with the halo of Saint Denis . Then a wheezing voice at his right elbow announces that van Dorff wishes to bestow his attention on him. Without much preamble – typical of the man's self-absorption - he regales him with the disgraceful price of various chemical compounds at the Jewish apothecary's. Jerome is himself a frequent customer of the Jew, Izaak, who has more or less a monopoly in Den Bosch of some of the various substances he needs for mixing his colours, as well as of some of the rarest spices and compounds for cooking and for potions. He falls in therefore gracefully enough with the topic, giving some examples of his own. He likes Izaak personally, but he doesn't have to like his prices. From the price of everything, they move tangentially along the topic of money to end up at the matter of who has it and who hasn't. Jerome isn't especially interested in such gossip, but van Dorff seems to know to the last penny what everyone in the room is worth. Leaning in towards him, van Dorff nods discreetly up the table towards the Abbess.

"There's a woman with money to burn. She's just buying a house off me now, and driving a hard bargain. But I'll do all right. She doesn't know how cheap I got it myself. It belonged to that old crone, Nijenhuis's widow. She died intestate and they had no children, so I made a quick offer to the nephews and nieces before they could start a family war over it."

Jerome nods politely.

"The Abbess is the wealthiest woman in Den Bosch," van Dorff adds with a wink, and then casts his eyes towards Lady Dreyer de Middelrode, who is clapping her hands gently in time with the minstrel's singing, innocent as a child. "She could buy up our lord and ladyship at the top table there ten times over."

Why this tone of indulgence – worse – admiration? He's irritated. The Abbess is supposedly a nun, dedicating her life to the service of God. Why should he nod and smile, and join in with the general acceptance of this woman's avarice? The two cups of spiced wine he has now drunk prompt him to a more robust response.

"For myself…" he says in a firm voice, "I find such grasping after money by the abbess of a convent to be abhorrent."

His remark chances to coincide with the final flourish of the minstrel and his accompanist and the momentary pause before polite applause follows. The words "grasping after money by the abbess of a convent" ring out as clearly as a bell in this gap of silence, not quite loudly enough to reach the entire hall, but certainly loudly enough to command the attention of everyone seated in the immediate vicinity. This audience obviously includes the Abbess herself, as a glance in her direction confirms. She meets his eyes for a moment with a look of such venom that if she were a snake, he is sure she would strike at that moment and sink her fangs in his throat.

The applause for the musicians begins, and the moment passes. De Bouilly begins to talk to him about the differences between music here in Brabant and in his native Chartres. Jerome is interested in the topic - he plays the lute himself, and composes small songs from time to time, just for the private entertainment of Aleyt and himself. While he converses, a small part of his mind continues to dwell on his accidentally public condemnation of their nearest neighbour at the high table. All in all, although it was unintentional, he is not displeased to have lodged a small barb in the ample flesh of the gluttonous, avaricious Abbess.

CHAPTER FIVE

The morning sun is shining with real warmth for the first time this year into the small walled garden at the back of the house. The shadow of the tall building creeps slyly across the grass and paving stones and by afternoon will smother the delicate pink and blue flames of the early-flowering cranesbills Aleyt has planted in old butter tubs along the far wall. But for now the sun holds sway over this little kingdom.

Mary sits near the house on a low stool, just in the sunshine. She pulls out the last of the Master's painting smocks from the soapy water in the bucket beside her, and squeezes out as much moisture as she can. Then she rubs and pummels the sodden cloth against the slats of the washboard. When her fingers start to cramp, she hoists the smock up to look at in the sunlight. It will do. She plunges it into the other bucket, the one with cleaner water, to rinse out.

At the other end of the garden, Aleyt is fingering the bedsheets hung over the washing line to see if they are dry yet. They flap and flounce like clumsy dancers in the mild breeze. It's a perfect day for drying laundry.

Mary decides she deserves a few moments' rest, and leans her head back against the garden wall to look upwards at the patch of blue sky above. There are a few clouds hurrying by, small ones. Little lambs, looking for their mothers. She starts to count them. Nineteen, twenty... It occurs to her that it must be her birthday soon. It comes in April, and surely she must be at least twenty? In fact, didn't her father tell her she was twenty about three years ago? She should really try to keep track of her age, because her mother died at forty four, and it would be well to know how much longer she'd got. Not that she would necessarily die at the same age as her mother. Her father, after all, who lives in the nearby town of Oss, is much older, and he's still alive, as far as she knows. She hasn't seen him since last Michaelmas, when he came to Den Bosch to see the mummers. They had a pie together in the Stricken Deer. Then they fell to drinking ale. Then they fell to arguing about her mother and whose fault everything had been. Then, almost, they fell to blows. Next, after the landlord had asked them to leave because the other customers didn't want to sit and listen to family rows, they fell into the street. And finally they fell into each other's arms, sobbing, and promising to love each other forever. All in all, this was typical of their encounters, which only occurred about once a year.

Mary closes her eyes. The warm sun on her face is a gift from heaven. The bells of all the churches and monasteries and convents and the cathedral start to chime. Midday – or what those nuns and monks call Sext. Thank goodness she doesn't have to go and pray eight times a day like them. Not that she doesn't pray. She prays fervently and often, but not according to any fixed scheme. She likes to keep her praying for when it's really needed; for when she's done something wrong. That is frequently enough. She wonders if...

"Mary! Mary!"

She opens eyes, startled. Aleyt is standing beside the flapping bedsheets with her hands on her hips, looking at her.

"Mary, you're asleep!"

"I wasn't Mistress. I was just resting my eyes a

moment from the sunlight."

"Have you done with the smocks?"

"Yes I have, Mistress."

She points at the bucket of dirty water, mute witness.

"Paint!" she exclaims, disapprovingly. "It's a wonder the Master has any left for his pictures, he gets so much on his clothes!"

Aleyt comes down the little garden towards her.

"I wish I had a groat for every time you say that, Mary!"

"I wish *I* had a groat for every smock I wash."

"Then you'd be richer than we are!"

"That would be a fine thing. Then I'd give the orders."

Aleyt smiles.

"And I'd be as big a mule as you are when it came to carrying them out!"

Mary puts on a look of mock indignation.

"A mule! That's the name I get for breaking my back scrubbing and cooking and carrying!"

"A very good name. Mary the Mule. The sheets are dry enough to take in now."

"Would you like me to do that with my feet while I scrub with my hands?"

Aleyt puts her hands on her hips again, and adopts her Stern Mistress look, which fools neither of them.

"I thought you said you'd finished with the smocks!"

Three light knocks on the high wooden gate at the end of the garden turn their heads. The gate gives onto an alleyway, part of the network of alleys and passages that lies hidden between the houses and backyards of the town. The alleyways aren't kept clean and clear like the cobbled streets. They are dark and strewn with rubbish, and not safe at night. But in the daytime they provide short cuts, and a way of getting about Den Bosch discreetly, for those who wish to.

Mary and Aleyt exchange glances. Aleyt looks anxious, caught off guard. Mary wonders what she will do. She has her own hopes and fears.

"Someone at the gate," she comments, giving away nothing.

The three light knocks are repeated.

"Go... go and see who it is," Aleyt says, agitated.

Mary stays where she is, challenging.

"Why don't *you* go, Mistress?"

Aleyt walks down the garden, dodges the sheets, and reaches the gate. It isn't enough time to compose her thoughts. Why has she not foreseen this, and prepared her words carefully? She unbolts the gate with clumsy fingers and pulls it open.

Like an eel, Hameel slips through the opening, and secures the door behind him. Then he turns, and his eyes seem to devour her. He glances towards the house. He can see Mary in flickering gaps between the waving bed sheets, observing them frankly. He speaks softly and quickly to Aleyt.

"He's in the middle of a meeting of the Holy Company - about the Good Friday procession. Then they're going to walk the route. He'll be away for ages."

Aleyt also glances down towards Mary. She can't yet meet Hameel's look. Mary knows all that has happened while Jerome was away working on his commission in Reims. It's far too late to help that. But Mary has been her maid since before she married Jerome. They are more like quarrelsome but affectionate siblings than mistress and servant. Mary acquiesced in the secret, and has done what she was asked to. She even became a go-between for them. Aleyt has never doubted that Mary would be discreet about this one thing, although in general she is as great a lover of gossip as any servant in Den Bosch.

Mary is not in the secret of her present thoughts and intentions –but no more is she. She had thought she had a plan, but... Hameel reaches out his hands to her, and she takes them in hers. She should have kept her hands at her sides. She feels all her resolutions instantly set at nought. Hameel smiles at her, and lets go of her hands to walk down the garden to Mary.

"Mary, would you like a groat?"

He takes the small leather pouch that dangles from his belt and holds it towards her. She makes round eyes and puts her hand delicately in front of her mouth. She'll play his game. She always has.

"That's a big purse!"

"Well?"

"A whole groat?"

"Yes."

She swivels her head a little to the side and rolls her eyes back to look at him coquettishly.

"What have I got to do for you, Master Hameel?"

"Just go to the market and see if there are any oranges from Spain."

"There aren't. I know."

"But you need to go again, and check every stall carefully. You might meet some friends and stop for a chat. You could be gone for some time. Until you hear the next bells."

Aleyt has followed Hameel down the garden, and stands behind him now. The colour has risen in her cheeks. Mary catches her eye, and Aleyt nods her permission, her eyes shining with – *lust*, Mary thinks to herself. Why call it love? *Love* is what Hameel feels. It cloaks him like a malady.

Mary stands up, dries her hands, and holds one out. Hameel loosens the string around his leather purse and fishes inside, bringing out a small dull coin. She takes the groat, makes an overly elaborate curtsey, and goes straight through the back door into the house.

A moment later they hear the front door out to the square slam shut. Mary's movements are always easy to follow at a distance.

Hameel turns to Aleyt. The sun illuminates a few strands of flaxen hair that escape her head cloth. Since Jerome's return, he has watched and waited for such a moment as this.

"You look so beautiful today!" he says, touching a hand to her cheek, gently.

Aleyt meets his adoring gaze for a moment, and then her cheeks dimple and she turns aside. She takes a couple of paces, speaking over her shoulder.

"Help me get these sheets off the line."

Hameel looks around. This garden is a fine and private place. The only windows that overlook it are those of the house, and the house is eyeless. He follows Aleyt. She stands beside a billowing sheet. He touches her back, just below the nape of her neck.

She feels her heart pounding. Why did she let Mary go? Why is she so weak? She speaks without looking at him.

"Hameel – it's different now that Jerome is back."

Her words clutch at his innards. He lets his hand fall and takes a step back. What does she mean to say? She turns towards him. A sheet flaps against his face, making him feel foolish.

"Aleyt... you still..."

He doesn't know what to say.

But Aleyt understands him anyway. His look of pain tugs her towards him. She puts out a hand and holds his arm

"Of course. Yes."

"Those weeks when... when we were together... have been the most blessed of my life," he says.

"And for me, Hameel... but..."

He interrupts. He wants no *buts*.

"I thank God he left you here. I might never have spoken of my true feelings for you otherwise. I had never thought..."

"Hameel – now he's back. I have to look him in the eye. Every day - and every night."

Hameel stares into *her* eyes, trying to read what is there.

"I think of you all the time Aleyt."

58

"I know. I could see it in your face when you came to the house that night for supper. God knows how Jerome couldn't see it. I was frightened."

"It was hard, being with you but unable to speak of what was in my heart. And now I feel so cut off from you. It's been three weeks since then. That's why I had to seize this chance."

Aleyt moves a little closer. It's as if she is drawn by some physical force, just as a heavy object is drawn to the ground. He takes her in his arms and their lips meet. Their tongues. Hameel pulls back a moment to whisper in her ear.

"Let me make love to you here! No one can see into the garden."

He pulls off his cloak and spreads it on the ground. They sink down onto it together. The sheets on the washing lines make a kind of room, with the blue sky and scudding clouds as a ceiling.

"Hameel..." she murmurs as he fumbles with the fastening of her gown. "You're like... like the serpent in the Garden of Eden." Then she reaches down and feels the stirring, rising movement in his breeches. "Oh, sweet serpent!" she breathes.

"And you are my Eve! Eve wore no clothes in the Garden."

They both giggle, and for a while, a short, blessed while, they make believe they are innocent of sin.

*

Mary stands for a few moments outside the door of the house, looking at the comings and goings in the market square. She feels at a loss with what to do with herself. Moreover, she feels disgruntled, in spite of the groat. She had been so confident that with Jerome's return, Aleyt and Hameel's liaison would gutter and expire, like a spent candle. But there they were, inflamed with passion once again, while she was dismissed to do as she pleased. Her hopes were dashed that Hameel might come looking for *her* one of these days, as he so often used to. She'd never told Aleyt that, and she doubted Hameel had brought it up. She wonders if Aleyt guesses it anyway.

She'd hoped so much that he might seek solace with her again. She isn't proud.

As she stands near the door, uncertain which way to turn, a man with wide shoulders and extraordinary vivid hair poking out from under his cap stops and catches her eye.

"Hello Princess!" he says with a wink. "Fancy coming for a drink with me?"

It's that Wiggers who works as a servant at the Holy Company house. Why is his hair orange? She turns her face into a haughty mask and walks away. It isn't until she's left the market square behind, and is walking briskly along Brugstraat that she decides where she is going.

Her sister Catalyn's room is in a tumble-down house down a side-alley beside the Three Hogs, a discreet location which is nevertheless well known to many men of the town. There are three other women who have rooms there, and, in the pecking order of such things, it is probably the best brothel in Den Bosch. The clients, at least, are men with heavy purses, and the women employ a man to stand at the door at nights and turn away riff-raff drifting from the inn.

At this time of day, there is no-one about, but Mary nonetheless looks anxiously up and down the street before ducking into the alleyway.

One of the women, Brigitta, is sitting on the step of the open doorway to the house, brushing her long black hair. She grins when she sees Mary.

"Ooh – look what the tide's washed in! A respectable woman!"

Mary laughs. Brigitta always chaffs her.

"Hello Brigitta. Is my sister at home?"

"No, I'm afraid not, My Lady. She's off on a jaunt somewhere."

Mary feels disappointed, and once more at a loss with herself.

"Oh, well... will you tell her I called by."

Birgitta looks at her with more attention, and speaks in a softer tone. "Is there anything wrong, Mary?"

"No, nothing's wrong. I was just going to pass the time of day with her for an hour, that's all. God save you."

"God save you as well, my dear. I'll tell her you came. I've a gentleman coming soon, or I'd like to talk longer with you myself."

Walking aimlessly down Pensmarkstraat, she feels crosser than ever. Then an excellent idea occurs to her. It will take her away for longer than she was instructed, but what does that matter? No one will be in any position to chide her. She lifts her chin as she walks. She has more strings to her bow than Hameel! Let him dally where he shouldn't - it was time she paid a visit to one of her *other* special friends. Farmer Gillis might be busy in his fields, or out and about somewhere like Catalyn, but if he is at home, and has a little free time, then he might be in for a pleasant surprise.

CHAPTER SIX

"Sister Theresa..." the Abbess says, and then turns around. Where is her pale mouse? Why isn't she in earshot?

Terce prayers have just finished, and there are three hours now until the prayers of Sext. During this late morning period, the Abbess likes, once or twice a week, to take a tour of her demesnes.

She glances over her shoulder at the nuns emerging from the chapel behind her. Sister Theresa has got trapped behind a knot of her peers and scuttles to catch up. She carries a sheet of paper clipped to a thin board, and a small bottle of ink and a quill in a leather quiver dangle from her belt. Good, she took these things into prayers in anticipation. This shows that even Sister Theresa can be trained, with perseverance. The Abbess likes a record to be kept of any notions she might have as she makes her rounds.

"Hurry up, Sister Theresa," she barks, and strides towards the kitchen. She's not really in any hurry, but Sister Theresa requires harassment, for the good of her soul.

She passes with her scurrying shadow along two sides of the cloisters, through the refectory, and down the covered walkway that leads to the kitchen building. She always starts in the kitchen. The main meal of the day, which follows Sext, will already be in preparation. A fresh breeze in the walkway makes her habit whisk about her legs, but it isn't a cold breeze. The morning is fine and bright - Lent is proving to be a foretaste of summer this year, and she has already tasted in her dreams the long absent savour of fresh green vegetables and fruit. A good proportion of the convent's grounds is laid out in orchards and vegetable plots, so there is always a time of plenty in the summer and autumn.

However, for now it is Lent, and the ingenuity of Sister Mary and her cooking assistants is put to the test to produce varied and flavoursome meals. The Abbess encourages some latitude on the theme of fish – beaver tails are permissible, and ducks when they can get them. She holds, along with many others in religious orders, that any watery affiliation is acceptable to God at this time. But the most important standby in Lent is the convent's eel pond, always well stocked with large, abundantly fed eels.

So, as she enters the stone-built octagonal kitchen, where already two of the fires are lit and water set to boil, she is not surprised to see Sister Mary contemplating a large basin of water with several fat serpentine forms slithering about in it.

"Ah! We dine on eel today I see, Sister Mary."

"Good morning Abbess. Yes, today and Friday, but prepared in different ways of course."

"Of course – I know you'll never bore us, Sister."

"I hope not – Sister Margaret! Where are you?"

A young nun with a slight limp bustles through a doorway and bobs an anxious bow at the Abbess. She is carrying a pitcher of liquid. She sets it down.

"Right, Sister Margaret. This one!"

Sister Mary and her assistant grab hold of one of the eels. It thrashes about, and tries to bite, but they lower it head first into the pitcher and hold it suspended in the spiced red wine within. After a few moments its frenzied lashing comes to an end.

If only one could dispose of enemies so easily, she thinks.

"Next one, Sister Margaret."

She leaves them to it. The eels, once drowned in wine, will be roasted, or perhaps smoked, and all the dangerous coldness and moistness of their humour will be expurgated. A fine dish to look forward to, especially served up with some tasty pottage. Sister Mary's pottages are in a class of their own.

She passes on through the door at the further end of the kitchen into the vegetable garden, where a couple of novices are hoeing the soil. She waits a moment until they see her and bow, bestows a gracious nod, and moves on towards the reedy edge of the stock pond. She is looking forward to the eel later in the day, but she is already tiring of the flavour, and will be heartily sick of it before Lent is over. She speaks over her shoulder to Sister Theresa.

"Make a note, Sister Theresa, that we are to have salted sea fish at least twice a week through the remainder of Lent, and also that Sister Mary should go and talk to Master De Vries to make it particularly clear that if he saves the best of his fresh river catch for us, then he will secure the best possible price."

He'll have a queue of customers trying to twist his arm, she thinks. How assertive is Sister Mary? She can hardly go herself to haggle for fish.

As she walks up the slightly rising ground beyond the pond to the tall tower of the dovecote, the thought of the tasty young pigeons in the squab pies at Shrove Tuesday's feast comes back to her. She must make sure that squab is on the bill of fare once more as soon as Lent is over. Inside the tower there is a subdued cooing that she listens to with pleasure. But something is niggling her. What is it? Something that has been conjured up by thinking of the feast.

Now she has it! It's that damned painter Jerome. How dare he censure her? She brooded on it in the days immediately following the feast and then managed to forget about it. But now his self-righteous face rises up again in her mind's eye, and his words ring in her ears: *Grasping after money…. Abhorrent.* He might be high and mighty in his own sphere, but what right does that give him to criticize her thus? Where does it say in the Bible that all monks and nuns have to live in poverty? Let the Franciscans have a monopoly on that! Where would Den Bosch be without her prosperous convent and its infirmary? And soon, the lure of St Alonsus will bring pilgrims flocking. Pilgrims need lodgings and food. They spend money. She is a public benefactor, and most of the town's citizens see that well enough. Her special contacts in the town – generally people who owe her money, or about whom she knows more than they would wish - report to her where she is admired, and where criticized. You can't simply trust what people say to your face. It's through her spies that she has learned of other ways in which Jerome has moved against her interests. It was he who privately helped out old Steenman when she had him over a barrel over his debt, and would have got hold of his house. It was he who spoke in private to council members at the Holy Company, raising questions about her suitability as a candidate for membership when she first came to Den Bosch. She gathers from Wiggers that Jerome was bending the ear of the Burgemeester about the Inquisitor at the recent feast. The Inquisitor and his assistant are her own paying guests, and she has some hopes of selling a building to them in the future. But, once again, that hell-hound artist is meddling in matters that didn't concern him. How good it would be to have him on a short leash in a dark kennel!

She pictures him, with a chain around his neck. As ever, her mental image blends Jerome with her own father, last seen many years ago. By now, she hopes, he's dead. The same haughty eyes and look of disapproval. She hangs the chain of this censorious composite man on an imaginary hook, to choke him.

A more pleasant thought arises. She has a new source of information about Jerome and his household. Perhaps today would be a good day to pay a visit to her special tenant farmer? She feels a little stirring sensation, a small warming glow from the fire within her. Yes, she is in the mood for that.

She turns to her mouse. She's staring into space in that foolish way of hers, and jumps when spoken to.

"Sister Theresa, we're going out to visit the cottage at Oostgebieden. Fetch my pattens."

Fifteen minutes later they make their way out of the east gate in the city walls and after a few hundred yards, they turn off the road onto the track beside the river that leads to Oostgebieden. The recent dry weather has saved them from mud. How pleasant to feel the breeze on her face, and to see the well-tilled fields with their neat lines stretching in all directions. How pleasant too, to think how many of these fields belong to the Convent of Saint Agnes.

Oostgebieden is the smallest of the tenant farms that pays rent to the convent and contributes to the tythe barn's contents each harvest. The farmer, Gillis, is a single man, and in his case she is prepared to go lightly on matters pecuniary.

He is a tall, well-built young man of twenty-four or five, with curly dark hair and a pleasing smile. He reminds her strongly of a boy she took a fancy to as a young girl, long before holy orders were in her mind. Gillis may not be the sharpest tool in the box, but he isn't a fool. He grows corn, and keeps pigs, chickens and geese, and is in general sober and hard-working.

Her spies in town have kept an eye on his doings there. She has found out that Gillis is a man with healthy carnal appetites, who seems in no hurry to acquire a wife. The most interesting fact that the Abbess's informants have unearthed is that he enjoys the favours of the servant girl at the house of Jerome.

This was worth knowing, as far as it went, but the Abbess could think of no use for the knowledge until a few months ago, when Gillis got into difficulties paying his rent. The young man, completely unable to meet his due payment, came and confessed in shame that he had fallen prey to gambling with the dice on the previous week's market day, and, fuddled with too much beer, had gambled away half a year's rent to a gang of men who would not hesitate to pay him a visit in the night with cudgels, or even knives, if he failed to honour his debt.

After reading him a homily on the evils of drink and gambling, the Abbess left him in suspense for a week. During that time she dwelt on a variety of aspects of the situation. In the end she decided that as he was young and repentant, he deserved a second chance. She sent for him, and proposed to him an arrangement that would see him through his difficulties and enable him to keep his tenancy of the farm, as well as providing him with a means of shriving any future sinfulness.

As she pushes open the gate to the yard of the modest thatched cottage, the flock of geese surges as usual around their ankles and puts the timorous Sister Theresa into a flurry of agitation. The Abbess is in a good mood once more.

"Ah – these birds look fine and fat, don't you think? We shall have roast goose after Lent, Sister Theresa."

Sister Theresa doesn't answer. She's too busy holding her habit tight around her legs, as if the geese might get under the cloth and peck at her spindly shanks. Well, let Sister Theresa spend the next half hour running away from the geese, it will keep her occupied. She always makes her wait outside the cottage when she visits Gillis.

"Go and sit on the fence in your usual place, Sister. The geese won't follow you over there."

Sister Theresa retreats, casting anxious looks over her shoulder. Some of the geese do seem inclined to follow her, and she breaks into a trot. Really, it's as good as having a court jester.

She moves towards the door of the cottage and calls out.

"Gillis? Are you here?"

A muffled voice responds from within, and she pushes the door open without more ado.

Gillis is seated at his workbench and looks up from his task. He is weaving a basket, it would appear. He puts aside the pieces of reed and the wooden base, and stands up. She's pleased to see that the room is swept and tidy. She's made it clear that she might drop in at any time without notice, and doesn't want to find any squalor.

"Good morning, Abbess Dominica," he says, with a respectful bob. She extends a bejewelled hand in his direction and he hurries over to take it and press it to his lips. The Abbess feels the firm touch of his fingers and inhales his slightly sweaty odour with pleasure. She ruffles his hair affectionately with her other hand. He smiles sheepishly and backs away, gesturing to the cottage's only chair, which she has paid for so she will have somewhere comfortable to sit when she visits.

"Well, Gillis, how goes it on my farm?"

She sits down. He remains standing.

"It goes well, Abbess. I've sown the seeds for the spring wheat this week, the same as what all the farmers around about are doing. The soil is soft and quite dry."

"Good. And your geese, I see, are looking healthy. Bring me a half dozen two days after Easter. I'll make sure Sister Mary expects you."

"Very well, Abbess."

She puts on an expression of mock sternness. There is no point in wasting time on pleasantries.

"Now, we must proceed to your penitential rites. Are you in a state of sin, Gillis?"

Gillis lowers his eyes. Is he acting? Or truly shamed? She can never decide, but both are delectable.

"I am, Abbess."

"Very well, then you must do penance as before. Take off your clothing."

She settles herself more comfortably in the chair to watch as Gillis kicks off his leather shoes and unlaces his hose from his leather jerkin to peel them off. He slips off the jerkin and pulls his tunic over his head and away. Finally he pulls down his short breeches and steps out of them. He knows better than to try to cover himself up with his hands, and she looks his naked body up and down. A pleasurable excitement is rising in her.

"This is good for you, isn't it Gillis? Do you feel humility?"

"Yes, Abbess."

"And remorse?"

"Yes, Abbess."

"Good. We will pray together in a minute. Now recount the details of your sin. Who was your fellow sinner?"

"It was Mary."

"Mary, the servant girl of Master Jerome?"

"Yes."

"Very well. Now, before we get into the details of your sinfulness, I want to know everything she said to you of the doings in that house."

Gillis raises his eyes to hers. She can tell that he's surprised by the question. He shrugs.

"There was nothing, Abbess."

"Nothing? Think again. It doesn't matter if it seems something trivial."

"Well... she talked of how much less work there was to do, while Master Jerome was away on his visit to... Reebs, I think it were."

"Reims, I believe."

"That were it."

"Of course. One less mouth to feed. One less set of clothing to wash. Go on."

He strokes his chin thoughtfully.

69

"She said as how she and her mistress Aleyt seemed to get on like a couple of old friends when the Master was away. How her mistress is a very lenient mistress, and doesn't stand on no formalities much."

"A most unsuitable way to treat a servant," the Abbess comments.

Gillis bows his head slightly, as if it were his fault.

"Go on."

"Nothing much else, really Abbess. She was saying as how Aleyt's cousin was a-having of a baby, and as how Master Hameel wasn't visiting the house so much, now that the Master was back from Reebs."

What? Hameel? Visiting in Jerome's absence? Is there the scent of something here? She realises that she has leaned forward eagerly in her chair, so eases herself back and speaks casually.

"Hameel, you say? But he's a frequent visitor to their house, is he not? You've told me that before, and indeed one would expect it, he and Jerome being lifelong friends."

"Well, that's as may be, but Mary says he's stayed away a bit since the Master's return."

"But while he was away... what did Mary say about while he was away?"

"Well, she didn't say a lot..."

His eyes won't meet hers. She feels sure she's onto something.

"Gillis... if I'm to help you to atone for your sins, I must have complete honesty and openness from you. I'm doing God's work. I represent God. You wouldn't lie to God, would you? You understand that, don't you?"

"Yes, Abbess Dominica."

"So, now, tell me plainly: what has Mary said to you about Hameel's visits to their household?"

Gillis studies the palm of his hand, and then meets her gaze at last.

"He was a frequent visitor – a very frequent visitor –

70

to Aleyt when her husband was away."

She nods, her face expressionless. Inside, she is getting ready to crow with delight.

"Always in company, no doubt? Always while Aleyt's father or cousins were about?"

Gillis shook his head.

"She didn't say that, no."

"Then…?"

"That's all I know."

"Are you sure?"

He's shifting his weight from foot to foot. He knows more.

"Are you *sure?*"

"Mary is very faithful to her mistress. She's a good girl – well, in that way. She said no more than what I've said to you."

"But it seems you think there was more to be said?"

"Now you're a-twisting my words, Abbess. I don't say as anything wrong has happened there, and nor did Mary."

She will get no more from him, but she has enough. Hameel and Aleyt? Here is some grist for her mill, perhaps. If she can gain more evidence of a taint of sin in that quarter, who knows where it might lead, and what its consequences might be for that insufferable painter?

She sighs, as if wearied of the sins of the world, and makes a sign of the cross. Then she allows her eyes to wander frankly over the naked young man in front of her.

"Very well, Gillis. Now it's time for your confession of your sin. I want no detail to be spared. Pass me the switch."

Gillis takes the flexible willow switch from its place and puts it into the Abbess's hands. She pats it against the palm of one hand.

"Good. Now, the details, Gillis. And if your manhood is aroused in the re-telling, what does that

71

mean?"

"It means I'm still sinning in my heart, Abbess."

"Exactly, and we must mortify the flesh in that case, must we not?"

Gillis nods.

"Go on."

He launches into a stumbling account of his last coupling with Mary. She watches his cock as it shows the first signs of plumping and extension, and feels her own parts becoming moist. He will not escape some cuts of the cane today. Of course he must do her bidding to keep his farm, and the poor fool probably believes that confessing to her is better than confessing to the priest, because she is higher in the Church. A little closer to God. But in addition to these persuasions, she suspects that he is learning to enjoy his chastisements for their own sake.

When she has heard every detail, and lashed him, and sent him into the cottage's other room with his bundle of clothes to pray, she hitches up her habit and slips the willow switch between her legs to pleasure herself. She closes her eyes and imagines it is Gillis doing this. Could she indeed, one day, make him complicit in this little sin? It's a delicious thought, but, sadly, probably incompatible with maintaining her moral authority.

When she emerges from the cottage a few minutes later, she walks through a sea of hissing geese to where Sister Theresa sits daydreaming at her accustomed spot, perched on the safe side of a stout fence.

"Come on, Sister Theresa," the Abbess says, "we don't want to have to hurry ourselves to be back for prayers at Sext. Have you heard the bells for the eleventh hour?"

"Just a few minutes ago," Sister Theresa replies. Why the peculiar sideways glance?

"Didn't you hear them yourself?" Sister Theresa adds.

"We were busy in discussion of the farm's rents," the Abbess replies.

"Ah – the rents…" Sister Theresa echoes.

The Abbess gives her a sharp look. Sister Theresa is more or less a simpleton, although she knows enough Latin to write down her instructions. Apparently she entered holy orders as a small child. She's never seen any sign that Sister Theresa understands anything of the world outside the convent. So these little remarks, this hint of some suspicion, seem uncharacteristic. Well, best to nip this in the bud.

"What's on your mind, Sister Theresa?" the Abbess demands.

Sister Theresa mutters something. She seems embarrassed. The only words that the Abbess catches are "Sister Ursula".

"Speak up, can't you?" she says with some asperity. "What's that about Sister Ursula?"

Sister Ursula is one of the convent's senior nuns. She had already made her way up the convent's hierarchy before the Abbess's arrival. She has gathered that Sister Ursula once had hopes of reaching the highest office herself one day, and there was no doubt that being overtaken on her way up the slippery pole had put her nose permanently out of joint.

Simple Sister Theresa fiddles with her ink bottle and paper, and clarifies her murky mutterings.

"Sister Ursula said that you visit Gillis far more often than the other tenant farmers. She said that I should go into the house with you when you visit. She said it was unsuitable for you to be on your own with a young man. She said it could cause scandal and bring disrepute to the convent."

The Abbess nods. More fool Sister Ursula to confide such thoughts to an idiot like Sister Theresa, who didn't have the sense to keep them private.

"Well – so that's it, is it? And what about you, Sister Theresa? Do you agree? Do you think I'm not to be

73

trusted on my own with a young man?"

Even Sister Theresa understands the correct answer to this question. She shakes her head vehemently.

"Of course, Abbess Dominica. Of course you're to be trusted. I'm only saying what Sister Ursula..."

"Yes. Well, from now on, I suggest you pay less attention to Sister Ursula and more to me. Sister Ursula is a bad apple. Do you understand me?"

"A bad apple – yes."

"And one bad apple can spoil a barrel, as the saying has it. You understand?"

"Of course, Abbess."

"So I suggest you rely on me to have a proper sense of what is and isn't fitting for an Abbess, and let Sister Ursula think whatever wicked thoughts such a bad apple would think. All right?"

"Yes, Abbess Dominica."

That will do for now. She sets off briskly, letting Sister Theresa keep up as best she can. As she walks, she mulls over how she might catch out Sister Ursula over some minor misdemeanour. Be it ever so small, she will find a fault. And as for a punishment... Her eyes fall on the straggling thorn bushes beside the path and she has a brilliant thought. A variant on an old theme. An improvement. She will talk to the tailor Johannes about it tomorrow.

CHAPTER SEVEN

The pale white light of morning seeps through the north-facing window into Jerome's studio. After yesterday's hurrying clouds and sunshine, a thin gauze of high cloud has spread over today's sky. He stares at it for a while, willing its featureless white to yield some image. But it resists his imagination, devoid of the steaming volcanoes, ships in full sail, flying witches, and shaggy-bearded faces of the day before. At least it is a good even light to work by. To make the most of it, he moves the easel that supports the panel of Hell closer to the window. As always, he steps back before he begins work on the day's detail, to see the whole.

At the top of the panel are his burning citadels, their black walls and towers silhouetted against an inferno that consumes the insides of the buildings and lights up the sky, where devils swarm overhead like summer gnats. Precarious bridges and walkways link one burning tower to another, and tiny figures carry pikes across them. Others climb ladders to feed the furnaces through fiery portals. On a bridge across a wide moat, an army gathers for an assault and behind them, from an open gate in the city wall, people flee the fighting and burning within. In the firelit waters, crowds of drowning sinners struggle for all eternity to draw air into their lungs. It is Den Bosch, its walls and ramparts and

75

battlements, its moats, bridges, windmills and water-wheels, that he imagines thus, transposed to Hell. The completed triptych, of which this will be the right-hand side panel, is destined for the nave of Saint John's Cathedral. Let those who will see it there in the coming years take note: Hell lies just beneath the surface of the material world we see daily, waiting to draw us down.

Below the flaming scenes at the top of the panel are the tortures of the damned. Naked and helpless, they are beasts saddled and ridden by devils; they are victims crucified on giant musical instruments; they are plunged into ice holes; they are eaten alive by lizards.

At the bottom of the panel, where he works now, gamblers are skewered on the knives of demons brandishing dice and backgammon boards. A monstrous bird sits on a high stool, eating a human body that farts smoke and soot-blackened swallows as it is devoured. Below, the sinners that have passed through the bird's body are defecated into a filthy cesspool. On the edge of the pool, a miser vomits coins into its murky depths.

All of this... for all eternity... without end! His heart shrivels within him at the horror of it, as if it were already exposed to the heat of Hell. What are the hours, the days, the weeks that he has been working on these images, compared with an eternity of drowning, of vomiting, of burning, of being impaled? What store can we set by the transient pleasures of the flesh, compared with the necessity of avoiding this eternity of suffering? God has sent him these visions to warn him, and to warn others. That is his task on earth – to castigate sin, and show its consequences.

Taking one of his finest brushes, he dips it delicately into the white lead pigment and limnes with a rim of light the hind leg of the grotesque creature he created yesterday. It is a kind of dog, but with something of a lizard or dragon about its back and tail. With an armour-plated companion, whose unicorn horn pierces

76

its round concave bonnet, it tears at the throat of a naked man prone on the ground.

When he is happy with the light on the dog creature, he steps back slightly and looks at the bottom right corner of the panel. He will prepare the pale ochre ground for this area next. This is one more part of Hell he is reserving for the monks, the nuns and the clergy. He has already made sketches of the figure he will work on tomorrow, a pig in a nun's wimple, lustfully nuzzling the ear of a man with a document on his lap. The pig wants him to sign the document, with a long quill it holds ready in one trotter. The man will sign away his wealth, in exchange for the Church's protection against the plague. If he refuses, a squat toad-like figure with an armoured helmet threatens him with St Anthony's Fire, the loathsome disease that will make his limbs wither and fall off. Already on its thorny spiked crest the creature bears like a trophy the foot of a sufferer, the leg bone protruding from the decayed flesh. All of these details he has already worked out.

He dabbles the fine point of his brush in a little dish of aqua ardens to clean it, and then places the brush carefully upright in a wooden beaker with the rest. Then he mixes new pigments and takes a slightly broader brush to create his ochre ground.

After a time, he reaches upwards with his arms, extends his fingers, and stretches his back. As he often does, he finds he has been working for too long in a single position, not aware that he was twisted and stooping. His back feels tight. To loosen up, he paces up and down for a few moments. How peaceful it is in his studio, unlike the bustle of the family workshop where he learned to paint under the eye of his father, Anthonis. His older brother Goessens and their cousin Willem still do their work there, and from time to time Goessens tries to lure him back. Goessens would like every painting to emerge as a collective work, a family effort. He has never understood how Jerome must withdraw from the world around him, how his works can grow only in silence and solitude, like seeds sprouting in the silent darkness under the soil.

One day, perhaps. One day, when Aleyt has given him a son, he will return to the family workshop and teach him there. He would like that. He imagines himself, Goessens and Willem as old greybeards, teaching the next generation. Perhaps God is making him wait, first giving him the time to bring forth his God-sent visions in silence.

He wanders over to the narrow bench where he keeps his alchemical flasks and retorts, to look at the potion he has made from the fermented mandrake fruits. It should be ready to drink in a few days. He picks up the glass, and swirls the liquid observantly. It is clear, and a good, deep colour: rose pink. It will certainly be quite potent. He feels a thrill of anticipation. This potion is God's instrument for his instruction. Once in its power, he might fly on the back of a fish high above the sleeping town of Den Bosch and up into the sky gardens that await the blessed. Or he might plunge down through dark tunnels as if sliding on ice, to where devils with the beaks of birds will seize him and flay his flesh from his bones. He is afraid of the potion, but it is God's will that he should bring back his visions for the enlightenment and instruction of the people.

He puts the glass down again, and returns to his painted panel. As his eyes range over its vibrant colours and extraordinary horrors, he tries to imagine that he is someone else, seeing it for the first time. How he would be shaken, and filled with awe at the artist's achievement! Yet it is he, Jerome van Aachen, Hieronymus of Den Bosch, it is *he* who has made this remarkable thing that the world will wonder at.

He hears a pitter-patter of little feet behind the wainscot. A mouse, or a rat? But no: it must be the Devil, with whisking rodent tail, who has come suddenly close to him. He has been ambushed by pride, one of the seven deadly sins. How swiftly and easily it overcame him. He kneels down on the hard boards and prays for forgiveness.

CHAPTER EIGHT

"The senses, Hameel, are the gateways for sin to enter our soul, and our senses are located about our head. We see with our eyes. We hear with our ears. We smell with our nose. We taste with our mouth. Only the sense of touch is more generalized, but to that also our head is highly receptive."

Hameel would rather be anywhere on God's earth than here in his workshop listening to the Inquisitor. The man has ferreted out his whereabouts and now stands at his ease. He has turned back his cowl in order to point as he speaks to the relevant parts of his own bony head. To his penetrating eyes, oddly grey in his dark face; to his slightly pointed and forward-facing ears; to his long straight nose; to his tight-set thin-lipped mouth, with the wandering thread of an old scar running diagonally downwards from the left corner to his jawbone.

"Therefore, when a person has admitted a devil into their soul, is it not fitting that they should be deprived of these gates by which sin passes?"

He has come clutching a roll of paper, which he now unfurls and smoothes open on the table in front of Hameel to reveal a drawing.

"My idea is for a helmet made with bands of iron, on which are positioned holes for the eyes, the nostrils, the ears and the mouth. Through these holes we will drive spikes, one at a time, of suitable lengths to destroy the sinning senses without killing the sinner. We will leave one ear and the mouth until last, so that the sinner can hear our exhortation and speak their repentance. Then we will seal up the final portals of sin, and they can go to their place of execution safe from any further transgression, to arrive in utter purity into the merciful judgement of God."

Hameel feels the same sensation as if rotten meat had been put before him. He cannot control his expression. He knows that Jacomo is watching him.

"Hameel, you must see this thing rightly. By this brief earthly torment, we are saving the witch or the heretic an eternity of worse torture in Hell. This is the curious contradiction you must understand. What appears to be cruelty is in fact kindness."

Hameel forces a nod.

"My sketches, as you can see with your artist's eye, are crude and inadequate. Do you think you can draw something more precise, so that Diederik and his workers will have a clear idea of what they are to make?"

There is no answer to this question but "yes", and Hameel forces it from his lips. The Inquisitor nods, satisfied enough.

"Excellent. Bring it to me as soon as you may. God be with you."

"And with you," Hameel replies, relieved that his visitor is leaving without further ado.

When the Inquisitor has gone, he rolls up the paper quickly, thrusts it aside, and returns to what he was doing before. But after a few minutes, his hand comes to a standstill in his drawing, like a wheel bogged down in mud. His attention keeps wandering. To the recent visit of the Inquisitor. To the warning cries of carters and the fragments of passing conversations from the street outside his workshop. To the dull ache in his wrist from yesterday's chipping, chipping, chipping away at the stone wings of Lust. To the nagging feeling that Anger, the gargoyle he is trying to draw now, keeps turning into an imitation of something seen in Jerome's work. To the memories of three days ago, of lovemaking with Aleyt, in the garden.

Aleyt.

She has taken the place of all his carefree thoughts and feelings. She has established herself at the core of him, so that all his other concerns circle uselessly about her image, just as he sometimes circles the streets about her house, or walks through the market square just so he can see her window. She is his lodestone, drawing him helplessly towards her. Only at night does he come close. In his dreams she lies beside him, above him, below him, her flesh pressed against his so intimately that they are one composite being. Half-waking, he thinks she is in the bed and puts out an arm. Touching emptiness, he groans, he weeps, incomplete, until sleep returns her to him.

On other nights he has dreams of separation, which linger in his mind long into the next day. Last night the sound of running water brought him to the reedy bank of a river. She was on the opposite bank. He was carrying a net, a child once again, a child standing beside a river, not knowing what to do. They both waited, looking across the water at each other. Then, in the middle of the stream his older brother Pieter appeared. He was swimming, catching silvery fish in his hands and throwing them to him. As they landed about his feet, he grabbed at the slippery, twitching creatures, putting them in his net. On the other bank, Jerome emerged from a wood, coming closer and closer to Aleyt. While he was a foolish child clutching at fish, she went away with Jerome. He knew he would never set eyes on her again.

The melancholy of this dream still clings to him. Anger, half-done, scowls up at him from the sheet of paper. The bells of Sext begin to ring from the myriad belfries of the town. With a sigh, with a feeling that time is slipping uselessly through his fingers, he puts aside his work and stands up. This morning he has an appointment with the tailor Johannes on Kruisstraat. His contract with the Abbess specifies that he is to be given a fresh suit of clothing at her expense, and Johannes is her chosen supplier.

He leaves his studio and walks through the streets of Den Bosch seeing nothing, until he arrives at the tailor's door and knocks at it. After a few moments he hears approaching footsteps inside, and it opens.

"Ah – Master Hameel?"

Hameel has never met Johannes before, but like everyone else he knows who he is, a flamboyant figure about the town, always dressed in bright colours. This morning he wears a jacket of dark blue with gold embroidery at the sleeves and collar. His leggings are red. Around his neck dangles a length of cord, knotted at intervals. His eyes take a journey down from Hameel's face to his feet and back again.

"Come on in. The Abbess has paid for a fine cloth for your tunic – a blend of cotton from Spain with fine English wool. She has already specified the kind of cut and colour she wants, so all we need to do now is to take your measurements."

Hameel follows Johannes along a short dark corridor to his workshop, where clothes in all stages of assembly are strewn on tables and pinned on wooden dummies.

"What colour has she chosen?" he says.

Johannes widens his eyes and holds up a finger as if a marvel is in the offing. He rolls down an arm's length from a bolt of dark green cloth.

"You have to be a tall, well-knit fellow such as yourself to carry this colour well. A small, fat person would look like a toad, and a lanky stooping fellow would look like a runner bean. On you, it will sit most handsomely."

He runs his hand across Hameel's chest.

"Hmm… a finer material than you have been used to, I think!"

He slaps his fingers against Hameel's tunic, and a little puff of stone dust comes off into the air. The tailor coughs exaggeratedly.

"Whoof!"

Johannes' breath is sweet, as if he has just been chewing on a liquorice root. Hameel feels crowded by his proximity.

"Now, let's see how you measure."

"What style of tunic…" Hameel starts to enquire. Johannes' comically raised eyebrows and pouting lips bring him up short.

"Well, the very latest style, of course! We should call it a doublet, rather than a tunic. The cut will make the most of your manly attributes. Broad shoulders with a little padding. Bagpipe sleeves, but not overdone of course. A tight fit on the torso, with eyelets and laces on the front opening. And of course not too long, so that your codpiece can be suitably prominent. You'll have the ladies of the town following you everywhere with their eyes. You're a single man, I believe?"

Hameel nods.

"You're to have fine new hose, as well. Two pairs – grey. The Abbess wanted green for those as well, but I said it would be too much. 'Green and grey,' I said, 'trust me – it'll look a lot more dignified. 'Well, dignity is what I want,' she said to me. 'Since he's in my employ, I want him to cut a fine figure about the town.'

Johannes lowers his voice and flutters his eyelashes a little.

"Between you and me, Master Hameel, I think the Abbess Dominica has rather a soft spot for you! Now – let's get this scruffy old tunic off you and get all your measurements."

Johannes deploys his knotted cord, and makes notes on a scrap of paper. Measuring Hameel's legs, he gives

84

one thigh muscle an unexpected squeeze.

"Where does an artist like you get such muscular legs?"

"They're the legs God gave me, I suppose. I used to run about everywhere, when I was a little boy, and I'd swim in the river every day all through the summer. We lived just beyond the city walls, in a cottage."

"How charming! And are your parents still there?"

"They're both dead now, in the last few years."

"I'm sorry to hear that. But they must have been very proud of what you've become – your father and mother?"

Hameel shrugs.

"My father was a stonemason. He'd have been happy to see me apprenticed as a mason too. But things turned out differently."

"Absolutely! Differently and better. Thanks to your friendship with the great Master Jerome."

Hameel feels the familiar tug of annoyance. Does no-one in Den Bosch see him as other than the protegé of Jerome? Is he just the lucky boy who happened to grow up fishing on the river with the great man?

"And you're a member of the Holy Company. Such an honour! You're the living proof that a man can improve his station in life, with talent and luck. I don't hold with these sumptuary laws they keep trying to enforce. Do you know, in Antwerp the tailors have a list as long as my arm of who is allowed to wear what!"

Hameel relaxes a little. At least the subject has changed.

"I suppose the nobility don't want the merchants and lawyers to wear finer cloth than they do," he says.

Johannes nods vigorously.

"That's exactly what it's all about. They like to claim that it's because everyone has their right station in life, determined by God. But really they just want to show off their status, and make the lives of poor tailors difficult by making lots of rules. Will you take a goblet of hippocras, now we've finished the measurements?"

"Well, I should return to work…"

"Faugh! So should I. But let's take a moment out of the day together. It's very good hippocras, made with a Bordeaux wine."

He thinks of his empty workshop, the unfinished drawing… of being alone again with his thoughts.

"Thank you, I'll join you in one draught then."

"The sun is shining – why don't we sit in the warmth? I have a little balcony at the back."

Johannes bustles off to another room, and returns with two goblets.

"This way!" he says with a toss of his head, and Hameel follows him up a narrow stair. Perhaps the tailor's exuberance can raise his spirits too.

The balcony looks across low roofs towards the city wall. They sit on a wooden bench painted a bright yellow.

"Good health and God's blessings!" Johannes clinks his goblet against Hameel's.

The wine is good, as Johannes had promised. The sunlight shines warmly on his face. But why does Johannes scrutinise him so closely?

"I can do you a small service, Hameel, if you wish," the tailor says. He leans in and runs his fingers through Hameel's thick dark brown hair. Again the scent of liquorice.

"Your hair is beautiful, and clean, and…" Johannes leans further forward, very close, and breathes in, "… and fragrant. And yet you are the landlord of a thriving colony of little head lice. Since I am the owner of a fine-toothed bone comb, why don't you let me evict them?"

"I thought I had felt an itching, but, please, I can go to the barber's on Brugstraat…"

Johannes puts his wine down and stands.

"It's no trouble my good Hameel! Allow me to do you this small service."

The tailor goes away for a few moments.

Well, let him do this thing, if he wants to.

As Johannes sets to work on Hameel's hair, he prattles about the foibles of some of his customers. Hameel closes his eyes. The sunshine warms him, and the slow, methodical combing of the tailor is soothing. The wine lifts his spirits, and he begins to laugh at Johannes' stories. For the first time since the garden, three days ago, the world seems a good place again. After all, Aleyt is in love with him. Whatever the agonies of the present time, that is something solid to hold onto. Aleyt loves him, and nothing can take that away.

CHAPTER NINE

"I'm splitting in two! Oh, Christ in Heaven! Don't let me burst!"

Aleyt presses the moistened cloth to her cousin Frida's brow. She wishes she could do something more, somehow take some share of Frida's pain to herself. Her cousin's breath is coming in rapid panting now, and every minute or so her face bunches tight in a grimace of pain and fear. At these moments she groans loudly, or even shrieks, and Aleyt feels torn herself.

The midwife remains calm, sitting on her little wooden stool – identical to a milking stool – at the end of the bed. Lisanne Damkot is the best in Den Bosch. Her services come at a slightly higher price, but all the best families call for her when a baby is due. A surgeon is notified, in case a Caesarean is needed, but he waits for a messenger, he does not attend. It is a very serious matter, to send for the surgeon. Many mothers die from the wounds he must inflict. As for the physicians, they are associated with a variety of inconveniences. Doctor Stemerdink insists on burning an expensive substance made from dried raven's dung immediately after a delivery, claiming that it calls forth the placenta. The smell lingers in the room for weeks. Doctor Slotboom consults an almanac of stars, and if the day or night is not auspicious for child bearing, he will refuse to attend.

Most families choose to engage Lisanne Damkot alone.

"Everything is going beautifully, Mistress Frida," she says with an encouraging smile. "Any minute now we'll see the baby's head."

There is a tap at the door, and Frida's mother goes to take the fresh basin of hot water from the servant girl. She doesn't consider it suitable to have a servant enter the room at such at time. She puts the basin next to the pile of clean cloths at the midwife's elbow, ready for use.

Aleyt speaks as calmly as she can in Frida's ear. Anything that comes into her mind, just a flow of words to soothe and distract.

"Soon, my dear, soon it will be over! Do you remember how we named our dolls together? How we talked about the children we would have one day, and how they would be such friends as we were? And now you... married a year only... how lucky you are, Frida! This will soon be over. Think how happy you're going to be..."

But Frida screams, and Aleyt knows that her words are just sounds without meaning to her. Lisanne urges Frida on.

"Push, now, my dear! The baby's on its way!"

Aleyt endures the fierce grasp of Frida's hand on her own. She looks into her cousin's eyes, but Frida's thoughts are all turned inward towards the river of pain that is flowing through her body.

"You're nearly there, now, my love!" Aleyt murmurs. She is terrified by this pain, but she strives to keep her voice calm. Frida's eyes flicker momentarily towards hers, and then the final surge of her labour racks her body.

The midwife utters a cry of delight.

"Well done, my dear! It's a baby boy."

The room is filled with a high-pitched cry. Aleyt looks at the face of Frida's mother and sees the same shock of joy as she feels herself. The midwife brings the bloodied little newcomer up to rest on Frida's chest.

Aleyt gazes in wonder at the tiny creature. She daren't touch it yet, although she wants to. So small and vulnerable! All her heart goes out to it at once. She feels as if she would lay down her own life to protect it if necessary.

*

That night as she prepares for sleep, her mind is still filled with the sights and sounds of the day. The cutting and tying of the cord; the washing of the baby; she herself helping to towel his little limbs dry; the visit of the priest to perform a precautionary informal christening. Most of all, she dwells on the experience of holding Laurens, the feeling of his meagre weight in her arms, his puzzled little face peering out at the world from his swaddling clothes. His eyes wandered without focus, and she tries to imagine the extraordinary confusion of his infant mind, exposed so suddenly and unexpectedly to the sights, sounds and sensations of the world around him.

She speaks of these things to Jerome, as he washes his hands in the ewer of warm water that Mary always brings up to their room before retiring for the night. On the table beside the ewer, unfortunately, is the bottle of deep rose-coloured mandrake potion and two cups. Jerome has delayed until now because Aleyt was needed at her cousin's labour, but now they will drain it to the dregs. Saint Anthony's Fire, please God, will be kept at bay by the potion. But what a miserable night of sickness and confusion lies ahead.

Drying his hands, Jerome glances at Aleyt as she sits on the edge of the bed in her chemise. Her talk of the new baby is creating in him a mounting sense of unease to which he cannot put a name. It is compounded of sadness, disappointment, frustration, and even a little anger. It makes him feel unsatisfied with himself. What exactly is wrong with him? Is God punishing him? He thinks uncomfortably of their last lovemaking: the night before he left for Reims. A long time ago now. Who had initiated it? His mind had been on the next day's journey, the commission, matters between him and his brother Goessens. But now, looking at Aleyt, it comes back to him. She sat on the bed just as she did now, and instead of putting on her nightcap, she unpinned her ash-blonde hair and let it cascade over her neck and shoulders. It was like a fountain of hair, a beautiful sight that was for his eyes only, and that rarely too. It was always uniquely arousing for him, more so even than the sight of her nakedness, or perhaps because of its association with that nakedness. She pulled her chemise over her head and held out her arms towards him, and he had gone to her. But their coupling had been hollow and passionless. He had felt it then, and he felt it anew now. The hopes that gave vitality to their lovemaking in the earlier years of their marriage had dwindled to almost nothing. And what was the point of lovemaking without issue? God had created this act, this strange conjunction, expressly for procreation.

He looks at her now, still talking of the birth, her cousin, the baby. Although she is just putting up her hair in her nightcap in the usual way, her animation makes her eyes shine in the candlelight, and her smooth arms and fluttering hands create a pattern of excitement in the air. But none of this excitement makes a connection between them. On the contrary, it seems to reinforce something he has vaguely felt since his return, a sort of new shyness between them. It is as if he has not completed the final part of his journey from Reims. Across this remaining distance, they have not yet reached out to make love.

He feels annoyance rising in him, and unjust and needlessly cruel though he knows it to be, he can't help puncturing her mood.

"A pity that your cousin's fertility is not catching."

Aleyt falls silent at once. She finishes putting on her nightcap, lies back on the soft goose feather mattress, and looks up at the canopy of cream cloth suspended

91

from the four substantial bed-posts. Her eyes wander to the carvings on the wooden posts themselves, with their design of leaves, branches, berries and fruit, a luxuriant, fertile woodscape. She listens to Jerome's movements as he puts the ewer outside the bedchamber door and closes it. She too now thinks of their last perfunctory lovemaking. It was only two weeks later that Hameel first came to this very bed. Was there ever such a contrast? Then she had felt like a vessel filled to overflowing with passion; like a rich, yielding field under the plough; like a mysterious flower that bloomed in secret at midnight in a burst of colour and scent. No extravagant image from poetry or song was vivid enough for what she had felt that night.

Jerome blows out all the candles except the one that they leave burning at night, and as she waits in the near-darkness for him to lie down next to her, her hands rest on her womb. Please, God, she thinks.

Now, obscure, he comes to the side of the bed, holding the two cups. She had forgotten the potion. She sits up in the bed, not looking at him.

"I'm sorry, Aleyt," he says quietly. "I'm sorry that I said that."

His voice, that tone of tenderness in it, still calls to her heart. She turns her head and meets his eyes. They catch the light of the single candle flame, and she sees her own pain mirrored there.

"I forgive you. And may God still bless us, Jerome."

She takes the cup he offers and drains it off quickly. The taste is sweetish, but not pleasant. However, to bring new life into the world, she must live herself. The potion will protect them.

Jerome drinks his own potion and puts the cups aside. He climbs into the bed. He lays a hand on one of her breasts and squeezes it gently.

"I love you, Aleyt," he murmurs. "I should show it more plainly to you. I'm sorry."

She lays her hand on top of his. After a moment, he

92

moves it down her body and she parts her legs slightly.

They make love, and Aleyt's mind darts away from her compliant body, confused, into a maze of sensations, thoughts, images and emotions. Perhaps the potion is acting on her already, scrambling her up. She loves Jerome. She loves Hameel. She is a sinner. God will forgive her. God won't forgive her. Then, as she feels Jerome approach his climax, a silent cry goes out from her heart to God. Give me a child! Give me a child! Give me a child!

*

Is he waking or sleeping? Beside him in the bed there is something. Jerome stares at the dim edge of the pale sleeping face in the flickering light of their night candle. It seems to shift its shape: it is growing a beak. It's an eagle! Its plumes rustle beneath the bed sheet. It will awaken and tear at him with that vicious bill. He is gripped with terror. He can't move any part of his body, not even a finger. Will this great bird eat him? But no - now the beak dissolves, and silvery scales cover the head. It's a fish, a huge trout, which will slip away into the river when morning comes. Sweet fish... he can hear the reeds shiver in the breeze at the margin of the stream, he can feel the plashing water, and he wishes he could be a fish as well, and slide under the cool green surface...

There is a sudden, surprising flash of light at the cracks of the wooden shutters. Then thunder rolls its heavy wheels across the roof, and rain, rain begins to fall on the slates. It's a battle in the heavens. A battle between angels and demons, with cannon shot blasting out in the clouds, and the blood of the vanquished streaming down from the sky and sluicing down the drainpipes and gutters of Den Bosch. Now he can hear the clashing of swords and bloodthirsty shouts.

He stares, wide eyed, as the door to their bedchamber slowly opens wide. The candlelight reveals two flickering demons standing there. They have green slimy skin, great trumpet-like snouts and whisking tails. There is a stink of sulphur, a taste of iron on his tongue. The demons prance gleefully into the room. He has a sense that more lurk outside, on the top landing of the stair. He hears music coming from there – a tambour and a flute – and the demons in the room dance a measure to the beat. Then one of them produces a great corkscrew from out of his anus. With cunning winks and looks of complicity, both demons sidle towards the bed. Then, with a swift lunge, one seizes Jerome's head firmly between his claws, and the other inserts the point of the corkscrew into his ear. Jerome tries to scream, but no sound comes out. The tip of the corkscrew is icy cold, an icicle, excruciating. It twists inwards until it has penetrated right into his head, and he feels something bursting in there, like a pig's bladder gushing blood.

At last he can move. He throws off the bed sheet and coverlet.

"No!" he shouts.

More demons come running in from the stairway to help subdue him. The fish beside him grows arms and grasps him

"Jerome…"

He struggles to free himself. The demons crowd closer.

"Jerome! Jerome – wake up! It's just the potion that's bringing nightmares."

It's a familiar voice calling to him. Aleyt's voice. But beside the bed a crack in the floor has opened up and he can see down through the different levels of their house, past the silent parlour below, past his empty studio, past the naked sleeping figure of Mary on the ground floor, through the wine bottles and cheeses in the cellar, down to a place where fire licks up, orange, red, and yellow. Devils swarm there like maggots on rotten meat. They have the bodies of men and the heads of birds, and with villainous curving knives they cut out the hearts of the damned and roast them on spits. Suddenly they all look upwards. They have seen him watching them! Now they are coming up, climbing, clambering, scrambling like scurrying spiders through his house. They are coming to cut out his heart!

He screams, and Aleyt puts both her arms around him.

"Jerome! Jerome my dear! Listen to me! It's Aleyt, your wife! Listen! Calm down! It's a dream!"

Jerome stares at her and his eyes seem gradually to focus. He blinks a few times and puts a hand to his brow, which is damp with sweat. After a few moments of silence, he whispers to her.

"Oh... oh, Aleyt! What terrible visions!"

"My poor man! This is the mandrake potion working on you."

Jerome nods. He glances nervously towards the door. It is closed. No demons have entered the room. He takes a few deep breaths. Rain is falling on their roof, and thunder booms in the distance. These things at least are real.

"The potion, yes. But the potion merely opens the gate for these visitors. Dreams are *sent* to us, Aleyt. Is it God, who grants me these visions to help me in my work? Or does he permit the Devil to sport with me?"

Aleyt strokes his arm.

"It's God who is working within you, Jerome."

He half turns to face her. He remembers that they made love, and feels a rush of tenderness. He kisses her forehead gently

"What an ordeal it is for you, sharing the night with me!" he murmurs.

He turns away and swings his legs out to sit on the edge of the bed. He speaks softly over his shoulder.

"I must sketch these monsters of Hell. I'll go to my studio now, and draw them, while their images linger in my mind. Once I have them trapped on paper, they'll leave me alone. Go back to sleep, dear Aleyt, go back to sleep. I'll come to bed quietly when I'm done."

He picks up the night candle, and lights a second candle from it. Then he puts on his soft gown, and slips out of the room. Aleyt listens to his footsteps descending the creaking stairway down the tall house.

She feels thoroughly awake now. Her stomach aches from the vomiting that came to her early in the night, but she feels she will not be sick again now. She lies on her back for a few minutes, revolving her thoughts. What manner of creature is she? She loves her husband, and yet she is unfaithful. What is wrong with her?

She must seek God's help, this very minute. Perhaps it is the potion that makes it seem so urgent. She gets out of bed and kneels on the hard floorboards in front of the crucifix on the wall. She crosses herself, and says a silent Lord's Prayer. She seeks for a long time in her memory for some suitable words to say to God, and eventually they come: some words from the Book of Psalms. She speaks them aloud, very quietly.

"Have mercy upon me, O God, according to thy loving kindness. According unto the multitude of thy tender mercies blot out my transgressions. Wash me thoroughly from mine iniquity, and cleanse me from my sin. For I acknowledge my transgressions, and my sin is ever before me. Create in me a clean heart, O God, and renew a right spirit within me. Make haste to help me, O Lord my salvation! So be it. Amen."

She remains on her knees in penitence, the floorboards pressing against her bones. She feels calmed by her prayer. Her resolution is made now, and she will not waver. God knows her will, and he will be ready to forgive. When she has been to confession, she will be washed clean of all sin. This certainty gives her strength. Only for a moment does the image of Hameel flicker like a candle flame in her mind's eye. Then, with God's help, she snuffs it out.

CHAPTER TEN

"God save me! God save me! God save me!"

Muttering this supplication under her breath, Mary hurries down Kirkstraat, splashing, skirts heavy and sodden. The rainwater runs over the cobbles like a shallow river and swirls clucking and scolding into the filth-choked gutters. It's pitch dark, but she knows the way, and from time to time a bleaching flash of lightning illuminates everything – the jutting gables of the houses that lean over the street whispering secrets; the rain-gushing clouds overhead; and the looming mass of the cathedral in front of her. Her heart is racing even faster than her feet, and with each boom of thunder she feels it jump a little with fear. She must get to the cathedral quickly, or she will be a lost soul!

At last she reaches the shelter of the cathedral porch. She's dripping, her hair bedraggled, her clothes sopping. When she cools down from her run, she'll probably start to shiver. But that's all good. That's all self-mortification, and it'll stand her in good stead. She pushes at the heavy, creaking door of the cathedral, open day and night to the faithful, and enters the nave.

Candles flicker in the gloom. As she had hoped, there seems to be nobody else here. Crossing herself and bobbing to her knees as she crosses the central aisle leading to the altar, she makes her way straight to the

Lady Chapel. Still panting from her exertions, she sinks gratefully onto her usual kneeler. It's three rows back – close enough to speak without raising her voice, but not so close as to seem impertinent. A single large candle burns at the feet of the Virgin, and Mary rests her eyes on that gentle sculpted face that always seems to come to life in the wavering light. She starts with a hurried Lord's prayer, and, slowing down, a Hail Mary. Then, glancing quickly around her, she addresses the Virgin in her own words, as she always does, when there are no priests about to overhear and criticize.

"Oh, dear Mary, Mother of God, don't let it be the Flood tonight! I've not had time to go to confession, and all my sins is piled up on me like sacks of... like sacks of sins. Oh, don't let me die by drowning, I'm mortal feared of drowning by water. You know I'm feared of water!"

There is a flash of dazzling light through the chapel window, and Mary's shadow and the shadow of the Virgin race together up the stones of the wall. Then, only a second later, the crack of the thunderbolt strikes her ears, and everything in the cathedral that isn't fixed down rattles. Even the main entrance door moans on its hinges. Mary looks imploringly at the Virgin. Is she safe, even here in God's house? She renews her pleas, urgently.

"Oh, dear! Let me off, please let me off! I seen what Hell is like, I seen it in the Master's paintings! Oh, don't let no devils be sticking their pitchforks into me! I'll mend my lustful ways at once, if you don't let me get all drownded in the Flood. I know I've been bad. But I don't go with no married men, only the young bachelor boys. I know it's still wrong, but it's not drowning wrong..."

She bows her head and begins a new series of mumbled Hail Marys. After a while, the pounding of the rain on the cathedral roof seems to ease slightly. Mary looks up hopefully. Is the Virgin answering her prayers?

"It's only rain, Mary, only ordinary rain tonight."

Mary stares, startled. The lips of the statue haven't moved. But yet she spoke. A miracle! After all these years of visiting and praying, the Virgin has finally vouchsafed an answer! As soon as the thought comes to her, she begins to doubt the evidence of her own ears. There is no-one else here to confirm this. It would be risky to tell anyone. These are not times to come to the attention of the Church, even as a witness to a miracle. Who knows what would happen to her?

"Holy Mother of God!" she says aloud, with as much reverence as she can put into the words. If the Virgin *has* spoken, she should acknowledge it, at least. To remain silent would be unmannerly.

"Father Crispin told me you prayed in this chapel, every time there was heavy rain. You are right to be afraid. The second Flood will come very soon."

It's the same voice. But now a human figure detaches itself from the shadows at the entrance to the chapel and comes forward. The faint illumination of the candle picks out a nun's habit, and a glint of gold at the wrist: the Abbess Dominica! What's she doing lurking in the cathedral in the middle of the night? How much has she heard?

It's disappointing that a miracle has not occurred. But a grand figure like the Abbess speaking to her – indeed, deliberately seeking her out – is almost a miracle in itself.

"The whole of Den Bosch knows you're building an ark, for you and the nuns," she says timidly.

It can be seen from all around, perched on the little treeless hill inside the convent's grounds. You couldn't get close to it because the convent's grounds are protected by a high wall. But as far as Mary and other curious townsfolk can tell, the ark is nearly completed. Of course she's never seen a real sea-going boat, but it looks large, sturdy and impressive - like the Abbess herself - who now comes forward to sit on a pew between Mary and the Virgin, turning her back to the statue.

"So we are, Mary. All over the land the wise are building arks. Soon we will reach one and a half millennia since the birth of Our Saviour. The day of our Judgement is long overdue, don't you think?"

Mary hasn't heard this idea before. She'd always thought the Flood could come any day, at random. She wants to ask what a millennia is, but feels stupid. If it's next year, perhaps she can sin with impunity for the rest of this year, and then reform her ways straight after Christmas? She looks again at the Abbess, who is standing up again now, dissatisfied with her perch. The seats of the pews are deliberately made narrow, to keep the faithful awake while they pray. Why is the Abbess deigning to speak to her?

"Would you like a place on that ark, Mary, when the Flood comes to wash away Den Bosch and all its sinners?"

Now truly a miracle is unfolding.

"What, *me*?"

"Yes."

"Why me?"

"Because you can do something for me, in return."

"What?"

The Abbess points to a broad stone bench at the side of the chapel.

"Let's make ourselves a little more comfortable, Mary."

She walks over to the bench and sits at one end of it, then pats the space beside her and beckons to Mary. She gets up to sit where she's bid. She feels ill at ease, so close to the Abbess. Even in the gloom, she can see how finely plucked are her eyebrows, how a fold of her jowl dangles over her high collar, how her ears are adorned with dangling golden crosses. She can smell her scent, a heavy musky odour. It doesn't mask the wafting garlic

100

of her breath as she leans close to Mary, almost touching, almost whispering.

"I just wanted a word with you about Hameel."

Mary is stricken with guilty panic. She blabbers quickly, unable to stop herself.

"Hameel? What have you heard? I've confessed it all. That's a sin that's been washed right away…"

Is the Abbess here to dredge up every fornication she's committed? They'll be here a long time in that case.

But the Abbess pats her hand and smiles a little. Perhaps she's trying to be maternal and reassuring, but the physical contact makes Mary even more agitated.

"Calm down, Mary. I haven't come to accuse you of anything!"

She pauses a moment.

"All right? Are you ready to hear me now?"

Mary nods.

"Hameel, I've heard, is a frequent visitor at Jerome's house."

Mary's mind races. If the Abbess isn't interested in her sins, then what's this conversation about? She knows very well, from listening at doors, that there is no love lost between her Master and the Abbess. She must take care. She wishes she had the courage to walk away, right now.

But the Abbess is waiting for her to speak. She chooses her words carefully.

"That's so. Of course he is. He's been close with the Master since they was children."

"But when the great Master Jerome was recently away for many weeks at the Abbey of Saint Denis, I hear that Hameel was an even more frequent visitor than ever."

Mary manages to hold her tongue.

"A pretty man, Hameel, don't you think?" the Abbess says with a smile, inviting complicity.

Mary nods, not smiling.

101

"And a great comfort to Jerome's wife Aleyt, I'm sure, while her husband was absent?"

"I suppose so."

"Go on, Mary. Tell me more," comes the low, insidious voice, still little more than a whisper.

"It's not my place..." Mary begins. She intends to use her lowly status as a defence, but the Abbess cuts her short.

"But it *could* be your place – *on my ark*. And look at this!" The Abbess fumbles inside her habit and brings out a small scroll bound with a thin ribbon of red material. She makes a sign of the cross with her free hand, and holds up the scroll reverently for Mary to look at.

"Do you know what this is, Mary?"

"A piece of writing, I suppose."

The Abbess smiles patronisingly, and taps the scroll with a finger. A finger adorned with a large signet ring of heavy gold.

"This has been touched by the Pope himself in Rome, Mary. Think of that! It's a Papal Indulgence."

Mary looks at the scroll in awe. The Pope himself has touched that! And she is within touching distance of it herself! A tingle runs down her back and even into her fingers. And – she can hardly draw breath - the magical power of such a scroll! She has heard of such wonders.

"Would that..." She hardly dares speak the thought, "...would that get you out of your time in Purgatory?"

The Abbess nods.

"Yes. And, Mary, Purgatory is a terrible place. All the torments of Hell itself. Not for all eternity, admittedly, but at least for hundreds of years. Just think of that - hundreds of years of excruciating pain."

She looks at Mary, appraising her.

"You have a bit of a reputation in Den Bosch. It has even reached my ears. For the sins of lustful women, the devils prepare hot pokers, Mary. Hot searing pokers to thrust into you where you have sinned. Think of that!"

The Abbess holds out the scroll towards her.

"But with this in your hands, you would never go to Purgatory at all."

Mary's fingers reach towards the sacred object, trembling, with a will of their own. She almost touches it.

She steels herself to look directly at the Abbess's face once more. In her dark pupils the reflections of the single candle in the chapel are burning. They look like the fiery eyes of a demon.

"What do you want?" Mary says, hoarsely.

"For now, just a little information. About Hameel and Aleyt."

Mary withdraws her hand carefully from where it still hovers near the scroll. It joins the other hand, on her lap, and they twist anxiously together. A Papal Indulgence! For a girl like her!

She must be firm, now, with herself and the Abbess. Her fidelity to Aleyt is not open to trading.

"I've nothing to tell you," she breathes.

"Nothing at all? For a place on my ark, and a Papal Indulgence?" The Abbess sounds incredulous.

Mary shakes her head. The Abbess stands up. She lets out a long sigh, and paces slowly to the statue of the Virgin. She puts a hand on the statue's foot and stands a moment in thought, the candle casting her wavering shadow like a dark stain onto the white stone. Outside, the rain has reduced to a pitter-patter, as if rats are running about on the cathedral roof. She turns back to face Mary, and once again her eyes reflect the flame.

"Well, let me put something else to you, Mary, since you hesitate to seize your good fortune. You know of our distinguished visitor in Den Bosch – our visitor sent by the Pope himself?"

"The Inquisitive?"

The Abbess seems to smile slightly, although in the darkness it is hard to be sure.

"Yes. Brother Jacomo. The Papal Inquisitor. Did

you see the witch burning on Saint Perpetua's Day?"

"Was there a soul in Den Bosch what didn't?"

"Brother Jacomo is keen to find other witches, Mary. He seeks them here, he seeks them there."

The Abbess pauses, and looks long and meaningfully at Mary. She shivers, and is suddenly aware of her cold, wet clothing and hair. One test of a witch is to see if she can breathe under water. Icy fear rises like a flood inside her.

"I've had nothing to do with that sort of devilry!"

"That's what every witch says. But under torture they soon squeal a different tune. And women of loose morals are often guilty of worse things. Your reputation will not be helpful."

"I'm a sinful girl, but that's the way God made me. I always repent, straight after. I go to confession every Saturday, before Sunday mass. And I pray in between times, as well."

"Nonetheless, I think Brother Jacomo might want to question you. Have you heard of the witch pricker? A very sharp and long needle. It's well known that witches have a place somewhere on their bodies that's insensitive to pain, Mary. You'll be stripped naked and chained down, and Brother Jacomo will use the witch pricker to find that place. You'll be stuck full of holes while he seeks it out."

Mary crosses herself.

"God save me!"

"Now, consider, Mary. I offer you a place on my ark. A Papal Indulgence. And I promise you that good Brother Jacomo will hear nothing of your sinful ways."

"What do you want? From me? Tell me."

"I want proof that Hameel and Aleyt have sinned. A little document, which I would draw up, and you would put your mark on it."

"Why?"

The Abbess strokes the Virgin's foot. It makes Mary's blood run even colder. She has such power, this woman, such confidence, that she handles Christ's own mother as a familiar.

"Do you know the game of chess, Mary?"

"I've seen it played. I don't understand it."

"There's a piece called the Queen. It's a very powerful piece, but often you just keep it in reserve. You might not use it until the end-game."

"What's that got to do with anything?"

"I'm answering your question. A little document, with your mark on it, would be something I'd like to have - even if I never used it. That's all."

There is a distant roll of thunder outside. Perhaps it's the storm retreating, or another one coming. Suddenly Mary is overwhelmed by desperation to get away from this woman, whatever the consequences. She stands up and moves quickly to the chapel entrance.

"Give me a little time! I can't think straight. I must get home. Please – give me time!"

"Mary…"

"Please… a little time to think…"

Before her courage can fail her, she flees the chapel.

*

The Abbess listens to her footsteps in hurried retreat through the nave. There is a muffled bump and an exclamation. She must have walked into the edge of a pew or some other obstacle in the dim light. Then the main door opens with its complaining creak and slams shut.

Loyal little fool!

Well, she might as well pray for a few minutes herself, since she is here. She makes her way out of the Lady Chapel and down to the choir. She prefers to pray to God himself, rather than to maternal or saintly intermediaries. She kneels on the soft rug that covers the broad stone step in front of the main altar and speaks aloud. There is no-one else there, after all. It is just her and God now. God will side with her, as he always has in the past. She begins.

"Oh Lord God, to whom vengeance belongs, show thyself. Deal bountifully with thy servant, that I may live, and keep thy word. Remove from me reproach and contempt, for I have kept thy testimonies."

She pauses, as the stony reverberations of her words die away and the image of the Master Painter rises before her mind's eye. He is seated at the feast of the Holy Company on Shrove Tuesday, smug, self-satisfied, judgmental. His words still ring in her ears. A loud, pointed remark about avarice, addressed to his neighbours at table but with his eyes fixed on her all the while. *Grasping after money by the abbess of a convent!* Well, suitable words for a man like Jerome can be found in the Book of Psalms. She speaks aloud again, sharing her thoughts with God and the echoing cathedral.

"Why boast you thyself, O mighty man! Thy tongue deviseth mischiefs, like a sharp razor, working deceitfully. Thou lovest all devouring words, O thou deceitful tongue. God shall destroy thee forever, he shall take thee away, and pluck thee out of thy dwelling place, and root thee out of the land of the living. The righteous shall see, and fear, and shall laugh at him. Lo, this is the man that made not God his strength, but trusted in the abundance of his riches, and strengthened himself in his wickedness."

She pauses again. She is getting angry, and anger is a sin. She takes a few deep breaths. She must be cold, calculating, and calm. Before God, especially, it is not fitting to show anger. He knows the justice of her complaint. She bows her head for a moment of quiet contrition, and then adds her final words.

"I am like a green olive tree in the house of God and I will praise thee forever. So be it. Amen."

*

Mary lies in her bed in the little ground floor room next to the kitchen. The rain has stopped altogether now, although thunder still rumbles far off. Sleep too seems far away from her. Unwelcome thoughts chase each other around and around in her head. She is a sinner, through and through, and she can only pray, and pray often, for salvation. Could that be true, what the Abbess says, about the hot pokers? The Abbess hasn't been to Hell, but she's read books and she's high up in the Church.

The witch pricker though! That's certain enough, and it's an agony in this life, not the next. Her skin goes into goose-pimples. The Abbess won't point her out to that Inquisitive, will she, without giving her more time to think? And her promises – the ark, the Papal Indulgence – she won't take them back, will she? Is she being a fool? What harm would she do, putting her mark on a document? But the Abbess hates the Master, and he hates her. It must be important for some reason she can't think of. No, whatever it is, it's not to be done. The Master and Mistress will protect her, if she's faithful to them. She can't put her trust in that creeping Abbess.

She hears her voice again. Her creeping voice.

You have a bit of a reputation in Den Bosch.

So, her private sins have reached the ears of strangers. How has this happened? She must change her ways, or sooner or later this reputation will follow her to the house of her Master and Mistress, and she will be cast out. And how is she going to find a husband, a decent young man, like Gillis for instance, if she has this *reputation* stuck onto her like the striped cap of a whore? That will be the end she'll come to, if she doesn't change her ways. She'll end up like Catalyn. To be sure, Catalyn seems happy enough, but it's not real happiness. It's just a brave show.

She'll have to give up her visits to Gillis. He can make an honest woman of her, if he wants her in his bed again. Her lips mumble a word.

"Chastity."

The word sounds like a winding sheet.

She was chaste, once. When she was an innocent young girl, just newly come to Den Bosch. Sixteen years old. Then along came handsome Hameel. He talked to her first on the banks of the river. She remembers that first smile of his, the sunlight full on his face. He showed her the fish he had just caught. He persuaded her – easily enough – to meet him again. He was several years older than her, but still a young man, and it was before he had such high ideas. He was apprenticed to be a stonemason – a good enough calling, but not one that put him high up above her. In those days, the idea of marrying Hameel one day had not seemed so very much out of the question. What a different life she'd have had then! Not a servant girl, but the young wife of a respected architect and artist, with a growing reputation. Not a *reputation*.

It has proved no more than a daydream though, in the end. Hameel had no thoughts of marriage. She found other nice looking young men to her liking. Men like Gillis. But Hameel always kept coming back to her, and she always welcomed him into her arms. Until the Master went to Reebs. Was it the Mistress he loved, all that time before? Did he think of Aleyt, when he was in bed with her? She turns over. She puts her hand on the place where he has lain; remembers their smothered giggles at the narrowness of the bed.

Now the Abbess comes again, and the scene in the cathedral plays itself through once more in her mind. Now she hears again the scream of the burning warlock in the town square, and the Inquisitive reading from his Bible. She sees the Master at his painting of Hell in his studio, and her Mistress Aleyt, all happy on her return from her cousin's house…

The Abbess… the Inquisitive… the Mistress… the Master… they circle in her head. They join hands in a kind of dance. They make a ring around her. And who is this, breaking through the circle and joining her? His arms enwrap her; his lips are on hers. They are on a bed. *This* bed. Her, and Hameel. Aleyt is watching them. She has brought spiced wine and luscious grapes to the bedside. Hameel dismisses Aleyt, and she fades away into nothingness as they make love. Her, and Hameel.

CHAPTER ELEVEN

In the Convent of Saint Agnes, the Abbess reclines on a couch below the window in her inner sanctum. She has had a bespoke wooden platform made, to raise the floor just enough for her to see through this window from the couch. She enjoys the view of the convent's immaculately tended and extensive garden below, where just now three nuns, like busy black beetles, are weeding the vegetable patches. In the unusually warm April sun, it must be unpleasant to toil in the unshaded vegetable plots in a heavy black habit and wimple. Well, each to their allotted task. She shuts her eyes for a moment to enjoy on her own more privileged skin the pleasant cooling breeze that comes through the opened shutters. Then she raises her neck from the upholstered headrest and plucks from the dish beside her another dried plum. It comes from last year's harvest of their own plum trees. It's rich with concentrated juice, and she dabs with a small handkerchief at her mouth and chin.

Her eyes wander from the garden to the newest of her tapestries, commissioned only last year, which hangs on the wall opposite to the window. The freshly dyed colours of its intricately woven strands look vibrant in the strong daylight. It depicts the Garden of Eden, which has been modelled at her instruction on the convent's own ample grounds. God waves a hand over the lush landscape, presenting it for the first time to the naked innocent pair who gape wide-eyed from the modesty-preserving foliage of some bushes. There are plum trees, and of course, an apple tree.

Her eyes drift from the tapestry and across the fireplace, to where they can feast on another recent acquisition, a circular mirror in a frame of gold set with amethysts and garnets. She accepted it last autumn in lieu of an entire year's rent when the Van Noorden family fell on hard times. Heavy rains had destroyed their crops. Well, it was their own fault for leaving the harvest too late. Apparently the mirror was a wedding gift from the wife's family, who were wealthy cloth merchants and traders in far-flung places. It's far too fine an object for a family of tenant farmers, however many daughters there are to primp and preen in front of it. She has saved them from the sin of vanity by taking it off their hands.

With a noisy suck, she finishes off the last dried plum and drops the stone to join the rest on the floor, where Sister Theresa will be able to see them when she comes in to sweep and clean after Compline. Well, back to her own work... she swings her legs off the couch, slides her feet into her soft leather sandals, and pads back to the large table where her task – not an onerous or unpleasant one – has been left half-finished.

She is still in a mood to appreciate her possessions, and as she sits down she runs her eye over the table itself. It is made of dark oak, but on its surface are inlaid patterns of lighter wood, and around its edges is a carving in low relief of acorns and oak leaves. Two neat little drawers are fashioned under the rim, to either side of where she sits. It is a very fine table.

On the table top is something that gives her more pleasure than all the fine things in the room put together. She looks happily at the two plump cloth pouches sitting to her right hand side, like oversized dumplings, takes another from the small pile of empty pouches to her left, and recommences sorting and counting the coins lying heaped all across the table, and putting them into piles ready for bagging. There are golden reals, florins and ducats, silver groats, schillings, briquets and double briquets, all to be separated, counted twice, and put into their own bags. It is a task that she would trust no-one else in the convent to perform. Only she knows the exact extent of their income, where it comes from, what is spent, and what is saved. Only she has the keys to the large chest with massive iron bands and locks that is bolted to the floor here in her own room. Only she keeps the account books, with her spidery black scrawl of writing, and only she ever sees them.

It's a long job, but at last the coins are counted, and re-counted, and carefully put away in the chest in their cloth bags. She returns to her chair and takes a small earthenware bottle from one of the neat little drawers. She uncorks it, and swallows a draught of the fine brandy inside.

There is a knock at the door.

"Yes?" she barks. Why must that woman move so quietly that one never hears her approaching?

The insipid voice of Sister Theresa seeps through the door panels from the other side.

"Hameel is here, Abbess."

Unhurriedly, she replaces the little cork in the neck of the little bottle, and the little bottle into the little drawer.

"Let him in!"

The door opens, and the tall figure of Hameel steps through. Behind him, the pale anxious form of Sister Theresa remains. Why does she not close the door and go away?

"Is there something else, Sister?" she says, brusquely.

"It's only to mention, Abbess, that Doctor Slotboom is here today letting blood – and wanted to know..."

"I'm too busy," the Abbess cuts in. "And my

humours are well balanced. I feel in excellent health. Instruct him, though, that Sister Ursula should have an especially thorough bleeding on this occasion – she strikes me as unnaturally choleric, and I'm sure a re-alignment of her humours through a good bleeding will benefit her."

Sister Theresa ducks her head and scurries away like a frightened mouse, forgetting to close the door. Hameel smiles, and closes the door himself.

Another of her well-merited possessions, the Abbess congratulates herself. She runs her eyes upwards along Hameel's sturdy well-formed legs, slim torso and broad shoulders to his open handsome countenance. He has rolls of paper tucked under one arm.

"Good afternoon, Abbess," he says. He puts the rolls down on the table, and she extends a hand, glinting with golden rings. He takes her fingers and bows his head to bestow the merest touch of his lips to them. The dangling locks of his dark brown hair tickle the back of her wrist. What a pity it is to be celibate! At least she still has vivid, and often revisited, memories from the days when she was young, before she took holy orders. And she permits herself certain thoughts concerning Gillis - although sadly not to be acted upon. But really, is celibacy in the mind the most important thing to God? If we serve him in other ways so well?

"Good afternoon, Hameel. How nice to see you!"

He releases her hand, and she points at the paper rolls.

"You have plans to show me?"

"I do. For the designs on the front of the font, and also some sketches of the next two gargoyles for your chapel parapet."

"Ah! I love gargoyles! Let's have a look at those first."

Hameel is nodding, but makes no move to unroll the papers. He has something else he wants to say, but he finds it difficult to begin. He looks towards the window,

113

and then back at the Abbess. Her fine, carefully plucked eyebrows are raised in enquiry. He feels as if he has let her down, although, God knows, he has tried his best.

"What is it, Hameel? Something's on your mind."

"I had some bad news a little while ago. I... I hadn't mentioned it, but perhaps you've already heard by now..."

"What? What sort of bad news, Hameel?"

"From Jerome. Jerome told me."

The Abbess guesses it immediately.

"Not the Overmaas commission?"

"Yes."

"So Jerome won it?"

"Yes."

The Abbess's face flushes red with anger. The bearded, pustuled features of the Dean at Overmaas thrust themselves into her mind's eye. After all she'd offered him! And the cathedral chapter certainly needed the money. They'd over-extended themselves, and now they have the fresh expense of the new window...

"The fools! I can't believe it. If they'd chosen you..."

Hameel cuts in. He feels embarrassed by his failure. Even with the Abbess's support, they didn't choose his designs.

"I know you did all you could for me," he mutters.

"It's dirt thrown in my face. I'll not forgive this. My gold not good enough for them!"

They mull over their defeat in silence for a few moments.

"Jerome has asked me to work as his assistant," Hameel says.

The Abbess snorts, and throws a sideways glance at him.

"Once more the second fiddle, eh?"

She observes his crestfallen face.

"I'm sorry Hameel."

There is another brief silence, and then the Abbess breaks the spell, slapping her hand down on the table.

"Well, let's see these sketches at least, shall we?"

Hameel unfurls one of the rolls. The Abbess fetches two heavy bronze candlesticks to weight it down top and bottom. Malevolent twisted faces squint up at her from the paper, leering, winking, and mocking.

"Hmm... interesting. You know, Hameel, I think I see the *influence* of your successful friend Jerome here. This fellow with the trumpet for a face – I'm sure I've seen him lurking in the corner of our big painting of the Passion in the refectory."

Hameel shrugs, irritated. The more irritated because it's true.

"Jerome himself draws on a long painterly tradition of depicting demons," he says. A feeble defence.

"Yes, but there's something unique, don't you think, about his little devils and monsters? You could really believe that he must have seen them with his own eyes, to paint them in such detail."

Hameel shrugs again. He isn't in a mood for graciousness towards Jerome. He hasn't been able to see Aleyt alone for ten days now. Since the garden.

The Abbess regards him closely. Her little dart has drawn a prick of blood, as she had intended.

"I'm sorry, Hameel! I didn't mean to belittle your own efforts. You and Jerome are very close. It's only natural that you should influence each other. How is his painting of Hell progressing?"

"Slowly," Hameel says.

The Abbess raises an eyebrow, inviting more.

Hameel gives in, grudgingly.

"It's a powerful work. Astonishing, in fact."

The Abbess nods. She toys with the little golden crucifix at the end of the ruby rosary beads dangling from her neck.

"And... those things we've spoken of before, Hameel. Does he persist in painting members of the clergy in a disrespectful manner?"

"He does, yes."

115

The Abbess takes the rosary beads from around her neck and lets them coil like a snake into her cupped hand. She glances again at Hameel, thinking.

Ever since she got wind of his adulterous liaison with Aleyt, she has been turning the information around in her mind, trying to tease out how she might use it best to hurt Jerome. Simply revealing the affair, if she can get hold of the proof of Mary's testimony, would wound him, certainly. But would it inflict the lasting, permanent damage she would wish to see? What if he was big enough to forgive and forget? She would herself certainly lose Hameel's loyalty – in fact Hameel might be driven away from Den Bosch altogether.

But she has come up with something else, another way to use her knowledge, and completely to disguise her own hand in the matter. Her idea is a touch complicated, somewhat uncertain, but with interesting possibilities.

Now, with Hameel smarting at Jerome's latest artistic triumph, it is perhaps as propitious a moment as will ever arise for her to put her speculative plan into motion.

She moves just a bit closer to him, lowering her voice as if they might be overheard. Of course, they won't. She once caught Sister Theresa apparently eavesdropping outside her door, and Sister Theresa will make quite sure that never happens again. But it's appropriate to subdue her voice, to draw Hameel in, to make him feel that she is sharing a confidence with him.

"It worries me, Hameel, the persistent anti-clerical thread in his work. Listen, let me put my cards on the table: I know very well that Jerome despises me..."

"Abbess Dominica, I'm sure you're wrong."

Hameel says as much out of politeness, but she waves a hand dismissively, and he gives up the attempt.

"Hameel - it's so obvious! Just watch him at the meetings of the Holy Company when I enter the room. He looks at me like an interloper, and then keeps as far

116

away from me as if I had St Anthony's Fire. I know he opposed my election. I know very well also that he slanders me behind my back. I hear it from my contacts among the merchants and the leading citizens of the town. I'm told he considers me avaricious, corrupt, and… gluttonous. These reported remarks I might forgive, although they're hardly pleasant. But, Hameel, what I can't forgive is that his work contains so much that is critical of the Church. What must the common people think, who cannot read, but see depicted in his paintings that the clergy, the nuns and monks, lead the riotous way to Hell? We, who in reality are showing them the way to Heaven, will be distrusted and despised if we are painted with such contempt."

She pauses, and looks at Hameel with an expression of innocent, open appeal to his good judgement.

"What do *you* think?"

Hameel glances down at the gargoyle faces on the paper, the only witnesses to this conversation. He hesitates, sensing some sort of trap. He always treads very carefully when speaking with the Abbess about Jerome. But he has to say something, and her assessment of Jerome's views about her is completely accurate.

"He's… self-righteous," he mutters at last.

The Abbess claps her hands as if in wonderment at his acuity.

"Well put, Hameel! Exactly so. And what a shadow he casts over *you*. If only you'd got the Overmaas commission! You need room to prove yourself. You're his equal as an artist – and as a man, Hameel. You're more than his equal as a man."

Hameel masters his impulse to nod. He gives no outward response. But isn't what she says true? Does not the proof lie with Aleyt? Why would she have fallen in love with him, if there were no failing in Jerome?

The Abbess moves to her next point of attack. Another public mark of honour has just yesterday been bestowed on Jerome, and she doubts if Hameel yet knows of it. One more ingredient for the little stew of resentment she is hoping to stir up.

"Did you know Hameel, that yesterday the committee of the Holy Company chose him to be the cross-bearer in the Good Friday procession."

"Oh?" Hameel mutters.

It's news to him, but he isn't surprised. Honours and distinctions seem to shower on Jerome from a liberal sky.

"I spoke against it in private, of course. I had the Burgemeester's ear. But he was outnumbered in the committee. What a travesty! An arrogant man like Jerome playing the role of our humble, suffering Lord Jesus Christ!"

Hameel feels uncomfortable with the direction of the conversation. It's easy enough to fall in with Jerome when he is mocking the Abbess in private, but he can't play the same game in reverse. He must try to draw a line under this topic.

"Abbess – forgive me – I understand your views. But *you* must understand that he's my friend. My oldest friend. He's been good to me ever since I was small. He was just the same age as my older brother Pieter. They were… they were close friends too."

The Abbess is taken aback. She doesn't like finding missing pieces to puzzles that she thought she'd worked out.

"I didn't know you had a brother," she says. With her own ears she can hear the slightly accusatory tone of her voice.

"He died when he was fourteen. Saint Anthony's Fire."

The Abbess nods, mollified. This Pieter must have died a long time ago, when she herself was just a novice, living far away from Den Bosch. It is not surprising she's not heard of him. Children are dying all the time. She gives her voice a softer tone.

"I'm sorry. And I'm sorry too, Hameel, to put you in an awkward position, criticizing Jerome in front of you. Let us put aside my...dislike... and your friendship, and I'll ask you a simple question. Don't you think it shameful, the way he depicts the clergy?"

Hameel almost smiles. If the Abbess had heard a fraction of what Hameel has heard Jerome say in private on the subject of the clergy, she might be more shocked still. She is looking at him expectantly, and he must choose his words carefully.

"Perhaps he goes too far. But he's headstrong. He says he paints the truth."

"The truth? Hmph! Well, I feel I want advice on what should be done. I'd like to know Brother Jacomo's views."

Brother Jacomo? Hameel is startled, as if the man himself has sprung out of a hidden door in the Abbess's room. What has the Inquisitor got to do with this? He feels that the jaws of a trap are lying somewhere directly in front of him, hidden beneath the Abbess's appearance of innocent concern. He must tread now with extreme caution.

"Jacomo's views? How does it concern him?"

"He's an emissary of Rome – of the Pope himself. His opinion will be most valuable. Will you describe Jerome's painting of Hell to him for me?"

Hameel avoids her eye.

"He's not a man... well... I wouldn't want Jerome to come to the attention of such a man."

"Because?"

"Jerome is outspoken, sure of himself..."

"Of course – a great artist! A genius!"

"He may speak provocatively."

Now it is the Abbess who suppresses a smile. How perfect that would be! She uncoils the serpent of her rosary, and lets the red beads – rubies of great value - trickle between her fingers like little drops of blood.

"I understand your loyalty, Hameel. But he may be

falling into a sinful error, which we can prevent. It's our duty to God."

"I'm not sure…"

She cuts in.

"You could say it was a duty of friendship too. Your friendship. A warning shot, alerting him to the danger of serious trouble. And, Hameel, *I'm* your friend also, remember."

She rests a hand on the edge of the paper with its sketches.

"And your *patron*. Can't you do this little thing for me?"

"Abbess Dominica, I owe you a great deal, and I'd like to do whatever you ask. But Brother Jacomo…"

He shakes his head, unable to express his fears precisely. Jacomo is a dangerous man to encounter, a fanatic, with extensive powers. A man to avoid at all costs, even if one's conscience is clear.

"Don't worry, Hameel. Brother Jacomo will be able to offer good advice on such a matter, and even Jerome himself might value such advice. Do you see my point?"

Now the Abbess leans forward towards him, placing both her hands on the paper. He looks down at it. The grotesque faces of his gargoyles leer up at him. They know. They know that the work the Abbess gives him is the surest way to make his name as an artist. They know that she could withdraw her patronage instantly, and even make his life in Den Bosch difficult or impossible if he crosses her. They know also, these dark, impish demons of his imagination, that there is something inside him that responds to the Abbess's appeal, that wants to make a little trouble for Jerome. They give him to understand, at last, that he has nowhere else to step but into the trap that has been laid.

"I'll do as you wish," he says.

Click.

The Abbess puts a hand on his arm, feeling the muscle there, squeezing it. She smiles at him.

"Excellent! I think it likely that Brother Jacomo will be in his rooms at this time. Why don't we go straight away? Then we'll come back and finish looking at your sketches."

Releasing her grip on his arm, she leads the way to the door.

He follows her, like a puppy dog.

CHAPTER TWELVE

The quill scratches into the silence as Jacomo moves it across the paper.

Cardinal Amandini,

Greetings from your brother in Christ.

When this finds you in Rome, God willing, my work will be much advanced here in the Duchy of Brabant. My secretary, Brother Bartelme, has made a copy of his detailed record of our doings, which accompanies this letter. But you requested that I write to you myself, and that I made as part of my matter some observations to you regarding the work of Abbot Geoffrey. I am sorry to tell you that I think the Abbot but a poor representative of the Holy Office here. As you commanded, I first visited him at the Abbey of Saint Anthony at Eindhoven, and since then I have travelled widely, both to the cities and in the countryside. I find the land in a parlous state, and that the competing factions of the secular powers leave much room for the Church's influence to thrive better than it does under Abbot Geoffrey. Satan is abroad here, and too often shows his face with impunity. As long as the sovereignty of these territories remains unresolved between the Holy Emperor Maximilian and the King Charles VIII, then the boy Philip cannot come into control of his Burgundian possessions. Meanwhile, the city states vie for primacy. There is peace, but it will remain uneasy and prone to ruptures until the matter of the succession is agreed – or imposed. God grant it will be the Holy Emperor who prevails, and I see many signs of that outcome – although I would hesitate to describe it a certainty.

I am lodged now at Den Bosch, where we have been these several weeks. The Burgemeester here, one Theofilus Piek, is most inclined to cede Rome's primacy in all matters of the Faith, being more concerned with keeping the roads safe for trade and promoting the interests of the many merchants and manufacturers who make this city their home. Den Bosch is a thriving centre for the cloth trade, and for metal working of all kinds. It is also known for its musicians and scholars, and a printing press was set up here in recent years. There is a goodly number of monasteries and convents, and yet, for all the outward show of piety, there seems little appetite for the prosecution of those who, in secret or more openly, do the work of the Devil. Nevertheless, I think that of all the cities I have visited here in the Duchy, Den Bosch is the most apt as a new centre for the present Inquisition. Looking about me for a suitable start to our work, I swiftly discovered a notorious warlock, possessed of demons, living quite openly as a beggar. At my application, Piek ordered his men to take him into custody without quibble. I worked as we have discussed in Rome, without the elaborate procedures instituted by Father Torquemada in Spain. I questioned him, and secured a confession, which he repeated without duress before a small jury of secular and ecclesiastical representatives. All this went forward smoothly. He was burned in the market square with all appropriate ritual and with the full support of the secular arm. This, I have been told, was the first such execution in Den Bosch in living memory, which tells you the extent of the accumulated work to be done in these parts. I have gathered, from interviews with Abbot Geoffrey, that no more than three executions for witchcraft have taken place in the entire Duchy of Brabant since the commencement of our present Papal Inquisition here. I know you will agree with me that this shows a lamentable lack of diligence in the service of our Saviour and on behalf of our Pope Innocent's Bull against Witchcraft. The hammer of God must smite hard and often

123

against these wicked practices, as it does in the German territories where the Malleus Maleficarum has been more influential.

His fingers are cramping, and he pauses to flex them. The scratching quill's cessation leaves behind it a gap of silence, filled only by his own breathing. He pays the silence more attention, and it yields its secrets. In the next room, Brother Bartelme coughs, very softly. Far off, on the edge of hearing, a dog barks somewhere. Silence, complete silence, is scarcely to be found; a rare benison. He has been born with preternaturally sharp hearing, and the slightest of sounds can disturb him. It is at times a burden, this faculty, but it saved his young life more than once, in the squalid, violent hurly-burly of his early years in Seville.

He shakes off this thought, before images can form in his mind's eye. He has done things that he knows God will never allow him to forget. He must have trust in His forgiveness. To suppress memory, and, worse, the lingering pride in some of his unspeakable acts, he scans his eyes around the bare room.

It's a great improvement on the place he'd been rented by the merchant Lammers. There, he was distracted by constant noise from the street outside during daylight hours. Then, at night, the walls proved woefully thin, and the disgusting sound of Lammers and his wife in lustful copulation forced itself repeatedly on his ears. He sees again Lammers' bulging eyes shifting sideways as he reminded him that Lent was not a suitable time for marital congress. Lammers slunk away, blushing, and the noises ceased. But he felt sure that they were still pursuing their filthy activities in conspiratorial silence. He couldn't abide to be separated only by a layer of lathe and plaster from such sin, and so the Abbess's offer of a room at the convent was most welcome.

He was cautious about accepting, nonetheless, until his advance inspection revealed that the room was in a separate building that had been incorporated into the convent at a relatively recent date, and had been converted for the use of visitors by the present Abbess. It has its own entrance, and there is sleeping accommodation for both himself and his secretary, Brother Bartelme. It is well away from the nuns' living quarters, and the windows look out onto nothing more than the side wall of the chapel. He wants no whiff of scandal to attend his lodging in a convent. Nor does he want to see or hear the nuns going about their business, although he is content enough to join them at their religious observances and in the refectory for the evening meal, which is conducted in silence. He ensures that Brother Bartelme records these irreproachable details in the account of his proceedings that Cardinal Amandini requires.

His eyes come to rest on the crucifix, with its carved figure of the Saviour twisted in agony. The crucifix is his own, nailed to the wall wherever he travels. He carries a small hammer about with him for this purpose. The figure of Christ is streaked with vivid red, where blood runs from the puncture wounds in the hands and feet, and from the crown of thorns. He painted these details himself. Christ's pain is an important matter. It demonstrates more than anything else that the only sure way to Heaven is through suffering. For the Son of God himself, taking on life in this human world had meant torture and a hideous death. That must not be lost sight of.

He looks down again at his letter. He pictures Cardinal Amandini's deep brown eyes perusing its contents. He will surely see the justice of his criticisms of the ineffectual Abbot Geoffrey. Like Kramer, author of the *Malleus Maleficarum*, like Father Tomás de Torquemada in Spain, like himself, Cardinal Amandini is a warrior of the Church. He will not rest while heretics and apostates, witches and warlocks are active and go unpunished. When his influence is brought fully to bear in the councils in Rome, surely there is every hope that he, Jacomo, will be appointed Grand Inquisitor in the Duchy of Brabant. Abbot Geoffrey is weak, not suited to the work. In a matter of months, perhaps as soon as the autumn of this year, he will have zealous, hand-picked assistants arriving from Rome to work under his direction. The dungeons in Den Bosch will begin to fill with the Devil's servants, and the cleansing of the land will proceed apace.

He feels uplifted by hope and holy joy, like a physical lightness in his body. His life's purpose, God's purpose for him, will be fulfilled. It is a moment in which to give thanks, so he kneels before the crucifix to pray, speaking the familiar words that he always uses aloud in a steady, low voice.

"Let the Unrighteous be confounded and put to shame. Let them be as chaff before the wind, and let the angel of the Lord chase them. Let their way be dark and slippery, and let the angel of the Lord persecute them. Let destruction come upon them unawares, and let their nets that they have hid catch themselves, into that very destruction let them fall. Blessed be the Lord my strength, which teacheth my hands to war, and my fingers to fight. My goodness and my fortress, my high tower and my deliverer, my shield, and he in whom I trust. Bow thy heavens O Lord, and come down: touch the mountains, and they shall smoke. Cast forth lightning, and scatter the Unrighteous; shoot out thy arrows, and destroy them. So be it. Amen."

As he ceases to pray aloud, he immediately becomes aware of a new sound. Feet – two pairs of feet – are approaching along the stone-flagged passageway outside. They halt, and then a knock sounds at his door. He levers himself up into a standing position using the edge of his table to steady himself. His legs prickle with pins and needles.

"Come in!" he calls out.

The door is opened a crack but no-one enters. He

126

sees the white wimple of a nun – the Abbess – through the gap, and behind her he can see just the arm of another figure, a man's arm. He feels irritation. He doesn't like surprises.

"Hello Brother Jacomo," the Abbess says. "We're not interrupting your afternoon prayers, I hope?"

"I'd just finished," he says, moving to the table. The ink is dry on his letter, and he turns it over. "Enter, please."

She steps forward into the room and motions her companion to advance. It's Hameel, the artist. The man makes a small bow towards him, keeping his eyes on the floor.

"We've just come to discuss a little matter with you, and seek your advice," the Abbess goes on.

He nods, and waves them forward.

"Shall we sit around the table? There are three chairs."

They sit, and the Abbess fingers her rosary beads. He feels like reminding her that they are an instrument of prayer, not a childish toy.

"It's a delicate subject," she begins, "but both Hameel and I felt we should raise it with you. As a Papal Inquisitor, it's a matter that is, we're sure, part of your remit."

Jacomo nods, and waits for more.

The Abbess glances at Hameel.

"It's delicate because it concerns a man held in the highest esteem here in Den Bosch, the Master Painter Jerome."

Jacomo inclines his head in recognition.

"The painter of the Passion that is on your refectory wall."

"The very same man."

Jacomo nods. In his mind's eye, Cardinal Grimaldi lumbers heavily into view, a man more concerned with his art collection than with the Church's interests. However, the Cardinal has convinced many others of the merits of the master painter of Den Bosch.

"He's held in esteem well beyond Den Bosch, Abbess. Even in Rome I've heard him spoken of. Spoken of highly."

Hameel shifts in his chair, as if uncomfortable. He still hasn't met his eyes since entering.

He addresses him directly.

"Hameel, you're an artist too. Is this a matter of art, that brings you to me?"

Hameel makes the vaguest of nods. Does that mean assent, or is it merely a twitch? He's annoyed. Many things annoy him. It's his besetting sin, the way that anger rises so quickly in him, like a fire in dry straw. Even a little thing like this can set off a spark. He takes a deep breath, and waits. He senses, from the movement of her fingers on her rosary, that the Abbess too is exasperated.

"It's to do with Jerome's paintings, yes," she says. Then she looks squarely at Hameel.

"Hameel –please - you can explain the matter best."

Hameel looks at his hands.

"Jerome's latest work..." the Abbess prompts .

At last Hameel looks up. He glances at both of them quickly, like a trapped animal. Jacomo can smell guilt, like a stinking privy. So, what is he guilty of?

"He's working on a triptych now," Hameel says, again preferring the sight of his hands to that of their faces. "It's for the cathedral here in Den Bosch. Not for the side chapel of our Holy Company, but to be placed right at the front of the nave, commissioned by the Bishop and chapter,. It's eagerly anticipated, and it will be seen by everyone who comes to masses in the cathedral."

"An important and prestigious work, then?" Jacomo says.

"Yes, and one whose content... whose content gives the Abbess... the Abbess and myself... some concern."

Jacomo leans forward on his elbows. He is beginning

to be interested.

"What does it depict?"

Hameel looks towards him at last. He can hardly avoid it. But his eyes appear to focus elsewhere, somewhere behind Jacomo's head. Jacomo almost turns around, to see what is there.

"On the left panel, God with Adam and Eve, and on the right panel, a vision of the torments of Hell."

"And in the middle?"

"So far I believe he's only made sketches for the middle panel. I haven't seen them. He speaks of some sort of garden – perhaps it will be the Garden of Eden, before the Fall."

"What is your concern?"

"If you look closely at his painting of the Passion here in Abbess Dominica's convent, you'll see a small example of... of what worries the Abbess... and myself. In the background of the Passion are some small figures – you might hardly notice them. There's a group of monks playing dice and also a priest and a nun embracing."

"Fornicating!" the Abbess cuts in impatiently. "Small figures they may be, and perhaps overlooked by many, but plainly suggesting that the clergy are more concerned with avarice and lust than the death of their Saviour."

Her voice trembles a little with indignation.

"Go on," Jacomo urges Hameel.

Hameel glances at the Abbess. She's got him on some sort of string, Jacomo thinks. He doesn't want to tell me this.

"In Jerome's painting of Hell," Hameel mumbles, "he's gone much further. Many of the damned souls are members of the clergy. Priests, monks, and nuns are prominent among the figures, and their torments are unspeakable – obscene."

The Abbess butts in again, eagerly.

"So surely you can see why we're concerned, Brother

129

Jacomo? Right in the heart of our own cathedral in Den Bosch, an attack on the very people who the common herd should look up to and respect! What effect will it have?"

She sits back and looks at him. Hameel seems lost in an examination of the table's surface.

Jacomo turns the matter around in his mind. Not only its substance, but the manner in which it has been brought to him.

"You were right to consult me. But with such an eminent man we must proceed with care. I'll visit Jerome tomorrow and speak with him. I'll ask to see this painting. Hameel... you're a friend of Jerome?"

Hameel nods, emphatically.

"I am."

Is this the explanation for his reluctance in coming here? Perhaps Hameel would have greatly preferred to leave this sleeping dog lying, but the Abbess has stirred him up to come to him. And of course, he is in her pay. Hence the guilt that sweats from his pores. He is putting difficulties in the way of his friend - at his patron's insistence. So far, so clear. But why is the Abbess so exercised by this matter?

"Hmm. Well, you do well not to let your conscience be blinded by friendship," he says to Hameel. "All friendships are fleeting things, when the fate of our eternal souls is in the balance."

The Abbess leans forward with her elbows on the table.

"There's another thing you should know about Jerome," she says. "He has spoken to the Burgemeester, Theofilus Piek, urging him to discourage your mission here."

"Discourage?" Jacomo raises an eyebrow, soliciting more.

"That's all I know. He was overheard raising the matter in private before the Shrove Tuesday feast of the Holy Company."

Jacomo nods.

"Thank you for the information."

The Abbess stands up and glances at Hameel, who jumps up with alacrity.

"Well, we mustn't disturb you any longer, Brother Jacomo," she says. "Will you dine tonight in the refectory?"

"I will," Jacomo assents, standing up also.

"We can take a close look at that painting of the Passion together then, if you wish."

He nods.

"Until then, God be with you!" she adds.

"And with you," Jacomo replies.

The door closes behind them, and he sits down again at his table, thinking over what this all means. One thing is certain: an overtly anti-clerical painting in the heart of a cathedral is a serious matter. He looks forward to seeing with his own eyes exactly what the painter is doing.

CHAPTER THIRTEEN

"Hello Mary!"

Gillis.

She finishes paying the stallholder for her pound of flour, and then turns to give Gillis a strictly provisional smile.

Since her encounter with the Abbess in the cathedral, she's wondered how that woman came by her information about Hameel's visits to Aleyt. Gillis was a tenant of the Abbess's, and therefore might be expected to have some dealings with her. Also, there was no-one else in all of Den Bosch in whom Mary had confided, not even her sister Catalyn. In fact, even in bed with Gillis, she'd not gone so far as to say that Hameel and her Mistress were lovers. She'd done no more than drop hints. Why had she done even that? She was angry with herself, because really there was no good reason. It was just idle talk, lying all comfortable in his arms and feeling relaxed and close. And her careless words had just been following her thoughts, which often turned towards Hameel in such moments, whoever's arms held her at the time. She couldn't help it.

So now she feels provisionally angry with Gillis, and unconditionally angry with herself, for being a prattling-jay.

"How have you been, my dear?" Gillis says, as they

make their way through the press of people in the market square. "It seems a long time since... since your surprise visit."

"I'm very well, Gillis. How are you?"

"I'm well. Busy. But I wouldn't be too busy to see you again one day soon."

"Well, perhaps you might. But I can't come and go as I please."

"Maybe your mistress will want you out of the house again?"

He grins and winks at her. Mary frowns and pulls him aside between two stalls. She checks that no-one is near enough to overhear them.

"I had a surprising talk with the Abbess Dominica a few nights ago," she says in a low voice, watching his face.

His jaw drops a little and then his eyes go wandering off like naughty schoolboys.

"The Abbess? What's the Abbess got to talk with you about?" he says.

"Keep your voice down, Gillis."

"Where did this happen, this talk?"

"In the cathedral. I was praying there in the night - that night when we was having the dreadful storm."

"And the Abbess..."

"The Abbess came up to me, right out of nowhere she did, like a boggart. She half-frighted me out of my shoes. Then she starts straight off asking me questions. She seemed to have a thing in her head about Hameel and my Mistress, and I wondered how that had got there, Gillis. Do you happen to have seen the Abbess recently? You told me once she visits quite often."

Gillis clears his throat and looks off into the middle distance.

"She came a while ago. The day after you came, it were. Or maybe the next day."

"Oh. Fancy that. So were you and her a-talking about anything in particular, Gillis?"

A deep flush of embarrassment reddens his cheeks. She presses her attack.

"Well? Did you pass on anything as you shouldn't have done?"

"Why would I?" Gillis mumbles.

"Well, *you* tell me, Gillis. I can't think what you and the Abbess should be talking about, unless it's fattening up geese or what she wants you to grow in your fields."

"The Abbess is a… she's a strong sort of a woman..." he says at last.

"Strong?"

"Well – what I mean - she's my Mistress, just like you're a servant to Master Jerome and his wife. I'm her servant. She could take away my livelihood tomorrow, if she snapped her fingers."

"What has that got to do with it?"

"Mary… listen… she knows about you and me. That wasn't my doing. Someone, I don't know who, had told her that we… that we saw each other at times. She seems to know everything what's going on in Den Bosch. And knowing about you and me, then she takes it into her head to ask me questions about… you know, your master."

"Which you don't have to answer, Gillis. She doesn't know what I do or don't tell you. You could say we never talk about the Master and Mistress."

"Well, I *didn't* tell her nothing."

"About Hameel?"

"I didn't say nothing more than what you said, Mary. I didn't cast no stones. I just said as how… as how he was a-visiting a lot... when the master was away. That's all. She kind of wheedled that out of me, and I didn't think as it was doing any harm to repeat it. You didn't say nothing about it being a big secret, Mary.

He seems struck by a thought, and looks her straight in the eye again.

"And anyway - if it *were* such a big secret, well – you wouldn't have said nothing to me yourself, would you

Mary?"

She's been a fool. A silly blabbering gossip.

"I've got to go now, Gillis," she mutters.

"But, Mary…"

She doesn't hear him out. She marches off quickly, so he knows not to follow.

When she regains the house and enters the kitchen she's still agitated. The pans from last night's meal await her, mute but recriminatory. She should have dealt with them before going to bed. Now the muck will be harder to scrub off. She needs to calm down properly first. She paces about the ground floor of the house, her little kingdom. Up and down the main hall where they all eat their meals. In and out of her little bedroom next to the kitchen, with its tiny window onto the garden, directly below the Master's painting studio. She comes to a halt at last at that window and peers out towards the back gate. Because the Master and Mistress's bedroom is right at the top of the house, facing the square, like their parlour, they are none the wiser when she lets in a nocturnal visitor through that gate. It used to be Hameel. Then it was Gillis. But now it looks as if it will be nobody at all.

She goes back into the kitchen and blows on the embers in the kitchen hearth until they glow. It will take a lot of hot water to deal with those pans. She casts her mind back to the last partner she'd had before Gillis: Jacob, the youngest son of the miller Jaap. Jacob was too frightened to come to visit her in the dark, and she'd scurried herself through the town's dark alleyways at night, terrified of being seen, or set upon by lurkers, to knock at his bedchamber shutters. Those were his first encounters with a naked woman – he was so young, with such soft skin and bright blue eyes. But he wasn't soft where it was important. Then one night his older sister had quietly entered the room and threatened to tell their father if Mary ever came again. Jacob was terrified of his father, whose forearms bulged from years

135

of heavy work and regular beating of his wife and children.

That was all a long time ago. Perhaps a year. She puts some kindling onto the glowing embers in the hearth and goes to pick up the pans that will need washing. She's still dwelling fondly on those secretive couplings with Jacob when she sets down one of the big iron pans carelessly too near the edge of the table and catches the handle with her sleeve. It clatters onto the stone floor like a peal of bells.

Her heart jumps into her mouth. She's been thinking lewd thoughts! They'd crept up on her unawares, and now this clattering pan is like a summons to the Devil on the roof of Hell! She walks around the pan without picking it up, making the sign of the cross and muttering the Lord's Prayer. She's so careless sometimes... the Devil could come and carry her off at any time, and she'd go straight to Hell with her sins unconfessed!

Suddenly she's aware of Aleyt standing at the kitchen door. She crosses herself one more time for luck, and then touches the pan gingerly. The Devil could have made it hot or icy cold to punish her. She looks at Aleyt again, who is smiling broadly now. She can't see why Aleyt should look so amused. Nevertheless, she feels a need to explain herself.

"Well – making a clatter on the roof of Hell! We don't want the Devil coming up to see what the noise is, do we?"

"No, we don't want the Devil in our house, you're right," Aleyt says, coming further into the room. "Did you get the flour?"

"Yes."

Aleyt goes to the little pantry and looks over its contents. She speaks over her shoulder.

"I have to talk to you about what we need for our feast for the council of the Holy Company on May Day."

"It's not for ages yet," Mary objects.

"I want to plan well ahead. It's a big occasion."

136

Too big an occasion, she is thinking to herself. The Holy Company is at the heart of Den Bosch's activities at the end of Lent, and since Jerome has the honour to be Christ in this year's procession, he has proposed a feast at his house on May Day, for the dozen or so council members of the company.

He'd discussed it with her before making the offer, and she had concurred with his suggestion. She sensed what his feelings were on the matter. Because he was such a private person, spending so much of his time working alone, he felt the need on this occasion to show his face to the world. The burghers and clerics of Den Bosch were proud of having the most renowned artist in Brabant living in their midst. It was for that reason that he was being honoured as the Christ in the procession, and it was appropriate to reciprocate in some way.

Mary is following a different train of thought.

"I ain't never cooked a swan before."

She's been privately anxious about this ever since she learned that a swan was to be on the bill of fare.

"The swan is being brought in," Aleyt tells her, emerging from the pantry. "They're cooking it at the Golden Keys and bringing it over here."

Mary finds herself dealing with mixed emotions.

"So, you and the Master didn't think I can manage?" she says.

Aleyt knows how to deal with this swiftly enough. She adopts a tone of tender concern.

"Are you disappointed, Mary? Well, we can cancel that and get a live swan brought here a few days before for you to kill and hang and cook yourself."

Mary feels outmanoeuvred.

"There'll be enough else to do, no doubt," she says.

"That's true."

"Perhaps the swan can be dealt with at the Golden Keys then."

"I agree. A good idea, Mary."

"What else does the Master want for the feast here?"

137

Aleyt picks up a wooden spoon and beats a little drumbeat on one of the pans with it, then shrugs.

"Too busy with his paint brushes to discuss it, I suppose," Mary suggests.

Aleyt strikes Mary as looking a little sad.

"He should give you more of his time!" she blurts out.

"Mary..." Aleyt says.

"I'm sorry. Not my place to say, I know."

Aleyt smiles ruefully at her. Whenever Aleyt smiles, Mary is struck by how young she looks. She could almost be a girl of Mary's own age, and at such moments she feels a great surge of affection for her Mistress. She smiles back at her, and Aleyt reaches out and holds her hand. Aleyt often makes such spontaneous gestures, and it makes Mary feel as if they are more like friends - even sisters - than mistress and servant.

"You know I don't hold you to your place," Aleyt says quietly.

Mary returns the pressure of her hand.

"You don't, Mistress. You're the best Mistress a girl like me could have! If I was to be somewhere that I had to know my place all the time, I wouldn't last for five minutes in that place... if you understand me."

Aleyt laughs.

"I understand you perfectly!"

She glances at the kitchen door, which stands ajar, and goes to push it closed. Returning, she looks at Mary and smiles again, more seriously.

"And *you* understand *me*, I think. You know all my secrets anyway. Or almost all of them."

"What don't I know?" Mary replies. There is nothing she doesn't know, and her heart goes out to Aleyt.

"You'll see. But I want your advice."

"About Hameel?" Mary guesses. They are both speaking in low tones, although Jerome never emerges from his studio at this time of day.

"About Hameel, yes."

"I know what you're going to say," Mary says.

"How?"

"Because I guess your secret."

"No you don't!" How could she?

"What about Hameel?" Mary prompts her.

She sighs.

"He loves me."

That is true, and obvious. Mary waits for more.

"Mary, I love him too. But..."

She falls silent and looks so hopeless that Mary helps her.

"But he has to be given his marching orders."

She feels a little joyful skip in her heart as she says the words.

Aleyt is grateful for Mary's powers of divination. She nods slowly.

"But how can I do that, Mary? It will kill him!"

Mary waves a hand at that.

"No it won't. He'll be sad, but he won't die."

Aleyt shakes her head.

"He'll be worse than sad. It'll make him desperate. Mary, I don't know how to do this. I *do* love him. But Jerome..."

"Who hardly notices he has a wife..."

Mary stops herself. As usual, she's letting her mouth run away with her.

"That's unfair to him, Mary. He loves me dearly. And I love him. More than I love Hameel."

She pauses. She's never said these words before, even to herself. There's something wrong with them. Mary is looking at her.

"Differently," she adds, and falls silent. Is that the right way to say it? She could say that her love for Jerome is like a steady, single candle flame, always there to ward off the darkness. But when she is with Hameel, all the flames of Hell possess her, and she burns like a

139

witch on a pyre. But willingly, deliberately, helplessly.

Mary feels sanctioned by Aleyt's silence to speak her mind.

"I know the Master loves you too, Mistress... but... oh, I feel so *angry* sometimes, how he leaves you alone so much. He *lives* in that studio of his. Painting away his life!"

"He won't always be so. When we have the country cottage at Roedeken finished in the summer, he's promised we'll go there every Friday afternoon and only return in time for mass on Sunday morning. We'll have all that time together - no painting or Holy Company business."

"Will I be coming?"

Aleyt is amused by the question. She's never considered Mary's attitude towards their future visits to Roedeken.

"Of course! I expect so. Why not? Or sometimes perhaps you could have a free day on Saturdays and have the house here to yourself, if you'd like that."

Mary gives Aleyt a sly look. It's time to show her hand.

"So, if I stayed here, it would just be the three of you at Roedeken?"

Aleyt tries to make sense of this.

"What do you mean?"

"You, your husband, and the baby," Mary replies.

Aleyt gapes at her. Mary meets her eyes, which brazen it out for a moment, and then flicker downwards.

"Mary! What are you talking about?"

The question, and the tone of bafflement, fools neither of them.

"That's your secret, isn't it Mistress! And I guessed it days ago."

The look on Mary's face, the smile, breaks down Aleyt's attempted reserve. She finds that she is smiling back, flooded with sudden joy, babbling.

"I've only known myself for a matter of days.

140

However did you guess? I'm quite certain though. It's happened at last!"

Mary puts out her arms, and she steps into them. They hug silently for a few moments.

"After all these years of hoping and waiting!" Mary says, patting her back. "Seven years isn't it, you been married? What do you think made the difference? Was it the Master being away in Reebs, do you think?"

"Mary!" Aleyt takes a step back.

"And nine weeks since Hameel first came to your bed. I been counting."

Mary is grinning openly now.

"Mary! Please, don't... don't make light of this," Aleyt appeals.

"I'm sorry," Mary says. But she isn't. After all, what harm in speaking the truth, in private like this?

Aleyt looks Mary in the eye. She makes her tone serious.

"The child is Jerome's child, Mary. The child we have both hoped and prayed for, for so long."

They exchange a very long look. At last, Mary nods. No more needs to be said.

"When will you tell the Master?" she says. "He'll be overjoyed!"

"Just as soon as I've broken off with Hameel. I must do that first."

"Hameel must be given his marching orders, as soon as may be, then."

Aleyt shakes her head helplessly.

"How will I do it, Mary? How can I do it kindly?"

"You can't. You must do it cruelly."

"I don't know how I'm to do it at all."

She feels a prickling sensation in her eyes.

"You must help me, Mary."

Mary wishes she had something wise or practical to say.

"*I* can't tell him, Mistress."

"I know. I know, Mary. It's just – I had to share this

141

burden."

"You did right, Mistress. You can share all your troubles with me."

They embrace again. Aleyt's tears are released, and she sobs on Mary's shoulder. Mary pats her back, and feels very protective and proud. After a while Aleyt stands back again, dabbing at her eyes with her sleeves.

"Oh Mary! You should see my cousin Frida's baby boy!"

"A child is such a blessing," Mary says.

Aleyt finds her lace handkerchief. She dries her eyes.

"It would make my life complete. I'm so happy! Oh, what a muddle my mind is in!"

She sighs.

"We'll talk about the preparations for the feast later. I can't think straight. I'm going to go upstairs and work on my tapestry for a while."

They share a last smile, and Aleyt leaves the kitchen. Mary listens to her light tread crossing the dining hall and diminishing up the stairs.

She returns to sorting out pans. Something of Aleyt's joy has found its way into her heart too. A baby! It will make the quiet house come alive, and give them all something to think about. For a while she amuses herself with considering where the cot could go, and how they should make the house safe for when the child begins to walk. She dwells on how she might help with bathing the little creature, and feeding and clothing it. From that, she soon falls to thinking about how she would love to have a baby herself. But a man would have to ask for her hand before that could happen. Would Gillis ask her?

Of course her 'reputation' – which has even reached the ears of the Abbess - might be a formidable obstacle to a proposal of marriage. Perhaps she should go to live in Oss, where her father ekes out his life. There she might start with a clean sheet. But then she'd perhaps get drawn into his drunken world - and he might beat her as well. At least nobody beats her here. And she would miss Aleyt. Beyond Oss, her thoughts don't dare to roam. The great city of Antwerp is not too far away, she's been told. But how would she get there? What would she do? No, the little play of her life would be acted out here in Den Bosch.

She thinks sadly of the time she fell pregnant herself and had to make a covert visit to old Gertruida Hooftman. Now *there* was a woman who might be burned as a witch, if that Inquisitive ever got wind of her! Living on her own with black cats as her familiars. But she knew how to stop a baby being born. She had different methods, all painful and unpleasant, and she always used two methods together, just to make doubly sure. It was a wonder she'd avoided the witch hunters all her life.

And what of Hameel? Aleyt was going to turn him away! No longer would she have to suppress her own feelings so rigorously. She hardly dared to give her hopes a square look. In his disappointment, could *she* catch Hameel's affections more strongly than before? Might he take her more seriously than he had done in the past? Would he exchange the mistress for the maid?

Could he ever think of *her* as a future wife?

There is a knocking at the street door. A smart double rap, peremptory and authoritative. Who could that be? No-one who knows the Master would interrupt him in his working hours, and Aleyt's occasional visitor Frida is more gentle with her summons.

Mary goes through the dining room and little hallway to the front door. When she opens it, she feels her legs turn to string. As if summoned by her ruminations on witch hunters, the Inquisitive himself towers above her in his black robes.

She puts a hand to her mouth and gasps. She can't help it.

"Oh my Lord!"

Jacomo is puzzled, and feels a little put out. He isn't

143

used to being stared at like an apparition by servants. He gives the girl a hard look. She colours up, like a little pink rose.

"This is the house of Jerome, the painter?" he says.

The little fool nods, but appears to be struck speechless. She starts crossing herself repeatedly.

"Whatever's wrong with you?" he says impatiently. "Do you know who I am?"

The girl nods again, her eyes on his feet.

"Well, please announce me to your master, if you're capable of speech."

Once more he receives only a nod for reply, and then – extraordinary rudeness – the door is closed in his face. He is left standing out in the town square, facing a closed door! He looks at its dark wooden planks. The shapes in the grain and the knots in the wood suggest faces to him, little grotesque faces making fun of him. He glances over his shoulder, to see if anyone is paying any attention to his undignified reception. Already he feels ill-disposed towards the master of this ridiculous servant girl.

CHAPTER FOURTEEN

Jerome is in the part of Hell reserved for the punishment of gamblers. Naked men and women flee an upturned gambling table. Demons pierce their bodies with vicious knives. One lizard-like monster with a single swelling woman's breast for a body brandishes a backgammon board above its head, ready to smash it down. Pinned to the gambling table is a man with a dagger thrust through his hand. Holding him by the throat, and pushing a sword into his chest is a hideous mouse in a spotted uniform. The mouse stands on wooden pattens, with a round shield strapped to its back. On the shield is mounted a severed hand impaled on a knife. The hand balances a die on its fingers.

Jerome bends close again, and adds more little white spots to the mouse's dark outfit with his delicate fine-pointed brush.

There is a timid tap at his door, so unexpected at this time of the day – his working hours – that he applies a little too much pressure, and the mouse acquires a spot that is a fraction bigger than the others.

"Wait!" he calls out. Quickly he dips another fine-tipped brush in the dish of aqua ardens and dabs away the mistake. Only when he is satisfied that it is gone completely does he call out again.

"Yes? Come in!"

145

Mary puts her head around the door.

"Someone to see you, Master. I've left him at the front door."

Jerome is puzzled. No-one who knows his ways would call on him at this time of the morning.

"But who is it?"

"Like a devil, he is, all in black robes. Oh, I thought I was going to die when I seen him standing there!"

Jerome stares at her.

"Black robes?"

"That's him. Black. A devil!"

Black? A thought comes to him.

"Do you mean the Inquisitor?"

"That's it. Yes. The Inquisitive."

"Go and bring him inside at once, Mary! Show him here. And don't let him hear you calling him a devil!"

Mary scuttles off, leaving his door open. He starts to clean the white lead off his brush. Why would the Inquisitor come here? He is utterly mystified. Footsteps advance with a measured tread up the first flight of stairs from the entrance hall, and then the tall figure of the Inquisitor stands framed in the open doorway.

Jerome bows very slightly, and sweeps an arm across his surroundings.

"Welcome to my studio."

"I am Jacomo, the Papal Inquisitor."

Jerome nods.

"Yes. I saw you at your work in our town square."

"*God's* work. I am only his instrument."

Jerome nods again.

"Burning a man to death."

Jacomo looks at him sharply. He feels subtly criticized, although the words are neutral enough.

"A vile and filthy warlock!" he says emphatically. "I suspect he had corrupted others too. They must all be rooted out. I may be in Den Bosch for some time to come, and…"

But the painter's eyes have drifted from his face to

146

something behind him. He half turns. The idiot serving girl is still standing there at the open door, gawping at them. She gives a little start, and slams the door shut.

Jerome makes a small apologetic gesture.

"What brings you to visit me, Inquisitor? I hope you don't think I'm a warlock?"

Jacomo responds with a tight-lipped smile. His eyes remain cold. Jerome looks into them for a moment. Pale blue irises, almost grey. Unusual in a man with the Spaniard's swarthy skin. He will paint a demon with those eyes somewhere in his Hell.

"I have been examining your work in the refectory at the convent where I'm lodging. The Convent of Saint Agnes."

"Ah - my painting of the Passion of Christ?"

"Yes."

What could this mean? Examining his painting? Jerome gestures to a stool, but Jacomo remains standing.

"Won't you sit down, Brother Jacomo?" he says. Perhaps he didn't understand his gesture?

Jacomo shakes his head.

"Thank you, no. What are you working on now, Master Painter?"

Jerome points towards the panel, where the white dots of the devilish mouse's costume are still bright and fresh.

"This is part of a triptych for our cathedral. The left panel, which is finished, represents God speaking to Adam and Eve, and this panel that I am working on now is a scene of Hell."

The panel is set at right angles to the studio's window. From where he stands, Jacomo can only see a swarming mass of tiny figures and peculiar shapes.

"May I look more closely?" he says, already taking a step towards the panel.

Jerome would prefer to keep him away, but can't think of any reasonable excuse for doing so.

"Of course," he replies, trying to keep resentment out

147

of his tone.

Jacomo notes the painter's reluctance. He approaches the panel and looks at it for a long time. He stoops close to the painted surface and his eyes range methodically across it. He is soon utterly absorbed, and the more he looks, the more astonished he becomes. He has never seen anything like this in his life. It is as if the painter has descended into Hell himself, and come back with a precise record of every horror to be found there. How can a mortal man conceive of such things? Surely they must be the record of visions, but visions sent by whom? By God? Or the Devil? His eyes drift down from the figure of a knight in armour being eaten alive by monstrous lizards to a gigantic creature with a bird's head. The ghastly monster is consuming a naked sinner, from whose fundament a flight of birds bursts forth amidst smoke and flames.

Jacomo feels his heart flutter as if it too were a bird, trapped against his ribs. Are these indeed the torments that await sinners in Hell? They are more hideous, more painful, more exquisite than he could have conceived of.

He takes slow deep breaths, and calms his troubled heart as best he can. He reminds himself of what he has come to look for, and indeed it is there in abundance. At last he draws back a little from the panel.

"Your Hell seems populated most particularly with the clergy. Priests, monks, bishops – and here a pig in a nun's habit! And who is this, being roasted on a spit by demons? An Abbess?"

"The fires of Hell will feed on all alike, if they are sinners."

"But do you think the religious life leads more surely to Hell?"

"The temptations are the same, and the fall from grace heavier."

Jacomo nods, thinking. It is already obvious to him that the painter is an intelligent man. He had anticipated as much. Now he must choose his words carefully. If he considers himself, at this moment, as a fisherman, then Jerome is like a crafty trout lurking in a shady pool. But one can be too subtle with a subtle fish. He decides to try a direct cast straight in front of the prey.

"As an example of this fall from grace," he says, moving to stand with his back to the window, "I believe you consider Abbess Dominica to be both gluttonous and avaricious?"

He studies the painter's face in the light from the window, aware that he himself is now no more than a silhouette. Jerome looks surprised by his remark.

"How do you come by that belief?" Jerome says, annoyed. He might have guessed that the Abbess had some hand in this visit.

"I speak to people in the town. The Abbess herself told me you hold her in low esteem."

He points to the painting.

"And this Abbess here – being basted with fat as she roasts…"

"That is not Abbess Dominica."

"But people here in Den Bosch might think of Abbess Dominica, when they see it, might they not?"

"That is for them to decide, not me."

Jacomo snorts.

"You are disingenuous, I think, Master Jerome."

"That at least is not one of the Seven Deadly Sins."

Jacomo laughs, amused by the joke, but even more pleased by the clue it gives him that the painter does not take his questioning too seriously. If Jerome thinks the game is frivolous, then more fool him. He could betray himself with one careless remark.

"Well, you're right!" he agrees. "But gluttony, and avarice - they are both deadly sins. Are they widespread in the Church, do you think?"

Does this interfering Spaniard expect to lure him into sweeping statements against the Church? It is such an obvious ploy. On the other hand, why should he be

149

intimidated into fawning acquiescence?

"Does one have to think that the institutions of the Church are perfect?" he replies in a brusque tone.

"Not at all, not at all, Master Jerome! We must strive towards perfection, though it be out of reach. But let me put this to you: should the ordinary people follow what the Church teaches them?"

"Of course."

"And will they be more likely to do so if they hold the Church in esteem?"

"Yes, but esteem must be earned."

"Indeed. But can esteem be earned if the ordinary people are given the impression that the Church is corrupted through and through?"

"The ordinary people – according to their wits – will form their own judgement."

"Ah, but *you* have a role to play, do you not? What you paint will be interpreted, particularly by those who cannot read. Your paintings are telling them a story. And in the foulest, most abysmal reaches of Hell, they see … "

He turns to the painting.

"Well… here, for instance, they see an Abbess being roasted on a spit. Will this help them to follow the teachings of the Church?"

"I paint the world as God reveals it to me."

Jacomo sees a ripple in the pool. The trout has just moved into open water. He must cast again, cleverly.

"But God's revelation is only visible through the rituals of the Church, and the prescribed forms of prayer. How else can God reach us?"

"God gave us eyes to see sin, and a nose to smell corruption."

Just the kind of response Jacomo had hoped for. He speaks quietly, but assertively.

"Those who believe God speaks to them directly through their senses tread a dangerous path, don't you think? The true voice of God is heard in the mass. Who knows what voice speaks in your head, Master Painter? You say you see the world, but what you are painting here is Hell. How can you see Hell?"

"I see it in my dreams. God has granted me terrible visions of the fate of those who sin."

"How do you know these dreams are not sent by the Devil himself to mislead you?"

"I must have faith in God."

"And paint what you think is the truth?"

"Yes."

A short silence falls, and then, like stones falling into a still pool, the bells of Den Bosch's many churches, monasteries and convents began to chime for the mid-afternoon prayers of None. The ripples of sound spread through the quiet studio, and both men cross themselves. As always, the cathedral bell sounds last, its measured deeper note chasing away its lesser brethren like undisciplined children.

Jacomo speaks at last.

"I have a different view. I agree that the Church is susceptible to corruption, like any earthly institution. Outwardly, it leads the common people towards Heaven, but within, it is sometimes in turmoil. Now, I would argue that it is best to allow the Church to reform itself in private, without outside interference, in order to maintain the esteem in which it is held."

"Vices must be exposed."

Jacomo shakes his head, as if sadly.

"You are dogmatic, Master Jerome. That is generally considered to be an Inquisitor's privilege. But I am flexible. Let me give you a parallel situation. Let us suppose that there is an influential man, a painter: a great painter, who holds a highly respected place in society. Let us suppose that painter is – much like the Church - in a state of inner turmoil. Racked, perhaps, with demonic visions that give him no peace. Would it be better to deal with that discreetly through prayer and self-mortification, or would exposure be the better course of action? Should the world be told that the painter is possessed by devils, and see him tortured and burned at the stake?"

An ugly threat disguised as a hypothesis. Jerome's indignation gets the better of his discretion. He can barely keep the anger out of his voice.

"You menace me, Brother Jacomo, but your zeal should be directed elsewhere. If I thought the Church was capable of addressing its own problems, perhaps I would be less critical in my paintings. You're an emissary of Rome itself, doing God's work, as you say, and yet you lodge at the convent of the most corrupted and avaricious woman ever to take holy orders! I've no doubt she's set you onto me out of spite and wickedness. She'd like nothing better than to see me in trouble. But why aren't you asking questions of *her*, Brother Jacomo?"

Jacomo keeps his face impassive. Now he's drawing out this wily painter a little! It will be interesting to explore further the nature of his antipathy towards the Abbess.

"What questions?"

"Can't you see with your own eyes?" Jerome can't stop himself now. "Does an Abbess normally wear jewellery?"

Jacomo considers the Abbess. He has paid little attention to her adornments, although her finely wrought rosary of rubies with its golden cross has caught his eye. He is an acute observer of human behaviour and failings, but, regrettably, he does not have an artist's gift of visual observation.

"She wears much gold," he says, remembering also a ring, and perhaps a bracelet.

"She drips with gold and jewels!" Jerome says emphatically. "And what do you make of the food served up in her refectory?"

Jacomo recalls his meal of the previous night, taken in silence at the Convent beneath Jerome's painting of the Passion of Christ. There had been eels in a sauce. A very tasty dish.

"The nuns eat well. Exceptionally well. I was surprised," he concedes.

"Dig deeper, Brother Jacomo. These are just the outward signs of corruption within. Make enquiries of her papal taxes. I'll wager she's not sending much to Rome. Did you know that she lends to merchants in Den Bosch – at usurious rates?"

Jacomo's ears prick up. Avarice and gluttony were broad fields of sin, with degrees of culpability. He had eaten the fine meal at the convent himself. If he ate in such a fashion every night, would he be a glutton? There was a gradation. But usury, on the other hand, was a matter of black and white. If you were a usurer you were on a path straight to damnation.

Is the painter a man to invent a slander?

"Do you have proof of this accusation?"

"I can get it. And she seeks to corrupt others. Only recently she attempted to bribe the cathedral chapter in Overmaas to favour her choice of artist for the design of their window."

The recollection of this raises the pitch of Jerome's frustration. He stabs a finger indignantly towards the Inquisitor.

"What is done about any of this? She's not the only corrupt cleric in Den Bosch. I could point out a dozen more to you. But she's the worst, and *you* are closely associated with her here."

He can't see Jacomo's expression against the light of the window, but he feels he has him on the back foot now. He goes on.

"You may not be aware that I made a pilgrimage to Rome last year. In Rome, my work was already well known to the Pope's closest advisors. I was well received there. I had several audiences with Cardinal Domenico Grimaldi, who commissioned a painting."

"Go on."

153

"You came to frighten me off being critical of the Church, but you've failed to examine the facts. You've been fed lies by the Abbess. My paintings are known and approved by powerful figures in the Church. If I attack the vices and failings of those who are not true followers of Christ, I know that there are those in Rome with the wisdom to accept that as legitimate."

Jacomo turns and looks once more at the terrifying panel of Hell. The painter's boast of influential connections is not idle. That self-indulgent Grimaldi certainly has the ear of the Pope. And yet, the Abbess, whatever her motives, and whatever her own failings, has a point. What will be the effect of such a work, placed in the cathedral where the common people will see it constantly? It's not something to which he can turn a blind eye.

"You make your views clear, Master Jerome. But I think that with this work you are venturing beyond boundaries you have previously observed. Let me suggest a way forward. Would you consider moderating this... this vision of Hell... if I could prove to you that I, for one, take corruption within the Church very seriously?"

"How would you do that?"

"Get me your proof of the Abbess's usury – I'll speak to anyone you suggest to me. I'll make my own enquiries also – into her papal taxes, and the lavish spending I see at the convent. If the Abbess proves as venal and corrupt as you allege, then I'll do something about it. I'll prove to you that the Church can act with vigour and discretion, and deal with its problems privately and quietly from within. Is that a bargain?"

Jerome looks back at him suspiciously. Is there some snare here that he isn't seeing?

"If I say no?"

Jacomo is ambushed by anger, the Deadly Sin that always lies in wait for him.

"Then you would make a dangerous enemy, Master

Painter!" he flashes.

They regard each other tensely for a few moments. Jacomo focuses on calming himself. When he was a feral boy with a knife in the slums of Seville, running with a gang of the dispossessed, anger was his master, the besetting sin that infused his whole being. Ever since, he has been dedicated to atonement, and a part of his offering to God must be to put away anger whenever it arises in him.

Jerome too is calming his indignation. The last thing he wants is for a man such as Jacomo to work against him with the Abbess. A compromise occurs to him, one that will not impede him too much in his work.

"I suggest this: I'll stop my work on Hell for now, but I'll change nothing at this time. While you prove your reforming powers here in Den Bosch, I can work instead on sketches for the middle panel."

Jacomo nods. This is a bargain he can accede to. His interest in the Abbess's goings-on has been piqued, and although witchcraft and heresy are his preferred quarries, he is not averse to hunting down a little corruption.

"Very well," he says. "I look forward to our next conversation."

He moves towards the door.

"I can see myself out."

They both hear a scurrying sound beyond the door, and as Jacomo throws it open, they glimpse Mary at the bottom of the stairs, heading into the dining hall. The Inquisitor snorts, whether in amusement or anger Jerome can't be sure, then descends briskly to the street door, and leaves the house.

CHAPTER FIFTEEN

"His little nose is just your own!"

"Nonsense. I can see Joris in that nose, and no-one else!"

"What does Joris say?"

"He's offered no opinion on the nose..." She giggles. "He's just relieved that everything is in its proper place down below, I think!"

Aleyt smiles. Laurens starts to squirm in her arms and then emits a sharp whining noise. She passes him back to Frida.

"Time to get Grieta back up, I think," Frida comments.

"It's time I left anyway, Frida. I can send her up on my way out."

"Thank you. She'll be in the back parlour, spinning."

Aleyt embraces her cousin, and makes her way out of the room. She has enjoyed the visit, but in the few days since the birth it seems to her that her cousin, Grieta the wet nurse and the baby have formed a kind of tight, inward-facing circle from which she is unintentionally but inevitably, excluded. She passes Frida's husband Joris at the door of the house as she leaves, on his way back from some business, and she wonders if he feels the same way. He asks her how things fare 'upstairs', as if hesitant to go and find out for himself. She hopes that

Jerome won't be so detached. Already she can picture him cradling a baby in his arms, and singing to it in his mellifluous, gentle voice.

When she gets back to her own house, Mary meets her on the stairs with a white face and an air of solemnity.

"The Inquisitive!" she says in a hushed tone, pointing at Jerome's studio door.

"What?"

"He's here. Talking to the Master. In his studio."

"What about?"

"I can't hear properly…"

Mary realises she has made an overly revealing remark. She looks at the floor.

Aleyt sits anxiously in the parlour upstairs until she hears the door of the house open and close, and goes quickly to look out of the window. Below her, the tall black robed figure strides briskly away across the busy square. People make way for him instinctively, drawing well back. She watches his lean stalking shape until he disappears along Markstraat at the opposite corner. Just as he does so, she becomes aware of a growing hubbub approaching the square from the narrow Kolperstraat. With a clamorous banging of tambours and a rattling of cowbells, a rag-tag procession of itinerant penitents comes into view.

They wear tattered robes – probably once white, but now soiled with every muddy colour that the fields and ditches of Brabant can exude. Both men and women are among their number, although since all have shaved off every scrap of hair from their heads they appear almost sexless. Most of them bear knotted lengths of rope, with which they lash at the backs of their fellows in front of them. At the rear of the procession, the only figures who are not lashed by ropes labour under heavy burdens wrapped in cloth – the scant worldly possessions of the band.

Leading the troupe is an old man with a wild, angry

expression. Once into the square, he shakes a wooden bucket aggressively in the face of every citizen he can find, and most dig into their pouches and produce a coin of some sort. She hears the door of their house open below her, and sees Mary dart out into the path of the penitents. She throws a coin – probably a penny – into the bucket and crosses herself, then returns to the house. The penitents carried away your sins on their own bleeding backs, if you gave them money.

After a while, Aleyt retires from the window and returns to her stool. She contemplates the tapestry stretched on the wooden frame in front of her. She has been working on it for more than a year, but now it is within a month or two of completion.

To her surprise, she hears feet on the stairs. It's Jerome's step. He must have been disturbed by his visitor, because he hardly ever leaves his studio before the midday meal. The door opens, and she turns and smiles at her husband as he comes into the room. He looks preoccupied, but he returns her smile and advances to the stool where she sits. He puts a hand affectionately on her shoulder and looks at the tapestry.

"Your Garden of Eden is almost complete. I haven't looked at it for a while. Your apple tree is beautiful, Aleyt! Where will you put the serpent?"

Aleyt puts her hand on top of his and shakes her head.

"There won't be a serpent. This is the Garden of Eden before the tempter arrived."

A memory comes to him, from his visit to Italy.

"Your garden reminds me of the gardens of Firenze. Filled with colour and a clear bright light that our poor Brabant can rarely attain."

He takes his hand from her shoulder and moves to the window. The sounds of the penitents' tambours and bells are diminishing down a side street. He stands there, lost in thought.

"Your painting was disturbed this morning?" Aleyt

158

says.

"Yes. I'm leaving aside my painting of Hell for the moment."

"Why?"

"Do you know who my visitor was?"

"Mary said it was the Inquisitor, and I saw him myself leaving the house."

"Yes. It seems he doesn't like my painting. He thinks I show the clergy in a poor light."

"Why is that his business? I thought he was looking for heretics and witches?"

"A Papal Inquisitor has wide-ranging powers. He's a dangerous man."

Aleyt looks at him sharply, alarmed.

"Not dangerous to you?"

"He made a veiled threat."

"A threat? But you're a godly man! A prominent member of the Holy Company of Our Lady. Why, you're even going to be Christ in the Good Friday procession!"

"Christ was innocent, but he was still crucified."

"Don't, Jerome. You're frightening me."

Jerome looks at her pale anxious face and regrets the levity of his remark. He should have kept this business to himself. He thinks of a way to allay her fears.

"Well, I turned his attention elsewhere, I hope. I think he saw the justice of my position. And he said he'd investigate my own accusations."

Aleyt is puzzled.

"Accusations?"

"Against the Abbess."

Aleyt feels confused. How is the Abbess connected with this?

"But Jerome - I know what you think of her, but you've always avoided… well…"

"An open confrontation?"

"Is it because of what happened about Overmaas, that you're angry? But you won the commission anyway.   And you're both members of the Holy Company. You have to meet and speak civilly to each other sometimes, surely?"

"I can still avoid open confrontation. But she works against me behind the scenes, and I must do the same in my defence. I'm sure it must have been her who tried to set this Jacomo onto me like a wolf at a sheep."

"So...   does he want you to stop painting... the Inquisitor?"

"He doesn't want to see any monks or nuns or priests in Hell."

"In your *painting* of Hell?"

"Yes."

"Couldn't you... I mean..."

"What?"

"Well... couldn't you do that? To avoid trouble?"

Everyone, even his dear Aleyt, seems willing to sweep the corruption of the Church under a rug and ignore it!

He speaks as calmly as he can. Aleyt observes the tense line of his jaw.

"God gave me eyes, and I can't help but see with them! Just take a look around Den Bosch. We've got dozens of so-called monasteries and convents, and how do their occupants behave? They're a haven for the idle and the corrupt!"

Aleyt knows what she wants to say. She can't remain mute if Jerome's stubborn rectitude is going to propel him into trouble with the Inquisitor. She dreads his response, but her anxiety emboldens her.

"But Jerome, your paintings aren't going to change that," she says.

Jerome stares at her, caught between anger and love. He knows why she has said that.

"But if my paintings don't contain truth, what's the point of them at all?"

He clenches both fists, uselessly, against an intangible enemy.

160

"Ah! It's maddening!" he concludes.

He walks over to the oak settle by the wall and subsides onto it, staring into space. Aleyt leaves her tapestry stool and goes to sit beside him. She takes one of his hands.

"Oh... Jerome. We have everything we want in life, don't we?"

Jerome nods, although of course the statement has to be modified, as they both know.

"Except..." he says, and leaves the rest unsaid. They talked of children often in the first year or two of their marriage. But now, after seven years, it is more a matter for silence.

"Of course," Aleyt says. "But we have each other, and our comfortable house, and the country cottage at Roedeken nearly finished. Your prominence in the Holy Company of Our Lady, your success as a painter..."

"You seem very serious," Jerome says, cutting in.

"I'm worried. I don't want our lives torn apart. This Inquisitor – you call him dangerous."

"I'm sorry. I shouldn't have told you."

Aleyt shakes her head vehemently and squeezes his hand. "Of course you should. We shouldn't have secrets."

They sit in silence for a few moments and Aleyt feels the truth of those words sink into her. She is the one with a guilty secret. But in a few months' time, Jerome will be happier than he can imagine just now, and so will she.

She speaks again, softly.

"Jerome - it's so good to have you with me, *talking* to me like this. You shut yourself away so much."

It is the merest, the mildest, of reproaches, but Jerome feels its justice.

"I know. I leave you alone too often, my dear Aleyt."

The lute hanging on its hook on the opposite wall catches his eye. He stands up and goes to it. He runs a finger over the smooth varnished wood of the neck, and

161

then takes it down. He sounds the strings idly. They are in tune, more or less.

"I feel like chasing away this sombre mood! Why don't we sing a little duet, like we did in the old days?"

Aleyt feels uplifted. They used to have such fun, once. And they would do so again, at Roedeken, with the baby. They would re-enter the Garden of Eden.

"Hark at you! What shall we sing?" she replies.

"Our old song, what else?"

He puts a foot on the crossbar of Aleyt's tapestry stool and bends forward, supporting the instrument on his knee, then strikes a chord. They sing together, but in each verse they divide the second line between them, Aleyt taking the first part, and Jerome the second. It is a song he composed himself, for the first anniversary of their wedding, and they know it as well as they know their faces in the mirror.

"In the Springtime we'll be happy,
Gathering little flowers, in love with all the hours
Of the morning.

In the Summertime we'll be drowsy,
Sleeping under trees, to the hum of the bees
In the afternoon.

In the Autumn we'll be busy,
Gathering the fruit, playing on the lute,
In the evening.

In the Winter we'll be cold,
Skating on the ice, wrapped in furs like mice,
All night long."

They look at each other, smiling with pleasure, and then repeat the first verse more loudly than before:

"In the Springtime we'll be happy,

162

Gathering little flowers, in love with all the hours
Of the morning."

They have always repeated the first verse, because it just seems right to finish the song with Spring, not with Winter. They laugh with delight, and Jerome hangs up the lute again.

"Well, I'll return to my studio for now, my love. Hell needs to be set aside, and I'll go on with my sketches for the middle panel of the triptych."

He kisses her cheek and leaves the room.

Aleyt returns to sit in front of her tapestry. She feels elated by the shared song, by Jerome's gentleness, by his confiding in her. She looks at the naked, innocent figures in the Garden of Eden she has woven, and the glowing, inviting fruits on the apple tree. Out of nowhere an overwhelming sadness wells up to smother her joy, and she covers her face with her hands, blotting out the light, and sobs helplessly until the emotion has been purged.

CHAPTER SIXTEEN

Jerome puts down his silverpoint stylus to rest his wrist, and contemplates the drawing of a mussel shell that he has been working on all morning. In front of him on his table is the shell on which he has been modelling his image. He has been dipping it regularly in a jug of water, so that it shines moistly, and the beautiful curving lines that subtly give definition to its surface are more lustrous. In his drawing, the shell has assumed a grander scale, and it is being carried on the back of a naked man. Inside it is a copulating couple with only their nude legs protruding from the half-opened shell. He has already decided where he will place this group: somewhere near the margin of the lake on the left part of the central panel, where enormous birds and diminutive human figures will gather to eat fantastical giant fruits and float in bobbing, hollowed out vessels on the water. His thoughts wander to other ideas that he has for this panel, images of fecundity and the mingling of opposites, God's Garden of Eden as it might have become but for the Fall, a riot of innocent pleasures, a melting pot of living and inanimate matter, out of which surprising hybrid creatures could spring to life.

The bells chime out for midday prayers, and remind him that today he will be finishing work early. Time drops away from his consciousness when he is in his

164

studio at his drawing and painting, and often the bells of Den Bosch seem to ring out at intervals so short that he thinks some imp must have got at the ropes and be ringing the half hours. He glances out of the window at the garden. The sun is shining on the small apple tree they put into the ground with a fanciful little ceremony last year, and a couple of goldfinches hop from branch to branch, twittering and trilling.

The street door opens below in the entrance hall, and he hears Mary speak, and an answering male voice. Familiar footsteps ascend to his studio door, and then a soft triple rap confirms that Hameel is on the other side.

"Come in!"

Hameel must have known of his intention to finish early today, or he would never have come visiting at such a time. However, he couldn't remember mentioning his plans for the day to Hameel.

Hameel half opens the door, a little sheepishly. He's holding a new peacock-feathered cap in his hands. He has new grey hose and an expensive-looking green tunic, and his hair has been freshly cut.

"Hameel – you're looking finely plumed! How did the ladies of Den Bosch let you pass unmolested? Come on inside!"

Hameel advances, closing the door behind him.

"I'm not disturbing you?"

"Not at all. I'm riding over to Roedeken shortly to see how the work on our cottage roof is progressing. I'll stop for a pie and a cup of ale on my way, at the Jolly Bargeman."

He is struck by a fine thought.

"Why don't you come with me?"

Hameel shakes his head.

"Come, Hameel! We'll pass the old woods along the river that way, where you and me and your poor brother Pieter all used to play and fish. I'll bet you haven't been out that way in years."

"I'm committed. I've got to show the Abbess some

165

more drawings this afternoon."

"The Abbess!" Jerome snorts crossly. "She's really got you by the balls, hasn't she! Well, I hope you're paid well – and promptly - for your efforts!"

Hameel nods, with a half smile. He strikes Jerome as being ill at ease, somehow. But his own thoughts are still in the old days.

"Remember that pike Pieter and I caught?"

Couldn't he persuade him to drop his visit to the Abbess and come with him after all? He pictures the riverside track, dappled with light and shade under the big willows. The two of them riding along, laughing.

"Of course," Hameel says.

"What a time we used to have, along the river! You know, it's as if the sun always shone on those days. I think that's why I'm so looking forward to our cottage at Roedeken. It'll take me back to those young, carefree days in the countryside. Are you quite sure you can't come?"

Hameel hunches up his shoulders and makes a glum face. He glances over to the corner of the studio where Jerome's panel of Hell stands unfinished.

"You've not been working on Hell today?"

Now it's Jerome who shrugs ruefully.

"No. Our Papal Inquisitor isn't fond of my Hell."

Hameel is taken by surprise by a sense of power - hidden power - which is not disagreeable. Jerome would be astonished to learn of his own role in causing the Inquisitor to visit his studio. There is a pricking shard of guilt too, however.

"He's come to you here?" he says, putting surprise into his tone.

"Yes."

"But why?"

"It seems the Abbess has stirred him up. We came to an understanding, for the moment."

"An understanding?"

Jerome waves a hand dismissively. He has no

aversion to taking Hameel into his confidence, but this subject is casting a shadow over his pleasurable afternoon: the ride out to Roedeken; the pie and ale; the spring sunshine. Who would wish to think of Inquisitors on such a day?

"It's not worth talking about, Hameel. I'll tell you another time. Anyway, for now, I'm leaving Hell and concentrating on my ideas for the central panel."

"May I see?"

Jerome gestures towards the drawings littered over the surface of his table. No-one else has seen them yet, and he feels a sudden eagerness to find out how Hameel will react to them.

"Rough ideas, that's all," he says, excusing the eclectic chaos of the images. "It's to be a fantastical garden filled with figures. A vision of a world of innocent pleasure, in part. I think of calling it *The Garden of Earthly Delights*."

Hameel leafs through the drawings. Wonder and admiration battle with envy in his breast. This is how he always feels when he sees something of Jerome's work for the first time. How can a man of flesh and blood, a man who he's known since he himself was a small child, produce such things? It isn't the technical accomplishment of the work – although that is extraordinary. It is the content. It tears a rent in the cloth of the world and reveals horrors and glories unimagined by ordinary men. And yet, what is Jerome outwardly but a working artist, a married man, a plain citizen of the town? Where do these things come from?

"I've never seen anything like these," Hameel says at last, after many minutes immersed in the drawings. He feels as if he is coming back to the surface to breathe. "How… where…?"

He gives up.

Jerome hears the little rodent scuttle of pride behind the wainscot. But what man can resist praise?

"Things come to me in dreams, Hameel. It's both a

167

blessing and a torment."

He looks out of the window again at the clear blue sky outside. Hameel's admiration has reinforced his own sense of work done well. Now it's a day for simpler pleasures.

"Well - it's time I left for Roedeken," he says. "Perhaps you've enough time to stay and talk a while with Aleyt before the Abbess expects you? She'll be glad of your company I'm sure."

"I have a little time, yes."

"Come on then, we'll go upstairs together and I'll say goodbye and leave you."

CHAPTER SEVENTEEN

Cleaning the parlour of the house is one of Mary's favourite tasks. It can only be done when Aleyt is out somewhere, because she generally spends much of her day in that room. Like the bedchamber above, it has a fine unobstructed view over the town square outside, and this is the only time when Mary has that window to herself and can enjoy the scene. She loves watching people, and she doesn't have much opportunity for that in the kitchen or the scullery or the little enclosed garden where she hangs the washing.

Now she leans luxuriously on the sill, enjoying the early Spring warmth. The shutters are not completely thrown open – she doesn't want everyone in Den Bosch to be able to glance up and see her idling there. Word might get back to her Mistress.

The market stalls below are busy, as the first fresh vegetables of the season are on sale. Mary can see celery, radishes, spinach, tomatoes... then a blob of orange catches her eye. It's that Wiggers again. Amidst all the bustle, he seems just to be standing and watching, leaning against an empty cart. Is he looking at the house? She can't be sure. He gives her a creeping feeling along her spine. He's like a big-eyed broad-backed orange bug, looking for a smaller bug to eat.

Taking her eyes from the unsettling Wiggers she

scans the square for Aleyt, who will be on her way back from her visit to Frida and the baby some time soon. Then her attention is drawn downwards to a group of children playing chain-tag just in front of the house. They are making a lot of noise, which is why she doesn't hear the voices of Jerome and Hameel until they are actually opening the door and walking into the room. Luckily she always keeps her cleaning rag in her hand when she's window-gazing, just in case. She starts wiping the sill vigorously.

Jerome takes in the empty room, and Mary at the window. She has been idling there, no doubt.

"Aleyt not in, Mary?" he says.

Mary bobs a curtsey.

"She went to see baby Laurens. She should be back any time soon."

Jerome scratches his chin. He really wants to be outside now, in the beautiful sunlight.

"Well, I've got to go. Hameel - why don't you wait here for Aleyt? Mary can bring you something to eat and drink."

"All right. Thank you."

Jerome gives him a brief friendly embrace, patting his back. Then without more ado he clatters off down the stairs.

As the sound of his footsteps diminishes, an idea forms in Mary's head. A rare thing in itself, and in the case of this particular idea, quite a brilliant thing, she feels. She should act on it as soon as she might.

To give herself a moment to gather up her wits, she looks out of the window again. The street door closes below, and she watches the top of Jerome's head as he walks diagonally across the square. She speaks over her shoulder to Hameel.

"There he goes, off to the stables."

Jerome disappears. There is still no sign in the square of Aleyt returning. Now is the moment to act on her brilliant thought. She turns to Hameel, who is standing in the middle of the room fiddling with some new fancy hat. In fact, all his clothes are new.

"Just the two of us here for now, then. Is there anything you desire, Master?"

She gives her eyes a bold run, up over his legs in their fine grey hose and then on across his chest to his own eyes. She knows very well the sinewy body that lies beneath his clothes. Their eyes meet frankly. His expression is amused. Well, let him enjoy his amusement for now, things are going to turn more serious in a moment. She brushes close beside him, ostensibly on her way to the door, and he puts a hand around her waist to stop her.

"Is Aleyt really coming back soon? Or are you teasing me?"

"Oh, she'll be back… but things have changed around here."

She disengages his hand from her waist and goes to stand near the Mistress's tapestry.

"What *things*?" Hameel says.

"My Mistress has changed."

"I don't know what you're talking about."

Good, his face betrays a touch of anxiety now.

"Give me a groat and I'll tell you a secret."

"You're a saucy maid!"

His light-hearted grin gives her a pang of guilt. But the bad news she has for him is a dose of physick that will do him good in the end.

He fishes in his purse and finds a coin. He brings it to her and she takes it, letting her fingers trail across his palm.

"You used to like me being saucy. Perhaps I can be saucy again with you, once you've heard the news. I can comfort you."

"Tell me the secret, then."

"My Mistress is going to have a baby."

Hameel appears almost to stagger. His face turns white and he stares at her as if she has sprouted wings,

171

or horns.

"What?" he breathes, as much to himself as to her.

"I said it plain enough, didn't I? She was going to tell you herself, and she thought it was going to be difficult. So I've done her and you a favour and I've earned myself a groat."

Hameel looks like a man in the grip of a dream. He walks to the oak settle and sits heavily on the edge of it, turning his ridiculous new hat around and around in his hands.

"A baby! And... what..."

Mary puts on a bright smile, and speaks as if joy is in the very air that they breathe together in the room.

"It's a wonderful thing, isn't it! A baby at last for the Master and Mistress! Master don't know yet, but he'll be so happy!"

"A baby... for Jerome..."

Hameel's eyes are looking at her but his gaze is turned inwards.

"Of course. Who else?" Mary replies, brisk and no-nonsense.

Hameel stands up and walks over to the window, then back to the door. He puts his hat down on the table, picks it up again, and puts it down again. Mary hears the street door open, and, immediately afterwards, light feet ascending the staircase. She administers more physick, while there is still time.

"Perhaps you can be the godfather? You won't be needed for anything else now."

Hameel stares at her and opens his mouth to speak, but then he too hears the footsteps on the stairs. The door opens, and Aleyt stands in the opening. She looks at Hameel wide-eyed.

Mary goes to the doorway quickly. This is not a moment for her to tarry.

"I'm going down to the kitchen, there's a lot to do," she says in passing to Aleyt, who stands aside, her eyes never leaving Hameel.

As Mary thunders downwards, Aleyt steps into the room and closes the door behind her slowly. Inside her head, all language has fled. She can't think of a single word to say to Hameel, not even a simple greeting.

He comes now towards her. His arms are outstretched to embrace her. She can't meet his eyes, and her gaze is drawn downwards, through the floorboards, towards Jerome's studio and to Hell beneath. In Hell there will be no pretty words.

"He's not here. He's riding to Roedeken," Hameel says. He seems to have read only a simple meaning in her downward look.

She wants to enter into the embrace of those beautiful arms. The father of the little child growing inside her! But all that must be put aside now. The wordless confusion in her head persists, and she turns towards the Garden of Eden on its stand.

From the corner of her eye, she sees Hameel's arms drop, and his head also.

"So Mary was right," he mutters. "I'm not needed here any more!"

Aleyt looks at him sharply. The power of speech returns.

"Mary? What do you mean, Hameel?"

He looks back at her. His brown eyes are watery.

"I've done my job, have I?"

"What job?"

"Can't you guess what Mary's told me?"

The blood rises into Aleyt's cheeks.

"She hasn't..."

She tails off. Looks away.

Hameel summons up a tone of resentment and sarcasm, but it rings like a cracked bell in a belfry of hollow misery.

"I'm privileged at least to *know*... to know before the father of the child himself has been told. A great honour!"

Aleyt goes towards him, but stops just short. How

173

she longs to put her arms around him, to comfort him!

"Mary should never have said..." she says softly, and then falters. This thing could not be unsaid

"You would have had to tell me yourself, Aleyt. You'd have had to tell me one day – and Jerome."

"I wanted a little time," she murmurs. "Just a little more time..."

"Time for what? For what?"

She has no answer. To tell him that everything between them was over? That had been her intention. But how impossible it seems at this moment. They stand so close together now, and their arms hang uselessly at their sides. It is all that Aleyt can do to keep her arms lowered. They are aching to reach out towards him.

"Time to get rid of me? Aleyt?"

Her arms lift slightly as if of their own volition. Hameel takes half a step forward at the same time as she does. Then they are locked in an embrace, her face buried in his shoulder.

"Aleyt, Aleyt, Aleyt..." he murmurs.

She weeps quietly now, and he strokes her back gently with one hand.

"I've always loved you," he said, "and I always will. Mary was wrong. You were never going to give me up, were you Aleyt?"

Aleyt draws even closer to his body. They are two, no three, bodies joined in a single communion. She whispers the words he is desperate to hear, words that come straight from her heart, true words that are pulled from her by an irresistible force. A force that cares nothing for other words that she should have said, that she had intended to say.

"I love you Hameel. And now I'm carrying your child in my womb."

Hameel holds her tenderly. He wants to be as close to this woman as it is possible to be. He feels a stirring in his loins, and presses towards her. The flames of Hell lick up inside her, claiming her, and she returns his

pressure with her own hips.   He pulls her gently
towards the door, towards the stair that leads to the
bedchamber.

"Come... my darling one... come..." he whispers.

Mary can't bear another minute of suspense in the
kitchen, imagining different conversations between her
Mistress and Hameel. She would give her groat and a
lot more besides to be a little fly with ears on the wall of
the parlour upstairs. She half expected to hear Hameel
thundering out of the house like a black storm cloud, but
all is quiet.   So has it all passed off not too badly,
perhaps? Has her revelation proved an excellent idea, as
she hoped, and are they taking it calmly up there? She
burns to know. Well - it's past the middle of the day,
and an ascent of the stairs and an enquiry about food
would be altogether in order.

She decides to take up a tray with a bottle of wine
and a couple of goblets, as an additional excuse for her
intrusion. As she locates a bottle and uncorks it, she
muses on the wonderful fact that Hameel is a free man
again. It would take him a little while, no doubt, to get
over his disappointment. He was very fond of Aleyt,
she can see that. But it's only been an affair of nine
weeks, after all. And Hameel bedded *her* from time to
time for *years* before that. She misses him so much.
Only now does she allow herself to see that clearly.
Going up the stairs balancing the bottle and goblets
carefully on the tray, she also allows herself the sin of
thinking lewd thoughts about some future encounter
with Hameel.

The door to the parlour is unexpectedly open. Mary
goes straight in without knocking and looks around,
puzzled. Where are they? Surely she would have heard
them if they'd descended the stairs? Also, if they'd left
the house, Aleyt would have called out and told her
where she was going. She sets the tray down on the
table, and looks out of the window, as if she might see

them in the square nonetheless.

She looks about the square in vain, and then the blood rises to her face as she makes a guess. She goes back to the open door and listens at the base of the further flight of stairs that leads up to the Master and Mistress's bedchamber. At first she hears nothing, but then there is a faint moan from up there. It's Aleyt. The sound could be mistaken for a moan of pain. Then she hears a lower note, the soft note of Hameel's voice murmuring something, and another moan from Aleyt, louder this time. A moan of pleasure.

Mary puts a hand on the wall to steady herself. She has a queasy feeling of being in a bad dream, and needs its firm solidity. She whispers aloud to herself.

"I don't believe it! I done everything for her, to make it easy for her!"

Indignation against them both overwhelms her. Worse than indignation. For the first time since Hameel has taken up with her Mistress she feels the bitterest pangs of true jealousy. Her own relationship with Hameel had been a casual, occasional thing. She had not shied away from other encounters and neither, she was certain, had he. But in this moment she feels utterly possessed by the desire to have him back for herself.

She goes back into the main room. Angry and restless, she pours herself a full goblet of the red wine, pulls one of the box chairs to the table, sits, and drinks it down. Who would dare scold her now? For nine weeks she has connived at Hameel and Aleyt's secretive, adulterous, lustful couplings! Why hasn't she recognised her own true feelings until now? How could she have been such a stranger to herself?

A second goblet of wine. She drinks it as quickly as the first, the Master's best wine. There is no-one to gainsay her. Jerome is away until nightfall, and Aleyt is sunk deep in her own sinfulness. She goes to the foot of the upper flight of stairs to listen again, and hears low voices and a laugh from Hameel. Fury sweeps through her like a storm.

One more goblet of wine, why not? She goes back to the table and pours it out. She's starting to feel a little dizzy. She sips the third goblet more slowly, staring at the knots in the wood of the table. She starts to see eyes. She can see the eyes of Our Lady, just like the statue of Our Lady in the cathedral, her favourite statue. That stormy night in the Lady Chapel at the cathedral comes back to her. The things she was offered by the Abbess. She speaks aloud to herself quietly. Hearing her own voice always helps her to get things clear in her head.

"A place on the Abbess's ark. A Papal Indulgence to get out of Purgatory... and I turned those offers away! And then, even worse, I'm running the risk that vicious Inquisitive will decide at any moment that I might be a witch! I'm doing all this for what? For them upstairs – so they can fornicate and adulterate like two goats in a field."

Hearing these words said aloud makes it sound like advice, sound advice, from a third party. Indeed, it *would* be sound sense to avoid being burned as a witch, to secure herself from death by drowning in the next great Flood, and to avoid the pains of Purgatory in the next life. What fool wouldn't take up such offers?

"You've been a little idiot, Mary!" she says firmly. "But you're not any more."

Downing the remainder of the third goblet of wine, she stands up, and walks unsteadily out of the room, down the stairs, and out of the house.

*

In the canopied bed upstairs, Hameel and Aleyt lie side by side on their backs, their hands clasped. Aleyt lets her eyes wander among the leaves and berries of the carved foliage on the bedposts. The bed came to them from Jerome's grandfather. Everything feels amiss. It should be Jerome lying at her side. Her husband Jerome. She directs her eyes back to the blank purity of the cream cloth bed canopy. Hameel arouses her senses in a way that she has never known with her husband. And the old wives whisper that there must be some fire in the lovemaking for a child to be conceived. Sadly, she thinks that with Jerome she might never have had a child.

Her whole body feels sated and deeply relaxed, but now that the exquisite sensations of their union have abated, guilt is wrapping its dark cloak around her once more. Again she is guilty before God of the deadly sin of adultery. If the world ended today, now, she would pass into Hell as surely as the most heinous murderer or heretic. The torments reserved for the lustful last for all eternity. Thousands of years of pain for every tiny moment of pleasure. It is a terrifying thought, one that almost impels her to rise from the bed this instant and run to the cathedral to seek the confessional box.

Adding its own heavy weight to this spiritual terror, burden upon burden, she can't stop herself from imagining him now, her betrayed husband, riding to Roedeken in the beautiful Spring sunshine, looking forward to seeing the progress on their cottage.

Poor innocent man. If only they'd had children...

She sighs, and Hameel squeezes her hand. A child! How she has longed for that, all her life, and now her wish will be granted. Wasn't that a good thing, a holy thing even, to bring a child into the world? A new soul for God.

It was that, after all, that had brought her to Hameel. It was that, not merely lust.

But why is she in bed with him once more, now that she is blessed and fruitful? There can be no excuse; there can be no reason now but lust, and she has fallen low in her own eyes. This must be the last time, the very last time ever, that she makes love with Hameel. She silently vows this before God, but a misting of tears comes into her eyes at the thought, and the canopy above is blurred.

CHAPTER EIGHTEEN

Jerome lets the horse amble along the road towards Den Bosch beside the river. At Roedeken, the builder has shown him all that has progressed since his last visit. It looks as if the cottage will be ready for occupation within a matter of weeks. The thatched roof is complete, and the work has now moved on to the interior walls and floors. He feels a quiet satisfaction at what he's seen. Now, as he sways with the easy rhythm of the horse, his thoughts turn to other matters. He must call at the apothecary's to get more ground lapis lazuli for the blue of the frozen lake in Hell. This thought unfortunately leads him straight to a less pleasant one: the impediment to his progress with the triptych. He recalls his promise to the Inquisitor. He said he would furnish evidence of the Abbess's usury. This is not so easy as he might wish. He has heard rumours, and has every reason to believe them, but he has only one hard piece of evidence to turn to. Therefore, after he has visited the apothecary, he must pay a call on old Steenman. He heaves a sigh. How much more pleasant life would be without Abbesses and Inquisitors. And how much more respect and love the Church would inspire if its core was not rotten with such maggots.

When he has passed through the town gates and left the horse at the stables, he directs his steps towards the

179

shop of Izaak the apothecary, on Brugstraat. He walks briskly, nodding in his reserved manner to one or two people he knows along his way. Reaching at last the old painted wooden sign, with its faded mortar and pestle, he ducks through the low doorway beneath it and enters the interior of the shop. It's gloomy in here, after the brightness outside, and he stands still for a moment to let his eyes adjust. Surely it's even darker than usual? More like a cave than a shop. He breathes through his nose slowly to savour the complex scented air, filled with the perfumes and exhalations of a thousand exotic substances. Outside, on busy Brugstraat, he hears a group of drunken men passing by, swearing and laughing.

"Master Jerome! How are you today?"

The apothecary materializes from the darkness behind his counter, like a spirit taking shape.

"Hello Izaak. I'm well thank you. How goes it with you?"

Izaak shakes his large bearded head a little, and points to a collection of wooden planks leaning against the wall. Some of them have obscured a portion of the window, which explains the dimness.

"I'm getting ready, Master Jerome. The Easter time is nearly upon us - already there have been – not directly to me – amongst us - threats."

Jerome understands, and, as a Christian, feels guilty.

"So you'll barricade your window as usual?"

Izaak nods sadly.

"And a few days earlier I think this year – not Good Friday – it's leaving it too late. From now onwards, we Jews, we must – a good friend of mine, Mordecai – he heard someone already – yesterday – someone called out 'murderer' after him in the street. It may be a jest. But – you know how it's been in some years – burning houses – stoning – some years there are deaths."

Jerome nods, and scratches his chin. He has half an idea forming.

"What will you and your family do, Izaak?"

"What will we do? We do what we always do. We get our food ready, and our water. We nail our wooden planks in front of the window, and we go into the back of the shop. We wait, and we listen, and pray to Hashem. The hours are long and slow."

"It must be a miserable time for you."

"The worst time – worse than the birth of Christ. When the end of Lent comes near, Jews everywhere must hide their heads. This is when all the old lies are polished up like – like gems - and brought out afresh. We are the murderers of Christ. We poison the wells and bring plagues and Saint Anthony's Fire upon the people. We take Christian children and slit their throats and drink their blood in our rituals."

Izaak heaves a sigh, and fixes a troubled eye on Jerome.

"But none of this is your problem, Master. I hear you are to be very honoured this year. You are the Christ, are you not, in the procession?"

Jerome feels less of pride than embarrassment, in the light of what Izaak has already said. He nods.

"Well – anyway - what can I serve you with today, Master Painter? I have no more dried mandrake fruits just now, only the roots."

"No, I've come for my painting materials today, Izaak. I need an ounce of ground lapis lazuli."

Izaak claps his hands, and a bright-eyed boy of about ten appears in a doorway behind him.

"David, grind me an ounce of lapis lazuli and bring it here. A generous ounce for the Master Painter."

The boy nods and retires. Jerome can hear him rummaging in a back room. He shares a slight smile with the apothecary, imagining how proud he must be, bringing up the boy in the knowledge and practice of his own craft. He can imagine how proud *he* would be.

He brings forth the thought that has been taking shape in his head.

"Listen, Izaak… tell me… would it be better for you and your family to be away from Den Bosch on Good Friday?"

Izaak looks at him, puzzled.

"Of course. Anywhere out of the city would be safer. But what can we do? We can't sit in a field."

"Izaak – I have a cottage being built – it's at Roedeken – near the river, at a turning off the road to Sint Michielsgestel. It's not completed – there's no furniture – but it has a roof, and it's out of the way. It's a beautiful, quiet place. If you can get a wagon, why don't you and your family go out there on Maundy Thursday, and stay as long as you wish? Come back perhaps on Easter Sunday?"

Izaak looks at him in a rapture, and then takes his hands in his own.

"Master Jerome! You don't know how happy this makes me! Of course we can get a wagon! This is – I can't – so generous!"

He continues to hold Jerome's hands, and to smile at him.

"Well," Jerome says, smiling back. "You'll need to take makeshift bedding and food…"

"Of course, of course!" Izaak nods. "That is all easy. Thank you! *Yasher Koach*, as we would say – may your strength be increased!"

Jerome shrugs his shoulders.

"I think it's the least that the Christ of Den Bosch could offer!" he says quietly.

With his little parcel of the ground lapis lazuli in his hand, he walks down to the end of Brugstraat and turns left into Waterstraat where Steenman lives. It's a street that has seen better days. Most of the houses are let to several families living together, and he hears children crying and voices raised in discord through opened windows.

At his knock, the old man opens the door of his house just enough to peer out through the gap. He hasn't dressed properly, Jerome observes. He's wearing threadbare slippers and some sort of grubby gown. His legs, what can be seen of them, are bare. He looks as if he needs a good meal. It takes him a few seconds to identify his visitor.

"Jerome! What brings you here?"

Steenman's attempt at a friendly smile is painfully weak.

"May I come in, sir?"

Steenman hesitates, but then opens the door wider and stands back.

"Of course, of course you must come in, Jerome. How does your father?"

His father died some years ago and Steenman was at the funeral. Jerome chooses to misunderstand the query.

"I'm very well, thank you."

Steenman nods, satisfied. He leads the way through the entrance passageway into a large square room, none too clean or tidy. Steenman's own paintings hang on the walls, conventional scenes of Biblical events for the most part, and one very flattering self-portrait of a smug young man in fine clothes and accoutrements. Steenman used to share a studio with Jerome's father Anthonis. Jerome has known him since he was a small child.

The old painter waves him to a chair, and sits down himself on a stool.

"Your father…" he begins again, and then stops, as if remembering something.

"I wanted to talk to you, Meister Steenman, about your dealings with the Abbess Dominica."

"The Abbess Dominica?" Steenman looks confused.

He will need to be patient.

"You do remember, don't you, how I paid off your debt to her? She was charging you usurious rates of interest, and I repaid the capital on your behalf and took on the debt with this house as security."

A sudden panic comes into Steenman's face.

"Have you come for my house?"

183

"Meister Steenman, you know that you can live safely here for as long as you will, and that no interest on your debt is accruing. You're an old friend of the family. Do you recall how you first taught me to draw a face?"

Steenman's features relax again.

"I taught you and your brother… Goessink?"

"Goessens."

"You were apt pupils. Your father had no patience…"

He pauses, and looks quizzically at Jerome.

"Your father…"

"He died, three years ago. You remember."

"Of course. So sad. Well… I should offer you something Jerome. A drink or something to eat. My servant… she's only here in the mornings. I can't afford… It's afternoon now, I think? But she leaves my supper ready. Would you like…"

"I'm only here on a short visit, Meister Steenman. I want to ask if you'll do something for me."

"What's that?"

"I wondered if you'd be willing to describe the events that led to your financial difficulties with the Abbess Dominica. How she made you a loan for your daughter's dowry and you made this house your security. How you didn't understand the usurious rate of interest she would charge. How you fell further and further behind with your payments, and were to be thrown out onto the street before I heard of your plight and set all right."

Steenman has his head in his hands now, as if it were all happening to him again.

"To whom must I describe this, Jerome? It's a matter of shame, not a story to be told with a light heart."

"Nevertheless, I'd like it told. To the Inquisitor newly arrived here in Den Bosch, Brother Jacomo."

Now Steenman's eyes are like those of a fish on a hook; his face is as white as the cleaner parts of his gown.

"I saw the warlock being burned, Goessens... Jerome!"

"You have nothing to fear from him."

"The whole town talks of him. They say he has killed hundreds, in the cruellest ways."

"People will make up tales."

"Goessens, he is a terror. I can't speak to him."

The old man is clearly terrified out of his wits. It is not the moment to press him. What would happen if he brought the Inquisitor to the house, unannounced? Steenman's testimony might be irredeemably tainted by this terror and confusion. He will need to think over how this thing might best be managed. Perhaps he can talk to Steenman of other things now for a while, and calm him down.

But the old painter is rocking himself forward and backward on his stool and muttering to himself. Perhaps he's praying.

Jerome loses his heart for the business, for the time being. He doesn't want to cause more distress.

"Well, we'll leave this matter for now," he says, standing up. Steenman makes no response. He makes his own way to the door. As he leaves the house, and looks up and down the street, he thinks he catches a glimpse of that orange-haired fool Wiggers in the distance. His path lies the other way, but after a few paces curiosity makes him turn to look back over his shoulder to be sure, but now there is no sign of him.

CHAPTER NINETEEN

The Abbess leans back for a moment to rest, and surveys the ledgers and scribbled sheets of sums spread across the table in front of her. Reckoning the accounts of the convent's infirmary is always a pleasant task. There are the inevitable expenditures to record of course – the food; the potions and ointments; the wood and charcoal to fuel the endless heating of water for laundry. But far more than counter-balancing such outgoings are the funds that flow in from the families of the patients: the donations of livestock, fine plate, sacks of grain, cases of wine, and especially gold and silver coins. When Saint Anthony's Fire strikes at a family with money, they will generally pay almost anything to have the sufferer taken away before the affliction spreads. Their consciences are paid off too, with the thought that their loved one is to be cared for in a holy place, and conveyed with dignity and prayer down the painful, inevitable, road to death.

Another source of profit, which has only recently become fully apparent to her, is the rate of attrition amongst the nuns who act as fever nurses. Rarely a week goes by without one of them succumbing to the disease. This creates vacancies for new novices to enter the order, and there is always a good dowry for Christ when they came from respectable families. The prestige of the Convent of Saint Agnes guarantees a steady stream of applicants from the whole of Brabant, and beyond.

As a measure to protect herself and the rest of the nuns, she has had the fever nurses housed separately in cells in the old stables, adjacent to the infirmary itself. The infirmary is a good distance from the convent's main buildings, and she has introduced the added precaution of setting up a separate sitting in the refectory, and a separate section of the chapel for these members of the community.

She stands and walks to the window thoughtfully. A corner of the infirmary building is visible, beyond the apple trees in the orchard, where early white blossom is already appearing. Perhaps she should introduce further precautions? Could the fever nurses eat and worship without entering the main convent buildings at all? How might that be managed? Their food could be carried on trays to the old stables, and a makeshift chapel could be set up somewhere in the infirmary itself. It could be done under the guise of providing a more formal place of prayer for the patients.

There is a deferential tap on her door.

"Yes? Come in!"

Sister Theresa opens the door a crack.

"There's a *person* to see you Abbess Dominica. In my opinion she should have been turned away at the gate. But apparently she was most insistent that you would wish to see her, and now…"

In my opinion! The Abbess can hardly believe this audacity.

"Does this woman have a name?" she interrupts.

Sister Theresa turns and speaks to whoever is behind her. The Abbess recognises the voice that replies.

"Mary," the voice says.

"Mary," Sister Theresa echoes.

"Send her in!"

The door opens wider, and Mary enters. Her face is

187

flushed, and she looks about her defiantly. She scowls back at Sister Theresa, who closes the door quickly, leaving them alone.

She approaches Mary and takes her hands in her own

"Mary! I've been remembering you in my prayers. How gratifying to see you here! Come and have a comfortable seat here, by my table."

There is wine on Mary's breath. Maybe she needed a drink to embolden her to come to the convent? In any event, if she's in drink she will likely be more malleable.

She leads her to a chair, where she flops down heavily.

"I never been in a convent before. They didn't want to let me in. Sneery, your nuns are. They didn't look friendly at me at all. But I said you'd want to see me."

"Oh, and I did, I did!"

She takes her little stone bottle from its drawer, and two cups. She sets them on the table and pulls the snug cork from the bottle. It makes a satisfying sound. She holds the opened bottle up in the air slightly.

"A little something to make you feel more welcome?"

Mary nods.

"Why not?"

She pours brandy into the two cups and they both take a sip. Then the Abbess puts her cup down and looks at Mary appraisingly.

"So, have you been thinking about my offers?" she suggests.

"And your threats."

The Abbess waves an appeasing hand and smiles.

"Oh, Mary, no! *Threats* is much too strong a word."

"They don't deserve me protecting them. She said she'd give him up. Well, what's she doing going into bed with him then? Tell me that?"

Mary stabs her finger at the surface of the table to emphasize her point. She is a little more drunk than the Abbess had at first thought.

"You're going a bit quickly for me, Mary. You're

talking about your mistress?"

"The minx!" Mary spits out.

"And... Hameel?"

"The traitor! But... oh, he's such a sweet man!"

Mary looks suddenly down at her hands. Our Lady save us, is she going to burst into tears now?

"I'm sure he's fond of you too, Mary," she says comfortingly.

Mary looks up, hopefully.

"Do you really think so? It wasn't just lust?"

Really, it's like dealing with a child. She leans forward and looks Mary straight in the eyes.

"I think it's love," she says in a voice as soft as velvet.

A look of sheepish gratification spreads over the girl's face. A rag appears in her hands and she dabs at her eyes with it. The tears have been averted, for the moment.

"He *says* he loves my Mistress. And now he knows all about the baby..."

"The baby?"

Mary stares at her, puzzled.

"My Mistress is going to have a baby. Didn't I tell you that?"

The Abbess leans back in her chair and takes another sip of the brandy. This is getting increasingly interesting.

"No, you hadn't mentioned that. That's very happy news for your mistress."

"So she should be getting rid of Hameel, shouldn't she!" Mary says emphatically.

The Abbess nods her head vigorously.

"Certainly."

"And *she* says she should, but she doesn't!"

Mary shakes her head, defeated by this conundrum. She looks down at her hands again.

"That sweet man..." she murmurs, and then drains her brandy.

The Abbess pours a little more into Mary's cup.

"We can *make* them part, Mary," she suggests.

Mary looks up eagerly.

"That's exactly what we should do. How?"

The Abbess goes over to her chest and unlocks it. She reaches in and brings out a small tightly furled scroll of parchment. She returns to sit across the table from Mary and unfurls the scroll.

"I've been hoping you'd come to see things my way, so I prepared a little document."

She pushes it across the table towards Mary, holding it flat with both hands. As she had anticipated, Mary only glances at it.

"I don't..."

The Abbess nods, smiling.

"Of course. Don't worry, I'll tell you what it says. It says *I, Mary, testify before God that Hameel de Groot, Architect and Artist, of Den Bosch, and Aleyt Goyarts van den Meervenne, wife of Jerome van Aachen, Painter, of Den Bosch, are adulterers.* And here at the end is a little space where I'll drip some wax from a candle and you can press your thumb there to make your mark."

Mary stares at the document for a few moments, and then looks up at the Abbess.

"And all what you promised?"

"Of course! No drowning for *you* in the second Flood, Mary! And no risk of Purgatory either, with your Papal Indulgence in your hands. Just wait there while I get a candle."

She goes to the door quickly. It's important to strike while the iron is hot, before the simpleton can change her mind. She throws the door open, and strides down the stone corridor to an alcove where one of the convent's many statues of Saint Agnes stands, with fat votive candles burning before it. Further down the corridor, stationed where she cannot be accused of eavesdropping, Sister Theresa stares. The Abbess ignores her. She plucks one of the candles from its black iron spike, and carries it back to her room, shielding the

190

flame with her other hand.

Mary addresses the Abbess as she sits down again, placing the candle carefully on the table next to the scroll. She has been thinking, apparently.

"And the Inquisitive? What about him?"

"Not a word, Mary. Why, you could even set up as a witch if you like, and I'd protect you!"

Mary gapes at her.

"It was a little jest, Mary," the Abbess says, putting on a reassuring smile. "The Inquisitor has no interest in you, and I will make sure that things remain that way. Now..."

She holds the candle over the scroll and lets some wax run onto it. Then quickly she reaches out for Mary's hand, and helps her to position her thumb over the melted wax and push down into it.

"Good, all done."

She waits until the wax has hardened, and then rolls the document up once more and returns it to her chest. She has no clear plan for what exactly she will do with it, but it could prove a useful thing to possess, and it is cheaply gained. She picks up another scroll from the chest and locks the lid again. As she does so, there is a knock at the door.

"Yes?" she calls out.

Sister Theresa's voice responds through the door.

"Brother Jacomo to see you, Abbess."

"One moment!" the Abbess calls back.

Briskly she picks up the two cups and the little stone bottle and puts them away in the drawer. She holds out the new scroll to Mary.

"Your Papal Indulgence, Mary."

Of course it's a worthless fake, but this uneducated serving girl will have no way of ascertaining that.

Mary's thoughts aren't on the Indulgence. She's watching the closed door as if it were a snake.

"That's him, isn't it?" she whispers to the Abbess.

"Don't worry, Mary. Come on, I'll see you out as he

comes in."

"And... my Mistress... Hameel..."

"We'll make them part, Mary, just wait and see!"

She puts an arm under Mary's, and helps her to her feet. Mary sways like a sapling in a strong wind, but the Abbess guides her firmly to the door and opens it.

"Come in, Brother Jacomo," she says, and the tall figure of the Inquisitor passes through into the room. As soon as he has cleared the doorway, Mary disengages from her arm and scuttles off along the corridor, past the startled looking Sister Theresa.

"God be with you my child!" the Abbess calls after her, and then speaks quietly to Sister Theresa.

"Follow her and make sure she leaves the convent straight away. Don't talk to her – she's been drinking and makes no sense."

Jacomo is staring after the retreating figure.

"Surely, that's..."

"A poor sinning woman, Brother Jacomo," the Abbess cuts in, "seeking my advice. Please – come and sit down."

The Inquisitor moves slowly into the room, his nose sampling the air like a bloodhound's.

"I smell... what, brandy?" he says.

The Abbess nods, frowning.

"I thought so too, Brother Jacomo. But she's trying to mend her ways."

They both sit down. Jacomo's eyes rove over the papers on the table in a way that she doesn't quite like. It seems the Inquisitor is in no hurry to start the conversation, even though it is he who has come calling. It's annoying. She feels impelled to say something.

"Have you questioned Jerome?"

Jacomo nods.

"I spoke with Jerome, and looked at his painting."

"A scandalous attack on the clergy, as Hameel warned us?"

His eyes are drifting now to the wall, across her new

192

tapestry and her gold framed circular mirror. He speaks without looking at her.

"His subject matter concerns me, but not so much as his apparent belief that his visions come straight from God. That is a dangerous belief, and is something I must consider further."

He shifts his gaze to the Abbess.

"However, that's not the matter I've come to discuss, Abbess."

She assumes an expectant look, but he doesn't carry on. Damn his little games! Probably Papal Inquisitors are trained in ways of unsettling people. Well, she isn't going to say anything until he does.

Jacomo indicates the papers on the table with a long bony finger.

"I see you are doing your accounts. You understand, I imagine, that my remit from His Holiness the Pope is a wide one?"

Where is this leading? She feels a prickling of anxiety.

"Your remit, Brother Jacomo? Well, yes. As a Papal Inquisitor, you're licensed to seek out witchcraft and heresy, wherever you may find them."

He's looking down at the papers again. Can he read the figures upside down? Can she think of a good excuse to remove everything from the table's surface?

"Witchcraft and heresy, as you say, are my primary concerns. But I'm also licensed to make investigations of other kinds. For example, into the financial practices of monasteries and convents."

He looks straight at her, suddenly, his eyes narrowed a little. As he no doubt intends, she feels flustered.

"Really? I hadn't understood that, no."

"Among other things, I'm charged by Rome to discuss – where I see fit – the levies remitted from our brothers and sisters in God. A three-way balance must be struck, you'll be well aware, between those taxes due to Rome, local works of charity, and managing what is left over to lead a humble religious life of self-denial and abnegation."

"Of course."

Even to her own ears, her words sound as if they have been choked out of her, so she repeats them more firmly.

"Of course. Indeed."

The Inquisitor stands up abruptly. He goes and stands in front of the mirror. She doesn't know if he's looking at himself, or at the gold frame set with garnets and amethysts. He speaks with his back to her. What rudeness!

"So I thought it would be helpful if I could see the accounts for the convent and for your infirmary, Abbess."

She is speechless.

He goes now to the door, and opens it. Sister Theresa isn't visible, but Jacomo's sallow-faced secretary stands there.

"Please come in, Brother Bartelme," Jacomo says. Really, this is outrageous! Who is Jacomo to determine who comes in and out of her room?

He turns to her.

"Brother Bartelme will wait here while you gather together everything I need to see. He will help you to make sure nothing is overlooked. I must go now. I have an appointment at the bell foundry. They are making an iron maiden for me."

He smiles coldly, as if inviting a response. What is he talking about?

"An iron maiden?" she says blankly.

Jacomo looks at her condescendingly, as if at a foolish child.

"I'll explain it to you later. May you go with God!"

"And you..." the Abbess responds to his brusquely turned back. She completes her benediction in the privacy of her own head. ...*may go to the Devil!*

The Inquisitor's angular figure vanishes down the

194

corridor outside, and Brother Bartelme takes up a mute and watchful station beside her table. Reluctantly, and without looking at him, she starts to gather together the ledger and papers recording the infirmary's accounts.

CHAPTER TWENTY

"Stop!"

The cry behind sounds like a seagull pursuing her. The sneery nun wants her to wait, but she just wants to get as far away as she can from that Inquisitive, as quickly as possible. She breaks into an unsteady run, turns right and left in a panic, and then at random dives through an open doorway. She stands, panting, against a wall in the dark room, and hears rapid footsteps, and the swishing of a gown, approaching and then receding along the corridor outside.

Her breathing slows, and her eyes become used to the darkness. A horrible odour in the room suddenly takes her throat and makes her gorge rise. She stumbles to a long stone bench surfaced with wood that runs along one wall, and into one of the holes cut in its surface she vomits up the churned mixture of red wine and brandy from her belly. Then she sinks to the floor, unable to do more for the moment than sit quietly and wait for her head to stop spinning.

Two nuns appear at the door.

"Here she is!" one of them says.

*

Brother Bartelme leaves the Abbess, carrying off her precious and hitherto private ledger and papers, and she sits alone, ruminating. The bells summon her to None prayers. After that, she has arranged a chance encounter outside the convent gates with Wiggers, to hear his report.

She sets off towards the chapel, and pauses at the end of the corridor leading from her room. There are voices just around the corner, and she stops to listen.

"Who *was* that woman we found in the necessarium?"

Sister Ursula, poking her nose into things that don't concern her. She is reminded of her intentions for this gadfly. Johannes sent word some days ago that he had finished her commission. She will go and see him after talking to Wiggers.

"A servant girl of some kind."

Sister Theresa, giving information that she had no permission to impart.

"A common drab from the town? What was she doing visiting our Abbess?"

Silence from Sister Theresa. The Abbess pictures a shrug of the shoulders and a hitch of the eyebrows. Sister Theresa has irritating, bushy eyebrows.

Now Sister Ursula again: "Abbess Dominica spends time with a number of unsuitable people. She's always out and about in the town. The Abbess of a convent should pass her days within its walls, leading her community in prayer and self-denial."

It's time to put a stop to this. She sweeps majestically around the corner. The two nuns jump like frogs caught out of their pond.

"Sister Ursula," she says with gravity, "It ill behoves a nun in holy orders to criticize her spiritual leader behind her back."

Sister Ursula inclines her head silently downward.

"Do not attend chapel. Go to your cell immediately and pray for forgiveness from God. I shall inform you of a more extended penance later."

Sister Ursula hurries away. The Abbess has long ago observed that Sister Ursula always moves slowly when approaching her, and quickly when retreating.

"A bad apple, Sister Theresa, as I've said before," she sighs, conveying regret more than anger. "We must do all in our power to stop her spoiling the barrel."

*

Mary totters away from the convent gates. She would give up a month's wages to lie down and sleep! Her hair is wet from the sousing with icy water the two nuns inflicted on her. The sunlight hurts her eyes, and her throat is parched. She thinks of the nearby fountain in Zuidwalstraat, and makes her way there. She tries to walk steadily and straight, and attract no attention. At the fountain, she scoops up handfuls of the cold water to drink. It would be good to rest awhile on the adjacent stone bench, but an old man sits there staring at her, and she knows from frequent experience that such an old man will try to engage her in conversation. Besides, he has a yellow cross stitched prominently on his tunic. Someone once told her what that signified, but she's forgotten. It's something bad.

What she really wants is to be lying in her little bedchamber at the back of the house, with the shutters closed. But she doesn't feel she can go back to the house just yet. She can't let the Mistress see her in this state.

The Mistress... Mary feels a pang of guilt at what she's just done. But she has the Papal Indulgence, tucked securely in the cloth pouch at her belt. And she is safe now from the Inquisitive's evil eye. These are substantial, weighty things to put in the balance against her act of betrayal. But still, she wishes she hadn't done it. She was all angry and hot-headed, but now she's cooled down.

She turns out of Zuidwalstraat into Sintjanstraat, feeling at a loss. Where can she go? She thinks of Gillis. Perhaps she could go and rest at his cottage? But then, she wouldn't want Gillis to see her like this either. And Gillis would want to do what they always did when she visited, and she isn't in any mood for that.

At the end of Sintjanstraat, she leans against a wall, temporarily at a loss again. The men's public urinals are a little further along, and she doesn't want to pass them. Already a tang of urine is in the air, and she can see a tanner filling his barrel with piss from the tap in the urinal trough. She turns back the way she's come, her gorge rising again.

"Mary! Mary!"

It's Catalyn approaching, with a grin on her face.

"Oh, Catalyn! What a day I'm a-having!"

"You look like something the cat found outside," Catalyn says, surveying her sister. Then she embraces her.

"You've been drinking wine, you wicked servant girl! The master's best Rhenish? Or a nice spiced red from Burgundy?"

"Oh, don't talk about wine…"

"There's a story to tell here, I'll guess? It's not your way to be staggering about the town with a sore head."

"I know it's not…"

"Do you want to come back to my room? I'm expecting one of my regulars, but not until after the mid afternoon bells."

"Oh, I'd like that of all things, Catalyn. A little rest, in a quiet place."

"Come on then, my wayward sister!"

*

The Abbess emerges from the convent gates and looks away down to her left. Wiggers is sitting there in the distance, beside the canal. He has a fishing rod extended over the water; a picture of innocence. She walks down that way slowly, glancing about her. When she reaches Wiggers she walks just past him and stops with her back to him, as if contemplating the canal. There is no-one else about, but one can't be too careful.

"Well, my red ferret?" she says. "What has been happening?"

"Hameel has visited the house again in Jerome's

absence."

"I know all about that. That's of no more value to me."

"Well, I do beg your pardon! I was only doing what you asked."

"I asked you to pay particular attention to the Painter. What of him? Where was he when he wasn't at home?"

"He went out of the city on a horse."

"Where to?"

"I don't know."

"Couldn't you have found out something at the stables?"

"I didn't think. But there's better news."

"What's that?"

"For my usual little commission, if it's useful?"

"I'll be the judge of that. Go on."

"I waited at the city gates until he rode back in. It cost me hours of my time."

"Yes?"

"After he'd stabled the horse, he visited the Jew."

"The apothecary? Where he gets his materials?"

"Yes. And then... he went somewhere else."

"I have money with me. Go on"

"He went to the house of Steenman."

Steenman? She gazes at the surface of the water. There's something fishy beneath the surface of this visit too.

"He was not long there..."

"Be quiet Wiggers! I need to think."

Steenman... the Inquisitor's sudden interest in her accounts... of course! That malicious painter has been looking for ways to make trouble for her with Jacomo. Well, she must tread carefully on this ground. Her money-lending has been as discreet as it has been lucrative. She has a good grip on the throats of her debtors – they wouldn't squeak without being ruined themselves. But Steenman... he's out of her power, thanks to that blasted Jerome. Well, there are no documents, at least. After he settled, she destroyed them. But if Steenman is persuaded by Jerome to come forward... if Steenman goes to any authority within the Church – Bishop Andreas, for example, or Jacomo – and if he's believed, then that could precipitate a considerable fall from grace for her. The Church looks on usury as a certain way to Hell, an offence which sullies even the hands of Jews, who are going there anyway. Anathema to all Christians.

So... Steenman...

If Jerome guessed that it was she who urged the Inquisitor's interest in him, then that would explain why he has turned his plough into this formerly fallow field. Why did she not foresee that he would fight her, fire with fire? She should have thought of this before.

She burns with angry self-recrimination. Now that battle is joined, she must be utterly ruthless.

Steenman is a frail old man. He has a roof over his head, thanks to Jerome. But what else does he have to live for? His mind is weak. He merely drags out his days.

"Wiggers?"

"Yes, Abbess?"

She knows things about Wiggers that no-one else knows. A vice, in particular, that he would not wish to have exposed. She has spies to watch her spies. And he'll do anything for money.

"There is a rabbit in a hole I know of, my red ferret..."

Wiggers makes a perfunctory show of shock and reluctance, but comes to terms soon enough. She puts five silver groats discreetly on the bench next to him, and makes her way to the tailor Johannes' place of work.

The Frenchman, De Bouilly, pops out of the door just as she is about to knock on it.

"Ah, Abbess Dominica. How are you?"

"Very well, God be thanked."

"And the shrine of Saint Alonsus? When will it be 'open for business' as you say here? I am troubled with such a pain in my legs – I have been telling Johannes here all about it."

The Abbess catches a glimpse of Johannes over De Bouilly's shoulder, pulling a face.

"I'm sure that a touch of the bones of Saint Alonsus will soon put paid to that," she says. "We'll have the shrine open straight after Easter."

"Excellent. You see, the damp climate here, it is not so good for the body as in my own town. I am suffering such pains. That doctor, Stemerdink, he has made me some linament, but it is disgusting. I'm sure it has the excrement of some animal in it. And the pains are the same."

"Prayer, Monsieur De Bouilly. Prayer is the answer."

"Perhaps you are right. I will pray to this Saint Alonsus. Do you think he will intercede for me even without touching his bones?"

"Perhaps, but come straight after Easter to the shrine, even if the pains are easier. There is no substitute for direct contact with the sacred bones."

"I will."

She offers no more comment, and turns purposefully to enter the doorway. Monsieur De Bouilly may make his adieux to her back.

Johannes shuts the door behind them with a sigh of relief.

"What a bag of wind!"

"But a good customer?"

"Oh, yes. He wants to wear the latest styles of Brabant. He tells me all the time how much better things are in Chartres, but he wants to cut a dash in Den Bosch. You've come to see the chemise, I expect?"

She follows him into his workshop, and he takes the chemise out of a drawer and displays it. Outwardly, it looks like an ordinary, if rather thick, chemise of coarse linen. But then he turns it inside out to reveal the lining of bristly woven goat's hair. The corners of his mouth turn down in an expression of distaste.

"It's a hideous thing - please tell no-one that it's my handiwork. I wouldn't make such a horror for any customer but you."

"No one will see it, except the wearer, my dear Johannes. Obviously it will be worn next to the skin, under the habit."

"Well, and a miserable time they'll have in it, I can assure you. I remember my grandfather John had to wear a hair shirt for a year, on the insistence of a Church tribunal. He nearly lost his mind, and his skin is still a torment to him to this day."

"He still lives, then?"

"Oh yes – and guess whose earnings are keeping him in bread and beer!"

"I think you've told me of your grandfather before, Johannes – wasn't he an Adamite? One of the Brethren of the Free Spirit?"

"That's right. He was the leader of some dreadful commune they set up. He was lucky he wasn't a heretic in these days of ours – he'd have been burned for it, not made to wear a hair shirt."

"Yes, Brother Jacomo would take an interest. But he must have recanted? He would have been executed even in the old times if he didn't recant."

"He did, but between you and me I think the old villain would go back to his old ways if he wasn't afraid."

"I'm sure I've seen an old man with the heretic's yellow cross stitched on his tunic. Is he within the city walls?"

"He's usually within the walls of the Three Hogs, if it's cold or raining, drinking my money. If the weather is fine, like today, he likes to wag his tail near the fountain in Zuidwalstraat watching the women come and go with their water jugs. He's an old lecher, in my opinion, but I suppose he does no harm any more. The cross on his tunic is a warning to all right-thinking people."

As he speaks, the tailor rolls the hair chemise into a neat bundle. The Abbess tucks it under her arm, and, after a few more pleasantries and an exchange of coins, takes her leave.

CHAPTER TWENTY ONE

Sweat gathers on Hameel's forehead. The Spring weather remains unseasonably warm, and he is working hard. He wipes his brow and pauses to rest his arms for a moment. He has been chiselling a groove in the wing of his lustful gargoyle for the last half hour, and the stone is dense and resistant, good quality limestone that will withstand the weather on the chapel parapet at the Convent of Saint Agnes. From the butcher's slaughter yard next door, he can hear Hans the butcher working hard as well, chopping at a carcass of a cow or a pig. The smell from the butcher's is bad in the summer time, and the flies too. Perhaps by then, if the Abbess will advance him some of his fee, he will be able to afford a workshop in a better part of the town – or even a little place outside the city walls, with some land to grow vegetables. He bends again to his task.

There is a double rap on the rough plank door. Hameel is puzzled – it's too early for the boy with his pitcher of beer and hunk of bread and cheese from the Horseshoe.

"Come in!"

To his surprise, it's the Abbess Dominica herself who pushes open the door and steps in, closing it behind her.

"I thought I'd look in to see how my gargoyles progressed."

She advances towards him. He slaps the dust from his hands with a rag. She extends her own elegant fingers, glittering with rings. A flowery perfume of some kind wafts to his nostrils. He bends to take her offered hand and bestows a kiss on the back of it.

"Well - I'm working, as you can see."

He releases her hand, which seems reluctant to leave his own, and gestures to the lustful gargoyle, which is nearing completion now. It is a winged creature with a thin body. One hand holds a strangled cockerel to its ribbed chest, while the other hand clutches at its groin. Its features are twisted into a lascivious grin; its eyes are hooded in ecstasy. The merest suggestions of goat's horns protrude from its forehead, little stony lumps of wickedness. Soon it will stand in the corner of his workshop next to its brothers, Gluttony and Avarice, and then he will begin tentatively to chip out the first rough outlines of Rage from one of the blocks of stone waiting in the opposite corner.

The Abbess runs an approving eye over his muscular chest in its singlet, and then over the gargoyle beside them.

"I know you work as hard as you can, for the glory of God," she says.

"I won't work this Friday, of course. Good Friday."

The Abbess nods.

"Yes. I know you'll be busy with the Holy Company's procession. You're Judas this year, I believe?"

"Yes. And you?"

"A Roman. Have you visited Jerome since Brother Jacomo talked with him?"

"I visited Jerome some few days past."

"And his good wife, Aleyt?"

"Aleyt? Aleyt was out, visiting her cousin who has a new baby."

"A new baby! How adorable."

The Abbess looks around her for somewhere to sit.

Hameel pulls forward a bench.

"Wait one moment, Abbess…"

He finds a clean square of sack-cloth and spreads it on the bench.

"And has the great Master Painter taken heed of his warning?" she says, when she has made herself comfortable.

"He has. He's stopped working on the panel of Hell."

"What does he work on now?"

"He's making sketches for his central panel. *The Garden of Earthly Delights*, he calls it."

"A strange title. What will it depict?"

The remarkable drawings he has seen swarm back into his mind, a fertile riot of imagery. He keeps enthusiasm out of his voice, however. The Abbess doesn't like to be reminded of Jerome's talents.

"It's to be a fantastical landscape, filled with cavorting naked figures."

The Abbess leans forward a little.

"Really? From which of our Biblical stories does this derive?"

"I don't think it comes from the Bible at all."

"Hmph! The arrogance of the man! He thinks he can invent his own subjects! Cavorting naked figures, you say?"

"Yes," Hameel affirms. He does not want to describe those things in more detail. The Abbess already has a good enough stock of stones with which to pelt the Master Painter.

The Abbess feels an agitation; the glimmerings of an idea. What is the bell that has been struck by Hameel's words? She needs a moment to let it ring out more clearly. She stands and walks a few paces to commune with Gluttony and Avarice for a moment. The glimmerings, the disparate parts of her idea, begin to cohere. She walks back slowly to interpose herself between Hameel and Lust.

"Has Jacomo been to see you at all?"

Hameel is surprised by the question.

"No. Why would he? He already has my drawings for his... devices."

"I've heard a rumour that he was going about asking questions. I'm told he's got the idea from somewhere that I'm a money-lender."

Hameel composes his features quickly into a look of shocked surprise.

"A money-lender? That's absurd."

"Of course it is. Yes. And I have reason to believe that it's Jerome who's trying to stir up trouble for me with such lies."

She looks down and heaves a sigh.

"You know, Hameel – forgive me for saying this of such a close and lifelong friend of yours – but I wish this accursed Jerome could be wiped off the map of our dear Den Bosch."

Now she raises her eyes to his.

"Wiped?" Hameel says, at a loss.

The Abbess rests a hand on the gargoyle's head.

"Have you ever thought of how things might be if he wasn't here any more? Just imagine: no Jerome. For a beginning, *you* would be the pre-eminent artist of the town."

She runs a caressing hand down the gargoyle's neck and gives him a sideways look.

"And you'd also assume your rightful place in his household."

Hameel maintains a blank expression with difficulty.

"What do you mean?"

"I think you're very close with someone other than Jerome in that house."

Hameel feels a sense of relief.

"Do you mean the servant girl, Mary?"

"Oh, I don't doubt that. A lusty man like yourself, my dear Hameel. But I had someone else in mind."

"I don't know what you mean."

He has to look away. He can't meet her gaze.

The Abbess transfers her hand from the gargoyle to his own arm. She grips it just above the elbow, kneading the muscle. She keeps her voice low, intimate.

"Hameel! Don't be afraid. Your secret is safe with me. *You and Aleyt!* And who could blame you? Such a beautiful, sweet woman. So much better than that pompous painter deserves."

Hameel feels confounded.

"I don't know where you've got hold of such an idea!"

But the Abbess has him on her hook. She gives him a sly pinch on the arm.

"Well, from your other little paramour, of course. Perhaps she's jealous. Like yourself."

"Like me?"

"Come on, Hameel! Don't bury your true feelings. You're passed over. Unjustly so. Look at that Overmaas decision. What if *you* were the leading artist in Den Bosch, admired by all, showered with prestigious commissions?"

Hameel is speechless for a moment. When he replies, his tone reveals more than he would wish; a tone of flat resignation.

"There's only room for one such man in Den Bosch."

"And only room for one man in Aleyt's bed, eh? What if you were to take that place?"

Hameel moves away from the Abbess so that her hand drops from his arm. She is speaking aloud of things that he hardly dares to speak of in the privacy of his own head. He sits down heavily on the bench. She has penetrated straight to the heart of his secret desire, and he has no words to deny it.

The Abbess sits down beside him. She takes out her rosary, and runs the ruby beads between her fingers for a few moments. Then she speaks again.

"Let me tell you a story, Hameel. There was a young girl, thirteen years old, from a family that lived on a farm. Her father was a proud man. He loved his daughter and she loved him dearly too. But she was no better than she should be, and she had a roll in the hay with a man or two. Her father found out, and all his fatherly love turned at once to anger and harshness. He despised her. He disowned her. He said she must go to a convent and become a novice. If she prayed and fasted and devoted her life to God, then perhaps she would be forgiven in the end and go to Heaven, and perhaps *he* would be forgiven for bringing her into the world. So she was taken away to a convent. The nuns knew her story, and so they despised her too, and set her to the meanest tasks. But the girl decided that she would change her place in the world. She decided that one day she would be respected not despised, powerful not powerless, rich not poor."

Hameel glances at her. Now he understands of whom she speaks.

"To get there, she had to do anything that was necessary. She learned how to get the ear of the powerful ones, and slowly, little by little, she learned to wield her intelligence and her ambition. In particular, she learned to be ruthless, Hameel. And when she had an enemy, she did whatever was necessary. Fortune favoured her in the end. Her chief rival in the convent was blinded in an accident. You never thought to ask, did you Hameel, how I came to be an Abbess, a member of the Holy Company, one of the most important citizens of Den Bosch? It's because I grasped the world by its balls, and squeezed until I mastered it."

She lets the silence prolong itself, to let her words act on him.

"Well. Why do I tell you this story, Hameel? "

"I don't know."

"Of course you do, but you're afraid to face it. It's because there's a way for *your* golden future to open up for *you*, Hameel."

He shakes his head. If only there was. But he is not

210

like the Abbess.

"There is no way," he says, almost in a whisper.

Alert to every nuance, she hears the hint of wistfulness in his tone as clearly as if it were the chapel bell ringing out the summons to Lauds at daybreak.

"Oh, there *is!*" she said vehemently. "I've been seeking so hard for a way to help you, Hameel – ever since I knew of Aleyt, and how much she's in love with you. And then it just came into my head a few minutes ago, as you were telling me about Jerome's *Garden of Earthly Delights.* Listen, Hameel, this is what you must do: the day after tomorrow, after the Good Friday procession, you must draw Jacomo aside and speak to him."

Jacomo? What has he got to do with this? Hameel feels as if a draught of cold air has entered the room.

"I don't want anything to do with him. He terrifies me."

"Nevertheless, you *will* talk with him You'll tell him of Jerome's sketches for this *Garden of Earthly Delights.* You see, they have put me in mind of that filthy heretical sect, the Adamites. I think it will be very fruitful for you to make that connection for Jacomo."

"The Adamites? But surely they're all finished here in Brabant. They've been eliminated, driven away. Why would I mention them?"

"There are rumours that they are active again!"

The Abbess stabs towards the ground dramatically with a finger.

"Right here, in Den Bosch!"

"I've heard no such rumours."

"You've just heard them, Hameel."

He looks at her. She nods, as she sees him understand.

"What of these... rumours?" he says.

"Jerome has confided in you that he has attended meetings of the sect."

The audacity of this idea almost makes him laugh.

Almost.

"What?"

The Abbess pays no heed to his incredulity.

"They are said to take place in complete nakedness, these meetings, since they consider themselves innocents in the Garden of Eden. The Devil knows what obscene rituals they carry out."

"It's preposterous! Why would a successful, respected man, a master painter like Jerome get involved with such things? He's pious to a fault."

"Jacomo doesn't know Jerome as well as you do, Hameel. If he got wind of him being in a secret sect – one specifically forbidden on the highest authority in Rome – then he would take a great interest. It's the most perfect wasps' nest for him to discover. Jacomo will extract a confession, there'll be a tribunal. And then..."

Hameel's hands are trembling. Is this what the Abbess meant by wiping Jerome off the map? In some black corner of his soul, he feels a demon stirring. But such dark desires must be crushed. He puts firmness into his voice.

"Jerome, tortured? Burned at the stake? It's inconceivable. I want no part of this!"

She holds him with her eye, speaking with quiet intensity.

"Then take a long, clear look at your own tortured future, Hameel. See! Jerome moving on, in all his puffed-up pride, from triumph to triumph. Feted and admired wherever he goes. Imagine a family portrait, painted some years hence. Painted by you, it might be. He's seated in his rich robes on a fine chair. Who is that standing tenderly at his side, her arm on his shoulder? Your beloved Aleyt, of course. And – look! There's a third figure in the picture, isn't there? Your own child – yes - your own child, sitting so sweetly on Jerome's knee. Looking up at him, loving him, piping in his little voice, 'Father!' A perfect family, Hameel. *Just imagine!*"

Hameel stares at her.

"My child! How do you know of this?"

The Abbess says nothing, but the answer comes straight to him anyway. There is only one person in Den Bosch who could have told her. Why had she done that? He feels completely mystified. He had no idea she had any connection at all with the Abbess.

"Mary! Mary has come and blabbed everything to you, hasn't she!"

"Never mind Mary. Think about the future I describe to you. Think of Jerome, the Master Painter, with your Aleyt and your child. And you with... nothing. How could you bear it?"

He stares at the ground, unable to dismiss her vision of the future. He will be like a stone falling down an endless well.

She speaks again, gently, persuasively, with a voice of honey.

"Hameel - friendship is a fine thing, but think of Aleyt. Your future *wife*, Aleyt. In your bed, Hameel. Think of that."

She puts her hand on his forearm.

"And I'll be such a friend for you, Hameel, a friend of much more use to you than Jerome! You'll find commissions will flow thick and fast. *You* will be the master artist in Den Bosch - perhaps in all Brabant!"

Hameel wants this future so much that it hurts to think of it. If only Jerome could be stricken down by Saint Anthony's Fire, or break his neck falling from a horse!

A powerful objection occurs to him, and he voices it in a confusion of relief and regret.

"Aleyt could never forgive such treachery. It would come out where Jacomo got his information, and then..."

The Abbess cuts in.

"Easily dealt with, Hameel. Surely you've heard that the accusers in an Inquisition can remain anonymous, if the Inquisitor thinks that's for the best? Jacomo is no fool. He'll bide his time, in the hope that you might wheedle yet more revelations from the heretical sinner in the guise of trusted friend. And then, when he arrests him, why would he ever reveal to Jerome who spoke against him? Hameel – take hold of the future you deserve! Speak to Jacomo on Good Friday, after the procession. That will be the perfect time to catch him, while the image of Jerome as Christ is fresh in his mind. He'll be outraged by such hypocisy."

Hameel tries to imagine this conversation. He can't.

"But – how could I make this credible? I know nothing of heretical sects. Jerome would have given me details."

"I've thought of that. Before Friday, speak to the grandfather of Johannes the tailor. He's often in the Three Hogs, apparently, or on fine days he likes to sit at the fountain in Zuidwalstraat. He's required to wear the yellow cross of the reformed heretic. It will a simple matter to strike up a conversation with this man – John is his name – and find out about the practices that got him into trouble. Johannes tells me the old fool still maintains that his beliefs were not really heretical at all, and apparently in private he's always keen to discourse on these things. He belonged to the Brethren of the Free Spirit. I imagine he was probably one of the last of that particular brand of heretics. They lived in some disgusting commune, doing who knows what with each other."

The bells of the churches and chapels begin to ring for Midday Prayer. The Abbess stands up quickly.

"Make good use of this man's conversation, Hameel. I must go now. I'll pray in the cathedral today, since I'm close by."

Hameel finds his voice as she reaches the door.

"Jerome…"

He intended to protest again, but the words have dried up in his throat.

The Abbess pauses.

214

"Jerome!" She spits out the word like a curse, and his image rises up in her mind's eye. The painter has always reminded her of her father. The first time that she set eyes on him, the physical resemblance struck her. But it went much deeper than that: both censorious, proud, setting themselves above others. In her dreams they merge into one *creature*.

She looks at Hameel. "Jerome is like the father in my story. Well, may they rot in Hell together!"

She goes, closing the door behind her. No sound of retreating footsteps comes from the little yard outside. It is as if she has drifted away into the air, a malevolent spirit conjured by his own desires. The stone gargoyle's wicked eyes meet his own, and the hairs on the back of his neck prickle.

He stares into space for a long time, and then, as the chimes of the bells cease ringing outside, he gets down onto his knees to make his own midday prayer. Words from the Psalms come unbidden to him, words that the Bible offers for a soul such as his.

"O Lord, rebuke me not in thy wrath. There is no soundness in my flesh because of thine anger; neither is there any rest in my bones because of my sin. For mine iniquities are gone over mine head: as in a heavy burden, they are too heavy for me. For my loins are filled with a loathsome disease, and there is no soundness in my flesh. Lord, all my desire is before thee, and my groaning is not hid from thee. My heart pants, my strength fails me, the light of my eyes is gone from me. I am counted with them that go down into the pit: I am as a man that hath no strength. Lord, why castest thou off my soul? Why hidest thou thy face from me?"

He bows his head and waits for divine guidance, for some inkling of what he must do to avoid the terrible sin that looms ahead of him. But God, as ever, remains silent.

CHAPTER TWENTY TWO

"Aren't you the grandfather of the tailor Johannes?"

The man nods, regarding Hameel with curiosity from heavy-lidded eyes.

"I thought so. Johannes has been making a suit of clothes for me, and he told me you often sit here by the fountain. You'll be pleased at the change in the weather?"

"It was a long winter," Johannes' grandfather replies. His voice is a little wheezy, as if air were escaping from a hole in some bellows within him.

"Do you mind if I sit for five minutes beside you there? I'm taking a little rest from my labours."

He looks pleased rather than otherwise and nods his acquiescence. Hameel puts down his empty water jug on the ground and takes his seat on the stone bench, worn smooth by generations of idlers. But they are the only two occupants today, so there is no danger of being overheard.

"My name is Hameel."

"John," the bellows wheeze.

There is silence for a few moments, apart from the tinkling fall of water from the fountain's spout into the stone basin below. How is he going to bring up the subject that interests him? *I see from the yellow cross on your tunic that you used to be a heretic*? It would be like commenting on a facial disfigurement.

In the end it's John who breaks the silence.

"What did you say Johannes is making for you?"

"He's already made a complete outfit – new hose and doublet, and for winter, he's making a houppelande."

"My grandson's tailoring doesn't come cheap. Are you a wealthy man?"

"My employer is paying. It's part of my contract."

"Ah – and who might that be?"

"The Abbess Dominica, of the Convent of Saint Agnes".

"You're working for her? What might you be? No… don't tell me… I'll guess. A pastry cook?"

Hameel makes a smile.

"No."

"A butcher? But you don't smell like a butcher."

"No."

"Well, my last guess is – one of these people who go around claiming to have miraculous cures from touching the bones of a saint."

Hameel snorts.

"That's hardly a way to earn one's bread!"

John shakes his head.

"No, it's not. But I have a feeling that the Abbess will be employing such people soon."

"Why's that?"

"Everyone knows she's opening a new shrine. She's got hold of some bones from somewhere."

"You're very well informed."

"You'd be surprised who comes and talks to me. This yellow cross has stopped me from gaining work, but it draws people to talk to me. They're curious."

John's rheumy eyes invite enquiry. This could prove easier than Hameel had expected.

"Well – it's an unusual thing, at least here in Den Bosch," he began. "I daresay there are others I haven't seen…"

"There were, there were. But I'm the last. They deal

with what they like to call *heresy* more harshly now, the *Church*."

He spits a gobbet of phlegm on the ground, as if ridding his mouth of a bad taste.

Involuntarily Hameel glances about them, but there is still no-one near. He lowers his own voice a little anyway, hoping that the old man will follow his lead.

"So – what were *your* beliefs? The beliefs that were condemned as heresy?"

The old man winks.

"The same beliefs as I hold today, whatever the Church may think. I believe that God is present in the world – and in ourselves – in *me*, even. Once you understand that God is within you, you are as innocent as Adam in the Garden. You can do no sin. Sin does not exist, for such a believer."

"The Church preaches that God is not on Earth, but in Heaven."

"And who is the Church?" the old man replies combatively.

"It's the body of men – and women – who take holy orders, and owe their allegiance to God's own Pope in Rome."

"Exactly so!" the old man says with a wag of his finger. "Just as you say, it's a body of men and women. And they claim to know everything about God, and to order the rest of us to believe the same as they do. How many brewers do you think there are in Den Bosch?"

Is the old man changing the subject? He gives the question a moment's consideration.

"Well, there are probably more brewers than bakers. I'll take a guess on a hundred."

"And how would it be if we only had one brewer in Den Bosch, and the only beer we could drink was their beer?"

A puzzling question.

"I suppose it would be bad – we would have only the one savour, and they could charge us any price they wanted."

"That's the Church. A poxy brewer. They force the same idea of God down all our throats, and they want our money for the privilege. They make me sick."

How does this old man stay out of trouble, if he's given to expressing thoughts such as these to a stranger on a bench?

"Do you agree?" John says, looking at him.

It's an awkward moment. Hameel looks at the cobbles at their feet and shrugs.

"It's hard to say. Tell me though, what you did – you and your fellows – in the old days. Did you openly defy the Church authorities?"

John laughs a wheezy laugh.

"Oh no! That would have been a short end to our fellowships. We were a secret network – we had communities of believers all over Brabant in those days, and beyond into Namur, Hainaut and Artois. We called ourselves Brethren of the Free Spirit, or Adamites. But we didn't make ourselves too obvious. They've persecuted holders of such beliefs for time out of mind. I think we were among the last of our kind."

"So – how did you gather, and worship?"

"We gathered where we could. It might be in a quiet forested place away from prying eyes, or perhaps in a barn belonging to a farmer amongst our number. You see, we didn't believe that churches and cathedrals were the only places you could worship God. Besides, the priests would never have let us worship in our own way in their churches. It was our belief that we should be naked as Adam and Eve in our services, and give thanks to God for our earthly senses. We were without sin, you see, because God was in us. So we could do as we pleased in all innocence."

"What do you mean, *do as you pleased*?"

John scratches his pendulous nose and one heavy eyelid makes a ponderous wink, like an old woman curtseying.

219

"Do you enjoy the pleasures of the flesh, young man?"

Hameel feels himself blush a little, ridiculously. He makes no response.

"Come on, don't be a plaster saint! You have carnal desires. That's part of how God made us. We believed that we shouldn't run away from our own nature. The Church denies our freedom to be ourselves. We freely expressed our carnal natures in all innocence, without sin. Think of that! Why, I'll tell you all!"

Without further prompting, John feeds him with details of the ceremonies of the Brethren. It's obviously a golden age for him, a time of intensity whose afterglow still warms him as he sits there, marked out by his yellow cross, a combative old relic of glory days.

After a while, the old man drops in a reference to the parching effect of so much talking, with a sly look. So Hameel takes him for a beer at the Three Hogs. Fortunately, in the more public space of the inn, the old man drops the subject of the Brethren and reverts to the gossip of the day. The plague of St Vitus' Dance that is supposedly sweeping the countryside to the south. The attempts to stamp out prostitution at the public baths. The plots of the Jews to poison the water supplies. Other old men join them, drinking companions of John, and Hameel is able to slip away and make his way back to his workshop.

He sits there for a time, motionless, staring into the empty air. If he is to set forth a lie, he now has the flesh with which to clothe its bones. But can he hoist up such a false scarecrow of Jerome? Would the piercing eyes of the Inquisitor be deceived by such a poor likeness of a heretic? Would his own conscience allow the attempt, or undermine him in its execution?

At last, wearied by treading these dismal circles in his thoughts, he returns to his work. For the rest of the day, as he hammers and chisels at the gargoyle of Lust, the Abbess's vision of his golden future glows at the back of his mind, like a little paradise that is his for the taking, if only he dares to reach out and seize it.

CHAPTER TWENTY THREE

"Get on your bloody way, King of the Jews!"

The lash of a whip strikes the street behind his feet. Swaying under the burden of the cross, he staggers forward a few more steps. His show of exhaustion is exaggerated, but nevertheless he is already looking forward to his crucifixion and deposition. The cross he carries is a small one, to save weight. A more substantial one awaits him just beyond the city walls, on the modest mound that serves Den Bosch as Golgotha each year on Good Friday.

Behind him, he knows, the members of the Holy Company follow in his steps. First come the two thieves, and then all the others in the guises of brutal Roman soldiers, preening Pharisees or disconsolate Disciples. Next will come Bishop Andreas ambling along in his fine robes of office, crozier in hand, accompanied by the Dean and the other members of the cathedral clergy. Behind them, the monks and nuns of Den Bosch will stretch out in a long sombre tail. The slow beat of a drum regulates the pace of all these participants in the official procession, although he himself is expected to exhibit an irregular and agonised mode of progress. The rest of the townspeople take their choice – some of them tag along behind the assorted clerics, while others line the route and watch all go by.

He is clad only in a loin cloth. A crown of thorns rests on his head, and pig's blood has been smeared on his forehead and also on his back, to signify the lashes he has received. His feelings are mingled. Sometimes pride predominates – a sinless pride, he hopes – that he is the citizen chosen for this highest of honours, the Christ of Den Bosch. He is the first artist ever to be given this role, usually reserved for the corpulent cloth merchants who bring wealth to the city or for some long serving member of the legion of tax collectors Theofilus Piek has gathered around him in the Staadhuis.

While pride has its moments, he is also smitten by waves of embarrassment. To have the eyes of the town on his almost naked body in this way can only be supported by the thought that it is not *him* they are looking at, but Christ. He is like a mummer in a play, and though his mask is paltry, he can at least hide something of himself behind it.

Now at last the north gate of the city wall is reached, and across the bridge outside he can see the cross. Soon he will be able to rest his poor bare feet on the little platform at its base and drape his tired arms comfortably across the wooden pegs on the crossbar. He slightly increases the pace of his staggering advance, eager for the end.

*

It's hard to see her husband thus. His white body smeared with blood. The body that she knows in all its intimacy, now bared almost wholly for all the town to see. This is harder than she had apprehended.

She knows she should be thinking on this day of Christ the Saviour, not of her husband. But his enacted suffering calls up pity and regret inside her in a way that the ancient suffering of Christ does not. She has betrayed him as surely as Judas betrayed his master. Her sin is still unshriven, her guilt a dead weight in her soul, pulling her downwards. She must unshackle herself from this, before it is all too late.

"Aleyt! Aleyt!"

A woman's voice. She looks around.

It's Frida, moving through the crowd towards her.

"Oh, Frida! How are you?"

"I'm well. Grieta is looking after Laurens. How exhausted poor Jerome looks!"

Frida's husband Joris appears too, behind Frida, and smiles at her.

"How do you do today, Aleyt? A strange day for the bride of Christ!"

He smiles at his own joke and she does her best to smile back.

"It's an honour, and it will only happen this one time. Perhaps it will be you one year, Joris."

She immediately wishes she hadn't said this.

Joris makes a self-deprecating gesture with his small white hands.

"I'm not one of the Holy Company of Our Lady. I'm not likely to be plucked from my obscurity into such eminence."

Aleyt catches a sideways glance from Frida towards him. Perhaps a censorious glance, as if he is speaking with sarcasm? She herself has felt in the past, privately, that Joris is a touch envious of Jerome's status, and resentful that he hasn't proposed him for membership of the Holy Company.

The moment passes quickly however, and the three of them are caught up in the flow of the crowd across the bridge outside the north gate. Ahead, the three crosses of Golgotha stand stark against the blue sky and scudding clouds.

*

Hameel is an outcast. He trails along at the end of the Holy Company's part of the procession, just ahead of Bishop Andreas and his clergy, and the townspeople hiss as he passes, like so many angry geese. Earlier, at the makeshift Garden of Gethsemane – a few tree branches suspended over the porch of the cathedral – he had consulted with two shadowy figures in cloaks, who flung a bag of coins to the cobbles at his feet. He slunk away with it, pursued by the jeers of the crowd, as Roman soldiers marched forward and swept Christ away to appear before Pontius Pilate. Now he carries the clinking bag of coins as a badge of his shame and betrayal. It is filled in fact only with pennies, to be returned later to the Dean of the cathedral.

The procession reaches the scene of the crucifixion. As Christ and the two thieves mount their crosses, and the crowd disposes itself in a broad semicircle, Bishop Andreas begins to intone the prayers for this station. Glancing around him furtively, Hameel finds the place where Jacomo stands. He stands alone, a little apart. Hameel suspects that others have instinctively made a space for him, as a man whose very proximity is like an unspoken threat. He would himself avoid him, but he cannot. Jacomo is the doorkeeper to an earthly paradise. Only through that forbidding portal can he reach the golden prospect of a future life with Aleyt. He must go to him.

The declaimed prayers are no more than birdsong or the wind in the trees. He is thinking only of the words *he* will use, the evidence he will present, and yet he still can't fully imagine the moment in which he will speak. At the start of the day, it occurred to him to say out aloud, in the privacy of his workshop, *the Master Painter Jerome is a heretic*, but even there the words wouldn't come out. He wishes he could have emboldened himself with drink, but that would have been too dangerous and unpredictable an ally. He thinks longingly of postponing his denunciation until later in the day – of visiting the Inquisitor at his lodging in the convent. But in the end he knows he must act out here, amidst the bustle of the day's observances. He senses that his resolve, weak and fearful as it is, will evaporate entirely if he has to seek a more formal moment.

Only seconds seem to have passed while his own

thoughts chased about his head, but already the body of Christ has been taken from the cross. Strong members of the Holy Company, led by Diederik the bell master, have shouldered his bier, and begun the doleful procession back towards his place of burial. As the crowd shuffles into place to follow, he takes advantage of the flux to draw alongside Jacomo's shoulder. Jacomo glances at him, and acknowledges him with a small nod of his head. It's enough to unlock his tongue, and he plunges into speech as if jumping from a precipice.

"Brother Jacomo," he says quietly.

Is that really his voice, so quiet and measured? He takes courage from this beginning.

"After the prayers at the Entombment, I'd be grateful if I could speak with you briefly in private."

The Inquisitor regards him blankly with his cold eyes.

"Concerning what, Master Hameel? This is not a day for discussing drawings."

"Concerning…" Hameel indicates with a cast of his eyes the prone figure of Jerome being borne aloft along the street ahead of them, "… concerning the Master Painter Jerome."

Jacomo makes no response. For a few seconds, he wonders if he's even heard him.

"The final station of the cross is in the cemetery beside the cathedral, is it not?" he says at last.

"Yes," Hameel replies.

"Then shall we withdraw from there to the vicinity of the cathedral porch, where you enacted your own role in the present ceremonies?"

" Near the cathedral porch, yes. I'll see you there."

They have arrived at the town's moat. The crowd of penitents funnels onto the bridge leading to the north gate, and he falls back behind the Inquisitor. He has crossed the Rubicon, and now there will be no return. Ahead in the crowd he catches a glimpse of Aleyt, following close behind the bier. After sadness will come

226

joy. He closes his mind to all that surrounds him, and thinks of his future of earthly delight.

*

Jacomo stands at the side of the porch, watching the crowd disperse after the entombment. Christ himself has arisen prematurely, and he can see him in the distance making his way homewards. A woman, presumably his wife, has thrown a cloak over his bare shoulders. Nearer to hand knots of young men are jesting and showing off, and in general there is a degree of unseemly rowdiness and noise. Good Friday is a holy day, but sadly it will be spent by such fools in the alehouses instead of in prayer. Well, the world may belong to the Devil, but he will not have it all his own way. When his Inquisition is well established and his power in Den Bosch has grown strong, he will find ways to put pressure on Theofilus Piek. On Good Friday next year, God willing, there might be no alehouses allowed open to do the Devil's business.

Now that artist, craftsman, draughtsman, call him what you will, is walking slowly towards him. He still has his Judas moneybag in hand, but he's removed the Jew's skull cap that exacerbated the crowd's opprobrium. No one is paying him any attention now, but he still looks furtive and guilty, and casts glances about him as he walks.

"Brother Jacomo," he says on arriving, and his eyes flit quickly away from his own. He feels, as he has before, that this man has something to hide.

"Well?"

"Do you think we might enter the cathedral, and speak quietly in there? Perhaps in a side chapel? There will be no mass said until evening."

Jacomo makes a nod, and allows Hameel to lead the way. The cathedral is deserted, and dim. Hameel turns into the smallest chapel on the left hand side, barely more than a room, where a stone statue of Saint Thomas stands uncomfortably in a niche too small for him, plain and dull, outdone by the profuse gilded adornments of the wooden retablo.

He takes a seat on one of the half dozen pews, and Hameel slides into place beside him. He would have preferred a place where he could have seen the artist's face more easily. It crosses his mind that Hameel might have planned their interview thus.

There is a pause, which becomes prolonged. He is usually comfortable with such silences. The way in which they break can be revelatory. However, a sideways glance at Hameel reveals that he is white-faced and that his hands tremble on his lap. He seems sick with some apprehension, so he decides to get him started on his road.

"You wanted to speak to me about Jerome, you said?"

"Yes."

Another long pause, and then, at last, more words come.

"I have some information – some terrible information – which I feel bound in duty to God to impart to you."

"Go on."

"It's hard. Forgive me. There are bonds, powerful bonds of… of friendship… of gratitude… that I must break to tell you of this. This pains me."

He feels his pulse quicken with anticipation.

"Hameel – your duty to God lies above all earthly ties of friendship. When you first came to me with concerns about the content of his painting, you showed that you understood this."

Hameel's profile nods slightly in agreement.

"Well, go on. Is this more matter of his work?"

"No. It's a worse thing, far worse."

"Yes?"

More silence. The taut cord of his patience snaps.

"For the sake of Christ, Hameel! Speak, will you?"

Hameel's whole body jerks, and the words come tumbling out.

"Jerome is a heretic. He belongs in secret to a sect proscribed by the Church. You'll know of it. They call themselves the Brethren of the Free Spirit, but they more often go by the name of Adamites."

Joy! That is the only word for the rush of feeling that engulfs Jacomo, and as soon as he identifies it he steps on it as if crushing an insect. This is no occasion for such emotion. He must be circumspect, sceptical, and thorough. He keeps his voice level and calm.

"Tell me everything, and speak only the truth."

CHAPTER TWENTY FOUR

"Well? Did you speak to Brother Jacomo?"

The Abbess has found Hameel sitting in the little yard outside his workshop. He appears to have no occupation. As he raises his eyes to hers, he looks so hangdog that she fears his courage must have failed him at the last. But he nods, and her spirits rise again.

"And did he seem to take your accusations seriously?"

Again, a nod only.

The bells of the town begin to sound faintly. They have all been muffled for today, the day when Christ was absent from both Earth and Heaven while he swept down to Hell to free the good heathens. She gives this doctrine scant respect. Why should the heathens have been saved? Why would those who lived before Christ's coming be redeemed by him? It beggared belief. However, she paid it careful lip-service, as became a spiritual leader.

"Well, I must return to the convent, Hameel. Preparations for the Easter feast tomorrow are under way and I should cast an eye over the kitchens. You will celebrate at the Company's feast?"

"I will be there, yes."

"Well, I'm sure Maarten and his kitchen assistants will provide you with something memorable. I'm sorry

I can't be in both places at once. Farewell for now."

Sister Theresa is waiting for her in the street outside Hameel's workshop. She cradles like a baby the heavy Paschal candle, which she has been sent to collect from the candlemaker.

"Come along Sister, don't dawdle!" the Abbess says animatedly. She feels invigorated by the prospect of trouble in store for that damned painter, and also by the prospect of good food and wine at last, after the long privations of Lent. She sets off at a good pace.

They re-enter the convent together through the small gate in the east wall, and she pauses for a moment in the east yard, where there is a sight to add to her felicity. The foundations for the little chapel to accommodate the thigh bones of St Alonsus are laid, and piles of stones have been delivered for the building work. A small wooden shelter beside the gate has already been constructed, where a rota of nuns will sit to take entry fees from the pilgrims when the season begins.

There is a flutter of movement, and a whisking black habit comes around the corner. Sister Ursula. She is probably on her way to the refectory from the cloisters. She watches her with interest. Her bowed head betrays nothing of the hideous discomfort she must be suffering from the chafing of the hair chemise. The Abbess sends Sister Theresa along to Sister Ursula's cell every morning to confirm that she has donned the garment.

A thought occurs to her.

"Sister Ursula!" she calls out.

Sister Ursula stops in her tracks with unnecessary suddenness. There is something defiant even about the way Sister Ursula obeys her orders.

"Come here a moment, if you please."

Sister Ursula approaches at an insolently leaden pace. "Yes, Abbess?"

Her face is flushed. With anger? Or something else?

"Sister Theresa!"

"Yes, Abbess Dominica?"

231

"Put the candle on the ground and lift Sister Ursula's habit."

Sister Theresa looks startled, and Sister Ursula takes a pace backwards.

"I just want to confirm that you're wearing your penitential chemise, Sister Ursula. Do you have any objection to that?"

Sister Ursula casts a glance towards Sister Theresa. Is there a plot here? She feels a swelling in her chest. She is in ebullient form this morning. One thorn in her side is in a good way to be plucked from her flesh forever. Why should she suffer lesser irritants to trouble her?

"I – please Abbess – could Sister Theresa conduct this proof in the privacy of my cell?"

"Absolutely not! What nonsense! Sister Theresa! Do as I bid!"

Her suspicions are confirmed by the manner in which Sister Theresa moves to the opposite side of Sister Ursula before raising the hem of her habit. She can't see.

"Yes, Abbess. All is as it should be," Sister Theresa pipes. She can smell fear at a hundred paces, and there is even more of a quaver in Sister Theresa's voice than usual.

"Are you quite sure, Sister Theresa? Come around to my side and lift the hem so that I can see for myself."

Sister Theresa looks as if she might faint with terror.

"It's my fault, Abbess," Sister Ursula says, her eyes now lifted to her own face. In spite of her blushing skin, her eyes still look defiant to her.

"I couldn't bear the chemise today – I have sores all over my body. I persuaded Sister Theresa to let me have a day of alleviation."

"Well!"

She turns to her black mouse.

"I wouldn't have thought this of you, Sister Theresa! Has Sister Ursula had any other days of *alleviation*?"

Sister Theresa shakes her head.

"But I don't know, any more, if you tell me the truth,

do I Sister Theresa?"

She is thoroughly enjoying herself now.

"I do tell the truth, Abbess," she murmurs.

"This penance was imposed on Sister Ursula for a good reason. But she has sought to evade it, and you have assisted her. Penance before God for our sins is an essential part of our holy vows, sisters. Not to mention the vow of obedience that you have both taken. Go to the chapel and pray. Stay there until midday prayers, and after that I'll deal with you both."

She has already had an excellent idea.

*

When the prayers of Sext are ended, she stands at the front to address the assembled nuns.

"There will be a change in Sister Ursula's duties," she announces, and directs an icy smile towards the miscreant.

"Her tenderness, selflessness, and qualities of leadership will be rewarded with a position at the head of the infirmary, relieving Sister Benedicta. From today, our dear Sister Ursula will take her place there among the poor suffering victims of Saint Anthony's Fire, where her dedication and humility will be as a shining beacon to those she has charge of."

Of course there is nothing said in reply – only she can speak aloud in the chapel, apart from the prayers and responses and hymns. But she senses the flutter of spirits in the place. The nuns will know very well how to interpret this apparent elevation. The present incumbent, Sister Benedicta, is dour, plodding and, frankly, rather stupid, so setting her aside bears scrutiny. But more to the point, everyone knows that the previous two managers of the infirmary died of Saint Anthony's Fire themselves.

She detains Sister Ursula and Sister Theresa as the rest of the nuns file out with averted faces.

"Sister Ursula – you are hereby released from your penance of the hair chemise. You will want all your strength for your new role. Go straight to the infirmary, and inform Sister Benedicta that you are now in charge. Take this note to her that I've written, which gives my authority for this change. Naturally you will lodge in the old stables beside the infirmary now, so remove everything from your cell here."

Sister Ursula turns on her heel without ceremony and stalks away. She doesn't bother to recall her for a reprimand. Let her sulk her way to her death bed.

She turns to Sister Theresa.

"You, Sister Theresa, will need to spend some time in self-mortification and penance. Go after Sister Ursula to her cell and collect the hair chemise from wherever you have both plotted to hide it. Then come with it to my room, where I will see you put it on. You will wear it day and night – and, make no mistake, I will check, Sister Theresa – until you have learned to repent fully of the sin of defying your spiritual superiors."

*

Hameel doesn't know what to do with himself. He would like to work at his gargoyle, but the sound of hammering and chipping would scandalize his neighbours. Work cannot resume until Hock Monday, after tomorrow's Easter celebrations. The Abbess had told him to await her visit in the morning, but now that she's gone he's free to do as he sees fit with the rest of the day. In times past, on such a day, he'd be as likely as not to spend time with Jerome and Aleyt, with perhaps a surreptitious return visit in the night to Mary's bedroom. But he can't go to that household now, he burns so for Aleyt. He can't trust himself to hide his feelings any longer.

He gets up and paces about the yard. He revisits in his head every word spoken between himself and the Inquisitor. It's intolerable. If only he could fly out of Den Bosch like a bird, and perch on a tree in a distant forest until... until all was done. Images of leaves and sunlight play in his mind. He should make use of the unwonted freedom of this day. Perhaps it would refresh his troubled heart to walk along the road towards Roedeken, beside the river, and take some victuals at the Jolly Bargeman? His limbs move as if loaded down with chains. Surely anything, any action, is better than this moping in his yard? He goes into the privy to relieve his bladder, collects his coin pouch from his room, and sets off.

*

Jerome knocks on the door of Steenman's house again. After another long wait, he's about to give up and leave when a woman's voice speaks behind him, and he turns. A tall bony woman with a long pointed nose and a thin neck. She could be a heron, looking for fish. She has small eyes like bright beads.

"Are you calling on Meister Steenman?"

"Yes."

"I wonder why he hasn't come to the door. Never mind, I've a key. I'm his servant. I live over the road and I sees you there out of my window. I says to myself 'why isn't Meister Steenman letting in his visitor?' and so I comes over now instead of when I usually comes which is just before the next bells."

She puts the key into the lock and twists.

"That's strange…"

She tries the handle, and the door opens.

"He usual keeps it locked."

He follows her in.

"Meister Steenman? Meister Steenman!"

Her raised voice is heron-like too, a harsh rasping cry. It elicits no response.

"I'll have a look in the parlour…"

Jerome waits in the hallway. There is a long pause, and then another bird-cry, a heron alarmed. The woman reappears at the parlour door, her hand over her mouth and her bead-eyes staring.

"What's the matter?"

"You'd better come and see!"

235

The room is dim. Steenman sprawls across his oak chair, both hands clutching a cushion on his lap. He has slid downwards, and one leg is bent at a strange angle. His face is paper white, his mouth gaping, his eyes closed.

Jerome approaches the figure. He puts a hand on the old man's. It's as cold as a stone.

Behind him, the woman starts to sob.

*

"Well, have you found out where he lives?"

Brother Bartelme nods.

"It's the third house along Kirkstraat. A fine big house."

"And was my request for an interview well received?"

"At first a servant tried to get rid of me, but then the Burgemeester himself appeared in the hallway and asked what was the matter."

"And...?"

"He said it should wait until Hock Monday, whatever it was, and you should come to the Stadhuis."

"And so you said...?"

"That it was a matter on which you wished to act as soon as might be. That of course it must wait until after Easter Sunday, but only as far as the morning of Hock Monday. That it was a matter of dangerous heresy, and involved one of the most respected citizens of the town."

"Of course he tried to get a name from you?"

"He did, and that was the lever I used to secure your interview with him today. He's burning with curiosity, I believe. He will receive you now, before dinner."

"Dinner! It would be more appropriate for a leader like him to set an example today by fasting with his family."

"He's not a Godly man. There was an aroma of cooking from the kitchens. The Easter Feast will be held a day early in that house."

"I daresay every day is an Easter Feast."

236

Brother Bartelme shrugs.

"And yet he's as thin as a bleached bone."

*

Theofilus Piek receives him in a small room at the back of the house. There is a desk at the window, so perhaps this serves him as a private office. The furnishings are opulent. The small unpleasant dog yaps at him for a few moments, and then settles into a basket. The aroma of cooking to which Brother Bartelme alluded pervades the air. Just such a house of Gluttony and Avarice as might be expected of the Burgemeester of a thriving Brabantian town.

"Please, sit down Brother."

The facing settles glow with brocaded patterns in gold thread. From a small table at his elbow Piek picks up a little silver ornament – another dog – and cups it in his hand. He is reminded of the Abbess and her rosary beads. This playing with objects annoys him.

"I understand you have a bee in your head, Brother Jacomo. Your fellow Dominican said the matter could not wait. How does it concern me?"

"I may need the support of the civil arm. I would wish to have some of your tipstaffs at my command, as before."

Theofilus Piek looks alarmed.

"Today?"

"On Hock Monday."

"Good God! We're not to have another witch burning in Easter Week?"

"No, that would not be appropriate."

"Well then?"

"Let me start with a question, Burgemeester. Do you believe you know most of what happens in Den Bosch? Would you consider yourself well-informed about the activities of its citizens?"

Piek rolls the silver dog from hand to hand for a moment. He makes a thin smile.

"I believe I'm adequately informed, yes."

"You would be shocked, then, if you discovered that, for example, the town's laws were being flouted, or the town's taxes were being evaded?"

"These things happen, from time to time. Illegal stills, for example are a recurring offence. We soon find out, and we act."

"It is the same situation for the Church. From time to time we find that our laws are flouted, and we must act. But our authority is more challenged."

"How so?"

"Well, in spite of the turmoil over the succession, and bickering between cities, Brabant has been at peace for some time now, has it not?"

"It has."

"No army will arrive at your gates. Trade thrives. The people can prosper."

Theofilus Piek nods, and there is a small smile curling the corners of his mouth, as if the fool thinks he could take the credit for all of this.

"By contrast, the Church is always at war, on behalf of mankind. The legions of Satan besiege us all, and would bring destruction on our immortal souls if they could. Our enemies are not open, they are covert. They conceal themselves within the hearts of men and women, and we must identify them as best we can."

"And you think you have found one of your lurking devils in Den Bosch, I suppose?"

He doesn't like the Burgemeester's tone.

"Do you make light of this?"

Theofilus Piek spreads his fingers and wards off this slur.

"No, of course not."

"I am only an outrider here, Burgemeester. You know of my intentions, and I rely on your support. Den Bosch will benefit both spiritually and materially when the Inquisition is established here in full force."

"How, *materially?*"

"The Inquisition's success in Brabant and the

238

neighbouring provinces is the will of Rome. If political circumstances change, if this part of the world is turned inside out again with war, Rome will protect its own. The French support for the autonomy of your city states may be withdrawn. The boy Philip may call on the support of the Holy Emperor to enforce his claim to all Flanders, and the cities, led perhaps by Ghent and Bruges, might resist. Would it not be advantageous to have the Pope as a friend should these difficulties arise? To be Burgemeester of a city whose eminence is not merely secular? With Den Bosch at the heart of our Papal Inquisition, even secular enemies will think hard before offending Rome. All men fear for their souls, and only Rome offers them the safe road to Heaven."

"Your interest in our politics surprises me."

"I have made it my business to know the situation here. War is a stamping ground for the Devil, but a time of peace is when he can best catch us unawares."

"Well, who *is* our devil in disguise?"

"I can't reveal that. The accusation may be false, and I would not tarnish the reputation of an innocent person."

A quiet tap on the door.

"Yes?"

A servant opens the door a crack. She speaks in a timorous squeak.

"The Mistress says that the food is on the table, Master."

"Good. Go."

The door closes again.

"Will you break bread with us, Brother?"

He could almost laugh aloud at the way in which Theofilus Piek draws this unwilling invitation from himself. It's like a rotten tooth being yanked out.

"Thank you, no. I break fast tomorrow, Easter Sunday."

The Burgemeester nods, unclouded relief shining from his features.

Jacomo stands up.

"I won't keep you from your family any longer. Can my assistant, Brother Bartelme, speak to your sergeant of Tipstaffs on Monday morning? Will he be expected?"

"Of course, do as you see fit, Brother Jacomo. My secretary will send word to the sergeant at the start of the day."

*

On Easter Sunday, Jerome and Aleyt attend mass at dawn. When they leave the cathedral with the rest of the large congregation, they are greeted by such a chorus of trilling birds in the adjacent cemetery, under such a cloudless sky, that the earth seems born anew. Everyone has donned their gayest clothing. After the sombre greys and drab browns of Lent, it is as if a living flowerbed has bloomed overnight in Den Bosch.

Poor Steenman, he thinks. He always came to this mass in that ancient red hat of his.

Amidst the bustling, chattering crowd, a bright mop of orange hair marks the presence of Wiggers, who is in the elevated company of the Burgemeester and his wife and family. Wiggers looks flushed and excited. Piek's dog yaps. As the crowd shifts and mingles, and the greeting 'Happy Easter!' is repeated a thousand times, a knot of the town's worthies gathers around the unlikely kernel of Wiggers. When this group starts to make its way along Kirkstraat towards the market square, Jerome and Aleyt fall in behind, with the rest of the congregation. As they progress, the crowd is swelled by the addition of folk who have not risen early enough to attend the daybreak service, or have attended it at other churches in the town. By the time they all arrive at the market square, there is a crowd as large as that which had gathered for the Good Friday procession.

Wiggers is led up the steps of the Stadhuis by the tall, thin personage of the Burgemeester, and the rest of the town's Council gathers on the flanks of these two figures.

Squinting, Jerome sees Wiggers as a block, the Burgemeester a pole. If both are made in God's image, then what is God?

The town crier appears with his gong, and behind him a man carrying a piece of rich red cloth. At a nod from Theofilus Piek, the crier beats his gong. The chatter of the crowd dies away, and the crier calls out his announcement.

"By authority of the city council of Den Bosch, it is hereby proclaimed that for the week of Easter Sunday until the first Sunday thereafter, Wouter Wiggers, servant to the Holy Company, shall be the Lord of Misrule of the city. His decrees shall be announced each day here in the market square, and shall be obeyed by all citizens under penalty of fines. Master Wiggers will now be enrobed, and will announce his first decree."

Wiggers, his face now plum red beneath his dyed orange hair, steps forward. The Burgemeester takes the red cloth from its bearer and shakes it out. It is a long robe, with gold embroidery as magnificent as that of his own robe of office. Moving behind Wiggers, he drapes it over the man's shoulders, and then comes around to the front to fasten the buckle at the neck. The crowd cheers and stamps and roars, until the crier beats his gong once more for silence. Wiggers speaks.

"Good people of Den Bosch! I am honoured to accept this honour, and to stand before you and above you today as your honoured Lord for a week. You will find me a fair ruler, not harsh. But beware! The honoured members of the Holy Company, and the tipstaffs, and the honoured members of the City Council, and the hon... the tipstaffs...no, I said that already... are all empowered by me to levy fines on such of you as defy my decrees."

Here he pauses to survey the crowd magisterially. There are one or two cries of "Hail the great Wiggers!" and some laughter. He holds up a hand for silence.

"Now, my subjects, take good note, the first of my

241

decrees is this: for the whole of this Easter Day, starting from this very moment and continuing until nightfall, all women not in holy orders are to wear their hair uncovered, and, to the contrary and opposite of this, men are to cover their heads. The penalty for not complying is a groat, and the tipstaffs and Holy Company and honoured members of the City Council will come among you in a matter of minutes with buckets to collect. All fines go to the good nuns of the Convent of Saint Agnes, to support their infirmary for the sufferers of Saint Anthony's Fire."

"One might have guessed that the Abbess would benefit," Jerome whispers to Aleyt behind his hand.

There is a flurry of laughter and excitement, and all over the square women take off their wimples or head coverings, and the men who are not wearing hats beg or borrow those coverings and drape them over their pates. Wiggers looks very pleased with himself. The Burgemeester leans towards him and says something quietly, at which Wiggers whips out a cap from under his robe and shoves it on his own head. Some of the more well-off womenfolk, who have donned elaborate headgear to celebrate Easter, start to fish in their purses, or in their husbands' purses, ready to pay their fine rather than look like a collection of whores.

At her place next to the steps, Mary takes off her head cloth as Wiggers descends in his robe of state. He catches her eye, and steps close enough to whisper in her ear.

"I wish I could decree the removal of more than your head cloth, my dear!"

Mary pulls a face and marches off back towards the house, where she can put her head cloth back on in private, and be damned to him! On her way she sees Gillis making towards her, but she pretends not to notice him and gains the house before he can speak.

Jerome looks after Wiggers as he moves away along Kirkstraat in his robes of state. Something is tugging at his memory. Yes, the last time he saw him. It was at the end of Waterstraat, disappearing around the corner. The street where old Steenman lived.

*

In his room at the convent, on his knees, the distant sound of the Easter bells brings Jacomo no joy. Is this a sin, not to feel uplifted on the most joyous day of the Christian year? But true joy, holy joy, cannot exist on this earth. A soldier of God may rest between battles, but he should not act as if the war has been won. He must not relax his vigilance. Only in death can he rest.

He gets up and goes to his table, where the letter that came a few days ago from Cardinal Amandini lies. Clearly it must have crossed with his own letter to Rome. He glances again at its exhortations.

...His Holiness troubles me almost daily with his complaints. He has always the same question. Why does he have reports of the prosecution of heretics by Grand Inquisitor Torquemada in Spain and accounts of Brother Kramer's war on witchcraft in Moravia and Bohemia, yet from Brother Geoffrey in Brabant we have nothing but silence?

I have already charged you to let me know your findings on the work of Abbot Geoffrey – perhaps you have already written. However, I advise you now that His Holiness's patience has worn thin. You know I have high expectations of you to end this weakness of our Inquisition. Innocentius believes that the enemies of God swarm openly like the rats that swim in the dykes and ditches of Guelders, Zeeland, Holland, Flanders, and all of those low provinces to which I have sent you. Brabant is the most important - the most influential - battleground in our war with the Devil in these regions. I expect victories from you, Brother Jacomo, and I expect to hear of them soon. I must have something to show His Holiness that will stand well beside the burning of witches in Salzburg and Bremen, and the trials of heretics in Seville and Cordoba. He wishes to be remembered as the Pope whose influence reached to every part of the Holy Empire, a Pope who was the scourge of heresy and witchcraft.

In the prosecution of Innocentius's wishes lies your future flourishing, Brother Jacomo. As I am his instrument, so are you mine. Neither of us must fail our master.

He lets the paper fall from his fingers, and gazes at the crucifix nailed to his wall. The world teems with witches and heretics, just as Innocentius believes, and God has furnished him, Jacomo, with all the weapons he needs. He has intelligence, and power enough to make a good beginning. His strength will grow as Rome sees and approves his work. The unmasking of heresy in an eminent man like Jerome, and the destruction of a vicious web of accomplices… well, he must not think of these things until they are achieved. He must not anticipate, but… surely, this would bring him the enhanced support from Rome that he will need for the Inquisition here to succeed. God does not mean him to be a foot soldier merely, He means him to be a general. He has believed this in his innermost being, in his blood and bones and soul, since Brother Domingo brought him to his vocation in the Monastery of Saint Dominic so many years ago.

He feels impatient for tomorrow, Hock Monday, Saint Ivo's Day. This Easter Sunday, he is like a hungry bird of prey, hovering, watching and waiting. Although he doesn't possess God's all-seeing eye, he can emulate the noble eagle, and apply a heightened acuity of vision to the world below. All day he must pray to God to guide him well, and, when the moment comes, to let him swoop down ruthlessly at evil, wherever it hides itself.

CHAPTER TWENTY FIVE

In the corner of the studio, a small fire is burning in the fireplace. Jerome holds a glass flask in the heat with iron tongs. A dampened rag is wrapped around his fingers for protection.

The flames lick around the sides of the flask. Inside, the pale pink liquid bubbles gently and releases an aromatic steam. He breathes in through his nostrils. Roses. Roses in a garden in Firenze. Another world.

Beside him, on his alchemy bench, are the mortar and pestle, the twisted papers of powder, and the little vials of liquid that he has used to make up the potion. A fertility potion. He has made it before, many times, to a formula given to him by the apothecary Izaak. He will give it again to Aleyt to take tonight. God will reward persistence. Aleyt is still young, and He must take pity on them eventually.

The potion has been boiling for long enough. He sets the flask carefully back onto its metal stand on the table. Once it has cooled, he'll decant it through a cloth filter. He opens a cupboard to look for one.

There is a clatter of ascending clogs and a knock at his studio door.

"Yes?"

The door opens and Mary's head pokes through the gap, eyes like twin full moons.

"It's that Inquisitive again, Master."

"The Inquisitor?"

"Yes, the devil in black."

"You've not left him standing at the street door again?"

"I wouldn't let him in the house if I were you."

"There's no choice in the matter, Mary! We can't turn him away like a pedlar. Now go at once and bring him here to me… and don't leave us until I've asked if he'd like something to eat or drink."

She withdraws, and he finds two chairs, which he places beside his work table near the window. Mary opens the studio door again and stands aside quickly. The tall figure of the Inquisitor looms in the opening.

"Good morning, Brother Jacomo, come in!"

Jacomo nods slightly, and moves forward.

"Good morning, Master Jerome."

Mary stands at the open door as she has been instructed, but like a bird about to take flight.

"Will you take some refreshment?" Jerome suggests. "A drink of something? My wife Aleyt and Mary here have baked some honey biscuits…"

The Inquisitor shakes his head.

"Nothing, thank you."

He turns and rests his gaze on Mary. Jerome makes a movement of his hand, and she steps back abruptly and shuts the door.

Jacomo's nostrils dilate. What is in the air? He turns his attention to the bench beside the fireplace. There is a clutter of alchemical retorts and stands, and a flask with gently drifting steam coming off the surface of a pink liquid. He is surprised.

He gestures towards the flask.

"You are on the alchemist's quest for gold?"

Jerome feels his hackles rise. Is there a mocking tone in the Inquisitor's voice? But there is no stricture of the Church against such things, as far as he knows. Plenty of monks waste their time in that way. He puts aside his annoyance, and answers blandly.

"No, no. Just a few herbal remedies."

Jacomo nods.

"In this part of the world, there hardly seems to be a man – if they have the means – who hasn't set up as an alchemist."

"It's a fascinating study, but I'm content to let others seek to transmute base metals to gold," Hieronymus says dismissively. The Inquisitor has not called on him for the purpose of small talk. "Won't you sit down?" he suggests.

Jacomo chooses the chair with its back to the window. Jerome remembers now that he had stood against the window the last time he had come. He moves the other chair a little, so that Jacomo is at least something more than a silhouette, and sits down himself.

"Has your painting of Hell progressed?"

"I've left it alone since you came. How goes your side of our bargain?"

"I'm looking into the Abbess's affairs, as I promised, and I'm still ready to hear any evidence you have of usury. But I'm not here to discuss that. Something else has come up."

Jerome waits. The Inquisitor's face reveals nothing. After a moment, he resumes.

"Might I ask if alchemy now occupies you entirely, or if you have started on some new painting?"

"I'm making sketches for the middle panel of my work for the cathedral."

"May I see them?" Jacomo says.

Curse the man's prying.

"They're only rough things," he says, not moving.

Jacomo smiles with his mouth only.

"Nonetheless I'm interested, Master Jerome."

He wishes he had said that he hadn't been working at all in recent days. It isn't that there is anything private about the drawings – after all, the finished work will be seen by all the world when it is installed in the nave of the cathedral. But he doesn't like Jacomo's interest. He might want to interfere again, as he has with the panel of Hell. *I'm damned if I'm going to have some monk dictating the content of my work!* He rummages crossly among the sheets of drawings on his work table and spreads some out, and then sits down again with crossed arms.

Jacomo stands to look at the drawings more easily, his long nose hovering above the table like the beak of a predatory bird. Jerome thinks he will make a sketch, when the Inquisitor is gone. A hybrid creature, part monk, part falcon.

Jacomo studies the works closely. At once he feels the thrill of discovering something illicit, and his excitement grows as he leafs through more drawings. There is abundant depiction of twisted and perverted practices, just as Hameel had suggested. Groups of unclothed figures cluster promiscuously around gigantic fruits. Owls and other familiars of the Devil unite in bestial acts with both sexes. A man plucks flowers from another's anus. Inside a sphere of glass, a man fondles a woman intimately. He feels a stirring in his loins and closes his eyes quickly in disgust.

"Lewd and lascivious acts - and everyone as naked as they were born. Strange matter for a work to be displayed in a cathedral!"

Jerome sighs. Why was he so foolish as to let this meddler see his work in progress? It was inevitable that it would be misunderstood by such a man. Now he will have to explain himself.

"You must understand the setting for these drawings, Brother Jacomo. They are the basis for the central panel of the triptych. To their left, Adam and Eve in the Garden of Eden, to their right, a vision of Hell. These images will form a part of what I call *The Garden of Earthly Delights.*

Jacomo waves a hand towards the drawings.

"So, these show us the sinful behaviour that leads

towards damnation?"

"Well…"

Jerome quickly checks himself from offering further exposition. Perhaps the Inquisitor's simple interpretation is best left to stand. Crude and inaccurate it may be, but if it satisfies the man, then so be it.

"Yes, you may see them as such, yes."

Jacomo strokes his chin. He picks up another of the drawings and studies it in silence for a little while.

"There seem to be rituals being enacted by your figures, and strange symbols amongst them. What is the source of these ideas?"

"God is my inspiration. He lets me serve him in my way, as you serve in yours."

Jacomo puts the drawing down, and resumes his seat.

"You and God together then, Master Painter. No one else is involved?"

"What do you mean?"

Jacomo observes his quarry closely. A man's eyes or the slightest of movements can betray his inner thoughts. He asks his leading question, making it ambiguous, potentially innocent.

"Do you belong to any associations of any kind, Master Jerome?"

Jerome is puzzled. What has this to do with his drawings?

"*Associations?* Well – of course: the Holy Company of Our Lady."

Jacomo's dark eyebrows hook upwards, inviting more.

Jerome stares back at him. There is something here that he doesn't understand, some sinister import in these questions.

"Only that, and the Guild of Painters," he adds.

"Are there other associations that you have heard of, here in Den Bosch, that have piqued your curiosity?"

Jerome's irritation boils up inside him again. What

right does this man have to come troubling him with these obscure questions? Is he, after all, no more than a tool of that malignant Abbess Dominica?

"You're talking in riddles to me, Brother Jacomo," he says, not troubling to disguise his impatience. "What sort of associations?"

"Have you heard of the Brethren of the Free Spirit – otherwise called the Adamites?"

Jerome nods.

"Of course."

"Of course?"

"They're well-known enough. But there are no such heretics in Den Bosch."

"How can you be so certain?"

"Such people couldn't be amongst us without rumours. The Church authorities would surely get wind of it. It's a sect that's been proscribed for... I don't know... since long before I was born."

"They are subtle and cunning, these Adamites. You know their doctrines?"

"They consider themselves to be like Adam and Eve before the Fall."

"Exactly so. Saints of the present day, liberated from the taint of mortal sin. Innocents. In direct contact with God, independent of the Church's teachings and rituals. Furthermore, in their Devil-inspired delusion, they engage in riotous orgies, naked as Adam and Eve, affronting Our Saviour with their lewd and lascivious behaviour."

Jerome shrugs his shoulders.

"So it's said."

"Your sketches..." Jacomo says.

He lets the words hang there in the air, and keeps his eyes on the painter's face and gestures.

Of course! This is the drift of the Inquisitor's questions! It's obvious. But because it *is* so obvious, and so ridiculous, he has failed to understand until now. He laughs out aloud at the absurdity of it. He could caper and turn somersaults at the very foolery of it.

"Because I have *drawn* such things, you consider that I am a member of this heretical sect?"

He fills his voice with incredulity. Mockery, even. Let this Jacomo understand what an ass he is making of himself!

But Jacomo's reply is like a flash of lightning out of a clear sky.

"It is alleged that you are."

Jerome stares in shock, and then rage, outrage, pours into him like molten metal into a cast. He almost shouts.

"*Alleged!* By whom?"

Jacomo speaks calmly.

"I have promised not to divulge my source."

Jerome can't stay in his seat. He stands up, and his rage finds its focus.

"This is another of the Abbess's slanders isn't it! She'll invent any lie to make trouble for me!"

Jacomo smiles his thin-lipped smile.

"I would discount the Abbess as a source of reliable information. It's clear to me she has some axe to grind against you. This comes from elsewhere. I take it then that you deny the accusation?"

"Of course I do! It's moon-madness! Whoever has said this... they must have their own reasons... they must be... *who* would say such a thing?"

He's spluttering and incoherent. He gives up and holds his hands palms outwards to the Inquisitor, appealing for the alms of information. Apart from the Abbess, he has no enemies in Den Bosch, or anywhere else, as far as he knows. And yet, *someone* has made up a preposterous lie to get him into trouble.

"My informer wishes to remain in the shadows, and that is their right," Jacomo replies brusquely. He takes a deep breath, and when he speaks again, his tone is softened, and almost wheedling. It's as if honey has just oozed down his throat.

"Master Jerome, if you were merely on the fringes of

251

this sect, and could point me to the ringleaders, then you would be doing the Church a great service."

Does this blasted monk think he is an idiot, to step into a clumsy snare like this? He retorts with intemperate loudness. He wants to break something with his hands.

"I don't know anything about it! There *are* no Adamites in Den Bosch. They were all driven out before I was even born. Someone is making a donkey of you for their own amusement."

"I am not so easily made a fool of!" Jacomo hisses.

"Well that's just what it looks like to me! A lie has been dangled before you and you've swallowed it like a fish rising for a fisherman's lure!"

Jacomo stands up abruptly. Jerome rises from his own chair, startled. He takes half a step backwards. It looked so much as if the Inquisitor was going to strike him. But instead the monk's hand stabs at the sketches on the table.

"My experience has taught me that where there is smoke, there is usually a fire."

Jerome is blindly furious now, the more so for having shown a moment of weak fearfulness in jumping out of his chair.

"Fire and smoke! The crude materials of your cruel work, executioner!"

"Do you jibe at me? Your arrogance is outrageous, Master Painter! You think you can paint a Hell filled with the clergy, and fill our cathedrals and holy places with obscenities? And then justify your warped images by saying that's what God tells you to do?"

They stand glowering at each other for a moment. With an effort, Jacomo brings his anger to heel, taking deep breaths in the rose-scented air. When he speaks again, his voice is calm.

"Be good enough to call your servant."

Jerome stalks to the door and opens it.

"Mary!"

She appears instantly, her face an open book of puzzled consternation. Jacomo scowls, and speaks directly to her over Jerome's shoulder.

"Go to the street door and admit the two men who wait outside."

Mary turns and runs down the stairs to the hallway.

"What is this?" Jerome demands.

"I'm going to get to the bottom of this."

"Get to the bottom of *what*? You can't..."

Jacomo cuts him short.

"I *can*. I remind you that I'm an emissary of the Pope himself. I am here to stamp on the sparks of evil, Master Painter, and I will stamp hard until they are put out."

Behind him, Jerome hears approaching voices raised in argument. He whirls around to see two burly men bustling towards him with Mary protesting in their wake. Their red tunics bear the woven green insignia of Den Bosch.

"Seize the painter!" Jacomo orders the men as they enter the studio.

Jerome struggles briefly as the men grasp him by the arms, but then desists. As if in one of those nightmares when all power of speech or movement is denied, he finds himself marched down the steps to the street door, brushing by the horrified Mary. He has no words at his command to utter to her.

Jacomo returns to the table and gathers up a handful of the drawings. They might prove useful later, at the tribunal. Then he sweeps out of the house, past the staring white-faced fool of a servant girl.

CHAPTER TWENTY SIX

"Our Father, who art in Heaven,
Hallowed be Thy name,
Thy kingdom come... thy kingdom come..."
Aleyt tails off into silence.

Only through sin did she achieve her own heart's desire. Why should He be listening now?

She is sitting near the window in the parlour looking out, her chair pulled back a little so that she will not be visible from the square below. Smudges of colour move down there in a meaningless blur. Are there people still who buy food in the market, and talk with passing friends? Are there people who breathe freely, without iron hoops seeming to constrict their chest? What do such people feel, or think? And yet she was one of them herself until today. Tears keep welling up, and she dabs them away with her handkerchief.

There is a sound of feet ascending the stairs rapidly, and then a knock at the door.

"Yes?"

Mary opens the door.

"He's here. I wanted to give you a moment first. Shall I send him up?"

Aleyt nods, and Mary descends, leaving the door open. A few moments later she hears the firm tread of Hameel coming up. She stands and puts away the handkerchief damp with tears. Then he is there, at the door, his hat in his hand.

They exchange a long look without speaking. It's like looking into a strange mirror; Hameel's face a reflection of her own anguish and uncertainty. Then he casts his hat onto the table and steps towards her, his arms open.

"Aleyt…my love…"

She returns his embrace, but it feels all amiss to her, and she pulls away again quickly.

"Did you find out?" she says.

Hameel looks away at the window.

"They've taken him to the prison. He was seen."

"Seen by whom?"

"Many people. In the market square – van Dorff for instance, he saw. The tipstaffs had their arms linked in his, one on each side. The Inquisitor came behind them. They disappeared behind the Stadhuis, and when van Dorff peered around the corner the prison door was closing."

Jerome… marched through the market square like a common criminal! She winces herself at the consternation and shame her proud husband must have felt.

"And… did you find out…?"

She can't bring out the word "accused". What does the Inquisitor think Jerome has done? It must be a wicked lie, whatever it is. Hameel still stares towards the window, and when he replies his voice is very quiet, as if that might soften and blunt his words.

"Heresy. I asked… the Abbess. The Abbess told me. Jacomo… the Inquisitor… must have spoken to her. She told me … she told me that Jacomo thinks Jerome is a member of a heretical sect."

Aleyt gapes at him.

"How could he think such an absurdity?"

Hameel feels afflicted with some dreadful sickness. He couldn't swallow food or even water this morning. His words ring dully in the room, like counterfeit coins dropped in a worthless heap.

"Jacomo is not like you and me. He sees evil everywhere."

He subsides into silence, unable to carry on with this.

Aleyt paces the room: to the window; back to the Garden of Eden; to the window again. At least now she knows where her husband can be found. But what can she do? She feels desperate to find some action that will help him. She turns to Hameel once more.

"I must go to Jerome. Will you come with me, to the... to the prison. I'm so afraid."

But Hameel shakes his head.

"You should stay away, Aleyt."

"How can I stay away? What must he be feeling?"

"There are dangers for you too."

"What dangers?"

"You're his wife. It might occur to Jacomo that you would have known everything that Jerome did. Perhaps that you too are a heretic. It's best you stay quietly here."

Aleyt looks wildly about the room. Like the square outside it's become a strange incomprehensible place. A prison in itself. She walks to the door and pushes against the wall beside it with both hands.

"Oh... I'll go mad in here... I don't care about myself."

Hameel feels as if a snake is winding around his entrails, constricting his breathing. Why had he not foreseen this suffering? Did he think she would don widow's weeds with joy? But it must all be gone through. Beyond this ordeal lies the Promised Land. He wills his chest to take in air, and steps towards Aleyt to put an arm protectively around her shoulder. She doesn't move away, and he takes courage. He speaks in a low, tender tone.

"Aleyt... you must think not only of yourself now. There's the baby to come. You must keep safe for the sake of... the child. Our child."

256

But at this Aleyt's whole body seems to shake him off, and she steps away again. She walks once more to the window, and back to the centre of the room. She's as restless as a caged bear.

"I don't care about the baby. Jerome needs me!"

"Don't speak like that. If you were tortured..."

He stops, his mind filled suddenly with horrible images of his own drawings for the Inquisitor. Aleyt stares at him.

"*Tortured*? In God's name, they won't torture him, will they?"

Hameel can't face her look of wild apprehension. He wants to run away from her - from Den Bosch itself. If only he could disappear, and not come back until Jerome is dead, and Aleyt is a grieving widow.

Her voice rises a pitch into panic.

"Hameel! They won't torture him?"

Hameel is still beside the door. His shoulders are hunched, as if against rain or sleet. She has a sudden inspiration, and goes to take his hand in hers.

"*You* must go to Jacomo, Hameel! Tell him everything you know about Jerome. He must listen to you. Tell him how Jerome has been your friend since you were children. How he was like an older brother to you when your own poor brother Pieter died. How he taught you to see yourself too as an artist. Hameel – you know Jerome is a good man. Surely *you*, of all the people in Den Bosch, can best convince him that Jerome is innocent!"

Hameel returns the pressure of her hand.

"Aleyt. I love you!"

What is he talking about? Impatience racks her. She withdraws her hand from his and pushes him towards the door.

"Oh, don't speak of that! Go! Please, go to Jacomo!"

Hameel hesitates at the top of the stairs, but he has no more false words left inside him. So he turns and hurries downwards.

He leaves the house and walks with apparent purpose across the square, feeling Aleyt's eyes following his back. But when he turns the corner into Kirkstraat, his pace slows and he finally comes to a halt, as if lost in a strange town.

Unusual sounds coming from up ahead catch his attention. He moves forward uncertainly. Carnival carts, like a line of brightly coloured beetles, are making their way slowly into position outside the cathedral, and the ridiculous Wiggers is declaiming something or other on the cathedral steps. Grateful for a few moments of distraction, he wanders to a vantage point, mingling with the gathering crowd. Suddenly, one of the carts bursts into noisy explosions and is wreathed in billows of smoke. Red-suited masquers with devils' horns jump out from hiding and run about, seizing children. The older ones laugh and go willingly, while younger ones look aghast, and one or two cry. The devils pen up all the children and dance in a circle around them in wicked glee, waving tridents. Then a trumpet blows a fanfare, and Wiggers enters the scene. He disperses the wicked devils with an imperious wave of his hand, and distributes comfits, marchpanes and ginger biscuits to the rescued captives. There is a good deal of laughing and cheering. A final explosion startles everyone, and signals the end of the entertainment. As the crowd begins to drift away, each happy, animated face that passes Hameel is like a reproach. He feels as if everyone must see how he is marked out, as if he bore a Jew's cap, or a heretic's cross, or the red, burning sores of Saint Anthony's Fire.

He walks the streets around the cathedral in great agitation for a long time. The smell of gunpowder lingers in the windless air. At last, he directs his steps towards the Convent of Saint Agnes.

*

The parlour walls seem to close in on Aleyt, as if the room tightened around her, minute by minute. An hour must have passed since Hameel's departure, and this confinement has become unendurable. She can't just wait for his report. She must act herself. She wants to rush to the town gaol and start tearing at its stone walls with her hands. Useless madness. What *can* she do? Who can she turn to? Her gloomy father would be outraged by what has happened, but when his tirade had burnt out he would have little idea of what to do. Any friends of influence that he once had are dead or in their dotage. She could go to Frida of course, where she would be sure of sympathy and good sense. But she wants more than solace, she wants some definite action. If only Goessens were not in Reims! Well - she must mobilise Jerome's friends in the town, and get them to protest against her husband's treatment.

The enterprise is daunting though. She has always been a quiet, private person. She goes through in her head various names that Jerome has mentioned to her, his fellow members of the Holy Company. She knows some of them, but she can't face knocking on doors and speaking to servants. Her thoughts keep returning to Diederik, the bell master. He's one of Jerome's oldest friends, and he's dined at their house frequently with his amiable wife, Birgit. Yes, she can bring herself to speak to him.

She pulls a light cloak around her shoulders and sets off for the bell foundry, telling Mary to send Hameel after her if he comes back before the next bells.

*

When one of the foundry men shows her to Diederik's workshop, he looks up in great surprise from a table covered with drawings.

"Aleyt!"

He stands and smiles, and prepares to make a courteous bow to her, but then he sees her drawn face and red eyes.

"What has happened?"

"No one has told you?"

"I've been here in my workshop since dawn. What is it? Has Jerome had an accident?"

"Oh, Diederik – he's been seized by the Inquisitor and cast into prison!"

Diederik stares at her in bewilderment.

"What? Why?"

"Hameel says he's been accused of heresy."

"Hameel?"

"The Abbess told Hameel."

Diederik takes a deep breath, and then frowns.

"Bad news from a bad source! But what caused this? Did Jerome say something to upset the Inquisitor?"

"I don't know what caused it. What can I do, Diederik? I'm frightened for Jerome."

"Sit down, Aleyt. Here's a chair for you. Let's think this through."

Aleyt sits down reluctantly. She feels held back, somehow, as if time were racing along at twice its usual pace. But of course they can't do anything without a plan. Diederik remains standing, but he looks calm now, after the first shock, and she feels she has made a good decision in coming here.

"Well," he says after a few moments. "Jacomo is a law unto himself here. He answers to no-one in Den Bosch."

He gestures to the plans on his table.

"He's even got *me* working for him, curse his hide! Working on evil contrivances when I should be making bells for churches. So far he has nothing from my hands, bar one small device, but I can't impede him forever."

He shrugs his shoulders, as if to rid himself of a burden.

"But you can still bring influence to bear on him, Aleyt. You must speak to the Burgemeester, to the Bishop, and perhaps also to Lord Dreyer de Middelrode."

He sees her look and immediately divines her anxiety.

"But of course, you'll want support, Aleyt. Do you want me to accompany you?"

She stands and takes his hands in hers.

"Thank you, Diederik. Thank you!"

"Well, let's begin this task at once."

He puts on his cloak, throws some swift instructions to his assistant in the yard outside the workshop, and then they make their way through the streets towards the centre of the town.

"We'll start with Bishop Andreas at the cathedral, I suggest," Diederik says. "He's a great admirer of Jerome's work – and of course Jerome is doing something for the cathedral now, isn't he? A painting for the nave?"

"He is. A triptych."

"Well, Andreas will want to know all about this turn of events, if he hasn't already heard."

*

The Bishop receives them in his rooms behind the chapter house. His study, which is quite small, is almost completely lined with books – more books than Aleyt has ever seen before in one place. In a corner, a small green parrot is preening its feathers in a cage. The Bishop listens to their story, toying with a lock of his long, curly grey hair, and shakes his head sadly. The parrot clucks softly behind him as he speaks.

"This is very difficult, I'm afraid. I'll speak with Brother Jacomo, and ask him about his reasons for this action. It seems absurd that a pious man such as Jerome should be in this kind of trouble. In fact, it seems outrageous. I had no wind of this at all. But I might have foreseen something like this would come up, with such a man as Jacomo. He doesn't need to consult me, you see. He's a free agent. As a Papal Inquisitor, he operates on a direct *mandatum* from Rome, and can call on the civil authorities anywhere in Brabant to assist him, without reference to the bishop of the diocese where he is operating."

"Then how do we put a stop to this quickly, Andreas?" Diederik says. "We can't apply to Rome – it would take weeks to get a message there and receive a response."

"Well, there *is* an intermediate authority between Jacomo and Rome. The Inquisition in Brabant is under the direction of Abbot Geoffrey at the Abbey of Saint Anthony outside Eindhoven."

"Eindhoven... that's quite close. A day's ride in each direction," Diederik says. "Can you send a message, Andreas?"

The Bishop looks anguished.

"I know Abbot Geoffrey of old, and I know what he will make of any direct appeal from me. He'll simply say that I'm attempting to interfere in the work of the Inquisition, and that it's no business of mine. He'll say that it's the Inquisitor's job to establish guilt or innocence, and that if we have some compelling evidence of Jerome's innocence, we should present it directly to Brother Jacomo."

"Evidence!" Diederik says contemptuously. "Why, the man's innocence speaks from his very soul. The Master Painter of Den Bosch, a heretic! It's madness!"

The Bishop nods.

"From all that I know of Jerome – although I don't know him as you do, Diederik, or of course, as you know him Mistress Aleyt – I must agree."

He raises a hand to quell further talk, and drums his fingers on his desk for a few moments, looking thoughtful.

"Although Abbot Geoffrey would give short shrift to a direct appeal from me, I do have a suggestion. If you were able quickly to gather some influential names on a petition – and of course I would add my own name to such a document – then perhaps he would take more notice. Within the Church, he is on secure ground. But if the civil authorities, and the nobility, showed signs of unhappiness with this proceeding, he might take more notice."

"That sounds like good advice, Andreas," Diederik says. "We'll go straight to Theofilus Piek now. If both you and he will sign a document, that will carry weight. And I can ride out to seek the support of Lord Dreyer too. Do you agree, Aleyt?"

"Of course. Thank you, Bishop Andreas."

*

After taking leave of the Bishop, they walk quickly to the Stadhuis. The glances that come their way in the streets feel to Aleyt like so many insect stings. The whole town must surely know of what has happened, and behind a hundred doors they would be talking of her husband, and the Inquisition, and heresy. She avoids meeting anyone's eyes, in case it might be a neighbour or acquaintance.

Gaining access to the Burgemeester is not as straightforward as speaking to the Bishop. Theofilus Piek has built up ramparts of petty functionaries to stand between himself and the troublesome citizens of Den Bosch, and Diederik and Aleyt have to lay siege to those ramparts for the time deemed appropriate. Aleyt is reassured by Diederik that his membership of the Holy Company will eventually effect a breach in the wall, and, after a period of frustration, his confidence is vindicated. They are finally admitted to the inner sanctum of the council chamber, which the Burgemeester, liking its stately proportions, uses as his everyday office.

Theofilus Piek listens to them, his thin, sharp face betraying no emotion. When he has heard all, he drums his fingers on the table in front of him for a few moments, as Bishop Andreas had done.

"Hmm. Well, I had already been informed of this matter by the sergeant of the tipstaffs, who reports to me on any unusual arrests made in Den Bosch. He doesn't bother me with news of drunkards and so forth, but obviously the arrest of such an eminent citizen as your husband had struck him as notable."

"But surely his men couldn't have made such an arrest in the first place without reference to you?" Diederik puts in.

Theofilus Piek shakes his head.

"You don't understand the power of the Inquisition, Diederik. My men have standing orders to act on the instructions of the Inquisitor. I can't countermand him without some exceptional reason. I certainly can't order the release of a prisoner of the Inquisition, even if he *is* held in our town gaol. I have to assume that Brother Jacomo must have his reasons for the arrest, however strange it looks to us."

"Who is the ultimate authority here in Den Bosch?" Diederik says crossly. "Is it you, our elected representative, or a Spaniard Dominican monk who arrived a matter of weeks ago and is, for all we know, a madman?"

Theofilus Piek sighs, and rubs his chin.

"You ask the wrong question, Diederik. It isn't a matter of individuals, it's a matter of Church and civil authority. Brother Jacomo is licensed by the Pope. The Burgemeester of Den Bosch is not going to defy the Pope."

There is a heavy silence. Aleyt looks helplessly at the wall of the council chamber behind the Burgemeester. Stern portraits of his predecessors glower down from their gilt frames, unhelpful. Dead.

Diederik breaks the spell.

"Bishop Andreas has suggested a petition, to be taken to Abbot Geoffrey in Eindhoven, who stands in authority over Brother Jacomo. Will you sign it?"

"How will this petition be worded?"

"I'll draw it up this very day. I'll say that the undersigned – all the members of the Holy Company that I can get hold of – deplore the arrest of an innocent man on an absurd charge of heresy, and demand his immediate release."

Theofilus Piek looks narrowly at Aleyt, and clears his throat.

"And – forgive me – Mistress Aleyt... why do *you* suppose the Inquisitor has arrested your husband?"

She twists her wedding ring on her finger nervously, but meets his eye.

"The only thing... the only thing I can think is that Jerome is critical of... he hates the hypocrisy of... of some of the monks and nuns and priests of Den Bosch. He might have been outspoken, in talking with the Inquisitor."

Theofilus Piek nods.

"I see. That doesn't surprise me. The Abbess Dominica, in fact, has mentioned something of the sort to me in the past. And Brother Jacomo might have... what, taken offence at this, and over-reacted?"

Aleyt can only shake her head miserably.

"It's possible."

Diederik cuts in impatiently.

"It can be nothing more than that. How could Jerome be a heretic? A member of a heretical sect, even, according to what we've been told."

Theofilus Piek simply nods, his expression revealing nothing.

"Well, draw up your petition Diederik."

"And you will sign?"

"Come back here with it, when you have gathered your other signatures, and we'll talk again. I'm sympathetic, of course, but I must tread with discretion, and not let personal feelings enter into the matter."

CHAPTER TWENTY SEVEN

"Seventy take away fifty five, then carry ... over... column one...."

She mutters to herself. The quill scratches at the parchment and the figures dance and dodge as if mocking her efforts. She stops to rub her eyes. This business over her accounts is spoiling all her enjoyment of Easter Week. Even at today's feast she felt she was chewing on bones and ashes. Jacomo's pale secretary Brother Bartelme has a quiet and self-effacing demeanour, but he's the very devil of a stickler for detail. He's gone into her records like a ferret into a rabbit warren, and there are corpses everywhere. Now she's trying to work out some notion of the potential Saint Alonsus income – a private calculation obviously, not to be shared with Brother Bartelme. Saint Alonsus, aptly enough, will have to foot the extra tax bill for Rome.

Her thoughts wander to other matters of money. One good thing is that she's covered her back on the matter of usury. The old fool Steenman can only blabber now to the worms. The other debtor she feared Jacomo might hear of has been dealt with too, the quack doctor, Stemerdink. He'd always resented the way she got hold of his orchard when he put it up as security for his debt. The interest she charged galloped away from him like a loosed horse. More fool him for gambling instead of paying it off. Anyway, she's returned the land to him at a bargain price on an understanding of silence, in case Jacomo comes his way. Just to be doubly sure, she had Wiggers call on him soon afterwards, to enquire how he would doctor his own legs, if they happened to get broken.

At least that damned painter is in trouble now. There's some considerable satisfaction in that.

Sister Theresa knocks on the door and calls through it.

"Hameel to see you, Abbess."

"Let him in!"

She turns over the sheet of figures and puts aside the quill.

As Hameel enters, she pushes back her chair and opens one of her hidden drawers.

"Excellent timing, my dear Hameel. A moment to reward the morning's labours with a little libation!"

She extends a hand to be kissed, and he comes forward and puts it to his lips. But he appears agitated and distracted, and doesn't speak. She extracts her stone bottle and two cups from the drawer. Hameel raises a palm.

"I won't…"

She raises an eyebrow, to let him know that he will. She pours two brandies, gives him his cup, and holds out her own to clink with his. He touches his cup to hers half-heartedly. What's the matter with the man? He should be cock-a-hoop.

"To a fortunate future!" she says firmly, and takes a draught of the brandy. It's very good brandy, from Cognac in France. She hopes Hameel is appreciative of its quality. He appears to be empty-handed, and she wonders why he's come. Never mind, he's always a pleasant diversion. There are no handsome men in a convent, which is one good reason why being out and about in Den Bosch is more congenial to her.

"Have you brought no more plans or sketches to show me?" she enquires, waving him to sit down.

Hameel sits, and takes a swallow of his brandy

"I came on ... the other matter."

The Abbess feels an irrepressible grin spreading across her features.

"Ah...yes.   I gather that the great Master Jerome finds himself in prison!"

This news came her way from Hugo van Dorff, who saw Jerome being led across the market square by tipstaffs. She wishes she'd been there herself.

Hameel takes another drink from his cup for courage, and tries to put some vigour into the words he has come to say.

"I can play no further part in this plot against him. He's an innocent man, a lifelong friend..."

The Abbess has heard enough.   She cuts him off briskly.

"And the only obstacle in the road of your passion for Aleyt. What's come over you? No thrust in your loins any more? I thought you were made of sterner stuff."

Sitting down is not right for what he's trying to do. He stands, to make himself feel taller, stronger, more determined. But the Abbess stands up too, and before he can assert himself she has moved close to him. Her arm goes to his waist, almost encircling it. Her perfume envelops him. He feels very uncomfortable.

"Hameel..."

Her voice is soft, wheedling,

"My dear Hameel... remember why you got into this. Remember that Aleyt could be yours – *will* be yours – all yours – very soon."

Her hip bumps gently against his own.

"As long as you don't spoil everything now."

Hameel shakes his head.

"She's distraught. I can't bear to see her like this."

"A temporary unpleasantness. Afterwards though...

268

who else but you should she turn to, once Jerome is gone? The father of her child. The first of many, I'm sure. A lovely family, Hameel. The wife and family of the finest artist in Den Bosch."

She runs her hand from his waist up to his shoulder and exerts a gentle downward pressure.

"Come now, sit down again and have another little drink, and let's forget this nonsense. It's all in Jacomo's hands now. You need do nothing more than stay in the background, keeping quiet."

Hameel sits again, and the Abbess pours more brandy into his cup. He drinks it down in a single fiery gulp. His throat and chest burn like a little internal Hell.

The Abbess watches him narrowly, still standing.

Hell. That is what he must fear, not earthly consequences. He lifts his head and regards her defiantly.

"I'm going to see Jacomo and withdraw my remarks."

The Abbess sits down again opposite him, regarding him in silence for a moment. This ugly flower must be nipped in the bud

"Withdraw?" she says with a sad shake of the head. "Hameel – you poor fool – do you think it's as simple as that? You'll go along to Jacomo and say *Oh, I'm terribly sorry, but I made a mistake about Jerome being a heretic.* And what do you suppose Jacomo will say to that? *Oh, that's all right my dear Hameel. I'm sure it was a mere slip of the tongue.* Do you think you can deliberately mislead a Papal Inquisitor without consequences? Imagine his reaction. What a temper he has! You'll achieve your heart's desire of a change of places with the Master Painter then, oh yes! Indeed, you'll find yourself in his place very swiftly. In a dungeon. The chains will come off Jerome's legs and onto yours. Away Jerome will run to his darling Aleyt, and you... well who would wish to be left in a dungeon with an angry Inquisitor? Jacomo is certain to think you have something to hide, once you've admitted lying to him. That's the way his mind works. Naturally suspicious."

Her words wrap him in a cold fog of fear. But... Hell... He tries to summon a bold tone of voice once more.

"I'll say I was drunk."

The Abbess waves this away like a bothersome fly.

"Feeble! He'll know perfectly well you weren't drunk. If you'd been drunk he wouldn't have taken such note of your remarks. He'll be furious that he's been led a dance. He has the ironworkers making all kinds of horrible new things - instruments of torture. You'll suffer as no-one has suffered before."

Hameel falls silent, eyes turned downwards. He looks terrified. Really, if she were a weaker person herself, she might even have sympathised with him. She pours him another full cup of brandy. Cognac is not cheaply come by, but the occasion warrants it. He pours it down his throat in three quick gulps, and then speaks again, less firmly, as if he were already broken on a wheel.

"I can't go forward with this lie. Whatever the consequences for me."

Well, It seems that even the terror of what Jacomo might do to him is not enough. The time has come at last to play her Queen.

"That's your decision?"

"Yes."

She puts her cup on the table between them with both hands, and then removes her hands from it. Hameel's eyes rest on it. Let him contemplate what that meant, the removal of her protecting hands.

"There would be consequences of that decision for others then, Hameel. I'm afraid the fact of your adultery with Aleyt would have to come out. Mary the maidservant has attested to it."

Hameel's eyes lift in surprise to her face. She maintains a blank look of neutrality, as if she were

270

powerless in the matter.

"*Attested?* What do you mean?"

"I have her mark on a document to that effect. I will have to take the document to the Church authorities – to the secretary of Bishop Andreas. I sin myself in concealing it. Before Jacomo gets hold of you, both you and Aleyt will be punished as adulterers, publicly, in the square of Den Bosch. I needn't remind you of the nature of such punishment. A very unpleasant ordeal. And afterwards – even if Jacomo eventually lets you off his hook – think of your situation then. Your prospects with Aleyt will be gone forever. You'll certainly have to leave Den Bosch after such a humiliation, and try to start again somewhere else. Perhaps physically crippled. Without your workshop, and with your disgraced reputation clanging like a leper's bell around your neck. And as for Aleyt... obviously Jerome will disown the child. You'll ruin Aleyt's life as certainly as your own."

Hameel stands up abruptly, and the room spins giddily. He puts a hand out to the table until he feels steady. His disgust with Mary and the Abbess are nothing to the hatred he feels for himself. Well – let him suffer the consequences! Let the sinning Hameel be punished as he deserves! He sets off towards the door, but it seems to recede as he approaches, and when he reaches it his resolve is already weakened. On the other side of the door is unspeakable pain, torture in a dungeon, and the end of all his hopes with Aleyt. His hand rests on the handle for a long time, but he has no will left to turn it.

The Abbess observes him closely. She has no more words of persuasion to employ. He is caught on the horns of his dilemma now, and must fall to one side or the other.

He turns, and walks to the window. White blossom is budding on the apple trees; a blackbird – two, three blackbirds – fly up from a branch into the sky; sunlight bathes all in glory. Would the memory of such innocent

271

beauty torment him when he burned eternally in the hereafter? He moves back towards the door, but this time more slowly. He doesn't even reach it. He stands still at last: trapped, irresolute, terrified.

The Abbess has thought of a little observation. Perhaps it will help him to make the right choice.

"Think of it like this, Hameel: your situation may feel complicated, but it's actually very simple. It's a matter of survival. It's you or him."

CHAPTER TWENTY EIGHT

This too is Hell. There are no devils, no fires, no torments. There is nothing here that Jerome could paint. It's Hell on earth: darkness, silence and bitter cold. It's as if he has been buried alive and forgotten about. He can hardly bring himself to believe that he's still in the centre of Den Bosch. Up above, life must carry on much as usual. He remembers the last he saw of the world of light and air. He was marched to the town's gaol, an ugly building crouching like a toad at the back of the Stadhuis. He'd barely been aware of it before, never speculated about what was inside those walls. The tipstaffs had pushed him along a cramped stone passageway with doorways on either side. A few of the doors were closed, but most were open, and he could see into the empty cells – miserable little kennels with tiny barred windows high out of reach. He'd expected to be shoved into one of these, but his captors chivvied him along to the end of the passageway. There, a heavy door that groaned in lamentation to receive him opened onto a winding stone stairway spiralling down into the earth, where the air grew dank and cold and the flickering rushlights burning in sconces seemed to fight for their lives against the moisture.

At the bottom of this stair was a door made of iron bars. Beyond was a windowless dungeon with a straw pallet in one corner and a wooden pail in another. It was much larger than the cells up above, but infinitely more oppressive. The tipstaffs had thrust him in here, locked the barred door and retreated upwards. A sorrowful groan and a thump as the upper door closed were the last noises that came down to his ears. After a little while, the rushlights in the sconces had guttered and died, and profound darkness embraced him.

At first he had strained his eyes to see any chink of light in the gloom, and strained his ears to hear any sound. But there was no glimmer of light, and no sound, not even the scratching of a rat. He thought that when the bells of the town rang out the hours, he would certainly hear them, but the hours came and went, as best he could judge, and no sound of bells penetrated the silence.

So he is left with his other three senses. By touch, he has made a circuit of his dungeon, feeling the rough-hewn stones slimy with damp, and the stone-flagged floor striking coldness up into his thinly shod feet. There is nothing to taste, since they have left him no food or water, but the thick air is both a smell and a taste at once, savouring of soil and decay. He wonders what other men have been incarcerated here, and what has become of them. It is a secular gaol, but of course the secular authorities are also the instruments of the Church. Jacomo no doubt would have free rein to use this place for his inquisitional activities. He recalls the recent witch-burning in the square. Quite probably that unfortunate half-wit had been held in this dungeon, and perhaps tortured here.

That thought sets his hands shaking. He clasps them together, intertwining his fingers to still them. Will Jacomo dare to torture him? Surely his status in the town, and the number and rank of his patrons will protect him? Nonetheless, he falls prey to hideous imaginings. What might Jacomo do to him? What instruments would he use? How fragile a thing he is:

what would he be, without his eyes, without his skilled fingers? What if Jacomo damaged him in some way? He would no longer be able to serve God with his special gifts. It would be an end of his work. *The Garden of Earthly Delights* would never take physical shape, for all that it is so vivid and bright in his mind, one among the many tributes to God that burn in his imagination.

He tortures himself most cruelly with these fears.

At intervals his fear turns into anger. He bangs his fists on the floor, and bellows like a bull. He is no longer a man, but a savage animal. If Jacomo were there with him in the darkness, unguarded, Jerome would pounce upon him like a lion, and tear him limb from limb, for daring to accuse him of ungodliness.

But these fits of anger soon consume themselves, and he falls to wondering how this appalling mistake has come about. He is as certain as ever that the Abbess has had some part in the affair – and yet Jacomo denied that it was she who had actually accused him. He racks his brains to think of who this lying, hitherto unsuspected enemy might be. To be sure, there might be those who envy him, in a general way, for his fair degree of wealth and reputation. Could his accuser lie within the Holy Company? But he is respected there, and well liked, as far as he can tell. Why else would he have been chosen as the Christ?

He thinks about everyone he knows, until the dark cell seems thronged with imagined faces and gestures, and his ears buzz with half-remembered snatches of conversation. He wearies himself engaging with this absent crowd, trying to discern any hint of hostile intent.

He gives it up. He will face Jacomo with the question again. He has a right to know his accuser, whatever the Inquisitor says. How dare Jacomo arrest him and throw him into this hole without revealing his source? He labours on a treadmill of imagined conversations with the Inquisitor, some calm and conciliatory, but others full of fury. Around and around he goes.

It must be night-time by now, surely? Hunger is a rumbling worm in his gut, and thirst a coating of dust in his mouth. What will Aleyt be doing now? Surely she must have gone to her father, or her cousins, and they will have started to seek his release. Hameel too. As soon as Hameel heard of this outrage, surely he would have spoken to other members of the Holy Company. What will his friend Diederik think? Does Theofilus Piek, the Burgemeester, know what has happened by now? Or Bishop Andreas? Surely, after all these dead hours, Jacomo must have had to confront a delegation of Jerome's friends and peers? Perhaps by now he has been persuaded of his error, and at any moment he will come to release him. Abject, apologetic, embarrassed. Yes, very soon the groaning door of this tomb will open, and a humbled and contrite Jacomo will usher him back to the world above.

For a while he strains his ears again, alert for the approaching sounds of his reprieve. But the night – if it *is* night in the world – wears on, and still there is no sound save that of his own breathing. The torment of thirst grows worse – how dare they deprive him even of such a basic need as water to drink! At last, lying despondent on the scratchy straw pallet, sleep comes to his relief.

Has he slept for minutes or hours? Now he is in a place without time. It's a foretaste of eternity.

"Help! Help me! God!"

His hopeless voice echoes in the stone stairway. His head throbs, and his hunger has changed from worm to claw, raking its nails inside his stomach. He has never experienced such hunger and thirst. Even in the hardest times of famine when he was a young man, he and his family had always had enough.

He stands gingerly, and takes a few faltering paces around his cell. However, he is light-headed, and fears falling over, so he gropes his way back to the pallet and lies down again. He drifts once more along the shore of sleep, and memories of happier times wash back and forth like the sea. He remembers his wedding day - the scent of the white roses that Aleyt carried into the cathedral; the words of the hymns flying up into the vaulted roof like birds; the sun on their faces as they emerged after the service, surrounded by beaming well-wishers. He wanders further back; back into the carefree days of his early youth, fishing along the river with Hameel's brother Pieter. The plash of the water as a trout surfaced. The deep green shade under the trees on the bank. Little Hameel was there too, carrying the basket for the catch...

He slides into the river, and lies there, inert, nothing but a stone with the water flowing over him.

There is a heavy groan. From his deep watery place he comes up towards the surface. Footsteps, several sets of footsteps, are descending to meet him.

He opens his eyes to see a fitful flickering light growing in strength, and the long shadows of those approaching are cast on the rough curving walls of the stairwell; grotesque and elongated devil-shadows, bobbing in an unholy dance.

When the first two men come into view, their faces are grim in the light of the torches they carry, and they don't look towards him. He recognises the two tipstaffs who brought him here. They are closely followed by a squat heavily-muscled man he's never seen before, stripped to the waist and carrying over his shoulder an apparently weighty sack. The sack clanks and clinks with some metallic contents. Next comes a monk, also unknown to Jerome. His hood is up. A black cloak whisks aside to show a glimpse of a white habit beneath. A Dominican, then. A quill and ink bottle dangle from the cord at his waist, and he carries a roll of parchment, and, awkwardly, a small wooden stool. Bringing up the rear of the little procession is Jacomo, his black cowl thrown back for once, revealing his lean tonsured head. His torch reveals something Jerome hasn't noticed before - an irregular dark line that runs from behind one of his ears down the side of his neck towards his shoulder. It could only be a knife wound, and one that had been unattended to, to leave such an ugly raised welt. The unexpected sight of this scar raises goose-pimples in his own flesh.

Jerome stands up, his limbs stiff and awkward, as one of the tipstaffs unlocks the barred door to his cell. The man is young, his face dotted with spots, and he fumbles with the keys. He's nervous, Jerome suddenly realises. Why is the young man nervous?

He gathers his thoughts. He must be assertive and confident. He has been unjustly subjected to an outrage, and God and justice are on his side. He speaks as the men file into the cell, his voice a stranger's croak after the long hours without water.

"Well – have you understood your mistake?"

The tipstaffs pay no attention, and busy themselves with setting everyone's torches securely in the sconces in the walls. Jacomo looks at him without responding. When the tipstaffs have dealt with the torches they turn to him for instructions and he gives a slight nod. They come forward and seize Jerome by the arms.

Fear sweeps through him like a cold wind. The muscles of his bladder and bowels go slack, but his body is dry and empty. The muscular man puts down his sack and stands gazing at him without expression. The monk with the quill settles himself on his stool in a corner just inside the barred door.

"I must apologise," Jacomo says with a slight thin-lipped smile, "for the inadequate space and means which I have at my disposal to conduct your interrogation. With God's will, Den Bosch will soon have a more fitting dungeon for the investigation of heresy and witchcraft, with the necessary devices as permanent fixtures. But for now, we must do the best we can with what we have."

He nods this time at the bare-chested man, who

bends to the sack and draws out a rattling metallic contrivance that glints in the torchlight. He lays it on the floor beside him. Jerome can't make out what it is.

"Before we go any further," Jacomo says, "I wish to let you know that you can make everything very simple and easy. You can make a deposition, which Brother Bartelme here will write down, laying out the details of your heresy, and the times and places when your heretical sect met for its obscene activities. You will make your signature on the document, and that will be the end of this part of our proceedings. We need only be here for a matter of minutes. Afterwards, I will order food and drink to be sent down to you, and you can then receive visits from those you wish to see – your wife, perhaps."

In the light-headedness of his hunger and thirst, he has a momentary sense that this is all an evil dream. He can't believe in these men and their intentions. He seems to float away somewhere.

"Well?"

Jacomo's voice, impatient, brings him back.

"And after that?" he replies.

"You will be able to make your peace with God."

"Who is my accuser?"

"I have already told you that you have no right to that information."

"It's a lie, and it can only have come from someone who wishes me harm."

"On the contrary, this information has come forward for the good of your eternal soul. Haven't I seen for myself the damnable evidence of your drawings? I have no reason to doubt the motives of my informant. Your own views, expressed freely to me in your studio, point me the way to your heresy. You believe that you are inspired directly by God, without need of the Church as intermediary. You make images against the Church, seeking to degrade it in the eyes of the common people. You believe that you yourself are pure, as Adam was in the Garden of Eden, and that because God lives within you, you can do no sin. This is the foul and misguided pretext for your sins of the flesh, which are in reality inspired by the promptings of the Devil."

"What are these sins of the flesh? My conscience is clear."

"Then we must stir up that conscience, which is corrupted and atrophied by disuse. Come now, Master Jerome, make a clean breast of these matters now, and avoid the suffering that is the lot of the hardened liar."

"But it's you who expects me to make up lies. If I am to confess to heretical activities that have never happened, I must lie to invent them."

Jacomo regards him for a long moment. Then he shrugs his shoulders slightly and speaks to the squat man beside him.

"Put him in the irons."

Jerome struggles in a sudden panic, but one of the tipstaffs, the older one, curses him and bats his head so hard that his ears ring. As he stands dazed, the squat man approaches with open iron cuffs linked with a short metal bar and pulls his hands into them. Clasps snap closed, and then he steps back to his original place.

"Brother Bartelme," Jacomo says, still with his eyes fixed on Jerome. "Begin your account of the proceedings with a note that the accused was offered the opportunity of a full confession without duress, and that he resisted his interrogators with physical force."

He turns again to the tipstaffs.

"Lay him on the floor, on his back, and restrain him. Ignatius, come forward."

Jerome struggles briefly again, but his legs are kicked from under him and he's lowered down. The older tipstaff holds his shoulders down. The younger one sits on his legs, facing away from him. He has never felt so helpless before in his life. The bare-chested man looms over him now. He has dark features, like Jacomo's. Another Spaniard?

"This is Ignatius," Jacomo says. He is out of the line of Jerome's sight now, just a disembodied voice behind him. "Think of him as an instrument of God's will, not as a person. He has no fear, no passion, no mercy. Mercy is for God himself, not for us, his instruments. Mercy will be shown to you in the next life, if you repent, but not in this. Do you persist in denying that you are a heretic?"

Blotting out his terror comes furious indignation.

"You fool! Can't you see that this is madness?"

"It is you who is mad, Master Jerome, if you prefer torture to a free confession. The bell-master has not yet produced the instruments I have commissioned, but we have simpler methods at our disposal. Ignatius, begin as we have discussed."

Jerome feels his foot seized and rough hands yank off the thin-soled slipper he has been wearing since he was taken from his studio. The young man sitting on his legs shifts his position. His spotty face is now turned towards Jerome, but his eyes are closed. *He doesn't want to watch.* The other tipstaff pushes down harder on his shoulders. He hears a clinking sound as Ignatius gropes once more in his sack. Then he feels the touch of cold metal against one of his toes. What is happening?

The answer comes with sickening suddenness. His foot is gripped at the ankle by one powerful hand, and simultaneously the touch of metal turns into a searing, wrenching pain.

The dungeon rings with his scream.

Then he is sobbing and gasping out, over and over.

"Jesus! Jesus! Jesus!"

He has never known such agony, and still he doesn't know what has been done to him. Have they cut off his toe?

"Show him," orders the disembodied voice of Jacomo from behind him.

Through his streaming tears Jerome sees something coming close in front of his face. It looks like a pair of

281

tongs, such as might be used to move coals on a fire, but smaller. Gripped in the tongs is a small fragment of bloodied material. At the same moment as he understands what it is, the torment in his foot seems to localise itself more precisely, and his empty stomach heaves as if it tried to expel the pain.

Jacomo moves into the line of his vision, above him.

"We could rip out by its roots every toenail and fingernail that you possess, one by one, Master Painter. But that would be mere play beside what I have in mind. Now you know what pain we can inflict here, and you understand that I am in earnest. We are soldiers of God and we do not flinch in God's work."

Jerome is sobbing helplessly now. Words blubber out of his lips without volition.

"Please... please.. please..."

"The next thing, Ignatius."

Now Jerome feels hands at the fastening of his breeches. The tipstaff turns away again, and shifts his weight onto his shins. Ignatius hauls the breeches down his shanks to his knees. Jerome's private parts are bared. Jacomo doesn't shift his gaze from Jerome's eyes. He speaks softly now. Kindly, you might think.

"Before we continue, let me explain. I have had to make you understand that we do not go lightly, but the use of torture to get to the truth is not a matter of careless brutality. It is a matter of understanding the nature of the sin, and tailoring the treatment accordingly. In your case, it is the sin of lust that has been uppermost in your thoughts and deeds. Your lascivious drawings recall and embellish the acts committed by you and your fellow heretics in your misguided and arrogant denial of implication in Original Sin."

"This is madness!"

"Show him the blade, Ignatius."

The man holds in front of his streaming eyes a small curved knife. Its blade catches the torchlight.

"Touch it to his sinful flesh."

Jerome feels the tip of the knife rest against the base of his member. It is just like the cold touch of the tongs against his toe.

"*No!*"

He tries to squirm away from the knife, but Ignatius presses the flat of the blade slightly against him and he desists at once.

"Stay very still if you wish to avoid injury," Jacomo says, "and listen carefully. Let us suppose that you persist in pleading your innocence. I am fully confident that you are not innocent, and so I will instruct Ignatius to remove your manhood, an entirely apt punishment for your acts. You will then make a full confession, or, if you are exceptionally idiotic, Master Jerome, we will have to inflict further damage on your sinful flesh. Eventually, make no doubt of it, you *will* make your confession. Now, if I have been mistaken, and you are somehow found innocent and exonerated by a tribunal, how will that exoneration benefit you? The damage will have been done, and cannot be undone."

"If you mutilate me in this wrongful way, you will be punished both on earth and in Hell!"

"That is a risk I will take. I know God's will. Now, confess at once, or bear the consequence of your lying denial."

CHAPTER TWENTY NINE

In the pale creeping light the workshop resonates with the chipping sound of his hammer and chisel as he works at Lust. He has barely slept. The bells of Lauds were welcome to his ears, a call to work. He will labour all day to keep his hands occupied and his mind empty. When it grows dark, he will go out and drink himself senseless. It is all he can think of doing.

There's a knock at his door, and Aleyt springs into his thoughts. She will wonder why he never returned yesterday. He looks around with mingled hope and apprehension. But it's Mary who lets herself in without waiting for him to answer. She wears a cloak against the cold of the early morning.

He lays down his hammer and chisel but doesn't stand up from his bench. He feels suddenly weary; too weary to stand and greet his visitor.

Mary approaches him. Her eyes take in the gargoyle for a moment, and then rest on him.

"Did you speak to that black devil as the Mistress asked?"

He shakes his head.

"He was away somewhere."

"You spoke to someone else, then."

"What?"

"The Abbess Dominica."

He stares at her. Her face gives nothing away.

"How do you know?"

"I followed you."

"When?"

"From when you left the Mistress yesterday. You went to the convent."

"I was seeking him. I'll see him later. The Inquisitor."

"*Will* you? Why didn't you go to seek him yesterday?"

There is something new in the way Mary is looking at him and speaking to him. She is more serious than he's ever seen her.

"Why have you come?" he says.

"I overheard something."

"You listen at doors too much."

"I heard the black devil say something to the Master."

"What?"

"About him being *in* something – I don't know what it was. Something sinful. But the Master said it must be the Abbess that had said he was in this thing. And that Inquisitive said no, it wasn't the Abbess. It was someone who wanted to remain in the shadows. Those was his very words. *Remain in the shadows.*"

He tries to meet her eyes. He feels the skin prickling on his forehead.

"So?"

"So, I just wondered if you might have any idea of who this person in the shadows is. Because..."

"Because?" he says. His face feels on fire. Mary's eyes are fixed on him.

"Because I been turning it over and over in my head, and now I think it might be you."

He looks at his hands, white with stone dust.

"Why would I?" he mutters.

"So you can have my Mistress."

He has no reply to make. His hands are so white,

they don't seem to belong to him.

But Hameel's silence speaks clearly enough to Mary. No words could be more bitter, and her heart feels like a great heavy stone. She has agonised about her suspicion all day. When it first occurred to her, she was swept by revulsion back to a vivid moment in her childhood. She'd found a beautiful blue-winged bird lying on the grass. She thought it was asleep, and picked it up gently to cradle it.

Its underside was churning with maggots.

That was the very feeling that had engulfed her, thinking that Hameel could have lied about the Master. Now she can see the guilt written on his flushed downcast face, and the memory of their intimacies makes her skin crawl.

She must put all that aside. She must be strong now, and deal with the horribly changed Hameel she has uncovered. She takes a deep breath, and speaks firmly.

"You've got to stop this. The poor Master..."

Hameel puts up a hand. His eyes are still turned downwards, and he shakes his head.

"Don't speak of this! It burns me inside like the fires of Hell."

"You can stop it."

At last Hameel looks up at her. The flush on his face has turned to a pale, hunted look. His next words shake her.

"Well, Mary, I'm afraid your own betrayal has made that very hard."

"What do you mean?"

"I mean what you did for the Abbess."

Now it is she who avoids a meeting of eyes. She looks over towards the grimacing gargoyles of Gluttony and Avarice, who watch from the shadows, like knowing witnesses.

"I don't know what you're talking about."

"Oh, you do! Why did you do it, Mary? Tell me that. Do you love your mistress?"

She lifts her chin. She can speak clear truth of this, at least.

"Of course I do. She's everything to me."

"But you put your mark on a document that accuses her of adultery."

Mary feels that weeping is almost upon her. Her voice sinks to little more than a whisper.

"It was the Abbess. She threatened me."

"How?"

"She said she'd tell the black devil I was a witch."

Now the tears pour out. Hameel makes no move to comfort her. He believes her. It is exactly the way that the Abbess would work on an ignorant girl. Perhaps there had been inducements as well, but a threat like that would be a terror to Mary. As she stifles her sobs, he speaks in a flat tone of despair.

"Well, now you see why I can't speak. She would produce that document. She has us all caught in her snare now."

Mary turns and walks away towards the door.

"Mary!"

She doesn't stop. After all, what words do they have left for each other now? The door closes behind her.

CHAPTER THIRTY

Aleyt slips around the edges of the square, hooded, avoiding the stallholders who are already setting up for the day. The rising sun touches the roofs of the tallest houses with a pink glow, but the square is still dim and chilly. She turns the corner of the Stadhuis and looks apprehensively at the town gaol lurking behind it. The darkness of night clings oppressively about its walls. She has a basket of bread, fruit, and cold meats under her arm.

She knocks on the heavy wooden door with her knuckles, not caring for bruises. Answering echoes ring from the back wall of the Stadhuis itself. She glances over her shoulder and the dark eyes of its windows look down at her without pity.

At last there is a turning of keys and the door opens a crack. A bleary-eyed man with heavy stubble on his jaw looks at her warily.

"What?" he grunts.

"Can I see my husband, the painter Jerome?"

The man shakes his head.

"Of course not."

"Can you... can you at least tell me how he is?"

"I can't do anything. The Inquisitor has left strict instructions. No communication with the prisoner."

"But, surely, you could tell me how he fares?"

The man shakes his head again, and starts to close the door. She puts out a hand.

"Stop – please – will you at least tell him I came, and... and give him this basket of food?"

For the first time the man looks a little abashed.

"If I break my orders," he says quietly, "there's no knowing what'll become of me."

Then he closes the door, and Aleyt hears the locks being turned against her again. So she has to hurry back home with the basket still in her hand.

The day passes with infinite slowness. Mary expresses her sympathy in little acts of kindness, and makes soup for their midday meal, but she seems lost for any words of comfort. Indeed, she is unusually preoccupied and silent, and moves about the house with a rare lightness of tread, like a thief.

In the afternoon her cousin Frida comes for an hour with baby Laurens. For a few minutes in this beloved company the anxiety that presses down on her is relieved. Of course they talk of Jerome's arrest, and of what is being done, but when Frida gives her the baby to hold, the little physical burden lightens her heart beyond all measure. Its wandering eyes halt to study her face, and joy, purest joy, floods into her as she remembers the secret child in her own womb.

After Frida and Laurens have departed, she resumes pacing the parlour. Why hasn't Hameel returned with any news of his appeal? How is Diederik's quest progressing?

"Mary! Mary?"

She calls out from the top of the stairs, vaguely hoping that Mary might have seen or heard something, but there is no reply.

She goes down the stairs. Mary isn't in the dining hall, or the kitchen, or her bedroom. She goes out into the garden. A solitary robin hops on the grass, cocking its head for worms, and the privy door is wide open. She feels a new pang of unease. It's almost unheard of for Mary to disappear like this, without a word. She wants to go out herself – but where would she go? She climbs the stairs slowly to the parlour as if to a prison cell.

Just as darkness is beginning to fall, a knocking at the door brings her running downstairs again to answer the summons herself. It's Diederik. He gives her a tired smile.

"I'm here at last Aleyt. It's been a long day."

"Come in, Diederik, come in."

He steps into the hallway, closing the door behind him. He smells of sweat.

"I've brought the petition to show you. I knew you would be anxious to know how I got on."

She musters a smile for him, and nods. He unfurls the document in his hand and holds it open for her to read.

We the undersigned deplore the unwarranted imprisonment of Jerome van Aachen, known as Hieronymus Den Bosch, pre-eminent painter of this city. We demand that he be released at once and let to be free until any accusations against him of any kind are conducted fairly and openly. We are confident that the sin of heresy, under which it is rumoured he is detained, can in no wise be imputed to him, and ask no more than that he be given the citizen's right of Justice.

A long series of signatures begins below this statement. Diederik speaks as she runs her eye down it.

"I made sure to get the high and mighty Lord Dreyer de Middelrode's name first. I went out on horseback to his place. You wouldn't believe the shambles they live in. Grand house on the outside, but a pigsty within. Then Bishop Andreas of course, he had no hesitation in signing. I thought that once Piek saw those names he'd feel that he would look weak if he didn't fall into line. But it was no good. He kept me standing for half an hour while he went on about Rome and civil authority and precedents and who knows what all else, until I felt like kicking him. Then he droned on about never knowing what was going on under the surface, and the Abbess Dominica, and her views about Jerome. I wouldn't be surprised if she has some hold over Piek - after all, she has half of Den Bosch at her heel. In the end, I grabbed the quill out of the inkpot on his desk and thrust it at him, and he folded his arms. He's lost any respect I once had for him, and I told him so. Anyway, I got most of the other important members of the Holy Company to sign, and the petition is as good as we can make it. The roads are too dangerous at night, but tomorrow at first light I'll ride to Eindhoven with it, and if I can speak to this Abbot Geoffrey in person, so much the better. I'll make sure he knows what a man Jerome is, Jerome van Aachen of Den Bosch. A heretic indeed!"

"You've been wonderful, Diederik! I can't thank you enough. You look exhausted – can I get you a goblet of wine?"

He takes her hands in his, and the kind look he gives her gives her strength.

"I must get back to Birgit. She will have food waiting for me."

She opens the door for him.

"We'll beat this Jacomo back to Rome, you just see if we don't!" he says as he steps through. As he moves off, Mary appears in the gloaming, walking quickly towards the house. Aleyt stays where she is, holding the door open, to let Mary enter. She feels hurt.

"Mary – I wondered where you were!"

"We needed bread, Mistress," Mary replies. Her hands are empty. She has a distracted look.

Aleyt lets the ridiculous excuse pass. She has no appetite for a quarrel.

"Did you… did you hear anything new?"

"Nothing, Mistress. Shall I prepare some supper now?"

"Yes. Yes, please do that, Mary."

Mary disappears through the dining hall towards the

kitchen. Aleyt feels like a boat left to drift. She feels sure that Mary is hiding something from her. Pray God it's not bad news. She climbs the stairs towards the parlour, but stops at the door of Jerome's studio. She puts a hand on the handle, and before turning it to enter she indulges a fantasy that he will be standing there inside, at his easel.

She looks into the studio. It's almost dark now, and there are shadows in the corners of the large room where a person could hide; especially a child, hiding in a game. But the room is lifeless.

The Vespers bells of the monasteries and convents start to call the clergy to their prayers. In the houses and hovels of the town, the ordinary folk too – or some of them – will be kneeling for a few moments to thank God for whatever they have, and to ask for more. Usually Jerome is at her side at this time, and they pray together in the parlour. She enters the studio and closes the door softly behind her. She kneels, and tries to feel Jerome's presence there, in the place where he spends so many of his hours. She welcomes the penitential pain of the bare floorboards against her knees. She bows her head and says the Lord's Prayer and a Hail Mary.

It isn't enough. She feels as helpless and hopeless as before.

She thinks of what Mary has told her: about how she prays to God in private in her own words. She hasn't prayed this way herself . She doesn't know if it can really *be* prayer. Perhaps God only understands the words of the Bible, the sacred, special words that the Church always uses. But in this moment of loneliness and despair, she needs to speak more from her heart, whether He listens or not.

"Dear God," she whispers. She feels shy and a little ridiculous, but she carries on anyway. "I'm sorry to use such plain words as these, but I beg you to return my husband Jerome safely to me. You know all that I've done – all the sin that I'm guilty of – but I believe your mercy is infinite, and you will forgive me. I've been weak, but now I will be strong. I abjure Hameel forever. I abjure adultery. I will be the most faithful, loving wife to Jerome, as long as we both live. I will be the most loving mother to this child I carry. It will make my husband so joyful; it will make our lives complete. Surely it will be no sin if in the eyes of my husband and the world, this child is his? Let it be the new bond between us, unbreakable, a bond of eternal love, like that which binds us to you. Forgive this sinful woman. Amen."

*

In a dark corner of The Three Hogs, Hameel drinks rough brandy alone. When he first entered, the inn was filled with working men drinking beer at the end of their day – tanners and brewers, ostlers and bakers, market-stall holders and gongfermors. The stink of bodies and bad breath was like a wall to break through. But he managed to find a seat on his own. The old man with the yellow cross on his tunic, John, came and stood over him, talking, but thank God some of his cronies called him away. They all left, at least two brandies ago. It's quiet in here now.

For a long time, it seems to him, he has been staring at the surface of his table in the feeble light of the smoky tallow candles. He wants to drink himself out of all memory and meaning and into a mere void, but the table keeps turning into a dark painting, where he sees faces loom in and out of the wood and beer stains. The Abbess. The Inquisitor. Jerome. Aleyt. Mary. Why won't they leave him alone? They hound him. He pours himself more brandy from the jug, and spills half of it down his tunic.

"Master Hameel! What brings you here?"

It's that tailor. Johannes? Is that his name? What the devil does he want?

Johannes is smiling. Teeth everywhere. What the hell is he wearing? The colours of vomit. Carnival

Week. Of course.

Fuck off! Hameel thinks, but no words come out. Johannes slides onto the settle next to him.

"I came in here looking for that old villain, my grandfather, but I see that he must have spent all my money, and gone to bed."

Cloves and cinnamon on his breath, teeth bared.

"You look as if you need company, if I might say so. What's the matter? Worn out by Carnival?"

Why has this fucking gadfly landed on him? He drains his cup and tips the little earthenware jug over it. A final dribble of brandy slops out.

"Well, if you can't have some fun in Carnival, when can you, that's what I say!"

Hameel nods, as if agreeing, and tilts the last of the brandy into his mouth. A hand lands softly on his arm.

"Listen, Hameel. I've got some good wine at my house. Why don't we go there for a drink? The inn will be closing in a few minutes anyway. Look – there's almost no-one here but us."

"Need… to piss…" His tongue is thick in his mouth. He can barely speak.

"Me as well," Johannes says. "We'll go together, and then back for some of my wine, eh?"

The Three Hogs turns sideways as he staggers out of the back door to the reeking jakes. Fighting nausea he fumbles with his hose, and a great steaming stream of urine gushes into the trough. Beside him Johannes fumbles too at his crotch, but there is no sound of pissing.

In the alleyway outside the inn, he no longer knows where he is. It's as dark as Hell. An arm comes around his shoulders and steers him along. He bumps into a wall. He stumbles over some obstacle. There's a noise. Words. Something about Carnival. Something about saying what is in your heart. Something about taking courage. It makes no sense. He allows himself to be led along.

294

From somewhere comes another voice. No sense in it either.

"A choice morsel, Johannes!"

Then there's another face, thrust into his own. Flaming orange hair.

"Wiggers..." he grunts. Is it Wiggers? Then the face turns upside down and he is on the ground. It goes dark. Arms are lifting him up to his feet. His feet move forwards, but all by themselves. He has no control of them.

When he next understands anything, he's at a door. He's still on his feet. Still two men with him. The tailor. The orange haired man. One of them is pushing a key into the door's lock. The other one is pushing a finger hard up between his buttocks.

"Soon be snug inside a bed..."

He lashes out with an arm and dislodges the orange-flamed devil.

"Hameel..." Johannes says.

He must get out of all this. He backs away, and then turns. The street is dark, but there's a flickering torch far off. He runs unsteadily towards it. Behind him, voices again.

"Go after him..."

"Fuck him. He'll only bring trouble. Let him go."

*

"What shall I do?"

Mary says the words aloud to the empty kitchen. The pans hanging on their hooks clank faintly in a slight draft. The beeswax candle's flame hisses gently. The embers in the fireplace crackle like insects stirring. Nothing gives her an answer. It must be near midnight, and she should go to bed, but her head won't let her. She feels guilty and angry, remorseful and fearful, all mixed up together. She won't be able to sleep. She *must* do something to help the Mistress and the Master – but what? Who can advise her?

The statue of the Virgin comes into her mind's eye,

with its gentle downcast eyes and half smile. Yes, perhaps in the Lady Chapel at the cathedral, the Virgin will guide her. Perhaps in the quiet gloom of the Chapel her riotous thoughts will calm down, and the way forward will be made clear to her.

It takes an effort of will, nonetheless, to put on her cloak and go out of the door. She doesn't like venturing out into the streets after darkness has fallen. She's done it many a time – to go and pray, or to fulfil some baser desire – but she always feels nervous as she leaves the haven of the house. Darkness is the Devil's time, the time when he and his minions roam the earth in search of sinners' souls to be snatched. The Devil could set a wicked man in her way, lurking around any dark corner to slit her throat and send her unconfessed soul to Hell. She thinks of her Papal Indulgence, safely stowed at the bottom of her little clothes trunk. Would it be of any use there? Should she carry it around with her? How could she wield its power if she were being carried off on the back of a winged demon straight to the fiery pit? She hurries towards the cathedral like a rabbit bolts for its burrow, and when she reaches the entrance she has to stand for a moment to catch her breath again.

She pushes against the heavy door. Of course it's unlocked as always for the faithful. Inside, there is no-one, only a few candles flickering like brave little angels in the gloom. They give her comfort and courage. She genuflects and crosses herself as she passes the top of the central aisle leading to the altar, and steps gratefully into the Lady Chapel.

Kneeling in her usual pew, she says a series of Hail Marys. The familiar words bring calm at last to her troubled mind. Now she feels ready to speak in her own words to the face of the Virgin, the kind face that looks down at her with compassion.

"What should I do, to help the Master and Mistress? Please tell me, Mother of God."

The answer comes almost at once. It has been in her

heart all along, but she hasn't listened to it. It was too frightening to face. But now, in the calmness and silence of this place, the Virgin has shown her that she has no choice but to do what is right.

Suddenly the heavy entrance door of the cathedral creaks open and shuts again with a bang. But no footsteps proceed into the nave. Instead there is a kind of dragging sound, a shuffling, and a man's voice groaning.

Mary moves quickly and silently to the iron grille that separates the Lady Chapel from the nave. The imposing tomb of some long dead bishop provides her with cover, and she peeps out from behind it.

The man is on the floor near the entrance door. As she watches, he staggers to his feet and leans against a pillar for support. Surely, she knows that shape? He's drunk, and muttering to himself. Then the figure moves erratically down the aisle towards the altar, and as the light of a stand of candles falls on it, her hunch is confirmed. It's Hameel. So, he's been drowning his guilt in ale or brandy. But what is he doing here?

She waits until Hameel is near the altar, a long way off, and then slips out of the Lady Chapel towards the door. She has no wish to encounter Hameel now, drunk or sober. She pauses at the door, where she can vanish quickly into the night even if he sees her, and looks back. Hameel has got down on his knees in front of the altar. He raises both hands upwards to Heaven and cries out to the hard stones of God's house.

"Forgive me!"

The echoes of his words chase each other around the cathedral, as if all the dead bishops and deans and worthies cry out with him from their tombs.

Then Hameel's head slumps, and his body sinks to the floor, where he lies still.

Mary opens and closes the door gently, softening its creaking voice, and hurries away.

297

CHAPTER THIRTY ONE

I confess that I have sinned most grievously against God and His commandments, and that I have led others astray and encouraged and abetted them in their sins also. I have abjured and forsworn the laws of God and the authority of God's Church on Earth, and clung instead in my wicked error to the proscribed sect of the Brethren of the Free Spirit, also know as the Adamites. I have hardily and most blasphemously partaken in rites, rituals and ungodly doings, and pursued perversions of lust and lewd behaviour most insulting to God. I freely confess to these most heinous acts, and embrace all impositions of castigation and redemption that the Church shall see fit to administer for the saving of my eternal soul.

Jerome van Aachen, also known as the painter Hieronymus Den Bosch.

Jacomo peruses once again the painter's confession, as recorded by Brother Bartelme. His secretary's style is a little ornate and repetitive. He will draw up himself in plainer language the document of accusation that he will present to the tribunal, along with Brother Bartelme's record of their proceedings.

The confession was not, in the end, hard to secure. The painter, as he expected, quickly capitulated once he fully believed that he would suffer emasculation. He congratulates himself that he found such a simple yet fitting way to get to the truth. There is no doubt now in his mind of the painter's guilt. Hameel was clearly greatly troubled by betraying the secret of his friend and mentor – it is much to be admired that his conscience overcame his scruples. And there is abundant evidence of Jerome's wicked and perverse obsessions in the drawings and paintings. The tribunal's verdict will be a formality.

One thing remains to be further investigated. Jerome is not a solitary heretic. As Hameel suggested, he must be part of a ring of Adamites, practising their vile rituals under a cloak of secrecy. This must be matter for further enquiry tomorrow. He has found – through trial and error – that it is generally more effective to conduct interrogations at intervals. The recollection of the first round of pain - and fear of worse - preys on the mind of the sinner. The mere sight of the torturer returning is often enough to open a blurting tap of further confessions.

There is a knock at his door. Surely it must be nearly time for the bells for Compline? A late hour for visiting. Probably the overly conscientious Brother Bartelme has turned up something in the Abbess's accounts that he wants to go over with him now.

"Yes?" he calls, unable to keep a note of irritation from his voice.

It is indeed Brother Bartelme who pokes his head around the door, but his announcement is most unexpected.

"A woman has come to see you, Brother Jacomo. Come from the household of the Painter Jerome. She is most insistent."

From the household of the painter? Who could this be? His wife, come to plead with him? She will find short shrift here.

"Let her in then," he says grudgingly.

His mood is not improved by the sight of the stupid servant girl. She enters the room with every appearance of a mouse entering the lair of a cat.

Brother Bartelme leaves the door open, as is proper. Jacomo listens until his wooden sandals have clacked away along the stone corridor outside.

"I know you. What are you doing here?"

The girl is actually shaking! Well, let her shake, if she is going to waste his time.

"Please don't be angry," she mutters, with her head down.

"Why should I be angry?" he says, angrily. This girl has a singular ability to infuriate him. She is sent by God to try his patience. He takes a deep breath to master himself.

"Go on," he says.

"It's none of it my fault. Or perhaps some of it is. But I been praying to Our Blessed Lady for help. Oh Lord... I been praying, hours and hours..."

Jacomo takes another deep breath.

"What is your point, woman?"

"There you go again. Oh, let me get my wits about me..."

Jacomo takes a few paces back and forth while the foolish girl pulls out a rag and dabs her eyes. He has rarely seen such abject terror – except in the torture chamber of course, or at the stake, where it is understandable. When he judges that she has gathered her courage a little he speaks again, deliberately softening his voice.

"All right. All right. Let's go calmly. Is it about the Master Painter?"

She nods, with a look of relief. Now perhaps they might get somewhere.

"Yes. I heard, you see, when you was talking to him."

"In his studio? You were eavesdropping, were you? What did you hear?"

"I heard what you said about someone in the shadows."

"In the shadows? You mean his accuser?"

300

"Yes, and I know who he is, and he's lying."

He stares at her. A nasty feeling, like a hunger pang, strikes at his gut.

"Lying?"

"God save me! Yes. It's Hameel, and he's lying to you."

He can feel blood draining away from his face. He must go carefully now. He observes her closely. Her eyes are wide, and red from crying. She still shakes slightly, as if from cold. Her hands wring together as if fighting each other. But in spite of her obvious terror, she meets his gaze now without flinching.

Of one thing he is completely certain – *she* isn't lying. But her revelation makes no sense. She must be labouring under some honest mistake.

"*Why* would Hameel lie? He's the friend of Jerome, his disciple one might almost say. It's a credit to his conscience that he has revealed this dreadful secret in spite of that. Now I've had it from Jerome himself that he's a heretic. He's confessed everything."

A look of anguish comes into the girl's face.

"You tortured him?"

He inclines his head slightly.

"Oh, the poor Master! He's not done anything wrong. Hameel made it all up."

"Why would he do that? You infuriating girl! *Why*?"

"Because he wants my Mistress, the Master's wife. Aleyt. He wants Jerome out of the way."

Jesus Christ! He sits down heavily. It is so unforeseen, so utterly unexpected... and yet it is immediately credible. He feels the most horrible misgiving, cold and heavy inside him. Has he arrested and tortured an innocent man on the testimony of a liar? And not just any man, but one of the most eminent painters of the age, a man with many friends in high places?

My God - what have I done?

He keeps his face impassive with a huge effort.

"Is this true?" he says.

Mary nods.

"Ask Abbess Dominica."

Here is another thunderbolt from nowhere.

"The Abbess?" he says, unable to keep astonishment entirely out of his voice. "What has the Abbess got to do with it?"

"She knew what was going on between Hameel and my Mistress. Then she got me to put my mark on a document."

"What sort of a document?"

"To say that Hameel and my Mistress were adulterers."

He's poleaxed again. Why in the name of God and all the saints would the Abbess want such a document?

"Why did she not simply report this immediately to the Church authorities? Adulterers must be punished, as an example to all who are tempted by lust."

"You'd have to ask her."

"I *will* ask her. I'll demand that she hands over this document. What is your name again?"

"Mary."

"You're not lying, Mary? Because I don't abide lying. Lying is a mark of the Devil at work. If I *did* find out you were lying, you would suffer the consequence."

He puts as much threat into his tone as he can muster, but he knows he's clutching at a straw. Sure enough, the girl crosses herself and looks him straight in the eye.

"It's all true, as God may save me! If the Abbess denies it, have her chest in her room searched. I seen her put the document in her chest."

What he needs now is time, to think this through.

"Go now," he says. "I'll look further into this. And - upon your life - speak to no-one else about it! Go, and pray!"

She scuttles towards the open door, once more like a terrified mouse. She pauses a moment there, half turns, and then changes her mind and is gone. He hears her feet hurrying away along the corridor.

He closes the door and paces his room for a while. Then the bells for Compline sound, and he kneels to pray. He needs God's help now. The long night stretches ahead of him. God will not want His Inquisition, *his* Inquisition, to founder on this rock. God means him to be a general in the war with Satan. With prayer and meditation a right way forward must be found.

CHAPTER THIRTY TWO

She smacks her lips with pleasure, and with the tip of her tongue retrieves stray flakes of leaf pastry from the corners of her mouth. The baker from Antwerp is a genius with sugar and almonds. Now that Lent is over, he is free to exercise his art to the utmost, and she is free to indulge herself.

She levers herself up onto one elbow, surveying from her couch the vegetable garden and orchard of the convent grounds. A land of plenty, and all the summer ahead to enjoy its produce. She peers into the basket at her side. Only one pastry left. She regrets the whim that she indulged when Sister Theresa brought the basket to her. She let her take one of the pastries for herself. A crumb of comfort to set against the misery of the hair chemise. Perhaps she will let her take it off in a week or so. Her lower legs, which she inspects periodically, are a blotchy mess of sores, and no doubt the rest of her scrawny body is even worse.

She eats the final pastry, and then lets her head fall back onto the upholstered headrest and allows her thoughts to drift where they will. Pleasant notions predominate. With that pernicious painter gone, her influence in Den Bosch can hardly fail to grow. In the town's inner circle, the Holy Company, she will have no more detractors – or, at least, no open detractors, which is good enough for her. In spite of the meddling attentions of Brother Bartelme, she foresees a period of growing prosperity and indulgence. Even if her papal taxes are increased, even if back payments are demanded for previous years, there are rivers of money flowing into her coffers from diverse sources. She is rich beyond Brother Bartelme's ken.

In her head she starts reckoning up these streams of income, but drowsiness creeps up on her, and she is soon meandering among drifts of coins piled up like snow, her feet sinking deep into the clinking little discs of gold and silver.

A knocking at her door startles her out of this beguiling dream.

"Yes?" she calls out, swinging her legs off the couch.

Sister Theresa replies through the door.

"Brother Jacomo wishes to see you Abbess."

Damn! She gets to her feet.

"One moment!"

She kicks the basket out of sight behind the couch. Wiping her mouth and dusting away crumbs from her habit, she goes to sit at her table. She opens her Bible at random, and then calls out again.

"Come in!"

Jacomo enters. As always she feels immediately ill at ease in his presence. His nose seems to sample the air, and she wonders if he can detect the almond aroma left behind by the pastries. His eyes travel around the room, take in the padded couch she has recently occupied, glance at the Bible in front of her, and come to rest on her face. She can't help feeling that he's deduced every one of her actions since Sister Theresa's knock on the door.

"I hope I don't disturb you, Abbess?"

"Not at all," she says, forcing a smile.

The Spaniard continues to stand there like a post, his face a blank mask.

"Can I offer you anything?" she says, when the pause

has stretched out for longer than she can endure. God blast his little games!

"No thank you."

"Please, sit down Brother Jacomo."

He nods, and sits on the chair facing her across her table. Once there, he seems in no hurry to talk, so she is forced to say something herself.

"Shocking news about our Master Painter."

Jacomo's eyes dart at her.

"What news?"

"His arrest, of course."

"Who told you of that?"

"Really! It's hardly a secret. The whole of Den Bosch knows, Brother Jacomo. The arrest of one of the town's most important citizens! I must congratulate you on not letting his status come into account. I expect he blustered a good deal. Has he confessed to his sins?"

"He has, under torture. Next, he must repeat his confession before a tribunal without duress."

"But if he refused..."

"Then more torture might be required to get to the truth."

"Who would have thought that vile heretical beliefs could be held by such an eminent man? In spite of the hostility to the Church that we can see in his paintings, I never suspected this of him."

"To what heretical beliefs do you refer?"

He looks at her suspiciously. Why? She feels herself getting flustered.

"Why... I don't exactly know, Brother Jacomo. But if he's confessed to heresy... well..."

He lets her tail off, his serpent eyes observant. Then he speaks himself.

"Apparently there's an active heretical sect here in Den Bosch. The Brethren of the Free Spirit. He must have associates."

"I imagine so... possibly."

"It's almost certain. I've been wondering about his

306

household – his wife in particular. He can hardly have kept such secrets from his own wife. Is she a virtuous woman?"

"As far as I know, Brother Jacomo."

"Are you sure?"

"I don't know her well."

"But if you had evidence that she was not?"

What is he getting at? He's on the trail of something. She feels uncomfortably warm. Perhaps she can divert him into generalisations.

"Lack of virtue and heresy are different things."

"Both are serious sins, however," he replies, "and both must be punished. Do you agree?"

She nods, and he goes on.

"You see, Abbess, I find myself in a slightly difficult position, and it seems you have had some part in putting me there. I think we might now need to help each other."

What does he mean? What does he know? His next words resolve her puzzlement only too clearly.

"Mary, the servant of Master Jerome, has been to see me. Apparently there is a document in your possession, Abbess Dominica. A document that accuses Jerome's wife – Aleyt, I believe she's called – with adultery. And her partner in sin is Hameel, with whom *you* are often in company, I'm told. Why do you have this document, Abbess?"

Damn Mary for a weak, treacherous prattling-jay! Why did she ever think such an idiot would be dependable?

Jacomo is watching her intently. She can't find anything to say.

He waves a hand slightly in the air between them – almost like a priest dispenses a blessing. He's dismissing his unanswerable question.

"Obviously it must be your intention to take it immediately to Father Crispin, clerk of the cathedral chapter and court. Perhaps you have been too busy, since it came to you?"

"I have been busy, yes..."

"I've certainly been busy myself. In addition to this business with the Master Painter, Brother Bartelme has been going through your accounts with me. The record of your income and expenditure at the infirmary appears to be, to say the least, incomplete. I don't want to have to raise this with Rome if we can work out something here in Den Bosch."

She feels the wings of hope fluttering inside her. Is he hinting at some kind of collusion? What a blessed relief that would be!

"No, I'm sure we can deal with things between ourselves... here in Den Bosch..." she says tentatively.

"Especially as there is, I'm told, a petition of some kind being got up by friends of Jerome in the Company of Our Lady. Word of my actions here will quickly reach Abbot Geoffrey at the Abbey of Saint Anthony in Eindhoven. He is not in sympathy with my mission in Brabant. When this petition comes into his hands I make no doubt but that he will use it as a weapon against me. Not only will he harass me with his own enquiries, but he will certainly send a letter to Rome. Have you heard of a Cardinal there named Domenico Grimani?"

"I don't believe so."

"Cardinal Domenico Grimani is a powerful man, who has the ear of Pope Innocentius. He is the patron and sponsor of your Master Painter here. It was in his rooms in Rome that I first saw a work of Hieronymus Den Bosch. Domenico Grimani will be alarmed. Abbot Geoffrey, and perhaps later the Cardinal himself, will ask questions about my proceedings. I want to make sure, Abbess, that all my doings in Den Bosch are above reproach. Do you understand me?"

"Of course."

"Therefore, as a beginning to set all this on the right path, I want you to take your document immediately to the Church authorities – specifically to Father Crispin, as

I have said. Once the facts of the case are known, the Church will issue a warrant to the secular arm for appropriate action. Adultery is a serious sin, and must be publicly exposed and punished, whoever the perpetrators, and whatever their status. The common people must see that no-one is above God's laws. You will do that?"

It's not a question: it's an order, however he dresses it up.

"I will."

Jacomo stands. She hopes he's going to leave. But instead he wanders over to the window and looks out at the grounds. He inhales deeply, as if allowing himself a moment of pleasure in the warm morning air and the sunlit scene. Then he speaks again, without turning to face her.

"I could be seen as failing in my duty to His Holiness if some adjustment is not made to the conduct of your convent's finances, Abbess. Brother Bartelme has all on record. I will require a twenty per cent increase in your contributions to Rome."

"Twenty per cent!"

He turns, and his thin lips form something like a smile.

"Seventy per cent would be nearer the mark. But we're helping each other, are we not? Furthermore, in anticipation of the petition causing an investigation of my doings here, I will require an adjustment in your own conduct, Abbess. Sister Ursula has told me that you've never crossed the threshold of your convent infirmary since the latest outbreak of Saint Anthony's Fire. This is sure to seem strange, should Abbot Geoffrey or someone from Rome itself make their way here and ask questions. My lodging here, and the investigation of your convent are now a matter of record. Brother Bartelme is a rigorous man. Even if I wished to do so, I could provide no cover for your failings. From now, you will work in the infirmary tending to the sick, just as your nuns do."

She stands, agitated beyond endurance.

"No!"

Blood rises in Jacomo's face like a spreading stain. His eyes are baleful.

"*No?* Do you hesitate to do God's work?"

"I am the Abbess of this convent. The conduct of its affairs is my concern!"

"Do you forget that our order, the Dominican order, takes its charter from the hands of the Pope in Rome? Do you forget that I am a Papal Inquisitor, charged with carrying out the will of His Holiness in these lands? Do you believe that you could remain Abbess here in the face of the report I would make?"

She feels herself wither in the blast of his glare. Her shoulders go down.

"No."

The thin smile returns to Jacomo's lips. How unpleasant a smile can be.

"Good. I'm trying to follow God's path, but there are times when the way is thorny and difficult to make out. In Den Bosch you are widely thought to be an enemy of the painter Jerome. If someone is sent here to second-guess my proceedings, that is certain to come out. What appearance will it have if I have prosecuted your enemy at the same time as being lenient with your failings? I must be even-handed. So now you fully understand and accept why you must work among the sick in your infirmary, Abbess Dominica?"

"Yes," she mutters with little grace. Already her mind is revolving how she might protect herself from catching the vile plague of St Anthony's Fire. Would prayer have any efficacy?

Jacomo hasn't finished with her yet.

"One final but very important matter, Abbess. Have you any idea who it was that accused Master Jerome of heresy?"

She thinks quickly.

"Of course not."

Jacomo meets her eyes and nods his head slowly.

"No, I thought not. If you were ever to breathe a word on such a matter, it would look very bad. Especially if that person had motives of their own for wanting Master Jerome out of the way. Do we understand each other?"

The Abbess thinks that they do, only too well. But what does he intend to do about Jerome? It's a black day indeed if she's brought all this trouble down on her head and not attained her object. Is he going to release the painter?

"Jerome…" she starts. She's not sure how to go on.

But Jacomo holds up a hand to silence her anyway.

"Leave him to me. This whole business can still go smoothly enough. Go to your work now in the infirmary. Sister Ursula is expecting you. I said you would welcome the humblest of tasks. God be with you."

"And with you," she replies. *And may you endure an eternity of torment in the fiery pit of Hell!*

He leaves her, and she sits down and stares into space for a long time. The hideous scenes doubtless awaiting her in the infirmary play out like a pageant in her mind's eye. She spots a stray flake of pastry still clinging to her habit, and brushes it away. In a few short minutes, her whole comfortable world has crumbled. She feels emotion rising within her, and quickly crams a handkerchief into her mouth, aware that Sister Theresa will be just outside the door. Then her body is convulsed with scalding tears of powerless rage, and fear.

CHAPTER THIRTY THREE

A vigorous hammering. Who can this be, as dusk falls? Mary leaves the candle she is lighting and opens the door. Two burly red-jacketed tipstaffs and one skinny one push brusquely past her and stand in the little hallway.

"What do you think you're doing..."

One of the burly ones winks at her, and displays the short staff of office that he carries with a vulgarly suggestive upward thrust. The others laugh.

"You see this, my dear? Can you see the device inscribed here on the side of my staff? That's the authority of the Stadhuis, that is. I've been in this house before."

Now Mary recognises him as one of the men who seized the Master on Hock Monday.

"What is it, Mary?" Aleyt's footsteps are running down the stairs, and then she appears herself at the turn in the staircase.

"Ah," the tipstaff says, "I believe you're the woman as we're looking for. Aleyt Goyarts van den Meervenne?"

"Yes," Aleyt replies, coming further down the stairs. "Is it about Jerome?"

The man emits a grim laugh.

"It's a matter that's of some concern to your husband,

yes. It's a matter that would be of some concern to me, if it was my wife that was in your shoes."

"What do you mean? And why do you speak so impolitely to me? "

"They burst in here like a herd of pigs!" Mary says.

"That's enough from you," the leader of the tipstaffs admonishes her. "We'll be coming for you as well one day, if you don't watch out."

He turns towards Aleyt again.

"Now, our orders is to take a hold of you and take you to the chapter house at the cathedral. There's some questions as is to be put to you there. And if you resist, I'm to force you to come. Are you going to resist?"

Aleyt feels her face burning with anger.

"Why should I resist? I don't know what this is about, but I'll come with you. Mary, get my cloak."

"I'll come with you," Mary says.

"No you won't!" the burly tipstaff retorts. "You won't be admitted into the chapter house, and you'll just have to come straight back again."

The light is fast fading as Aleyt walks in silence, flanked by the three men, along Kirkstraat. The street is deserted. The cathedral is a black looming shape against the sky, but next to it the chapter house windows show a faint amber glow. She is trembling with apprehension. She wonders if Jerome is in there. She would have felt hopeful, but the rudeness of the tipstaffs has unsettled her. They are acting as if she were a miscreant herself.

Once through the chapter house door, the air holds a memory of incense, and mechanically she makes the sign of the cross. She has never set foot in here before. It's a high-roofed octagonal space, illuminated unevenly by stands of candles. There are a dozen or so clerics inside, standing in small groups, and the low hum of their conversation reduces to whispers as she enters. They make no acknowledgement of her, but move at once to take up places on the carved high-backed benches arranged in three rows around the circumference of the space. Their candle-cast shadows move like great winged creatures above them in the roof space.

A priest she knows, Father Crispin, comes forward. He often takes a midweek mass in the cathedral and she has exchanged a few words with him from time to time.

"Father Crispin," she says, attempting a smile. But his mouth is a tight line turned downwards at the corners, and he avoids her eye.

"Please – come forward and take your place here," he says, and leads her to a table in the octagon's open floor area. He leaves her standing there, and the other clerics watch her like a line of crows from the benches. Their faces are half familiar, but she doesn't know their names. She feels herself begin to tremble, and clasps her hands together in front of her. What is going on?

"Bring in the other one," Father Crispin calls out. Aleyt hears several sets of footsteps coming through the chapter house door behind her, and turns to look. At first she recognises none of the newcomers, but then one familiar figure is propelled forwards by a series of pushes on his back. His garments are dishevelled, his hair a bird's nest, and he has marks like bruises under his eyes.

He comes to a halt beside her at the table.

"Hameel?" she says. "What's going on?"

He looks at her as if he'd never seen her before in his life, and now she smells the aura of alcohol coming from him. He seems to judder, his eyes widen, and he looks at her again with more recognition.

"Aleyt?" he mumbles, as if asking himself the question.

Father Crispin now stands on the opposite side of the table to them, backed by the faces of the clerics on the benches behind.

"Are you ready to take the record, Father Anselm?"

A small pot-bellied priest hurries forward with a quill, a little lead inkpot, and a piece of paper. He puts everything on one end of the table, sits down, and nods.

Father Crispin turns to Aleyt.

"You are Aleyt Goyarts van den Meervenne, wife to Jerome van Aachen, of Den Bosch?"

"Yes."

He turns to Hameel.

"And you are Hameel de Groot, architect and artist, of Den Bosch?"

Aleyt sees that he is swaying on his spot, like a slender tree in a strong wind.

"Yes," he mutters.

"A document has been passed, through me, to Bishop Andreas. The Bishop has read it, and has seen fit to delegate to me all matters pertaining to it. The members of the cathedral chapter now gathered here have the authority of the Bishop to recommend an appropriate course of action."

Aleyt listens as if she is in a dream. What kind of document? And what does any of this have to do with the arrest of her husband? Out of the corner of her eye, she sees a familiar figure taking a seat on one of the side benches. A tall, thin figure. Theofilus Piek, the Burgemeester. Something very serious is afoot, if he is here too.

"I am going to read the document to you. Father Anselm?"

The little priest passes a scroll to Father Crispin, who unfurls it, and reads out:

"*I, Mary, testify before God that Hameel de Groot, Architect and Artist, of Den Bosch, and Aleyt Goyarts van den Meervenne, wife of Jerome van Aachen, Painter, of Den Bosch, are adulterers.* This document bears the mark of the servant at the painter Jerome's house, Mary, who, plagued in her conscience by the sin she had witnessed, made a full testimony of this matter to the Abbess Dominica. The Abbess has now passed on this testimony to the Bishop. Do you accept or deny this accusation?"

She can't speak. It's as if a spear has pierced her side. Why has Mary done such a thing? Her own Mary!

Beside her, Hameel makes no sound.

"Silence will be taken as an acknowledgement of the truth of this. Speak now then, if you deny this charge. Be aware that the severest measures will be taken against the girl Mary if she has concocted such a wicked slander against you."

Aleyt half turns to Hameel. Their eyes meet, and fall away. She feels tears gathering. Tears of embarrassment and confusion now, which presage tears of grief later. Jerome will learn of this, and then what will become of them?

"Silence then, is your answer?" Father Crispin says after a moment.

"We are guilty of love," Hameel declares. The words ring out in the stony chamber. There is a stifled snort from one of the tipstaffs behind them.

Father Crispin's face takes on a more severe expression.

"You are guilty of *adultery*, which is a mortal sin. You must seek absolution from God for that, when you are in a right mind to pray. But adultery is also a civil offence, forbidden by the laws of our land, which are God's laws. Therefore, if the Church court agrees, I have no more to do than to hand you over to the custody of the Burgemeester and his officers, who will make all arrangements for the publication and punishment of your crime."

He turns to the benches behind him.

"Do I have your agreement, Fathers?"

"Aye," come back the voices all together from the benches. Father Anselm's quill rasps noisily on his piece of paper.

Father Crispin's look softens a little.

"Remember, you have only to seek God's forgiveness, my children, and the way to Heaven will open before you once more."

316

He turns and makes a slight bow to Theofilus Piek, who now stands up and comes forward like a daddy-long-legs. At his stern look, Aleyt feels the tears that have been barely dammed up starting to course down her cheeks.

"I very much regret this matter," he says. "The Master Painter, your husband, who is himself in such a predicament, has not deserved this of you. His own wife - and you - his friend and protégé. You bring shame on all of us in Den Bosch who try to lead a decent life and follow God's will."

He makes a signal to the tipstaffs, who come forward.

"Well... we will get this unfortunate matter over with quickly. You will be held - separately of course - in custody. The proclamation of your offence will be read out tomorrow morning in the market square, and your punishment will take place after the bells at None. After that, your slate is wiped clean as a civil matter, and your sin is a matter between you and God alone. Of course - and I'm sure I need hardly say this - any further congress between you would result in banishment from Den Bosch."

*

This is the first time Mary has ever been in the house alone at night. In vain she lies down on her straw mattress and tries to sleep. Then she gets up to pray, but what exactly should she pray for?

The world seems to have gone mad, and she can't understand anything anymore.

So she wanders about the dark empty rooms vaguely, as if looking for something. She goes into the bedroom at the top of the house, and straightens Aleyt's shift lying on top of the bed. She puts her head in at the door of the Master's studio. She wishes she had gone with her Mistress, in spite of the tipstaffs. She could have followed behind, and waited outside the chapter house. Where is Aleyt now? Perhaps she's been taken

317

to share a cell with the Master?

She thinks of laying a fire in the parlour. She could sit there herself, with the Master and Mistress gone, but that thought seems to make the strangeness of the empty house even more intense and she returns to her usual haunts of the kitchen and her own little room. She eats a few cold spoonfuls from the small iron pot of vegetable broth that she made yesterday. She's numb, not tasting anything, her thoughts dashing wildly from one speculation to another.

The idea comes to her of seeking out Hameel. Perhaps he will know something of what is happening? She wraps her cloak around her shoulders and hurries through the dark streets to his workshop. In her anxiety for news she hardly feels her usual fears of the night. She knocks gently against the wooden door of his workshop, and when she tries it, it isn't locked. Some moonlight penetrates the room within, and she advances gingerly. Gluttony, Avarice and Lust watch her advance to the door of Hameel's sleeping chamber. She calls his name softly, and then opens the door. The shutters are open, and moonlight falls on the empty bed. Hameel too has disappeared.

At a complete loss, she returns to the empty house in the main square. In the morning, she will have to go out again and seek answers to her questions. An awful sense of foreboding hangs over her. Does any of this come from her visit to the Inquisitive? She lies down again to sleep, but for a long time sleep evades her. She feels she has hardly closed her eyes when the cockerels of Den Bosch begin to crow.

CHAPTER THIRTY FOUR

"…let them take what's coming to them…"

"… high and mighty…"

"…eggs is good, but stones is better…"

"… carry on as they please…"

Mary hears these snatches of conversation as she stands pressed into a doorway on the opposite side of the square to the house, which she's left locked up with all its shutters barred. She has the hood of her cloak pulled well over her face. The square is filled with the dregs of the town. The clergy and the decent people have stayed away. In the eager faces of the crowd Mary can read easily enough the emotions that have brought them here. There is a smugness about all these ignorant onlookers that makes her want to lash out with her fists, and demand to know what makes *them* so superior to any other sinners.

"Mary…"

It's Gillis. How has he recognised her? It's disappointing to see him here.

"Come to watch the show?" she says, unable to keep bitterness out of her tone.

He shakes his head.

"I came into town with goose feathers for the pillow maker. Why is this crowd gathered?"

"Adulterers to be punished," she says, glad that he

didn't come for this.

"Poor devils!" he says. "Will you come away with me?"

"What?"

"Come away from this, back to my cottage?"

"Now?"

"Yes."

"Gillis, I can't. But thank you."

"You seem upset."

"Gillis, I'm sorry, but leave me alone just now. I have some important... I have to do things here."

He gives her a long look, and then shrugs.

"You're a woman, and a woman's a thing that I don't rightly understand. Never mind, come and see me whenever you want to."

As he walks away quickly, the bells ring out for the mid-afternoon prayers of None, and the transgressors are brought into the square. There is a great uproar of jeering and hooting. Mary says Hail Marys under her breath, praying for it all to pass quickly.

Hameel and her dear Mistress are barely recognisable. They are clad only in coarse pieces of sack-cloth with holes for their heads to poke through. The sacking hangs open and flaps about, revealing their naked bodies beneath. They are daubed with white ashes that make them look like two corpses brought back to life. Aleyt's hair is uncovered and bedraggled. Their hands are tied in front of them, and each is pulled along at the end of a rope around their neck by a tipstaff. On their backs hang placards daubed with a word in bright red paint. Mary doesn't need to be able to read to know that the word is 'Adulterer'.

They are led around the periphery of the square, where the mob has gathered in the lee of the houses. Eggs, rotten fruit, and some stones are thrown at them; they are spat at, and frequently someone emerges from the crowd to belabour them with their fists or a stick before the tipstaffs drive them back. They don't intervene in these attacks until a few good blows have landed, and Mary gasps in dismay as a heavy old woman wielding a broom brings Aleyt to her knees with a whirling thwack to the stomach.

After they have run the gauntlet of the crowd, Hameel and Aleyt, bleeding and stumbling, are dragged to the centre of the square, where Father Crispin declaims something at length in Latin. The mob, excited by its exertions, barely pays him attention. When he's finished, he stands aside, and the town crier standing beside him beats his gong and cries out in a voice loud enough to penetrate the crowd's noise.

"Drag them to the bounds of the town and release them. Let them creep back when darkness has fallen, and let no-one molest them thereafter. With this punishment they have paid the earthly price of their sin. Let them now pray for God to forgive them!"

Detaching herself from the shelter of the doorway, Mary follows the tipstaffs and those who have chosen to accompany Aleyt towards the north gate. Hameel meanwhile is being pulled away in the opposite direction, towards the east gate, with his own following of jeering louts.

At the threshold of the gate, Aleyt's wrists are unbound, and with an unceremonious shove she is propelled out of the town onto the muddy road that leads to the fields and farms of the surrounding tilth. She is pursued by a final volley of curses and crude jests, and one or two rotten eggs that have been held back for this final valediction. Then the boisterous crowd turns back towards its daily life, exhilarated by the edifying sight of the high and mighty brought low.

Mary waits until they have dispersed. When the tipstaffs are satisfied that Aleyt is moving away from the town as required, they turn away too, not noticing Mary as she slips quickly out of the gate to take the road. Her Mistress is a forlorn figure some few hundred yards away now, moving along slowly.

As Mary comes up with Aleyt, she hears her emit a load groan. Then she clutches her stomach and falls to the ground, rolling almost to the edge of a water-filled ditch.

"Mistress!"

Mary rushes to her. Aleyt's eyes stare up at her in misery and pain.

"Mary… Mary… it's the baby…" she gasps.

Mary kneels and holds her Mistress's hand tightly until it is over, and then uses her cloak to clean her as best she can, and cover her. As Aleyt lies exhausted and sobbing, curled up on the ground, Mary sets the foetus aside. It is hardly recognisable as human, just a tiny, bloody, already lifeless thing. She is too preoccupied with comforting her Mistress to think what should be done with it. But that question is answered quickly, as a mangy sand-coloured dog comes running across the road from nowhere and steals off with the fruit of Hameel and Aleyt's love.

CHAPTER THIRTY FIVE

Is it day or night now? The darkness in this underground dungeon gives no clue. In his intervals of fitful sleep Jerome has nightmares about going blind, and when he wakes, it's as if the nightmares continue.

The cell stinks from the bucket of his own urine and faeces that he has to find by touch in the furthest corner. His hands are chained together by heavy links, and on the rustling thin straw mattress he can find no comfortable position. The pain from his injured toe shoots up his leg periodically, as if a sharp-toothed rodent keeps biting it.

At long, long intervals, the gaoler brings him a hunk of bread and a cup of water. He comes by candlelight, followed down the echoing circular stone steps by a shadowy dancing demon. He pushes the offerings through the bars of the cell door. He never speaks or looks at Jerome. He leaves him again in darkness.

Perhaps Hell, contrary to his colourful imaginings, might be just such a place as this? Completely dark, silent, stinking, uncomfortable and lonely. An eternity like this would be as terrible a punishment as any that his waking or sleeping mind has hitherto dreamed up. The world up above him has receded to an infinite distance, and the life he'd led there is as strange as a traveller's tale. He tries to think of Aleyt getting up in the mornings, washing her face in the bowl of hot water brought up by Mary from the kitchen, sitting at the window of their room looking out at the busy market square. But she is like a figure in a dream, elusive, and her features are indistinct.

He has been lost in such thoughts when he hears the heavy door at the top of the steps groan on its hinges. This time there are two sets of footsteps descending, and the shadows of two demons caper on the rough stone walls. Jerome's whole body tenses. Is this Jacomo returning to inflict more suffering?

But when the flickering candle comes into view, he wonders if he has died and gone to Hell indeed. The gaoler is pushing a chained figure in front of him. It is wearing a rough open gown of sack-cloth and it has the white bloodless face of a corpse.

The barred door of the cell is unlocked, and the deathly figure is shoved unceremoniously forward. It stumbles, and sits down heavily on the stone flags.

"Some pleasant company for you, Master Painter!" the gaoler comments as he re-locks the barred door. His footsteps recede slowly back towards the distant world of light and air, and the last gleam of candlelight disappears. With a groan and a slam, the upper door closes.

In the silence, he can hear the corpse-like newcomer breathing. He is too surprised and mystified to say anything. Ridiculously, he feels embarrassment at the stink in the cell, as if it were his own fault.

After a few moments, when the man's breathing has steadied, he hears the rattle of chains as he crawls across the floor and leans back with a sigh against the wall.

"Who are you?" he says then.

There is a slight snort in response. Has he said something amusing?

"Can you guess?" comes the reply after a few moments. Jerome is shocked.

"Hameel! What in God's name has happened?"

324

"They've told you nothing?"

"I don't even know what day it is, or if it's day or night. But... you! I can't believe my ears! Has the world gone mad out there?"

"The world? The world goes on its wicked way to Hell, as ever."

"Have you been accused wrongly too, Hameel? Why are you in here?"

There is a pause..

"Jacomo wants to put some questions to me."

"Then God help you, Hameel!"

"They say you've confessed to heresy."

"I have. I would have confessed to every sin known to the Devil, Hameel. I would have begged for an eternity in Hell rather than another minute with Jacomo."

He shakes his head as if he could dislodge from it the memory of how his resolve crumbled into abject pleading when the torturer turned the point of the blade to prick his naked flesh. He had saved his manhood, but been unmanned of his courage.

"The world is a place of sin and perversion, Hameel. We can do nothing but submit, and fix our hopes on the life after death"

There is silence for a few moments, and his thoughts turn back to Hameel's appearance as he came into the cell. Was it some strange trick of the candlelight that had made him look like a corpse?

"Hameel... it appeared to me that you... you were daubed in white and wearing sack-cloth. I thought you were a dead man."

The links of Hameel's chain stir a little.

"Ashes," he eventually replies. "I was daubed in ashes."

"By whom? On the authority of the Church?"

"Yes."

"Then, that means they already..."

Hameel interrupts.

"Yes. It was alleged that I was caught in sin."

"What sin?"

"Adultery."

Jerome almost laughs. If Hameel had said 'heresy' or even 'witchcraft', then his prospects at the hands of Jacomo would have been bleak indeed. But adultery, in the circumstances, seems a trivial charge. He chides him, but gently.

"Hameel! I know you've been a rogue before now. A lusty, single man. But with another man's wife! That was foolish. Foolish and wrong."

"I know it."

"Well, you've paid a heavy price. Were you paraded and beaten in the square?"

"That was the way of it."

"And the poor woman too, no doubt. Who was she?"

"She's felt shame enough. At least let there be one person in Den Bosch who doesn't know her name."

"Well. It's of small concern in the present circumstances. Me, a condemned heretic, and you… why do you think Jacomo wants you here? What questions does he want to ask you?"

"I don't know."

Jerome shifts his weight uncomfortably. The chill of the stone wall numbs whatever part of his back is in contact with it.

"How's Aleyt, Hameel? Did you see her before this dreadful ordeal of yours?"

"I did. She's well."

"How she must be worrying, the poor dove! And what is happening among my friends? Has anyone gone to the Inquisitor?"

"There was talk of a petition. I didn't see it myself."

"A petition?"

"I know no more."

"Nothing?"

He waits, but Hameel remains silent. As for himself,

words are straining to burst out, like leaves from a bud. After God knows how many days and nights in this black pit, Hameel's company is manna from Heaven. He would like to go to embrace him, but feels too awkward. He has an overwhelming desire to reach out to him in some way. Perhaps with well-chosen words he can shine the light of their past happiness into the darkness of the present moment.

"You know, Hameel, as I've been lying here in this dungeon, my thoughts have often turned to our old times. You, your brother Pieter, and me. Fishing... running about the woods... the sun always seemed to shine in those days. Happy times!"

After a few moments, a single word comes back out of the darkness at Jerome.

"Happy!"

It is barely more than a whisper, a hissing, venomous little dart of a word. He feels mystified.

"What?"

"Those *happy times*, Jerome. You and my brother Pieter. So close, you were. Little Hameel could tag along, but it was the two of you."

Now there can be no mistaking the bitterness in Hameel's voice. Jerome feels a pang of unexpected sorrow. Could he have been mistaken? Those were idyllic days, for all of them. He's gone through his whole life with those days illuminated in his memory, like a precious little scene in a landscape. Twice he's put three tiny figures of boys fishing in a stream into the backgrounds of his paintings. Pieter, Jerome, and the even smaller figure of Hameel.

"Hameel... it was always the three of us."

"Pieter idolised you."

"You exaggerate."

"It was always 'Jerome this' and 'Jerome that'. Sometimes he hardly noticed he had a brother."

He contemplates the ugly crack that has appeared in the bright image of his remembered idyll. It had never

327

occurred to him that Hameel didn't share his love of those days. He feels crushed, his shell broken.

"I didn't realise. I'm sorry. My memory of it all is so different."

Now he wishes he hadn't spoken about the past. He wills Hameel to say no more. But Hameel seems now to have got the bit between his teeth.

"Sometimes I wished you would die. I remember once I prayed for it."

Jerome holds up an unseeable hand in the darkness, warding off the words.

"There's no need... after all these years..."

"There's no need. But what's the harm in the truth, now?"

After a pause, the words come again at him, invisible arrows.

"And then it was only a few weeks after that...after my prayer... that Pieter's face broke out in boils, and we knew he had the Fire. That's exactly what I'd prayed would happen to you. I wanted St Anthony's Fire to carry you off, so my brother would love me instead."

He feels a constriction in his breast, and draws breath with an effort.

"Those feelings, Hameel. Surely... they're long gone. These are the resentments of a child."

"I'm still that child, Jerome."

"Well - forgive me, Hameel. I meant no harm."

"No, you've never meant me harm. You couldn't help but overshadow me."

"After poor Pieter was dead, Hameel, I... well... I felt so sorry for you. Surely then I made amends, if I'd unintentionally stood on your toes before?"

"Oh, yes. You were my new big brother. Always there - whether I wanted you or not."

Jerome swallows the lump in his throat. Another bright image ruined – that of his younger self, the beloved friend and comforter of poor bereaved little Hameel.

"This is bitter," he mutters.

Hameel snorts, and goes on, scattering more treasured memories like so much chaff in a winnowing wind.

"And when I was apprenticed as a mason, it was you who persuaded my father - and me - that I should raise my sights higher. That I could be an architect and an artist."

He can muster a protest at this at least, though sick at heart.

"Every man should use his best gifts in the service of God. You have these gifts, Hameel."

"But in how much lesser measure than you, Jerome! You didn't let me become myself. By becoming an artist, I was doomed to stay in your shadow forever."

"You underrate yourself."

"No. In your heart Jerome you know that's not so. You know I'm your inferior as an artist."

The truth of this proposition strikes home to him. Would he have been so keen to encourage Hameel, if he had perceived in him a rival in talent to himself? Hameel's work was competent but uninspired. It was a match for the work of the majority of men who called themselves artists, painters, architects and sculptors. But it would never rank alongside his own achievements.

"Did you know I was one of your rivals for the Overmaas cathedral commission?"

Jerome is startled. Yet another recasting of his beliefs about the past, this time more recent. He feels as if he has been walking for a long time unawares amongst snares and pitfalls. How many tactless blunders has he committed?

"Of course I didn't know that, Hameel! Then straight away I asked you to work as my assistant... I'm so sorry."

"It was in *my* favour that the Abbess tried to bribe the cathedral chapter. But her gold wasn't enough to divert them. They wanted the greatest artist in Brabant – in all the Provinces - to design their windows. You, Jerome."

Jerome feels his heart go out to Hameel, little Hameel. In his mind's eye he sees his face again, the day of Pieter's funeral, and feels again the protective love that had overwhelmed him then.

"I always wanted the best for you. If only I'd been more perceptive! Can you forgive me?"

When Hameel's answer eventually comes, it comes softly, with none of the truculence that resounded in his earlier revelations. It sounds as if he is close to weeping.

"No – you've done nothing that needs my forgiveness. I would forgive you anything. It's myself I can't forgive."

"Why, Hameel?"

"It's God who gives and takes away. How stupid I've been. What a fool I was to go through life feeling as if you'd taken away my brother Pieter! And to wish... to wish that somehow I could take something away from you."

"Listen to me: you wallow in this too much, Hameel. It's only these... these desperate circumstances... that make you bring these feelings out. I value you even more Hameel, for your honesty."

Now Hameel's voice is barely a whisper.

"Jerome... Jerome. I'm worse than you think. I'm not worthy even to share a dungeon with you."

CHAPTER THIRTY SIX

"Take hold of the foot firmly, Abbess Dominica! You'll be of no use otherwise!"

God is punishing her, and no doubt she has deserved it most thoroughly. She glances at Sister Ursula's frowning face and tightens her grip.

When she first arrived in the infirmary, Sister Ursula – initially amazed, and subsequently triumphant - set her to work in the room at the back where the most desperate cases were laid on pallets, groaning in pain, or shouting in delirium. Her role is to bathe them with soothing cold water infused with henbane, to attend to their intermittent feeding, and to cope with the discharges of blood, pus, vomit, urine and excrement that seem to be in constant flow somewhere or other among the dozen or so sufferers in the room. Most of them have lost limbs already, and she was shown where their withered but carefully labelled arms and legs were hung in the cold cellar beneath the infirmary, ready to be reclaimed on the Day of Judgment.

Now she is holding the lower right leg of Vincent Lammers. She was there when he limped in only yesterday in a spitting mood, supported by his wife. Apparently the Inquisitor had happened to be passing on the street outside, and had the 'damned arrogance' to advise him that God was punishing him for fornicating in Lent. This morning Sister Benedicta pointed out that the disease was spreading fast towards his knee. An amputation is essential, and he has been dosed with mandrake in wine to send him into a deep sleep. Sister Benedicta has advised the Abbess that sometimes when the cutting begins, a patient will start out of his stupor, and start to fight. So together they have strapped Lammers' hands and arms to his sides.

This is the first cutting that the Abbess has seen. Obviously Sister Ursula is determined that she should have the closest possible view, so she has charged her with the job of holding Lammers' right foot, while Sister Benedicta, grim-faced but dauntless, wields the saw.

She has wrapped a rag around the foot to avoid touching the diseased flesh, and now she grips it tightly as she has been ordered, and closes her eyes. She feels the vibration through her fingers as Sister Benedicta begins her task, and hears the rasping teeth of the saw as they bite through the leg bone. It seems to go and on. Lammers' whole body twitches violently and repeatedly, and he emits inarticulate moans and gasps, but doesn't come to consciousness. It's almost unbearable. She distracts herself with prayers to Saint Anthony that she will avoid this loathsome disease herself, in spite of her constant exposure to it.

At last she feels the weight of the foot increase in her hands as the saw takes its final bite, and then she is holding the whole of the Lammers' lower leg. Except it isn't his, any more. Blood has spurted and flowed freely into the wooden tub beneath the point of amputation, and both she and Sister Benedicta are liberally stained with red. Sister Beatrice approaches with the cauterising iron, which has been heating in a brazier, and the smell of burning flesh and sinew fills the air as she applies it to the stump. Suddenly the Abbess can stand no more, and dropping the severed limb to the ground, she scrambles to her feet and runs, gagging, out of the room and into the little yard outside, where she gulps down fresh air as if it were the finest wine she had ever tasted.

Behind her, she hears footsteps.

"Sister Dominica!"

This is new. That upstart Sister Ursula has obviously decided to drop the title of 'Abbess' from her address. She shrugs inwardly, and decides to let it pass. All the wind has gone from her sails since she docked here in the infirmary. Surrounded by so much suffering and death, earthly status has diminished to a trivial matter.

"Sister Dominica!" the voice comes again, peremptory. She turns to face her.

"I'd like you to write the label for Vincent Lammers' leg and find a place for it in the cellar. After you've done that, I think it's time some more quicklime was added to the cesspit. You know where it's kept. Then hurry back to your duties in the ward."

She nods, eyes cast down. Sister Ursula takes a step closer to her. She hadn't really noticed how tall Sister Ursula was, before. Now she speaks down at her in a low voice, trembling with spite.

"I don't know what hold that Inquisitor has over you, Sister Dominica, but it must be a good one. I wonder which of your sins he discovered? Could it have been Avarice? Could the rumours of the interest you charged on your loans to merchants in the town turn out to have been true? Or perhaps he disapproved of your intention to exploit gullible pilgrims by passing off some pauper's bones as those of a saint? But then again, could it have been Lust? For example your improper dalliance with that tenant farmer? Or maybe it was Gluttony? Was he scandalised by the revelling in fine food and drink with which you made a mockery of your vows of poverty and abstinence?"

She lets her have her pleasure. She has no will to dispute anything. She still feels the weight of that leg, falling from the body. A step on the road to death.

"In fact," Sister Ursula goes on, taking best advantage of her passivity, "I suspect it must be some sin even worse than these things, if such a thing can be imagined. Why else would you topple from your pomp so swiftly, and without protest? I look forward to finding out more. Pray God we will soon get an Abbess worthy of the name to replace you! Get on with your duties!"

Sister Ursula turns on her heel and flounces away, no doubt to pre-empt any response. She needn't have bothered. She has no response. She takes out her precious rosary beads for comfort, and loops them around her fingers. Why do the beads feel sore against her skin, as if they burned? She looks down.

In the gloom of her cell and amidst her busy work in the stinking ward, she hasn't noticed. But here in the clear light of day, she can see all too well. Her hands are slightly swollen, the bones of the knuckles grown indistinct beneath plump pads. The skin on the backs of her fingers is peeling, and there is a raw, red look to her fingertips. She presses them together. They feel numb.

CHAPTER THIRTY SEVEN

"Well? Have your enquiries borne fruit?"

Brother Bartelme nods. His pale, earnest face, usually a blank wall, now betrays some anxiety. Or perhaps Jacomo is only seeing a reflection of his own state of mind.

"Yes, Brother Jacomo. At the Stadhuis I learned from a clerk to the Burgemeester that a petition has been taken to Eindhoven. And from Bishop Andreas I learned that a missive has arrived from the Dean at Overmaas. The Master Painter was to execute a commission there, so both he and Bishop Andreas have common cause to question this proceeding of ours."

"What is your own view, Brother Bartelme?"

His assistant's face registers surprise. He rarely seeks Bartelme's opinion.

"Of what, Brother?"

"Of the painter."

He replies without hesitation.

"The painter is most surely a heretic. A dangerous and influential servant of the Devil, who might do much damage to the Holy Church. We should not let his status divert us from God's work. Perhaps he has corrupted others amongst his acquaintance."

"Very well. Thank you, Brother. I would like some time alone now, to pray and consider our next step."

Brother Bartelme withdraws, and Jacomo sits at his table to think. On the roof, pigeons distract him, parading with their scratching claws, and cooing to each other. Also he hears Brother Bartelme coughing in the next room. It occurs to him that Bartelme might be a little unwell – surely he has heard him coughing before now, in the night? He must send him off to the apothecary to seek some soothing syrup. It strikes him, suddenly, how he takes for granted the diligence, the quiet efficiency, and the general *solidity* of his right-hand man. With this thought comes a fresh insight: Bartelme is very like himself. He's a man who has stepped away from his human persona, with all its failings and inadequacies, to become, as nearly as he can, a pure instrument of God's will.

He dismisses the coughing, and the cooing, and concentrates on turning his thoughts into their proper channel. That foolish maidservant! Who could have thought such a weak vessel would pour forth such a potent brew of truth! And her words *are* true, he has no doubt. That Hameel covets Jerome's wife is a motive for betrayal so plain and simple that it could stand out in the open, like a tree in a field, without ever being noticed. Why had it never crossed his own mind? He has been guilty of jumping to a conclusion, of seeing only what he already wished to see.

He understands now how he was well primed to be suspicious of the Master Painter. The Abbess's insinuations were enough to prick his interest, and then talking to the man himself had hardened his misgivings. Jerome's obdurate arrogance; his near-heretical belief that God spoke directly to him; his disturbing obscene images: all these had led him to a readiness to swallow Hameel's lie.

He contemplates Hameel. From what he has learned, Hameel owes much to the patronage of the older painter, and has been treated as a member of his own family. To betray a lifelong friend and benefactor in such a way; to send him to torture and death - this is wickedness so dark that the Devil must have been at work on him for a long time. It is a sin beyond the scope of ordinary human evil.

And now, by the Devil's hand working through Hameel, he finds himself in a predicament. He has arrested and tortured the most eminent artist of Brabant, and in spite of the man's confession, he is certain now that he is innocent. For this to come out will destroy the very foundation stone of his mission here.

Must it come out?

He has the signed confession of heresy. Hameel's adultery with Aleyt has no known bearing on that. There are only three people beside himself who are aware that Hameel was Jerome's accuser. He has Hameel himself in a dungeon. He has the Abbess under his thumb. Only the servant girl, Mary, is matter for concern. If a delegation from Eindhoven is sent to Den Bosch, then she should be kept well away. If they did get hold of her, she might not be believed, or her information might be regarded as flawed or irrelevant, but that was not to be relied upon.

Perhaps, before matters advanced to such a point, he might have her taken up, tried, and burned as a witch with all her spiteful falsehoods.

But he sees in her no sign that she is a witch, even though their ways are cunning and hidden, and they are myriad. No, he has no reason to think that of her.

It would be best then to avoid a delegation if at all possible. Should he go, even now, unbidden, to explain himself to Abbot Geoffrey, show him the drawings in his possession and seek his support for the next steps: a tribunal and execution? After all, other eminent men have fallen in the way of Inquisitors, and the world has moved on undisturbed. Jerome would soon be forgotten, and his paintings, tainted by his heresy, would be removed from the monasteries, palaces and churches where they now hung. The content of his new work – his so-called *Garden of Earthly Delights*– suggests that he is going to a persistent thorn in the Church's side.

Would he not be serving God if he could pull out the thorn now, before infection spreads? Would he not be serving God well, if this proceeding, supported by Cardinal Amandini in Rome, leads to the secure foundation of his Papal Inquisition here? Will not God be pleased if these lands are emptied of heretics and witches? Does the fate of a single man – a man who, in his own way, is troublesome to the Church – matter very much beside such weighty concerns?

These questions torment him. He prays for a long time for guidance, but God sends no clear answer to his soul.

He must rely then on his native cunning. After all, that was given to him by God. It was his wily intelligence, God's gift, that raised him up from a street boy in Seville to a Papal Inquisitor. He must have confidence in his own powers now, in this difficult test that has been sent to him.

There is one thing he might try. If God still has possession of any tiny portion of Hameel's soul or mind, there is one thing that he might not be able to bear.

*

The morning is fine and breezy, and Mary, all unaware of how she preoccupies the Inquisitor's thoughts, is hanging washing in the garden and wondering what is to be done with her Mistress. She brought her home from the ordeal of the day before, heated water and bathed her in the wooden tub, and tried to persuade her to rub one of Doctor Stemerdink's ointments on her cuts and bruises. It was an ointment made with raven's dung – a favoured ingredient of his – and one which she had bought from him to combat the tooth worm that was gnawing at one of her back teeth. But Aleyt would have nothing to do with Doctor Stemerdink's ointments, and this morning had sent

Mary off to Izaak the apothecary to ask for some healing balm. When she got there, Izaak told her he needed to prepare a new batch, and he would bring it himself later.

Now Aleyt is sitting on her own in the parlour upstairs, probably staring into space. Mary tried to get her to come and sit in the garden – it is warm enough – but she had just shaken her head and continued to fidget with her fingers in a distracted fashion.

When the washing is hung, Mary returns to the kitchen. Perhaps she'll prepare a pottage with some spring vegetables. It's strange, having to make her own decisions. Usually Aleyt would give her directions every morning, and there would be some fun to be had in disputing what was the best way to do things, or how the day's work should be organised. Such carefree times seem a long way off now.

There is a knock at the door, and Mary goes to answer it.

Izaak, the apothecary, stands there, the obligatory star of David a bright yellow on his cap. He has a small bottle in one hand, and a basket in the other.

"Good morning again, Mistress Mary. I've brought the unguent you wanted. Is it possible, do you think, to see your mistress?"

"She's not well, but I can ask."

"I'd just like to say a word, if I can. Tell her I'll not take up more than a minute of her time."

"Come and wait in the hallway, then, Master Izaak."

Mary runs up the stairs and taps at the parlour door before entering.

Aleyt is seated exactly as she was an hour ago. Her eyes lift to Mary's face, like dark pools with no light in them.

"Izaak the apothecary would like to see you for a minute, Mistress. He's brought the ointment."

"But he wants to see me?"

"Yes, he seems anxious to do that, Mistress."

"Send him up then."

339

She adjusts her head cloth, and wipes her eyes as she hears footsteps ascending the stairs. She barely knows the apothecary – it was Jerome who had dealings with him, over substances for his painting, and for his potions.

At the open door, Izaak smiles at her with a warmth that lifts her spirits. He puts his basket and little bottle down on the table as he walks forward to take her outstretched hand. Mary has followed him up, and peeps curiously over his shoulder.

"My poor lady. I am so sorry about what has happened. Whatever you have done, it is a shocking – a barbaric thing – that you were treated so. These 'Christians' – I'm sorry, but I must say this – so unforgiving, so in love with cruelty and punishment. You can see why we Jewish folk are afraid of you. Anyway – I'm sorry – I have come simply to say that in our humble way – we, my family and I – we're so grateful – what you and your husband did for us on Good Friday – and your support, at all times – I'm not making sense, I'm sorry…"

On an impulse, Aleyt captures his hand again, which has dropped her own and is waving about in the air in a vain attempt to clarify his confused sentiments.

"My good Izaak. I understand. I'm grateful that you should have come here to see me. No one else will come now."

He nods, and returns the pressure of her hand. He looks relieved to be understood. Then he lets go and gestures to the table.

"A balm for your hurts – and - a basket here, you see. I've taken the liberty – my wife and I – we've ventured to – some foodstuffs. Some of our traditional Jewish food - I'm sure I - we'd both be – delighted if you would accept this little gift from us, in this time of trouble."

"Thank you , Izaak, that's so very kind of you."

She lets go of his hand.

"I won't stay now – a painful time – such savagery.

Your husband – forgive me – your husband is a good man. I hear that his friends are doing what they can. I hope – well, of course – I hope he is soon freed from these inquisitions. When you – forgive me – when Christians are not turning on the poor Jews, it seems they are turning on each other. I don't say we are faultless people, we Jews, but - burning witches? What is a witch? It's all wrong. Sorry, I will go. I hope – pardon me, I speak of that which is not my concern – I hope that your husband is freed, and that as a man of great heart, he will - he will forgive you for whatever you have done in error, my good lady."

She smiles again, but Izaak appears to be struck with a sudden apprehension that he has said far more than he should have done, and starts to beat a hasty retreat, backing into Mary who has advanced into the room behind him, since no one told her to go away.

"I'm sorry, my dear Mistress Mary. So clumsy! If you could return the basket itself, perhaps, when it suits you? Just the basket of course. I'll leave now. Goodbye Mistress Aleyt. God bless you! The real God is a forgiving God. He would not countenance this savagery. Farewell!"

Aleyt hears him descending the stairs, still muttering and apologising to Mary, who has picked up the basket. Finally the street door opens and closes, and he is gone.

Mary takes the basket of food into the kitchen, and stores the offerings within in the pantry. There are interesting flatbreads and pastry parcels and jars that when opened exude an enticing spicy aroma.

Once more there is a tap on the street door. A quiet tap, but then repeated several times in quick succession, as if the person knocking is in a hurry.

Aleyt's cousin Frida is standing close to the door as she opens it, with a hood drawn over her head. She glances at Mary and whispers.

"Let me in quickly, Mary, if you please."

Mary lets her pass, and closes the door behind her.

"Not a word to anyone about this visit, Mary. My husband Joris has forbidden me to see Aleyt. How is she, the poor creature?"

"She's upstairs, and it will do her a powerful bit of good to see a friendly face," Mary says.

"You're sure she'll want to see me?"

"I'm certain of it."

"Then I'll see myself up the stairs, shall I?"

"Of course. And I'll bring up two mugs of small beer, shall I, and some biscuits. Try to get her to eat something with you, Mistress Frida, if you can."

"I will. I can't stay for long though, and, Mary – when I leave – I think you'd better let me out at the back garden gate, if you please."

Mary nods.

"And – complete secrecy, Mary!"

"Of course Mistress Frida. I understand."

CHAPTER THIRTY EIGHT

His punishment has been carried out. Why then was he re-arrested when he crept back in through the city gate at nightfall? Why was he thrust into this dungeon? Why the same dungeon as Jerome? As the long dark hours wear away, this question gnaws at Hameel's mind more horribly than the hunger and thirst that afflict his body. On whose orders was it done? The tipstaffs refused to speak as they marched him here.

Why did the Abbess produce Mary's document? She knew what the consequences would be. Has she withdrawn her protection from him, then? Why? He thinks back to their last talk. Was there any clue there to her actions? Her final words ring still in his ears: *It's a matter of survival. It's you or him.*

He shivers and clutches the coarse sack-cloth to his body, but it doesn't warm him. He can hear Jerome breathing deeply and regularly on the other side of the dungeon. Asleep, then. He summons the fantasies of the future that the Abbess conjured in his mind: himself married to Aleyt, the new leading artist of Den Bosch. A proud father. Jerome a fading memory. It is so hard to think of such a future, with the man living and breathing here in the darkness with him. He's glad he's asleep. It spares him from Jerome's attempts to hold him in conversation of some kind. He has no words left for

Jerome. He could only offer him more lies, or a confession, and he has no will to do either.

He falls into an uneasy half-sleep of his own, in which visions of a different future torment him. He is in an icy river, wading, or swimming. He can't get anywhere. On the bank is Jerome, fishing. A little boy is standing beside him. Hameel's son, now the son of Jerome.

A door opens and closes somewhere.

He opens his eyes. Flickering light appears on the rough wall at the base of the steps, and several sets of footsteps can be heard descending.

The first man to come into view is stripped to the waist. The powerful muscles of his chest and arms are sculpted in the light of the small open brazier he bears before him in gloved hands. He sets it down on its three short legs outside the bars of the cell, while his companions come down behind him. There are three more men bearing torches, and then, behind them, the black-gowned and hooded figure of Jacomo.

Hameel is gripped by terror so physical that it's as if the icy river of his daydream is now pouring through his body, and he is unsure if he has soiled himself or not.

The door of the cell is unlocked, and the group enters. The three men with torches place them in metal sconces on the dank stone walls, and the dungeon is illuminated so brightly that Hameel, habituated to darkness, squints half-blinded at the newcomers. On his thin pallet of straw, Jerome raises himself on one elbow. He too peers at the men through eyes like slits.

When the torches have been set, and the brazier brought in to stand in the centre of the cell, the men look to Jacomo for their orders. Hameel notices for the first time that the Inquisitor holds some object in his hand, made of dull metal.

Jacomo points a thin finger at Jerome.

"This one!"

Two of the men move swiftly to drag Jerome away

344

from his pallet by the wall and thrust him onto his back on the floor near the brazier. His head hits the stone flags with a thump. One of the men sits on his legs, while the other pushes down on his shoulders. Jerome grunts at the blow to his head, but otherwise makes no protest.

Hameel stares as Jacomo approaches the helpless figure. He is holding the metal object in both hands now. It clanks a little as he turns a screw. It's some kind of a clamp.

"What are you doing?" he blurts out.

Jacomo half turns towards him.

"This wretched man has already confessed to membership of the heretical Brethren of the Free Spirit. Now it's time to draw up a list of his associates."

He returns his gaze to the prostrate Jerome.

"Will you willingly tell me the names of your fellow sinners?"

"There are no fellow sinners!" Jerome replies.

Jacomo shakes his head, as if sadly. He looks again at Hameel.

"A hardened liar, you see, Hameel. He gives me no choice but to use force. Ignatius!"

The muscular man standing by the brazier squats on his hams to add his strength to that of the men already holding Jerome down.

Hameel's heart races. He can't help but look at Jerome's face turned sideways against the dungeon floor, his eyes screwed tightly shut, and his mouth open in a grimace of fear and despair. He is trying to prepare himself for this torment and he has no way to avoid it. What could he do? Blurt out the names of his friends and associates in Den Bosch at random, knowing that with each name he condemned another man to the same fate as himself?

Hameel finds words tumbling out of him, seemingly of their own accord.

"No! Listen to me first!"

345

Jacomo looks at him keenly, his eyes shining redly in the torchlight from within the shadow of his cowl.

"Well?"

Hameel's courage fails him. He shakes his head helplessly, and bows his head.

"Take me out of here," he mutters.

Jacomo turns back his cowl and shakes his head.

"No, Hameel. You'll stay and watch. You'll see the treatment meted out to one who lies to the Pope's representative. It's like lying to God himself. Who could excuse that?"

The Inquisitor kneels beside Jerome and holds the metal clamp close to his face.

"Open your eyes! You see this, Master Painter? It's the first thing your Den Bosch ironworkers have made for me, and a very suitable device for your case. It will crush your fingers, you see, so while we extract the truth we'll also be punishing those delicate hands for their sinful drawings."

Moving a little on his knees, he positions himself beside the painter's arm. The muscular Ignatius pushes it down to the dungeon floor. Jacomo draws the hand into the device. Then he speaks softly, almost regretfully.

"Now, Master Jerome. This is your final chance. Name your fellow sinners in this heretical sect!"

Tears of helpless despair are coursing down Jerome's cheeks. Hameel stares at them, and then closes his eyes. His friend's voice quavers, like a child's.

"God help me! I lied to make my own confession, but how can I condemn other innocents? God help me!"

Hameel's eyes are jerked open by Jerome's horrible scream of pain. He finds his body acting as if without any volition of his own. His legs propel him upwards from his sitting position, and his feet carry him to where the Inquisitor kneels over Jerome, with his back to him.

"No! No!" he hears himself shouting, as he slips his hand chains over Jacomo's head and pulls backwards to

346

choke him.

The Inquisitor is caught with his back against Hameel's chest, hands groping desperately for the chain. For a moment he thinks he will really kill Jacomo, but the guards quickly spring up and overpower him. They pull the chain back over the Inquisitor's head, and Ignatius hurls him like a doll against the wall of the cell with a bruising force.

Jacomo stands for a while, massaging his throat and coughing. Then he turns on Hameel, his face fierce and imperious, like a hawk.

"So, Hameel. You can't bear to see an innocent man tortured, is that it?"

Hameel shakes his head helplessly. Jacomo looks at him, and his hand clenches, as if he would wish to run him through with a dagger.

"Answer me, you dog! Is Jerome innocent?"

"Yes."

"And you, his *accuser*, are you a lying dog?"

"Yes."

There is silence for a few moments. Only the sound of breathing can be heard. Jerome is the first to speak, his voice strained with pain.

"Hameel – no!"

Jacomo speaks to the guards brusquely.

"Release the painter!"

He quickly unscrews the clamp himself, and the wrist chains are unlocked. The men help Jerome to his feet. He is swaying unsteadily, and his eyes never leave Hameel.

Jacomo speaks again, his face and his voice clenched.

"Master Jerome, I've been the unwitting agent of a plot against you. I'll do all that I can to make reparation."

Jerome doesn't appear to hear him. His eyes are fixed on Hameel's face as if he were trying to read something there, something written in a language he has never learned.

"Hameel?" he says. It is as if he isn't sure, now, to whom he speaks.

Hameel bows his head. He can't meet that uncomprehending gaze.

"Get him out of here," Jacomo says to one of the guards, who takes the Master Painter's arm and pulls him gently towards the cell door. Jerome veers, off balance, towards Hameel, but the guard tightens his grip a little and steers him easily out to the foot of the stairway. As the two figures disappear up the stone steps, Jacomo turns to look at Hameel.

"This was wickedness indeed, Hameel," the Inquisitor says softly. "The Devil has entered your soul and made it his own, and we must drive him out with the fires of righteousness."

CHAPTER THIRTY NINE

There is no ceremony in his release. He hesitates at the open door of the gaol, looking out at the blank windows of the back of the Stadhuis. It seems to be dusk, but his eyes still need time to adjust to this much light. The guard who has escorted him here coughs to draw his attention.

"I need to shut the door behind you and lock it, Master."

Jerome takes a step forward and the door of that underworld closes behind him. He feels like a resurrected wraith.

In truth it is nearly dark, and there's no-one else about. He is glad of that. He doesn't feel quite ready for the world of the living. He moves gingerly, keeping his weight easy on the foot that has been tortured. He can see now that his slipper is caked with dried blood. His fingers too throb painfully where the clamp has compressed them, but he doesn't think any bones have been broken. Either by design or accident, the Inquisitor seized his left hand, not his right. He will be able to resume his work as soon as he wishes.

As he limps slowly towards the market square, he goes over in bewilderment what has just happened. Hameel his *accuser*? That makes no sense to him at all. It is true that Hameel revealed to him a string of

349

resentments going back to their childhood days. But could such things hold the explanation for what he'd done?

He thinks with a shudder of Hameel still down in that foetid dungeon. What will Jacomo do to him? Is there anything he can do, to stop him? Only the Burgemeester could intervene in the gaol, but he won't oppose Jacomo's will...

He stops. In his preoccupied state, he has somehow gone in the wrong direction. He has turned right instead of left on leaving the gaol. Well, he might as well carry on this way now. It will bring him back to the market square by a different route.

As he moves on, he is filled with longing to see Aleyt. How overjoyed she will be to see him, and to learn that he is no longer in danger! What will she make of the news that it was Hameel who lied to Jacomo about him? He quickens his pace a little, as best he can.

This narrow street terminates, in the opposite direction, at the gate of the Abbess Dominica's convent. Perhaps that is why, when he sees a substantial woman's figure moving towards him in the gloom, burdened with a heavy sack, he immediately thinks of the Abbess.

The figure labours towards him, its head bowed and partly concealed by a nun's wimple. She doesn't cast a glance in his direction. In spite of the straitness of the street, she seems oblivious to his presence. But as she comes level with him, Jerome sees her face clearly. The skin is red and blistered, but what he had dismissed as a passing resemblance is more than that. This *is* the Abbess herself.

"Abbess Dominica!" he says aloud. It is more an exclamation of surprise than an address. But the Abbess turns the full pustuled horror of her ravaged face to him, and her eyes widen in surprise. She lets the sack slide from her shoulder to land on the ground with a heavy thump.

"You!" she spits out. "What are you doing here? I thought they had you in prison."

"It was all lies. It was Hameel... Hameel had lied about me. But - why are you like this? Your face..."

"You know the signs. The Fire of St Anthony has found me out."

He gestures to the sack.

"But... carrying burdens, like a labourer..."

"Kindling for our fires. I perform all of the meanest tasks. It's all the fault of that devil Jacomo. He ordered me to labour in the infirmary – and how swiftly I became infected! They say the Fire only picks out those who are sinners."

The note of despair in her voice moves him to pity.

"Can I help?"

The Abbess draws herself up a little, and summons what she can of scorn into her eyes.

"Help? I don't want your help! Get on your way. Where's Hameel?"

"Jacomo has him in prison."

The Abbess blinks, and makes a sign of the cross.

"In prison? God help him then! Such a pretty man, Hameel. No wonder Aleyt preferred him to you."

The name of his wife, so recently in his thoughts, startles Jerome. On the Abbess's lips, the word is like drinking water streaming from a stinking privy.

"What?"

Suddenly, a rictus of pleasure twists the Abbess's grotesque visage into a mask of wicked delight. He stares at her, uncomprehending.

"My God, don't tell me you didn't know!" She turns her face upwards and clasps her hands in a mockery of prayer.

"Oh, thank you Lord for giving me this last little pleasure!"

Jerome feels foreboding like a cold blade sliding into his guts.

"What are you talking about? What about Aleyt?"

The Abbess pauses a moment and licks her scabrous lips as if savouring the words in her mind before speaking them.

"Your darling wife was Hameel's whore."

Jerome wants to strike her. His hand actually lifts a little. Another of her evil calumnies!

"You're lying!" he says vehemently. But the cold blade twists in his guts nonetheless.

The Abbess opens her hands in a gesture of innocence. Her face takes on a new mask, this time an insulting look of tender sympathy.

"Ask anyone in Den Bosch if you don't believe *me*. The two of them were paraded about the town square. Your pretty Aleyt took quite a battering. When Mary saw me afterwards, she was furious. As if it were *my* fault. She said Aleyt had lost the child."

Jerome stares at her again. With every word she seems to tear down a wall of his being. The street in which they stand is like shifting sand beneath his feet.

"What child?"

"Your son and heir. Or daughter, it might have been. Except of course it was Hameel's child, not yours."

Now the very roof of his existence caves in, and as if to protect himself from a shower of rubble he sinks down onto his knees with his arms across his head. Tears begin to prick his eyes, and the coldness at the core of him spreads to engulf his whole body. In his self-imposed darkness he hears the Abbess shouldering her heavy sack again with a grunt. There is a moment's silence, and he tastes the salty droplets running down his face, and feels them dripping off his chin onto the cobbles of the street. Her voice, low and insidious, penetrates his Hell.

"This is where pride and arrogance have brought you. Master Jerome, the Great Master Painter! The great man of Den Bosch! Well, you couldn't even command the fidelity of your best friend and your wife."

He hears her begin to move off. Her voice reaches

him again, a little further away

"Now that the Fire has me, I'll spend the rest of my days in prayer. They say God's forgiveness is infinite. What about you, Jerome? What are your powers of forgiveness?"

The Abbess's shuffling footsteps recede until he can hear them no more. In the silent, dark street he lets himself sink completely to the ground, huddled against the wall of a house, and he lies there for a long time. Violent sobs rack his whole body, and in his heart he suffers torture worse than any that Jacomo could have inflicted.

At last he picks himself up and makes his way to the town square. It is deserted, but a tall pole in its centre puzzles him for a moment. Then he realises – today must have been May Day, and the square would have been filled earlier with revels and games. For a moment he tries to imagine the happy laughing crowds, the excited children running about, the music and bustle. But no image of such things comes to his mind's eye. The pole stands like an abandoned symbol of happier times long passed away.

On the far side of the square he can see the outline of his house against the sky. Stars are sprinkled across the heavens, and a light shows faintly too between the shutters of the parlour window, where Aleyt must be sitting alone. He gazes now at this familiar scene as if he has never seen it before. He feels like a beggar from another country who has wandered into a strange town and has no idea where to lay his head for the night. For a moment he thinks of turning away, and simply walking out into the countryside, away from Den Bosch for ever. But he is cold, and hungry, and in pain. He limps across the open space like a slinking injured fox, and taps quietly at the door of his own house

*

From above, Aleyt hears Mary open the door, and her heart jumps when she recognises Jerome's voice down in the little hall. She hurries to the top of the stairs and calls down.

"Jerome?"

The voice that comes back to her is Mary's.

"The Master's back, Mistress! I'm going to heat water for him to bathe."

Aleyt runs swiftly down the stairs. After the blackness of the last few days, all she can think of is how she longs to be in her husband's arms. Pray God he has not been told of what has happened! Whatever the future might hold, she can then at least tell him in her own words of her sin, her regret, her ardent desire to be forgiven.

But Jerome's face when she sees him standing there in the hall is enough to tell her that these were idle hopes. Her hurrying footsteps, which would have carried her to him, falter, and she stops on the last step. Still, she reaches out to him with her arms. Please, God, let him forgive her!

Jerome looks at the woman with whom he has shared the last seven years of his life. He has lived with her in this very house. He barely recognises her. Her hair, usually so carefully combed and covered with a head cloth, is an exposed nest of rats' tails. Her face, usually soft and glowing like a ripe peach, is white and lined with anxiety. Her eyes, usually clear blue pools into whose depths he could look with confidence, are like muddy puddles into which a stone has been thrown. He can read nothing of what is below their surface, and as her eyes seek his and then drop and turn away at his gaze, he feels he knows nothing about this woman at all. He shrugs his shoulders slightly, and turns into the kitchen, where Mary is already working with the bellows to re-ignite the glowing embers of the kitchen fire. He closes the door behind him, to indicate that Aleyt should not follow.

Aleyt looks at the planks of the kitchen door. In the fitful light of the candle at the foot of the stairs, the knots resemble eyes and mouths looking back and gaping at her. But there is no speaking with faces in a door, so she turns and walks slowly back up the stairs with burning tears running down her face.

CHAPTER FORTY

He has returned to Hell. Two cowled monks, their robes a pale blue, stand near the edge. One is seated on a naked man and reads from a book. The *Malleus Maleficarum*, he thinks it might be, but no-one will know that, the detail is so small. The other has a long beak ending in a paddle, like some strange wading bird. They supervise a fat gleeful demon who swings on a rope. The rope is attached to a bell suspended from a ruined building. From the inside of the bell, the legs of another naked man dangle helplessly as his head rings the hours.

He will need more lapis lazuli and white lead from the apothecary to complete the monks' robes. He sighs, and stares out of the window for a while. He won't go out himself, so he'll need to speak to Mary. He prefers not to speak at all.

Only Diederik has been to talk to him. Bishop Andreas and others were keen to congratulate him on his release, and to commiserate with his present situation, but he told Diederik he would be keeping to himself for a time and to ask everyone to stay away. Diederik is his best friend – after Hameel – and he knows the bell master well enough to sense that he is disappointed in his lack of fight. Diederik had got the bit between his teeth over the business of the petition, and he was full of how he was going to do all that he could to drive Jacomo from Den Bosch, in spite of the Burgemeester's spineless paltering. Jerome listened to his friend as if to news from another country.

He freezes now with tension as he hears footsteps – Aleyt's footsteps – descending the stairs. She keeps to the top two rooms of the house mostly. Mary has made up a bed for him here in the studio, and brought down such clothes as he needs. He hasn't exchanged a word with this stranger since his return to the world. They will have to speak, of course, but he's not ready for it yet. *What are your powers of forgiveness?* He doesn't know the answer to that question. He has lost his understanding of what she is, and of himself.

The footsteps carry on downwards without a pause. She will be going to the privy then, or to say something to Mary. She never leaves the house, and no visitors call. Even her own family will be shunning her now. He feels a pang of what might be sympathy, but it's quickly overwhelmed by anger and confusion.

*

Mary feels like a gaoler, with two prisoners in her charge. With Jerome she barely dares to speak, and he hardly meets her eye or says a word to her. She carries food and drink to him, that's all. What's passing through his mind, she can't begin to fathom. He appears to be in pain, from his face, but is it physical pain from the after-effects of his torture and confinement, or the pain of his betrayal? Perhaps it's both. She wishes he would rage at Aleyt, and then forgive her. How will this end, otherwise? Perhaps he will order her to leave his house. There are nuns that will take in a fallen woman, and set her on the road to her new husband, Jesus.

Is she going to end that way herself, one day? A bride of Jesus? She hopes not, with all her heart.

With Aleyt, she has desultory conversations. Her Mistress wants to know what is happening in Den Bosch, and what people are saying. She has written a letter to her father, but just as Mary leaves the room to deliver it, she changes her mind, and decides to wait instead for some word or act of forgiveness to come from him. She sends Mary instead to her cousin Frida, to ask if she might visit again, this time with the baby. But Frida shakes her head sadly when Mary hands her the note. She is sure that Frida would have come, she can see that in her face. But her husband Joris and his mother are visible in the hallway behind, watching. The baby is crying, in another room.

Her Mistress looks so wan that she prevails on her to see Doctor Stemerdink. He stands in the bedchamber now, with his stoop and his thinning wiry hair, and looks appraisingly at Aleyt over the half spectacles that cling precariously to the end of his long nose.

"A superfluity of black bile, Mistress Aleyt. This is why you are lethargic and sad. It's Saint Augustine's Day today, and this is a particularly auspicious confluence of the stars for restoring your balance."

He takes three cups of her blood and decants it into a flask. He follows Mary to the street door.

"My tooth worm still gnaws, Doctor Stemerdink," she says in the hallway as she opens the door to let him out.

"Are you applying the ointment daily?"

"I am."

"Then I suggest twice a day, and at the same time as you apply it, pray to Saint Appolonia. Come back to me if you need more ointment. I will study your Mistress's blood, and advise whether more cupping is required. Come tomorrow, and I will advise you – and pass you my bill to deliver to your Mistress."

She watches him walk away, bent forward with a quick scuttling gait, like a scavenging insect of some kind. A beetle.

Later in the day she ventures out to the market stalls to buy vegetables and some meat. It's the butcher who gives her the tidings, as he hands her a little parcel of bacon. He nods and points his eyes, little piggy eyes, at the pile of wood in the middle of the square. She hadn't noticed it.

"Here, you look as if you've seen a ghost!" he says, as she thrusts the coin into his palm and hurries away. She goes quickly into the house, dumps her purchases on the kitchen board and hides herself in her room, sobbing, until she has no more tears to shed.

She will have to tell Aleyt, and soon. She'll probably be sleeping now, recovering strength after the blood-letting. But when she wakes, she'll hear unfamiliar sounds in the square outside, once the market stalls have been taken down. She'll look out of the bedchamber window and see the tipstaffs constructing the stake and the pyre. Can she soften this pain for her, with any words at her own command?

Gathering her courage as best she can, she heats up the last of yesterday's pottage, puts it into a bowl, and takes it on a tray up to her Mistress. She helps her to sit up, and watches over her as she spoons the thick soup into her mouth. She must nourish and fortify her. Only then does she speak of what she has heard and seen.

"Witchcraft?" Aleyt says, looking at her as if she has invented a word, a word never spoken before.

"They say he confessed it willingly to the tribunal."

Then grief sweeps into the room like a raging wind, and they cling together against its violence.

When Aleyt can speak, she strokes Mary's head, lying against her shoulder.

"Ever since you told me, Mary... that... what Hameel did. That it was he who lied to the Inquisitor... since then I've tried so hard not to think of him. I looked at myself this morning in the peer-glass, Mary. And I thought – how could the love of such a thing as myself weigh heavier with Hameel than a lifelong friendship and the fate of his eternal soul?"

Mary whispers the only explanation she can think of.

"Perhaps... perhaps the Devil *did* get into him

somehow."

She continues to lie for a long time on the bed next to Aleyt. Not mistress and servant now, but two suffering souls together. Outside, hammering noises and the shouts of the tipstaffs announce that work has begun on the pyre.

CHAPTER FORTY ONE

As darkness seeps into the house, Mary lights candles, but they cannot staunch the rising gloom inside her. She takes food to Jerome in his studio. He looks as wretched as she feels, staring out of the window into the garden at the back of the house. He won't have heard the noises in the square.

She should tell him, but she can't. In the morning, that will be time enough. And perhaps he will find out for himself then, without need for words from her.

This is Hameel's last night on earth. Her revulsion for what he has done is all swallowed up now in pity and regret. She paces about in the kitchen and dining hall. She can't bear the thought of him passing away from her without any words of farewell. She drinks a cup of the Master's brandy. Just one. Dutch courage. She offers a short prayer to the Virgin and then goes up to speak with Aleyt.

She's sitting in the parlour in front of her Garden of Eden. Mary wonders if Aleyt will ever work on it again, she seems so bereft of will and joy. Aleyt's eyes stay on the tapestry as Mary speaks.

"I'm going to the gaol, Mistress, to try and see Hameel. I pray that wicked Inquisitive won't be there, or get told about it after. But I can't not go. He shouldn't be left all alone now, without a friend. What do you think? Am I right to go?"

Aleyt looks at her now.

"You're a brave girl, Mary. You're right to go. I can't visit him myself. Yet I still want to see him – is that a sin, Mary?"

"It's not a sin in my eyes, Mistress. But I'm not one to say what's a sin and what isn't, an ignorant girl like me."

"Will you say one thing to him for me, Mary?"

"If it's not too long and I can remember it."

"Let me think."

Aleyt shuts her eyes for a few moments.

"Say this, Mary. Say that I thank him for his love, and that now he must forget me and turn his thoughts only to the love of Christ, Our Saviour."

"That's a mouthful to remember, Mistress."

"You don't have to say the exact words, Mary. Say simply, if you like, I thank him, but now he must think only of holy love, love of Christ, as I do. Can you tell him that?"

"Very well. I'll say that."

"Thank you Mary, and…"

"Yes, Mistress?"

"It might… perhaps… comfort him to think… well…"

Her hand goes to her belly, and Mary divines her thought.

"I'll say nothing, Mistress, concerning that."

After Mary leaves the room, Aleyt's gaze returns to the figure of Adam in her tapestry. She has not woven features to his face; the figure is too small. But perhaps there is more of Hameel than of Jerome in his bearing. As for Eve, who holds his hand, she seems now to represent a younger Aleyt who has faded away into the past. A foolish woman who loved two men.

*

The young man who opens the gaol's door to Mary seems pleased to see her. Perhaps he was expecting worse. When she explains herself, he takes her offered coin without demur.

"There's no need, is there, to mention this visit to anyone?" she says, looking him in the eye.

He shakes his head, rubbing nervously at a spot on his chin.

"No need, like you say. You'd better not stay long. No one's said he can't have visitors, but then no one's said he can. I've got myself to be careful of."

"I'll be quick, I promise."

He leads her along a passage to a door at the end, and stops to light a rushlight from a smouldering brazier beside it. He unlocks the door, and a smell of urine and fear wafts from the darkness within.

"You'll likely find him a little changed," he says. "He's gone through – you know – a harrowing. That Brother Jacomo you know…"

He glances along the passageway behind her, as if he might suddenly appear, then whispers.

"He's a devil, in my opinion. A devil in disguise. Perhaps *the* Devil! Mind you say nothing. My views on the matter are private views."

"I'll say nothing."

She follows him carefully down the spiral stone stairs, and watches him unlock a barred door at the bottom. She can't see past his back, but she hears a slight stirring from inside the cell, and a weak voice.

"Who is it?"

"A visitor," the gaoler replies.

He stands aside to let Mary enter, and puts the rushlight into a sconce in the wall.

"I'll wait up at the top," he says, not looking at the prisoner. "I'll give you a few minutes."

He closes the barred door, and goes up the steps slowly in the darkness, having forgotten to provide himself with an additional light.

She peers at the half-naked figure stretched on a straw pallet on the floor. A square of sack-cloth covers his lower limbs. In the flickering light he looks like an old man, the man Hameel might have become in thirty years time. His hair has all been shaved off, and his once handsome face is trenched with lines of pain and smeared with dark congealed blood.

"Mary?"

His voice is different, muffled and unclear.

"Yes, Hameel."

She sinks to her knees on the floor beside him, and touches his face with a trembling hand.

"What have they done to you, my poor man?"

Hameel smiles, and she sees now that his sunken old man's mouth is toothless.

"They've driven out all the wickedness from me, Mary. I'm purified, and ready to meet my Maker and ask for forgiveness."

Mary can only nod, and takes one of his hands to stroke it.

"I was possessed, you see, and that's why I committed one of the Deadly Sins. A devil of Lust had got into me. Jacomo has driven it out, and saved my soul."

Grief fills her eyes and her voice.

"I… I always loved you, you know. There, I've said it now because I couldn't live the rest of my life if I'd never said it to you. I know I was always just a game for you…"

"Mary…"

"No, don't say nothing. I don't mean it badly of you. But you never thought of me as… as someone to marry and have a family by. I know that. But still, before… you know, before… you… die…"

His face twitches, perhaps in pain.

"Say, rather, before I am born into eternal life, Mary."

"Yes, that. Well… I wanted to have my say and I've said it!"

"Mary – I loved you too, in my weak sinful way. You were always dear to me, even after… "

The mumbled words peter out. She squeezes his hand.

"My Mistress sent a word by me."

In the dark centres of Hameel's eyes, the reflections of the rushlight seem to flicker with a life of their own.

"What word, Mary?"

"She said she thanked you for your love, but that now you must think only of the love of Christ, as she does. There, that's exactly it, I remembered it well."

"Thank you, Mary. Can you carry the very same message back to her from me? The love of Christ…"

He turns his head from side to side, as if he would rid himself of something.

"But yet… I'd wish…"

"What?"

"She said nothing of coming here, to say farewell?"

"That's a thing she can't do. It's hard enough for her already, without such a thing as that. The Master has set up his camp in his studio, and she keeps to the upstairs rooms. She talks of going to a convent."

Hameel closes his eyes for a few moments. He hardly seems to breathe.

Mary squeezes his hand again. If only death could come so gently.

"Please, Mary, tell her this. I want to set eyes on her for one last time. When they take me to the square tomorrow, will you ask her to stand at her window? She need not acknowledge me, and I will make no sign. But when she has seen that I have looked her way, then she may pull the shutters closed and pray. Will you do that?"

"Of course, I'll tell her. Oh, Hameel…" She wrings his hand. "What shall I do? All the joy is leaving the world."

"We're wrong, Mary, to seek joy here. It was in seeking earthly joy that I fell into sin."

Suddenly his eyes widen, and she feels his hand shaking in hers. Then his whole body trembles, and she

365

lays herself down full length alongside him, holding him like a baby. He whimpers, and she can only understand stray words from his toothless mumbling mouth.

"Mary... confessed... God will be merciful... pray for me... pray for me..."

CHAPTER FORTY TWO

From out of darkness he comes to his place of conflagration. He comes to that moment when his spirit will take flight as the mortal flesh is melted by flames from his bones and his blood is boiled to a vapour. He comes with hope, but with more of terror.

As he rounds the corner of the Stadhuis, the clanking of his chains announces his arrival to the nearest members of the crowd in the square. They set up a roaring and shrieking and stamping and jostling that spreads like Saint Anthony's Fire across the multitude. They look to his eyes like devils, devils in Hell. But he is not for them. He is for God and the saints above. He has been purified by suffering. The Inquisitor has saved his soul.

God. Heaven. God.

He keeps repeating the words in his head.

But the terror... he cannot rise entirely above that. His racked body will be tormented one last time, and it will be beyond imagining. At the centre of the square he can see a little column of smoke rising into the air, where the brazier is already lit. He watched this scene only weeks ago. The executioner will be standing there now, beside the brazier, with his arms folded. He has watched, a mere devil himself, as all of this was done to another man, a bearded man like Jesus.

Many of the devils have faces he knows well. All are turned towards him. All observe him closely. He passes one after another as the tipstaffs march him through the crowd. These faces belong to the world of the living, and he belongs to the world hereafter. They are no more kin to him now than the stone faces of saints and gargoyles staring from the walls of the cathedral.

Here is Johannes, the tailor, a brightly patterned handkerchief in his hand, red and green. He brings it up to his mouth and nose as he passes, as if he has something to hide. At his side, the yellow cross prominent on his tunic, is his grandfather. His face is blank and his eyes unfocussed, as if he is looking at some far-off vista.

Here is a huddle of Holy Company men. Meerdink, the cloth merchant; Hugo van Dorff, the lawyer; and Meister Diederik, the bell master. Their faces are hard as flints, and Diederik deliberately seeks his eye and scowls.

Here is Wiggers, with gaping mouth and orange hair standing up on end, as if he has rushed through a hedge with it. Here is Hans, the butcher from next door to his workshop. There is animal blood on his apron, and pity in his eyes. Here is Joris, the husband of Aleyt's cousin Frida, frowning at him as if he would kill him with his own hands. The small old man beside him, surely, is Aleyt's father, turning his face away from him now as he passes.

He raises his eyes to the steps of the Stadhuis, where the clergy are gathered. Father Crispin stands as still as a statue, his face cast down and his hands clasped in prayer. Beside him is Bishop Andreas, his hands gesturing in some animated conversation with Theofilus Piek, the Burgemeester, who listens with his head tilted to one side, like a bird listening for a worm in the ground. They will be speaking of some earthly matter. He will be in Heaven before any earthly matter of this day is finished.

God. Heaven. God.

As for the myriad faces that he barely knows, or doesn't know at all, many are shouting and hissing, alight with the self-righteous thrill of seeing wickedness punished. Others are filled only with curiosity, straining to see over each other's shoulders exactly what a man about to die looks like.

Now he has one more farewell to make to earthly delights. He looks up, across the sea of bobbing faces to the line of houses on the eastern side. Like a statue of the Virgin in a holy shrine, she stands there at an open window.

Aleyt.

She is dressed all in white, and it seems to him that she gazes towards him with such light in her face that she shines like a beacon. For a moment only, he is transfixed by that sight, and permits himself to remember her gentle voice; her warm embrace; her loving eyes. Then, as if drawing a dark curtain, he lowers his head back to the ground. He begins to intone inwardly the prayers that will consume his last minutes on earth.

*

As soon as she sees Hameel look away, she draws the parlour shutters closed. Then she takes herself up to the bedchamber, whose shutters are already fastened, and in the gloom kneels at the side of her bed as if beside a grave. Her first prayer is that Hameel's suffering will be brief. Then she prays for his soul.

*

Next to the pyre, Jacomó stands motionless. Within, he is seething with impatience for all this to be over. He has his Bible open on a lectern before him, but his eyes have ceased their attempt to follow the text, and his thoughts refuse to follow the path he prescribes for them at such a juncture. He should be pleading with God to accept his intercession on behalf of the sinner, pleading that his soul will join the blessed in Heaven, purged by

369

him, by *him*, of its sin.

But instead he cannot shift his thoughts from the guilt that is wrapped around him like a shroud around a corpse. The wretched man now being led forward was undoubtedly possessed by devils until he drove them out. In that he is secure. He has acted honestly as a soldier of God, to that degree. But Hameel is also in some measure a scapegoat for his own mistake, and from that circumstance comes the guilt that enfolds him.

Alongside the guilt is bitterness. Thanks to the wickedness of Hameel, his mission has suffered a grievous setback. Abbot Geoffrey, in his capacity as the representative of the Pope in Brabant, and head of the Inquisition, has recalled him to the Abbey of Saint Anthony in Eindhoven. He must take the road with Brother Bartelme this very afternoon, when all is done here. Clearly the influential friends of the Master Painter have themselves painted the blackest picture of his persecution of that eminent and godly man. His hopes of establishing a new centre for the investigation of heresy and witchcraft here in Den Bosch are in jeopardy.

He returns his eyes to the Bible, and tries to rid his mind of the bitterness he feels towards Hameel, bitterness that has already been vented in the town's dungeon, and yet will not leave him, like the lingering aftertaste of some meal tainted with rotten meat.

Bitterness and guilt.

*

Mary stands, as not so long ago, pressed into a doorway in a far corner of the square. She can't bear to be elsewhere, but she can't bear to be any closer. Catalyn, who knows all, is here with her, holding her arm and squeezing it from time to time.

Gillis appears in front of her blurred eyes. He nods an acknowledgement to Catalyn, and then speaks gently to her.

"I'm sorry, Mary. I know – I know as how that

man... I know as how he was someone... someone to you."

Mary nods.

"I won't interfere, Mary, with what you're feeling. I'll go away, right now. But I wanted you to know... well... come and see me again. Come soon – as soon as you feel well again in yourself. I miss you. And, this isn't the time – but I want to talk with you."

She nods again. His words mean nothing. She has no room in her mind for anything now but what is happening in the square.

Catalyn follows his retreat with her eyes.

"You could do worse than a young man like that," she says.

*

Jerome is wearing his winter hood, which partially shields his face. He has edged his way forward through the press until he stands close to the pyre. Jacomo is only a few feet away, and he avoids looking that way. He feels no fear of the man. He simply detests him, and all that he stands for. Yet now that he knows what lies the Inquisitor was fed, he will not deign to pick up a useless burden of resentment. A beast of prey will act according to its nature. He wants no further dealings with him – he would like to forget that he even exists.

The Dominicans on the Stadhuis steps commence their chant, and looking over his shoulder Jerome can see the tipstaffs in their red tunics pushing their way forward through the throng, their big-chested leader like the prow of a boat breasting boisterous seas. Then, with a catch of his breath, Jerome sees Hameel. His head is bowed, and his mouth moves silently. He must be praying.

Jerome sees not only what is before his eyes, but the Hameel made up of all his memories: the eager child carrying a basket of fish by the sunlit river; the modest young man he encouraged as an artist; his closest, most beloved friend, who, like himself, fell under the spell of

371

his beautiful Aleyt.

As Hameel arrives at the foot of the pyre, Jerome takes a step forward and turns back his hood. The guards, seeing who he is, don't intervene. Hameel's face lifts to his, and his eyes widen a little, as if in fear. Jerome meant to say something, he wasn't sure what, but he finds his voice has died in his throat, and burning tears are springing into his eyes. So he simply takes a second step, raising his arms, and Hameel, his own arms weighted with chains, steps forward into his embrace, and buries his face in Jerome's shoulder.

"I'm sorry. I'm sorry, Jerome".

Jerome hugs him hard, and then moves away to arm's length, his hands on Hameel's shoulders. The tears course freely now down his face. He smiles, and releases Hameel.

"May God be with you!" he says.

*

The guards push Hameel forward once more. He makes no resistance, and plants his unsteady foot on the first rough step of his path upwards. The board sags a little beneath his weight and suddenly diverse sensations rush at him: the shooting agony of his toothless gums; the smell of charcoal in the brazier; the deep voices of the monks, chanting. He dismisses all of that, and fixes his eyes and his hopes on the stake, where Jacomo now stands waiting for him. The fire that consumes his earthly flesh will free his soul from its prison, and it will fly like a released bird to God. He looks further upwards, beyond the stake, to the sky above. The deep blue of the waiting firmament is dotted with small white meandering clouds. So insubstantial. So beautiful.

CHAPTER FORTY THREE

Jerome keeps his place to the end, although driven back a little like the rest of the crowd by the heat of the fire. He stands directly in front of the steps, where Hameel could see him if he wishes to. He doesn't know what comfort that might be, but it is the only thing he can think of, a silent gesture of shared humanity.

But Hameel's eyes remain fixed on the sky above, and gradually the thick smoke rising from the flames at the base of the pyre obscure his figure. By the time the flames climb to the stake itself, there is no cry of pain, only silence. Hameel must have choked in the heat and smoke, and his spirit has fled already, leaving only his earthly husk to be consumed by fire. When he is certain of this, Jerome draws his hood once more over his features and weaves his way back towards his house, noting that the shutters of the parlour and the bedchamber are closed. Just short of the haven of his door, he is accosted by Diederik, who takes his hand in sympathy.

"Well, Jerome, a difficult day for you. I won't venture to guess your feelings towards that poor sinner in the fire, but I'm sure you'll be glad when a new day dawns."

"I will, Diederik," Jerome mutters.

Diederik regards him closely.

373

"I see you're upset. I won't detain you. But I'll just mention that this will be the last burning in our square conducted by that black devil. He's recalled to Eindhoven – and hopefully thereafter to Rome to explain himself. I had this from Bishop Andreas, who had it from Abbot Geoffrey. It's a relief to us all, I'm sure, but in particular to me. I'm going to the foundry this very afternoon, and we'll hammer into pieces the moulds that he forced us to make. There'll be none of his implements of torture and no inquisitorial dungeon in Den Bosch now, thank God and his saints. Farewell, Jerome. I'll see you soon in better times."

"Farewell, Diederik, and thank you," Jerome replies. He enters the house and closes the door behind him with relief.

He goes straight to his studio, and turns his hand to making more drawings for his garden of earthly delights. He works on the figure of a naked woman, resting against a tree. Her hand is on her womb, and a naked man bends towards her, offering her an enormous ripe strawberry. Behind them, other unclothed men and women pluck fruit from tree branches. He concentrates all his thoughts on this image, to the exclusion of all else, and makes the hours pass.

Mary brings him a simple meal on a tray, and after eating he moves on to another part of the garden, where armoured knights with fishes' tails float in a serene pool, balancing huge dark berries on their heads. Eventually the light begins to fade, and he calls Mary back to bring him a candle.

Now what will he do with himself?

A wind is rising outside that makes the open shutters of his studio window rattle against their metal fastenings. A sudden splatter of rain drives into the diamond-panes of glass.

He lights more candles, and notices his lute sitting beside the window. Has Mary brought it down? Why? Idly, he picks it up, and sits on his painting stool cradling it on his lap. He plucks at the strings, and turns the pegs to bring the instrument into tune. They are good pearwood pegs in tight holes, and the lute is never far out, even when left unplayed for weeks at a time.

He strums the strings, and the rain beats hard at the window. He should really close the shutters, because the driving rain will eventually seep through the seal of the glass and drip onto his studio floor. But instead he starts to sing, quietly at first, and then more loudly.

"In the Springtime we'll be happy
Gathering little flowers, in love with all the hours,
Of the morning.

In the Summertime we'll be drowsy,
Sleeping under trees, to the hum of the bees,
In the afternoon."

He hears a creak on the stair, and wonders if it's Aleyt. But his song has its own momentum and he carries on regardless.

"In the Autumn we'll be busy,
Gathering the fruit, playing on the lute,
In the evening."

He hears the studio door open behind him, but doesn't turn to look. The music is weaving a spell over him, taking him away from the bleakness of the day, and he won't break it.

"In the Winter we'll be cold,
Skating on the ice, wrapped in furs like mice,
All night long."

He senses now that there is someone standing at the opened door, and knows that it must be Aleyt. He begins the first verse again, as ever. They had always sung the first verse twice, to finish the song in the Springtime. Behind him, he hears Aleyt's voice, softly joining in.

"In the Springtime we'll be happy,
Gathering little flowers, in love with all the hours,
Of the morning."

He stands up from his stool, puts the lute down carefully, and then turns around to face the door. Aleyt has come a little way into the studio, and stands before him in her night shift, her hair dressed carefully as it always used to be, and covered with a white night cap. She looks beautiful, he thinks, and somehow quite serene. Her eyes meet his, questioning.

He kneels on the floor, and turns his gaze towards the heavens. From the corner of his eye, he sees Aleyt kneel too. They join their voices in the Lord's Prayer.

CHAPTER FORTY FOUR

"This corner is as good a place as any, Sister Theresa, don't you think?"

It is a part of the orchard near the wall, where windfalls are thrown to go rotten. Early wasps buzz in the air, and Sister Theresa holds her wimple close about her face.

"If you think so, Sister Ursula."

"Who is to gainsay us?"

"Some of the other sisters…"

She peters out.

"What, Sister Theresa?"

"Some of the other sisters expect a tomb in the chapel, as for the other abbesses."

"They might expect all kinds of things that don't come to pass."

"Or… at the very least… a headstone."

Sister Ursula waves the idea away like a wasp.

"The woman was a disgrace to our order. Do these *other sisters* take that into account?"

Her eyes narrow a little.

"Or do these *other sisters* in fact state only your own thoughts on the matter, Sister Theresa?"

Sister Theresa feels alarmed.

"No, indeed, Sister. Let's do as you think fitting."

"Good. Get three or four of the novices out of their

hoeing and weeding in the vegetable garden and bring them over here to dig the pit. We'll want a large hole and a deep one. I'll come and inspect it when you tell me it's ready."

Sister Ursula sweeps away to give orders somewhere else. She has put the infirmary back in the hands of Sister Benedicta. Her star is in the ascendant, Sister Theresa thinks, and it's no bad matter that *she* is entrusted with carrying out her orders. Sister Ursula is the sort of person to recognise and reward fidelity and selfless service.

She looks sadly at the unkempt corner where Abbess Dominica's remains will lie unmarked. She feels disloyal. But then she remembers the glorious morning when she didn't have to don the hair chemise: the morning that the Abbess was confined to her duties in the infirmary and couldn't check on her obedience. Now she has quietly cut the horrible garment into small pieces, and smuggled them into a bag of rubbish to be carried away. Her skin is recovering its softness, and her spirit is joyful.

All things considered, it's for the best that the Abbess Dominica has departed this world.

*

Jacomo squints along the darkening road ahead. He takes long strides, and Brother Bartelme, urging on the donkey that carries their worldly possessions, has almost to trot to keep up.

"Come on, Bartelme! There are woods ahead of us and it will soon be black as pitch. The abbey is still a long way off."

Damn that Abbot Geoffrey for insisting they leave today, too late to complete the journey in daylight! They might lose their way easily in the darkness, not to speak of footpads and wild beasts. The Devil and all his creatures would be abroad.

He would have defied the Abbot, but he is on thin ice after that accursed petition. He must keep the weak old fool sweet for a time, until he can convince Cardinal Amandini by his letters that trust can still be reposed in him. There may yet be hope, given a little time, of establishing a properly rigorous Inquisition here, if not in Den Bosch then in another city of Brabant.

Two figures take shape in the darkness ahead. Two men, standing on the road. Not moving, just standing. Tall men with cudgels.

Brother Bartelme makes a kind of squeak behind him, then hisses, "Brother Jacomo! What shall we do?"

"We can do nothing but carry on, Bartelme, and trust to God."

Nevertheless, in case God is looking elsewhere, he slides a hand under his robe to where his knife hangs in its leather scabbard.

"Good evening, brothers!" one of the men says, as they draw near. The men are blocking the path, and so Jacomo and Bartelme come to a halt.

"What do you want with us?" Jacomo says.

"Why, nothing with you or your companion. We want only your donkey and its burden."

He smells drink on the man's breath. Anger is rising in him like a tide, unstoppable. He was primed for anger already by this very journey, taken under compulsion against his better judgement.

"You would do wrong to us and the Holy Church. Let us pass, and seek forgiveness from God."

The other man utters a short false laugh, and brushes past Jacomo to seize the donkey's reins from Bartelme. Bartelme doesn't resist, but the man deals him a swingeing blow to the head with his cudgel anyway, and he crumples to the ground with a moan.

Jacomo has his knife up and under the man's ribcage in an instant. He delivers the well-remembered twist of the blade and withdraws it. As the man falls dying to the ground beside Bartelme, he glimpses the other man's cudgel flashing towards him, and ducks under it. It comes down painfully but harmlessly on his back. He is crouching now, almost off balance, but the man's leg is close by, and he sinks the knife into the thigh and feels the point jarring against bone.

The thief screams and drops his cudgel to clasp at his leg with both hands. Blood, black in the gloaming, wells out of his wound.

Jacomo stands, panting, knife still in hand. Ignoring the injured man, who folds over and squirms away like a snake on the ground, he goes to Bartelme.

"Bartelme… Brother…"

He puts his ear to Bartelme's mouth, but there is no sound of breath. He lays the side of his head on Bartelme's chest, but there is no movement. He has been killed, pointlessly killed. Rage consumes him. He pushes the murderer's body with his toe – he is dead already. He looks around for the other man. He's twenty yards off, scrambling along the ground.

Jacomo strides towards him.

The man looks up, pleading.

"Brother… you're a man of God. Mercy, please."

Jacomo spits onto his face.

"God may show you mercy, but I am only a man."

He stoops and slashes his blade across the man's defending hand, and then across his throat.

In a minute of calm that he knows will not last, he tethers the donkey to the trunk of a small tree.

Then he kneels amidst the three bodies, and contemplates what he has done. He has succumbed again to Deadly Sin. Anger. He had no need to kill the second man. It was done in fury, and done for revenge.

After all his years of prayer, he has come full circle. He feels as if the growing darkness around him is seeping into his very soul.

He clasps his hands in supplication.

"My God! Do not abandon me!"

*

"By Easter Sunday, I says to myself. If there's nothing by Easter Sunday, then… well, then it must be…

and I'll have some hard thinking to do. And then... everything what happened, Mistress... I couldn't tell you nor no-one."

"Mary, you know I'll help you in any way I can."

"I don't want to put this one out, Mistress. Whatever happens. But I'm scared of what folks will say. I'll be a disgrace."

Aleyt strokes her hand tenderly.

"Well, you must talk to the young man. What are your feelings for him?"

"I don't know, Mistress, really I don't. He's a handsome man, and a hard worker, and I like him well enough. But, with everything... I've stayed away from him for a while now. But he did say in the square, when... when we was in the square... he did say as how he'd like to talk to me."

"You must go today, Mary. The sun is shining. You look lovely, Mary. Go and see what he has to say."

"But – you might think this foolishness, Mistress – but I don't want him to propose marriage to me when I've told him. If he's to say such a thing, then I want it to be because he *wants* me, not because he thinks he's gone and got himself caught in a trap."

"And you think he's already minded to ask you?"

"I don't know. Catalyn – my sister – she says he looked at me like he was mad in love. But she likes a good story, and she's fond of me. She would say that."

"What will you do then, if he doesn't ask you? Will you tell him then?"

"I don't know..."

Her eyes fill with tears, "... I want my baby. I'm not going back to that witch, that Gertruida with her black cats, to have it put out."

*

He has prayed and God has answered. Not in words, but by pouring the balm of forgiveness into his heart. He looks across his pillow at Aleyt, who lies serenely, looking upwards. Candlelight flickers against the wall behind her, limning her hair, and the profile of her face.

They have slept in the same bed for a week now, and they have tonight made love. He feels calmed by this act, as if some broken thing had been made whole again.

She turns her head slightly towards him. He reaches out a hand beneath the bedspread, and their fingers intertwine.

"I have some news about Mary, Jerome," she says softly.

"Mary? What has she done now?" he says lightly.

"She's found herself a husband."

"She's got married?"

"No, of course not. But she has a husband–to-be."

"Who'd have thought it! Who is he?"

"A young farmer. Gillis, he's called."

"Gillis? I don't know that name. Where does he farm?"

"At Oostgebieden."

"Not far off then. She's kept this young man very secret."

"Would you have expected her to talk to you about it?"

"Well… of course not. But I have ears and eyes."

She thinks of all that he has failed to hear or see, and says nothing.

"Well, has she told her father? Or asked his permission, I should say?"

"She doesn't want him to know until it's all done. He's a difficult old man, given to drink, and a brute. She's afraid he'd do something to upset Gillis."

He lies motionless, still looking at her profile, still holding her hand.

"There's more," she says.

"More what?"

"Mary is going to have a child."

He's speechless for a while. This news fills him with such emotion he feels as if he could weep. It's a flooding of joy, something born of the reconciliation between

382

them, and he lets it wash over him, sink into him, cleanse him.

After a few moments, his thoughts move on to other consequences.

"So we've lost our only servant, who's been with us all the years of our marriage. What will you do, Aleyt?"

Now she turns her face more towards his.

"I've been thinking about this, Jerome, and I've talked about it with Mary. I'd like... I'd like very much... to keep her as our servant, and when the child is born... well, I'd thought of our cottage at Roedeken. Perhaps she and I could spend time there, with the baby. You would come out on Saturdays -and more days too, I hope - as we've talked of in the past. You know, I feel that I'd like to be away from Den Bosch for a time, now that it's possible. I feel... you've forgiven me... but the people... the way they treated me... I felt hated."

He squeezes her fingers a little, and lets all this new information swirl in his mind and slowly settle, like particles suspended in a liquid.

"I have an idea," he says after a while.

She jumps a little.

"I'm sorry Jerome, I think I was drifting off to sleep."

"I have an idea. Does this Gillis own his farm? Is he wealthy?"

"I don't believe so. He just makes enough from the land to pay his rent and live. Mary said it's a holding that belongs to the Convent of Saint Agnes.."

Jerome snorts a little.

"Like half the fertile land for a mile around... and his rent will be high enough. Well, it occurs to me that there was talk of land at Roedeken. I wasn't interested at the time, but there were twenty acres we could have had from an old man... I forget his name. He has no sons. The land is too much for him. I know he still wants to sell."

"So..."

"So... it's only a notion..."

383

"That Gillis might farm that land instead?"

"There's another cottage – in disrepair - worse than ours was - and smaller, but…"

Aleyt rolls closer to him in the bed and puts an arm over him and settles her head on his chest.

"We must talk more of this tomorrow, Jerome. I have a picture in my head. A beautiful picture. But now I need to sleep."

She kisses his cheek, and rolls away again to settle. Within a minute, he can hear her breathing grow slow and regular.

He lies there a little longer before sleep claims him. In his head too is a picture. It might be a real vision of the future, or perhaps it's no more than a little scene that he could place in some corner of a painting. In a sunlit cottage garden, two women swing a small child from their arms. Over a hedge, a man is guiding a plough with the help of an ox across a field of rich, brown earth. Inside the cottage, glimpsed through a window, is a man at work. In his hand is a brush, and he is peering closely at a panel set up before him. A painter.

The sounds of this tranquil scene flow into his mind. The songs of blackbirds; the scrape of the plough as it forges through the soil casting aside small stones; the cries of delight from the child. The colours grow brighter and brighter, the sounds fill the whole arc of the sky below the heavens, and at last he falls asleep in this garden of earthly delights.

THE END

Look out for Robert Dodds's forthcoming collection of short stories: **Secret Sharers**

64324718R00236

Made in the USA
Lexington, KY
04 June 2017